DATE		

sea room

A Novel by Norman G. Gautreau

Cover art: Painting by Richard Myrick, who splits his time between Deer Isle, Maine, and Washington, D.C., and exhibits his works at the Deer Isle Artists Association during the summer.
From the collection of Margaret and Peter Allen.

MacAdam/Cage Publishing
155 Sansome Street, Suite 620
San Francisco, CA 94104
www.macadamcage.com
Copyright © 2002 by Norman G. Gautreau
ALL RIGHTS RESERVED.

Library of Congress Cataloging-in-Publication Data

Gautreau, Norman G., 1941 —
    Sea Room / Norman G. Gautreau.
        p. cm.
    ISBN 1-931561-07-9 (alk. paper)
    1. Fishers–Fiction. 2. Trials (Murder)–Fiction 3. Fathers and sons–Fiction. 4. Maine–Fiction. I. Title.

    PS3607.A98 S43 2002
    813'.6–dc21

                                                            2001058697

Manufactured in the United States of America.
10 9 8 7 6 5 4 3 2 1

Jacket and book design by Dorothy Carico Smith

sea room

A Novel by Norman G. Gautreau

MacAdam/Cage Publishing

San Francisco ◆ Denver

To Susan

wife, friend, partner, confidant, and gentle critic;

and to Marc, Steve, Ma and Dad.

With gratitude.

author's note

One of the primary settings in this novel is variously named on maps and nautical charts as Buck Harbor, Bucks Harbor, and Buck's Harbor. I have chosen to use Buck Harbor, relying on the *U.S. Army Survey* of 1940 and the *Maine Atlas and Gazetteer* published by DeLorme Mapping Company. In addition to being the name used on period maps, it avoids confusion with the Bucks Harbor that is farther Down East near Machias, Maine.

Locals will know it was Hurricane Carol in 1954 which wreaked havoc on Revere Beach, not Hurricane Clara in 1950 as I have it in this story, and that on its heels came Edna, not Della. I am confident they will permit me the liberty.

For photographs of the lovely Blue Hill peninsula, a picture of Gil's half-model, the lofted lines of *Trobador*, and more, please visit my web site at www.nggautreau.com.

part 1

1941-1945

And, behold, there came a great wind from the wilderness, and smote the four corners of the house, and it fell upon the young men, and they are dead; and I only am escaped alone to tell thee.

— Job 1:19

chapter 1

The fog that day stayed offshore. It loitered round Bucksmaster Neck and the dozen or so little islets and rocks ringing it, and it brooded in Jericho Bay. The air throbbed with the sound of foghorns punctuating the steady, underlying thrum of lobster boats going about their business.

Ten-year-old Jordi Dupuy stood in the stern of the *Zabet & Lydie* alongside his grandfather Pip, who shifted his balance in time to the roll of the swell. Jordi's father, Gil, gripped the wheel, steering them out of Eggemoggin Reach into the mist. Veils of fog brushed over the boat, leaving on every surface beads of moisture that quivered with vibrations from the engine.

Emerging from the murkiness ahead of them, another lobster boat plowed its way homeward throwing spray from its bow. Its tiny riding sail smacked the air uselessly.

"Seems in a mighty rush, Pip," Gil called from the wheelhouse. He was a tall man, at least three inches taller than Pip and less leathery of complexion. A touch of Brylcreem in his hair lightened the brew of sea smell he had inherited from Pip.

Gil reached out with a yellow-slickered arm and nudged the throttle with a hand white and wrinkled with sea-damp. The *Zabet & Lydie* rose slightly onto her bow wave and accelerated, with a gentle hiss along her waterline, toward Blue Hill Bay and the waiting lobster pots.

Watching the other boat hurtle past, Pip said, "That's that damned Virgil Blount." His "th"s came out as "t"s or "d"s. Like his wife Nana, Pip had a Franco-American accent. Fortunately, he and

Nana were married in a French service. Otherwise, "With this ring I thee wed" would have been damn near impossible, as Gil often teased. Pip seemed sprung from the ancient granite crevices that edged the coast; he was all lines and edges, little difference between bone and muscle. His complexion was the brown of dried rockweed and he carried the mixed smells of the sea about him—salt-caked breezes, baited traps, barnacled rocks, and the vagueness of low-tide decay. Though a lifetime of Maine coastal winds had chiseled out the features of his face, the corners of his eyes were creased with a thousand traces of laughter and his eyes possessed a glint as fresh as a baby's.

"What's he doing out in the deeper water?" Gil asked Pip. "It ain't cold enough yet for the lobsters to be out that far."

"*We* have traps set out there."

"I know. But that's just in case. Do you figure he's copying us?"

Pip shrugged. "Where that jerk goes, that's his problem." He threw a bucketful of seawater over the trap skids for Jordi, who was brushing away the remains of chum, and made his way forward, gripping the gunwale, to secure the snatch block divot which was pivoting and jerking with a rhythmic squeak. "Jordi, this is your job. Make sure everyt'ing is secure like I told you."

"Okay, Pip. Sorry." Jordi joined his father and grandfather in the wheelhouse. All three of them wore yellow slickers they donned when the rain started earlier that afternoon. Now, however, all three slickers were open in an effort to dry the clammy shirts under them. The trouble with rubber was it kept the outside wetness out, but created its own condensation on the inside. Either way, you were wet, particularly when fugged inside a mizzling fog as they were now.

"Now will you look at that," cried Gil.

Drawn by the reverential tone of his father's voice, Jordi looked up to see a sleek ketch with a gleaming white hull and white sails materialize, wraithlike, out of the fog. In the light northeasterly breeze, she was sailing close-hauled on the starboard tack—main, mizzen, and huge overlapping jib all drawing nicely. The leach of her jib shivered. She had, as sailors say, a bone in her teeth—the water parted at her bow, a double sash of white foam spreading out like trailing scarves.

She moved steadily through the water, a fancy of pure, graceful power. Reflections of rushing water danced along her hull.

Jordi sucked in his breath.

"I saw one like her in *Rudder* magazine," said Gil. "I think she's a Herreshoff design."

"She's beautiful!" said Jordi.

Pip said, "I think it's the way she fits in wit' the wind. She uses it like it's a friend, not an enemy."

"I wonder what it would take to build something like that?" asked Gil.

Jordi gazed at his father with excited eyes. Was it possible?

"A hell of a lot of time and a hell of a lot of money—" replied Pip.

"Yeah, but look at her! Look at that sheer line!"

"—and a hell of a lot of skill."

"*You* have the skill, Pip," said Jordi.

"Just because I worked part time at the boatyard don't mean I have that kind of skill. I'm no Ogden Gower when it comes to boatbuilding."

"But, Pip, you built this boat," said Jordi.

Pip smiled with a great deal of pride. Nevertheless, he said, "The *Zabet & Lydie* was easy compared to somet'ing like that. *Jésus, Marie, et Josef*, she's all curves."

"Aw, you could do it and you know it," said Gil.

"And where would we get the money, eh? Tell me."

"Uncle Chrétien?" Jordi asked tentatively.

"Chrétien? Why would he give us money to build such a boat?" demanded Pip.

"You know him, Dad. He'd *make* money on it," said Gil. "We'd sell it for a profit after we sailed her for a season or two. For us, it's the building of her that would count…and Uncle Chrétien would jump at the chance."

"Where the hell does he get his goddamned money anyways?" It was a question that had been asked by every member of the family for years. But Chrétien would never tell them, claiming that he really didn't have a lot of money, at least not compared to some. Yet he always seemed to have enough to help out in any family crisis. Once, after many beers, he said mysteriously, "I owe it all to Sue Harper." But that had only provoked a deeper question—who the hell was Sue Harper and why was she giving him money?

"Is my brother mixed up wit' some kind o' loose woman?" Nana had asked. "Pip, you talk wit' him."

But Chrétien would not answer Pip's or anyone else's questions, and Sue Harper remained a mystery.

"Well, wherever it comes from," Gil said as he eased the throttle back a notch, "there ain't no doubt he has it."

"And you can be sure I ain't gonna ask him for none of it."

Gil smiled, shrugged, and turned the boat toward the pots they set near where Eggemoggin Reach spilled into Blue Hill Bay. Ahead of them, the fog thickened so Gil approached cautiously, his speed slow enough that the *Zabet & Lydie's* bow hardly stirred the water. They worked their way close by Hog Island. Though they guessed it was too early in the season for the lobsters to migrate to the deeper water, they had set a few traps in the fall and winter beds just to be sure.

As they entered a thick curd of fog, a snarl of mist curled about the boat. Gil slowed the *Zabet & Lydie* to a crawl. The world shrank around them. They still heard foghorns and the faint thrum of other engines, but the sounds seemed to belong to another universe. All three peered into the void, more likely to see floaters in the vitreous fluids of their own eyes than anything in the outside world.

"I hate fog wit' all my heart," Pip muttered. "We'll never find the goddamned pots."

No sooner had he said it, however, than they approached an area of brightening sky.

"Looks like the sun will burn it off soon," said Gil.

It took an hour to pull and re-set the traps before Jordi and the others started groping for home. They had gone only a short distance when two more lobster boats emerged from the fog at breakneck speed, their bow waves curling steeply, spray flying as high as their gunwales.

"What the hell are they doing?" asked Pip.

"I dunno. First Virgil Blount, now them. What's going on?"

Before Pip could answer, they were startled by the ear-splitting blast of a ship's horn. It seemed to come from directly above them like a Doomsday trumpet.

"What the Christ?"

Jordi was too frightened to say anything.

"That's one big ship," said Gil. "What the hell is it doing in Blue Hill Bay?" Then, with alarm edging his voice, "And *where* the hell is it?"

One of the speeding lobster boats turned toward them. As it steered to pass alongside, they recognized her. The *Susan May*.

"It's Travis Lathrop—"

"Looks like that ship's horn scared the crap out of him too."

Slowing only slightly, Travis Lathrop steered his boat past the *Zabet & Lydie*, cupped his hands around his mouth, and shouted, "It's the whole goldang German Navy! I saw 'em! Dozens of warships! They're invading!"

"You're crazy. We ain't even at war yet."

"We are now! You better get out of here. Go get your shotguns." With that, he jammed the throttle forward, and the *Susan May* leapt onto her bow wave and shot toward Naskeag Point.

"What the hell is he talking 'bout?"

Gil chuckled. "Is the fool trying to tell us that the Germans would blow their horns to announce they're here? Why don't they just send a telegram or call on the telephone? Hey, Americaner, *das var ist beginnink*."

They all laughed. And when they stopped laughing, they squinted into the fog.

"I don't see not'ing," murmured Pip.

But as he spoke, a dark gray mass resolved out of the undifferentiated white of the fog. Slowly it materialized and took on details like a photo in a developing bath. It seemed to be made of droplets of mist that were bonding together and transmuting themselves into molecules of metal.

It was a warship.

The long hull took shape, then the tall navigation bridge, then the two forward gun turrets. Finally they saw a thick column of smoke coiling from a funnel and stretching out over the stern.

Another shape appeared. A smaller warship. Then another. And another. Gradually, a total of six ships materialized out of the mist. Pip, Gil, and Jordi all stood, mouths open. The sun had shredded larger holes in the fog and they could now make out the ships' details. From photos in *National Geographic*, and from ships they had seen at Bath Iron Works, they recognized one cruiser and five destroyers. They saw a flag. It was American.

Gil laughed. "They're ours."

"It could be a trick."

"Oh, come on, Pip. You don't really think…"

They had drifted close enough to the largest ship to read the name. *Augusta*. A man's voice, amplified by a megaphone, hailed them. "Ahoy there, in the lobster boat. Best steer clear, we're anchoring."

"Speaks good English for a German," laughed Gil.

"Who the hell said they was German?"

"But you said it might be a trick."

"I was just foolin' wit' you."

Gil waved to the man with the megaphone. He eased the throttle forward and steered the *Zabet & Lydie* back toward Naskeag Point and Brooklin. "I can't wait to tell Travis and Virgil Blount what fools they are."

Soon they were approaching the entrance to Eggemoggin Reach.

The reach, a narrow wedge of water, stretched about ten miles on a northwest to southeast axis. With the clean abruptness of a butcher's cleaver, it separated the mainland from Deer Isle, Vinalhaven, Isle au Haut and scores of other islands off the coast of Maine. The reach was a water corridor about a mile wide in most places, but it narrowed to less than half a mile at Byard Point where Jordi remembered happily watching with his whole family as the bridge over to Little Deer Isle was built in 1939.

At the entrance to the reach, they again saw the white ketch. She now had the wind on her beam. Her sails were eased and she coasted majestically in the diminishing breeze. As they passed her, they studied her lines and the graceful way she moved through the water.

They entered Center Harbor. Just as Gil was making his final approach to the dock, Virgil Blount untied his boat and powered past them, riding his bow wave away from the dock. He peered at them through wire-rimmed glasses. A cigarette was wedged between his ear and temple. He had a thin mustache—the sad, wispy result of his effort to impress a woman who had raved about Clark Gable. He wore a perpetually dour, vengeful expression as if his ill-favored mustache was somebody else's fault. For all that, women found him strangely attractive. None of the men could understand or really believe it.

"Unfriendly cuss," said Gil as he edged the *Zabet & Lydie* against the dock and threw a line to Niall Macgrudder, the lobster buyer. The line shed a mist of vapor as it snapped taut after Niall wrapped it around a piling and brought the *Zabet & Lydie* to a stop.

"There's somet'ing about that Blount I don't like," said Pip. "Grew that poor excuse of a mustache because he overheard Lucy Evans make a silly remark outside the movie house. He has the hots for her, and she's a married woman."

Gil nodded. "He's trouble."

"*Il est un pète-sec!*"

"What's that mean, Pip?" Jordi asked.

"Means he makes dry farts. Always frowning an' complaining."

Niall Macgrudder smiled and said, "Heard 'bout the Germans?"

"Yuh," said Gil. "Here, tie up the stern and I'll tell you all about them." He tossed another line to Niall who looped it around a second piling.

Niall Macgrudder had a bald pate, mottled with brown spots, and a bulbous nose, all framed by a cascade of white hair and white beard. The broken capillaries on his cheeks, like watermarks on paper, testified to countless evenings in the convivial company of his lobstermen clients. It was Niall, friend to all, who had become best friends with Pip and Chrétien and who paved the way for their acceptance as Franco-American Catholics in a predominantly Yankee Protestant community. The fact that in the '30s Chrétien had lavished a great deal of his bootlegged whiskey on Niall helped to lubricate the process. Still, some, in the privacy of their kitchens, derided the Dupuys, but none would express these feelings openly for fear of angering Niall.

Stepping onto the dock, Gil said, "There are six warships out there, but they're American. The cruiser *Augusta* and five destroyers."

Niall laughed heartily. "That the whole of it? I figured as much. Gorry! Virgil come honking in here like his pants was on fire. Left in a awful huff when I told him he was crazy. Others too. They was some ugly!"

Seeing other boats approaching the dock, they quickly sold their lobster catch to Niall and returned to Naskeag Harbor. After putting the *Zabet & Lydie* on her mooring, they rowed ashore, beached the dinghy, and piled into their battered 1932 Ford pickup truck. In Brooklin they stopped at Gott's Market. Pip pulled a sodden piece of paper from his shirt pocket, carefully unfolded it, and announced that Nana wanted them to buy some Oxydol, Crisco, and vinegar. Gil picked up a copy of the *Bangor Daily News*. It told of new advances by the Nazis on two fronts.

"They're going to win this damned war before Mr. Roosevelt can get us into it," Gil said.

"Does Hitler have all of Europe?"

"Damn near," said Gil. "Hell, I wish we could do something." Gil scanned the newspaper further. "According to this, Mr. Roosevelt just met with Churchill up in Newfoundland. Maybe we'll be in it after all."

"Will you go if we get in the war, Dad?" asked Jordi, a slight tremor in his voice.

"I don't know if they would take me, being a father and all."

"But would you go if they asked?"

Gil put a hand on his son's head. "I'd have to."

"How the hell you gonna build your boat if you go?" asked Pip, narrowing his eyes at his son.

Jordi's shoulders sagged almost imperceptibly. Even at this early

age it was obvious he had inherited the slender good looks of both Gil
and Lydie Dupuy. The only flaw was a misshapen nose accidentally
broken at the bridge when Pip threw an Indian club too ardently during one of their barnyard games. But people never noticed his nose
because of the clarity of his unusual blueberry-blue eyes. Now, those
eyes were clouded.

Outside Gott's, they climbed back into their truck, Pip behind the
wheel with Jordi in the middle between him and Gil. As Pip pulled
onto the road, Gil said, "Let's go down to Center Harbor. I want to
see if that boat is there. Looked like she was headed this way when we
passed her."

"The ketch? We'll be late. The women will be expecting us."

"Nana and Lydie can wait just a few minutes."

"Christ, you'd think you found a beautiful woman."

"I wouldn't know what to do with another beautiful woman, Pip.
I got Lydie. But I sure as hell would know what I'd do with a boat like
that."

"What, Dad?" asked Jordi.

"We'd sail out way beyond Eggemoggin Reach, that's what we'd
do."

Jordi smiled at the vision of them slicing through the waters, his
father at the helm and him on the bow clutching the forestay.

At Center Harbor, they walked by the yacht club and scanned the
two dozen or so boats squatting on their reflections in the undisturbed
water. They had to squint, for the fog had not penetrated the harbor
and the sun glanced off the water. The dazzling white boat was not
hard to spot. Her masts stood taller than anything else in the harbor.
Two people sat in the cockpit lifting glasses and chatting.

"Jeez! Look at her lines," said Gil. He studied the boat for another few moments and said, "Both masts are raked a little." As he spoke,
the ketch swung on her mooring in response to a shift in the current.
It was as though she were posing, displaying all her lines to best advantage.

"Some boat," said a voice behind them. It was Ogden Gower, the
best boat builder on the peninsula. He had a long, straw-colored beard

that came to a point at his belt buckle. It had been cultivated on a five-year around-the-world solo sailing expedition. His tough, thin body showed the effects of a five-year diet of dried meats, thin soups, raw fish, and only occasional fruits and vegetables. His eyes bulged as though they had exceptional peripheral vision, perhaps like a fish, and he spoke with the conciseness of someone who had gauged the value of human speech in the silent center of many storms. His thumbs hooked the straps of his soiled coveralls, shaking a mist of sawdust from them. He looked like a man patiently waiting for Judgment Day.

"Herreshoff design?" asked Gil.

"Eyuh. Name's *Mistral.* Built down in Essex, Massachusetts. Forty-five plus overall, thirty-eight, nine on the waterline. Mostly white oak. Knees and other frame members of hackmatack."

"What does she draw?"

"Five feet. Pretty shallow. But sails fine, I'm told."

The ketch swung further on her mooring, showing her full profile. Reflections danced along her hull like flashes from a diamond ring.

"Who owns her?"

"Doctor from away. Boston."

They studied the ketch in silence. Then Ogden turned abruptly and with a broad smile said, "Good seeing ya. Ain't got time to chat all day." He started to walk back up the road but stopped and said over his shoulder, "Hello to your women folk." Then he was gone.

"Not exactly a chatterbox," said Gil with a smile.

"Old Yankee," answered Pip, imitating Ogden Gower's clipped speech.

After admiring the ketch a little longer, the three clambered back into the truck and headed for home. As the truck bounced along the dirt road, an image of the three of them building such a boat played in Jordi's mind.

Pip drove slowly along the rutted dirt roads, the truck trailing a cloud of dust. Up ahead, the road went down a hill, made an "S" curve, and climbed another hill like a long, narrow scrawl on the landscape. As the truck rumbled along, a half-dozen crows lifted up from a dead squirrel with a flutter of wings and squawked at the passing truck, their cries as harsh as rusty nails pulled from a board.

Pip's hand was cupped tightly over the gearshift. If he let go, the old truck would fall out of gear. Jordi studied the landscape of Pip's hands, the ridges and valleys of the long bones, the brown patches, the cracked crests of knuckles, the puckered veins, all interwoven with muscle. They were hands that seemed to have an intelligence of their own whenever they gripped a saw or guided a smoothing plane or angled a spokeshave. Jordi knew Pip had the skill to build a boat like *Mistral.*

Gil kept talking about the ketch, calculating what it would take to build such a boat. Jordi listened quietly, hopefully. The truck wheezed up Caterpillar Hill, barely making the summit, before descending to Route 176 where they made a left.

Ahead, they saw a scattering of cars and pickup trucks parked along the road.

"What's going on?"

"Accident, maybe?"

"Could be. Let's stop."

Suddenly, Jordi cried, "Look!"

Pip and Gil turned and gasped.

At the mouth of Buck Harbor a huge motor yacht sat at anchor, dwarfing the sailboats and all the other craft that drifted around it like flies around a cow.

"Don't you recognize her?" asked Gil. "That's the *Potomac.* It's Mr. Roosevelt! We've just been talking about him and, son-of-a-bitch, here he is. I bet those warships were his escort."

Jordi glared at the presidential yacht. What if Roosevelt decided to go to war? What about their boat then?

chapter 2

Pip and Jordi scrambled after Gil down the steep, rutted path. When they arrived at the docks, they saw a crowd of people watching as a motor launch rubbed against the pier with a deep rumble from its engine and a mist of water spitting from its exhaust. As the launch came to a stop, two sailors leapt off to whip lines around pilings.

Jordi recognized many of the people—Travis Lathrop, Niall Macgrudder, others. Virgil Blount was standing nearby. Travis Lathrop was saying, "Them ships was sittin' out there big as Billy-be-damned."

"Every one a honker," added Burl Babbage, bug eyes staring from an ancient, scarred face. "I shoved that friggin ol' exhilerater something fierce an' got the hell outta there."

"Godfrey mighty!"

"German, too," said Niall Macgrudder with a grin.

"Wan't!"

"Leastwise, that's what Virgil Blount said. Went on about it longer than a hard winter."

Virgil Blount scowled at Niall. The others snickered. Then everyone moved out of the way as the two sailors began to walk up the road.

"Need any lobstah?" asked Niall.

One of the sailors, a pimple-faced boy no more than eighteen, grinned, shook his head and said, "The president wants some ice cream."

Ray Gray ran an ice cream parlor from his white, porch-fronted home at the top of the path where it met Route 176. His ice cream was famous and had long ago gained the attention of Roosevelt, who frequently ordered the presidential yacht to stop at Buck Harbor on the way to his retreat on Campobello Island.

"Here comes Ma," said Jordi.

Lydie Dupuy, still wearing an apron over fashionable culottes and a rayon blouse, descended the path. A wisp of hair floated on her forehead, creating a faint, fleeting shadow. She wore a red bandana around her slender neck. A hush fell over the crowd as all the men turned to look at her. If not for the animation of her face, her features would be too perfect to be beautiful: high cheekbones, shapely chin, deep-set piercing eyes, and a straight nose. She gave her husband a hug and said, "Little Robbie Culver came over to tell Nana and me. Have you seen Mr. Roosevelt?"

"Nah, only a couple of sailors getting ice cream for him."

"Where's Nana, Ma?" asked Jordi.

"She has bread baking in the oven. Said it's more important than some president."

Before long the two sailors returned, carrying a large tub of chocolate ice cream. Gil approached them. "Say, tell Mr. Roosevelt for us that we'd like to know when we're going to do something to stop that Hitler fellah."

Lydie linked arms with Gil. "I'm sure he's doing what he can."

"Nah, we oughta be at war already."

"Vah!" said Rufus Metcalfe who had lost a son at Verdun and another at the Somme during the Great War. "That's just *their* business over theah, not ours. Just like the Christless Great War wan't none of our goldang business."

Virgil Blount stepped forward. "Rufus is right. Ain't none of our business." He looked at Lydie Dupuy as he said it.

Jordi looked sideways at Blount, watching the man stare at his mother. He felt a surge of hatred.

"Somebody's got to stop Hitler," said Gil.

"Well you can," answered Blount. "You can go get yourself killed for nothing. I ain't gonna."

The launch pulled away from the dock with a deep-throated rumble and made for the *Potomac*. "Come on," Lydie said to her husband

and son, "Nana will have supper on soon."

Gil, Lydie, and Jordi started up the path. Jordi saw over his shoulder that Pip wasn't following, so he went back to urge him on. As Jordi approached, he heard Pip and Niall Macgrudder talking in low voices.

"Saw the way Virgil Blount looked at your daughter-in-law. That man is some stemmy, like as though he eats nothing but oysters. I saw him talking up Delores Ludlow once. You know her, God made her as ugly as he could then kicked her in the face. Even has very-close veins all over her legs, but goldang if that don't matter none to Virgil Blount so long's she's female. But your daughter-in-law, she's a looker. An' that man's a zero."

Pip laughed. "Don't worry 'bout Lydie, she has eyes only for my son, always has."

"But that's the whole of it, Pip, them eyes. A lighthouse may want to light the way for one boat, but others can't help but see its beam."

Pip laughed. "That's a god-awful metaphor."

"What'n goldang hell's a metaphor?"

"Making a comparison like that. Jeez, I'd think you were talking about yourself and Lydie the way you're going on."

"Me? You're number'n a hake. I'm too old for such things."

Jordi backed away from them, feeling a flush of anger and embarrassment rise to his cheeks. He turned and chased after his parents.

The Dupuy farm was a saltwater farm in South Brooksville on the edge of Buck Harbor. It was bounded on three sides by stone walls and fences and open on the fourth to the sea. Down a gentle slope toward Eggemoggin Reach from the barn and the farmhouse sprawled a series of rectangles, each devoted to a different crop. Behind the barn was Nana's and Lydie's truck garden—tomatoes, beets, onions, potatoes, pumpkin, squash—sitting in a splay of long shadows from the branches of the big oak tree. Behind it was the pasture which, in addition to groves of maple, oak, and beech, contained a dozen hardy Dorset sheep, four Nubian goats, and a chicken coop housing two dozen Rhode Island Red hens with a rooster to service them. Beyond the pasture was a frog pond, then a rock-strewn meadow where wild strawberries and low-bush blueberries grew among the juniper and lambkill. Adjacent to the meadow sat a barren area where wind-blown salt had etched away the lives of plants. From there, the land sloped more steeply down to the percolating clam beds before submerging and continuing out to the lobsters' scuttling grounds and finally to the deeper water of the shrimp, scallops, flounder, and mackerel. Late afternoon sunlight draped itself over the scene like a fine, clinging cloth, fitting itself to every contour, dipping into every crevice and hollow, rising over every swell.

Living on a saltwater farm, they were always keenly aware that they existed in a marginal world ruled by the diurnal suck and shove of the tide—and by the wind. The sea regularly lifted skirts of fog over the farm, cutting them off from the rest of the world.

Jordi and his parents entered the farmhouse and an embrace of yeasty warmth. The bread Nana had just pulled from the oven sat on the table. A blue checkered cloth was draped over the loaves and a shimmer of heat rose from them. The aroma of fresh bread dominated all kitchen smells except the sharp, acrid odor of kerosene from the summer stove; the big coal stove, cast iron with chrome trim, emitted too much heat for the warm months. A base of wainscoting with wallpaper above lined the walls. The floor was brittle linoleum, curling at the edges and crazed in radiating circles where the four cast iron legs of the coal stove settled heavily into it. Above the table a ribbon of brown flypaper seemed always dappled with dead flies even though Nana changed it daily. Hanging below a naked light bulb, it swayed in an errant draft. Gil reached up and pulled the string to turn on the light. The bulb swayed in a small arc tracing a faint light across the four walls, dipping into the corners and brushing across the telephone and the coat hooks and hanging pots. Two flatirons perched on the cool stove plates and, hanging from a nail above the oak ice box, was a Frothingham Fertilizer Company calendar with the slogan "For *all* your dressing needs," which always made Jordi laugh.

"What's for supper, Ma?" asked Gil. "Besides your wonderful bread, I mean." He bent over to kiss her on the forehead.

"Beans n' franks." Zabet Dupuy, born Elizabeth Bastarache,

leaned forward to offer her forehead to her son. Soft hair, the pure, alabaster white of statues of the Virgin Mary, framed a doughy face hollowed and mounded by years of gentle stove heat. An apron, secured in a tiny knot at the very limits of its ties, cinched her yeast-swollen waist. Knowing, mischievous eyes, round and dark as plums, peered from under bleached eyebrows ready to tease the humor from any situation.

"Nana, you should have been there. We saw President Roosevelt's yacht."

"*Jésus, Marie, et Josef,* he's only the president," Nana said, tousling Jordi's hair. "I have more important t'ings to do, like cook your supper. Now wash your hands."

Jordi balanced himself on a stool before the sink and worked the handle of the pump. It wheezed like an asthmatic goat several times before a gush of water flowed from its lip. Jordi lathered his hands with Nana's homemade lye soap, rinsed and dried them. He handed the towel to his father who repeated the process. Together, they held out their hands for Nana's inspection. When she nodded her approval, Jordi sat at the table holding his hunger, waiting for everyone else to be seated.

Past Nana's shoulder, the sepia-toned photograph of his Aunt Emily, propped on a shelf next to a jar of stove polish, a bottle of lamp oil, and a statue of Saint Francis, caught Jordi's eye. As he gazed at the photograph, a shivering shadow cast by the flypaper bisected the image of Emily. A familiar feeling, like a moth fluttering around his insides, came to him. It was a kind of irresistible dread, like reading a horror story—a tale he played over and over in his mind. Jordi remembered overhearing Pip and his father talking about it once over glasses of whiskey when they thought Jordi was sleeping.

One day in 1919, not long after Pip had returned from the Great War, Nana took their three-year-old daughter Emily to the photographer to have her portrait done. Three days later, Emily was dead of pneumonia, a victim of the influenza epidemic. After the funeral, Nana and Pip had gone, arm in arm, to the photographer to claim the finished portrait. When the man asked cheerily, "How is your lovely daughter?" Nana had replied, "Happy now, and in Heaven where not'ing will bother her no more. It's very lucky that we brought her here when we did."

Now, every time Jordi looked at the photograph, which he did often, he thought he could see a dark knowledge of death in Emily's eyes. It was almost as though she had *known* she would die. Jordi wondered if such a thing was possible, and he wondered what happened to people after they died—their bodies, their thoughts, their souls. It was the mystery that most preoccupied him.

To relieve his mind, he thought once more of the *Mistral* and what it would be like to build such a boat with his father and Pip.

Once Pip came in, washed, and submitted his hands to Nana's inspection, they all sat down to eat. They ate in silence until Gil and Pip slid their chairs back with loud scrapes and got up to get second helpings of the beans. Gil returned to the table, set his plate on the red-checkered oil cloth, and said, "Saw a great boat today. A ketch."

Jordi raised his eyes to his father.

Gil described the way the boat moved and how Pip had said she fit herself to the wind and how he'd learned that it was owned by somebody from Boston. "I'd like to build a boat like that. Ain't often you can build something that works with the wind instead of being torn apart by it," he said.

"We got a lobster boat," said Nana.

"That's different, Ma. Can't go nowhere with a lobster boat 'cept to catch lobsters an' maybe do a little shrimping. And besides, lobster boats and wind ain't friends."

"Where else you gonna go but lobstering an' shrimping?"

Gil turned to Lydie and said, "Wouldn't you like to sail someplace? Take a cruise?"

Lydie laughed. "That's for rich people."

. "Not necessarily. If we built it ourselves…"

"And who has time for such a crazy t'ing?" demanded Nana.

"We could build it over the winters, on days too stormy for lobstering or shrimping."

"What do you mean 'We?'" asked Pip. "This is your crazy idea, not mine."

"Aw Jeez, Pip..." Gil turned to Lydie. "Do you think it's a crazy idea?"

Instead of answering, Lydie touched the sleeve of Gil's shirt. She stretched the fabric between her hands and smiled, exploring a hole with her index finger. "You've torn your shirt. Take it off when we're through eating and I'll mend it while we listen to the radio."

"And you take your shirt off too, Pip," snapped Nana. "*Jésus, Marie, et Josef,* it smells awful. I gotta wash it."

After supper, the whole family filed out to the porch where Pip had set up the radio for the summer months. He, Gil, and Jordi often sat out and watched the sky as they listened to Red Sox games. Lydie settled into a rocker with her mending kit and went to work on her husband's shirt, arranging the fabric across her lap. The others settled in around the Philco.

Jordi watched a moth flutter frantically against the screen.

Out of the kitchen and away from the aroma of bread, the essential smells of the farmhouse reasserted themselves, spilling out the living room window which opened onto the porch. The walls retained the scent of a hundred years of vegetables stored in the cellar: barreled apples, raw potatoes; of the coal stove and wood smoke; of earth tracked indoors, and of ever-present mould; and of generations of human sweat and breath—a smell dusted with years of the wind-blown dirt that was always threatening to bury the farm.

Jordi recalled when Pip first brought the radio home. He had walked proudly into the kitchen and put it on the checkered table-cloth with a flourish.

"What is that t'ing?" Nana had cried.

"That's a radio."

"But we ain't got no 'lectricity."

Pip rubbed his chin thoughtfully and said, "Yuh, that's a problem, I guess." Then he smiled and raised his eyebrows toward his brother-in-law, Chrétien, inviting him to speak.

"Zabet," Chrétien said, "I made arrangements for them to hook us up. They'll be here next week."

"Where did you get the money for that? You been seeing that Sue
Harper woman?"

"Zabet, I got the money, that's all."

Nana gave him a suspicious look and muttered, "Lights and radios
are one t'ing, but, *Mon Dieu*, I ain't gonna have no 'lectric stove."

On the porch, Pip turned the radio on and adjusted the dials. At
first, nothing but hissing and crackling came from the fan-shaped
sound opening. Then a few strange whistles came as if the radio was
warming its voice. And finally a scratchy voice rose out of the static.
Their disappointment that it was not Edward R. Morrow changed to
joyful shouts of surprise when the voice said, *"We now send you to
London where our new correspondent, Teddy Thibodeau, is standing by.
Are you there, Teddy?"*

"My cousin!" cried Lydie with delight. "He said he had a new
assignment, but—"

"*Mon Dieu!*"

"Sshh, listen."

*—speaking to you from London. Life in this great capital is gradual-
ly returning to normal since April when the Luftwaffe stopped its savage
bombing. No longer do we have searchlights slashing the sky, sirens wail-
ing in the gloom, a roar of fire, a crash of crumbling walls, the god-awful
whistle of falling bombs like the sound of wind through a crack-riddled
barn. Even the birds sleep normally now, whereas before, they awoke and
sang when the searchlights turned night into day. No longer do the patrons
in swank hotels bed down in the basements. No longer do we hear the
whining, shuddering roar, like a hurricane, of the high-explosive bombs,
or see the sizzling blue-white flares of cluster incendiaries, like lightning,
or see mines descending slowly under green silk parachutes. Even the stench
of the Thames, fouled after the main sewer system was destroyed last fall,
has gone away.*

*No, these nightmares are no longer nightly occurrences. But the mem-
ory of them is still here in the haunted, hunted faces of the people that you
pass in the street, in the rubble of shattered buildings, in the tangle of bro-*

ken pavement, in the piles of timber, lath, and plaster, and in the glitter of broken glass. And though the British people display amazing courage and resilience, though hope and optimism burn in their hearts, nothing can erase the horror of Hitler's madness.

Jordi looked at his father, then at Pip. They were both staring at the radio. He turned to see his mother, biting her lower lip, and Nana clutching her rosary beads.

Last evening, I was walking along one of the streets near Saint Paul's Cathedral when I came upon a remarkable sight. Before me stood a town-house whose street-side wall had been ripped away by a blast. I was look-ing, uninvited, like a voyeur, into some family's exposed dining room, nor-mally reserved for them and their invited guests alone. The pale wallpa-per carried a leafy theme in rose and green, which was mirrored in the upholstery of the dining room chairs. Miraculously, the room appeared undamaged. The table was set with plates and silverware, napkins, glass-es, as though the family was just about to sit down to dinner. Curtains still hung over a window in the far wall; they were whipped around by the invading breeze throwing frantic shadows across a wall which had never before been brushed with sunlight. Only a few shards of plaster on the sideboard gave any evidence of what had happened there. There was so lit-tle interior damage, I guessed that the family had survived and would be back to gather their belongings. But however much they might salvage, they had lost their privacy; it had been violated. For that is what war does. It transforms a private tragedy into a public display. And it destroys dreams.

As I started to leave, I saw a member of the Home Guard. I asked him who had lived there. A family of five, friends of his, he told me—Mom, Dad, three children, two boys and a girl. I asked him how the family had made out, where they had gone. 'All killed in the blast,' he said. Oh yes, and he told me their names. But out of respect for their privacy, let me just say they were an ordinary family, on an ordinary street, caught in an extraordinary time—just additional poor, long-distance victims, among legions and legions, of one madman who must be stopped.

This is Teddy Thibodeau in London. And as you sit down to a family dinner, please say a prayer for these folks on the other side of the pond and all the others like them. Good night.

Lydie wiped a tear from the corner of her eye. "He sounds so sad," she said. "Poor Teddy."

Gil slammed his fist on the arm of his chair. "Aren't we ever gonna clobber that Hitler? When is Mr. Roosevelt going to do something?"

"It's only a matter of time, if you ask me," said Pip.

Lydie turned her eyes to her husband and asked the same question that Jordi had asked in Gott's Market. "But you wouldn't have to go, would you? With a family and all?"

Gil exchanged glances with Pip and placed his hand over Lydie's. "Don't know what the government will do, so there's no point worrying about it now."

"But you wouldn't *want* to go, would you?"

"And, Dad, what about the boat?" asked Jordi.

Gil said nothing. He shook his head, caught Pip's eye again.

Jordi turned away and watched the moth still flinging itself against the screen, toward the unreachable kitchen light. And he saw, out in the barnyard, fireflies like far, far distant flashes from gun barrels.

chapter 3

Jordi's special project that summer was to bounce a baseball off the barn roof and catch it a hundred times in a row. A week or so after Roosevelt's visit, he went out to the barn in the unexpected September heat which fell upon him with a bother of bluebottles and dragonflies, and a thrumming of cicadas. He stuffed his left hand into the outfielder's glove, which still smelled of the linseed oil Pip had used to soften it, and made his first throw. He heaved the ball up to the tin roof where it landed with a dull clunk, hesitated a moment, then rolled down, bouncing wherever the tin was dented. It gathered speed and shot from the roof's edge. Jordi caught it with a plop in the center of the glove's pocket.

"One."

A skittering of barn swallows came fluttering out of the loft. He lifted his leg and hurled the ball up again. It clattered off the roof and into his glove.

"Two."

He imagined they were fly balls off the bat of Joe Dimaggio and that the "Yankee Clipper" was out every time. It was never Ted Williams who was out. That was against the rules. He had not yet reached a count of ten when an anger, like a blue haze, fell upon him. The previous night's news heightened his fear that the war in Europe might take his father from him. The president had announced that the American destroyer *U.S.S. Greer* was fired at by a German U-Boat, and he had ordered American warships to *"shoot on sight."*

"It's about time," Gil Dupuy said.

No one else said a word.

Now, Jordi changed his game. Instead of throwing the ball onto the roof, he started to hurl it against the side of the barn with such force that the ball's already frayed stitching started to unravel, creating a blur as the ball spun toward the barn. He imagined the coiled knot halfway up the third board from the corner was the face of Hitler, and he aimed for it. He heaved the ball repeatedly. It struck the barn with tiny sprays of long-embedded dust. The wood around the knot became mottled with small dimples. When he managed to hit the hardened knot, the board resounded with a sharp crack instead of the hollow thud of the softer wood.

"Jordi! What're you doing?" It was Chrétien. Small and wiry, he had black currant eyes that had a looking-for-a-deal alertness; they sat placidly in a face which showed the effects of three packs of Old Gold cigarettes a day for forty years. Despite appearances, he was a compassionate man. If he stood in the barnyard along with a dozen other people, all the knowing animals—cats, dogs, goats, sheep—would sidle toward him.

"Just playing," replied Jordi.

Chrétien bent down to field the ball as it rebounded from the barn's siding and rolled in the dust. He examined it. "Stitching ain't looking so good. Needs some tape. Jeez, you been t'rowing that ball pretty hard. What're you so mad about?"

"Nothing."

"Aw Jeez, you can't fool me. I know somet'ing's got you all mad an' everyt'ing."

Jordi took the ball from Chrétien. "Will there be a war?"

"So that's it. Well, there already is a war, except we ain't in it."

"But will we be?"

Chrétien nodded. "I think so." He paused then said, "And you want to know if your dad will have to fight?"

Jordi nodded.

"Well it ain't easy to say. I guess he won't *have* to go 'cause they probably won't draft dads, at least at first. But will he *want* to go? That's another question."

"I think he'll go."

Chrétien shrugged. "Maybe. It's in his blood, both from the Dupuy and Bastarache sides. Me and Pip, we went over to fight in the Great War back in '17. A man's gotta do what he's gotta do. If you was the right age, I bet you'd want to go, too."

This surprised Jordi—he knew Chrétien was right. "But I'm afraid…"

Chrétien put a hand on Jordi's shoulder. "Yuh, I know. But let me tell you somet'ing else about the Dupuys and the Bastaraches: We have a lot of luck when it comes to t'ings like this. Pip and me was in the Meuse-Argonne offensive, couple of General Pershing's boys. It was ugly as hell, lots of men killed and wounded, but me and Pip— not a scratch. So you see? The Dupuys are lucky, especially when they're mixed with Bastarache blood like your dad."

Jordi thought about this. "You know that boat Dad's been talking about? Do you want to help build it?"

Chrétien laughed. "Sure, why the hell not? Then after we are finished using it, we could sell it to some rich guy from Boston. Make a nice profit."

Jordi laughed. "That's what Dad said you would want to do."

"Only makes sense."

"Then let's do it! You and me and Dad and Pip."

"Aw Jeez, not so fast," said Chrétien. "We can't do not'ing until we know what's happening wit' the war."

"But—"

"That's the way it is, Jordi. War interrupts t'ings."

Later that morning, Jordi went into the barn to escape the heat of the humid, sulky day on which the sun appeared fur-edged and faint behind a gauze of cloud. From the moment he entered the barn, he was filled with its ancient, musty smell, a smell that always made him think of decay. He sat down next to the tractor and studied the way dissected sunlight shouldered through the gaps in the vertical boards of the east wall. When the light slanted in this certain way an entire universe of tiny insects, swarms of them, was revealed to him. Usually, they went unseen, but now they swirled and darted through the barn.

But then a breeze pushed through the cracks in the siding and the insects were swept away.

The light fell on a collection of old license plates nailed to the west wall. Several barn swallows, who had returned after the morning commotion with the baseball, flitted among the rafters. Jordi thought about what he had done, throwing the baseball at the barn and pretending it was Hitler and, he had to admit to himself, pretending also that it was Virgil Blount.

When Jordi returned to the farmhouse, Nana said, "Look at you. You're all dirty. Have you forgotten about the fair? Change your clothes."

Jordi *had* forgotten. He rushed up to his room to change. The Blue Hill Fair in early September was one of the great events in the year, and Nana would almost prefer to miss Sunday Mass than miss *it*. She was arrayed in her Sunday best, a blue dress stippled with small white dots that Pip always said looked like a map of the Milky Way, a broad-brimmed hat, and sensible black shoes. The box of blueberry donuts she was entering in the baking contest sat on the table.

When Jordi reappeared in the kitchen with his other pair of dungarees, he found his parents and Nana gathered impatiently around the table, dressed and ready to go.

"Where's that Pip?" Nana demanded. "Do you know, Jordi?"

"Oh, yes. He's at the library, Nana."

She raised her eyes to the ceiling as if seeking divine sympathy. "That man and his books. Well, go get him!"

Jordi ran the short distance to the South Brooksville library and found Pip sitting at his customary place at the table by the window, a small book open before him. Sunlight stirred a shaft of dust particles and fell across Pip's face which rested on his closed fist. He was asleep. Jordi lowered the shade then gently shook Pip's shoulder. "Nana says it's time to go to the fair."

Pip raised his head. "Eh? Fair? Aw Jeez, yuh, time to go."

"What are you reading?"

Pip closed the cover of the book and held it out for Jordi:

"Evangeline" by Longfellow.

"But you've already read that a bunch of times, Pip. You've even read it to me."

Ignoring him, Pip said, "It's about how the English stole our ancestors' farms and sent us out of Nova Scotia and Prince Edward Island and everywhere. That's how we ended up here in Maine. Listen to this:

Waste are those pleasant farms, and the farmers forever departed!
Scattered like dust and leaves, when the mighty blasts of October
Seize them, and whirl them aloft, and sprinkle them far o'er the ocean…"

Jordi remembered long evenings sitting by the light of a kerosene lamp, when Pip would read the entire poem to him. This passage near the beginning always left Jordi feeling uneasy. Every time he heard it, he thought of how the wind shook their farmhouse, threatening to reduce it to dust. During these readings Pip also instilled in Jordi the notion of never going along with authority just for the sake of comfort. "Our ancestors refused to bow to the English. You always got to think for yourself and do what's right no matter who the hell's in charge at the time. You always got to make your own choices—take action." Pip returned the books to the shelves and threw his arm around Jordi's shoulder. "C'mon, let's not keep Nana waiting."

Nana was in a huff. She insisted they all pile into the truck and leave immediately for the fair. So with Jordi, his father, and Chrétien sitting in the open bed of the pickup, along with the Dorset lamb that Jordi planned to enter in the 4-H contest, Pip drove with Lydie and Nana sitting beside him in the cab. It was a short trip to Blue Hill and soon the truck was sputtering and lurching up the hill to the fairgrounds, a long line of impatient drivers behind it. The sky suddenly darkened and a flash of lightning lit up the western sky.

"It's a way off," said Pip. "Looks like we have enough time to get under cover if we hurry."

At last the truck bumped over the field and into a parking spot.

One by one they filed out of the truck, straightened their clothes, and started for the Exhibition Hall where the baking contest was held. But they went only a few steps when a gust of wind lashed at them and they were hit with a cloudburst. They ran back to the truck where Pip, Jordi, Nana, and Lydie crammed into the front seat while Gil and Chrétien pulled a tarpaulin over themselves in the back. The few seconds it took to get back to the truck left them drenched. Steam rose from their clothes, the windows fogged, the rain splattered the windshield.

"Damned luck," Pip said.

"Not to worry, it's gonna end soon," said Nana with confidence.

"What makes you such an expert, eh?" asked Pip as they watched the wind lash the rain horizontally against the truck.

"I said a little prayer."

Pip waved his hand dismissively. "Vah!" But within five minutes the storm did, indeed, end. Sunshine returned and Nana smiled at Pip's dour expression. They spilled from the truck and gratefully inhaled the freshly-washed air.

Later, the whole family watched Jordi show his lamb in the sheep pavilion. As the judge ambled past the row of lambs, Jordi knelt in the sawdust trying to encourage the animal to stand with a proud forward lean. But the lamb wouldn't cooperate. When someone else was announced the winner, Jordi didn't notice because he was so distracted by Virgil Blount who had approached to say hello to his parents. Jordi saw that Virgil didn't take his eyes off his mother, and he wanted to run over and shout at him to stop.

Lydie stepped over and said, "I'm sorry, Jordi."

"It's not your fault, Ma."

She raised her eyebrows quizzically. "Of course not. Your lamb just couldn't stay still. You just need to train her more."

He looked at her, smiled weakly, and shrugged. "I'll bring her to the pens then we can go see the midway."

"I'll go with you," Pip said.

On the way back from the pens, they passed the fenced-in area used for oxen and horse pulls. The ox pull involved pairs of oxen pulling weighted sleds back and forth in front of the grandstand. The team that could drag the sled farthest in five minutes would win. The pair of oxen now pulling struggled mightily, hoofs slipping in the dust, spit bubbling at their mouths and nostrils. Their driver urged them on with furious shouts and vicious cracks of a switch. The oxen heaved in their yokes, heads lowered, huge, sad eyes seeming to beg mercy from the watching crowd.

Jordi winced with every blow from the switch.

"*Jésus, Marie, et Josef,* I hate the oxen pull," Pip said. "They ain't like the horses. The horses, they love what they're doing. There ain't no need to whip them. They do it by *choice*. But the oxen, they don't make choices." He placed a hand on Jordi's shoulder and steered him away from the place. They hurried to catch up with the others.

After an hour or so amidst the riot of smells and sounds that was the midway they headed toward the small track where the over-4,700 pound horse pull was about to begin. On the way, they passed a pavilion where cows reclined in straw against the inner wall.

Jordi asked, "Can we get a cow?"

"What would we do with a cow?" asked Lydie.

"We could put it in the barn, get our own milk and butter."

"And I suppose you would get up every morning to milk her, and then again in the evening?"

"Yes, I'd love to do that." Jordi turned to his father and Pip. "Can't we get a cow?"

Gil laughed. "I doubt it. But we'll talk about it later. Right now it's time to watch Cousin Denis."

Denis Dupuy was a second cousin who lived near Rumford. Most Franco-Americans of Maine lived inland in communities around Bangor and Rumford, working at the paper mills, or they lived and worked in the northern logging towns. Nana had wanted to stay near Bangor. But Pip dreamed of a saltwater farm, saying, "It's our heritage. The Acadians of Nova Scotia and P.E.I. always worked the land and the sea at the same time. They didn't work for no Englishmen in no goddamned paper mills." So Nana was forced to live among Yankee Protestants, a forty-five-minute drive from the nearest Catholic church.

They returned to where Jordi had been shocked by the ox pull and climbed the steps to the small grandstand. They took their places on a long wooden bench. Shortly after they sat down, there was a stirring in the crowd as the three-horse teams began to enter, their drivers following on foot with the reins grasped tightly in their hands. Denis Dupuy was third in line, leaning back, walking on his heels behind three huge Belgians like a man trying to hold back a hurricane. Even from the grandstand, they could see the roped muscles of Denis' lean forearms tense as he struggled to control the horses. He grimaced as acrid smoke from his cigarette curled under his nose. The horses, two chestnuts and a sorrel, were heavy-bodied, thick-muscled, short-legged. They were each at least eighteen hands, and looked powerful enough to pull down the entire grandstand if they'd had a mind to.

Following Denis Dupuy was an even more powerful-looking team of matched bays with black manes and tails. The man behind them wore suspenders that bulged over his huge belly, an engineer's cap, and dungarees that fit loosely over his incongruously slender butt.

"Bad luck for Denis," said Chrétien. "That's Ben Campbell. He never loses."

Of the seven contestants, Denis was the fifth to try his team against the weighted sled, or what they called a boat. Made of oak, it was shaped like an oversized toboggan, curved upward at the leading edge. Officials had placed heavy boulders on the sled which, for the first round of pulls, totaled five thousand pounds. Denis' horses had no difficulty pulling the load the required twenty feet and, to the loud cheers of Jordi and his family, he moved on to the second round. Three officials piled another thousand pounds of rocks onto the sled and called for the first contestant.

All of the teams pulled the sled with ease through the first four rounds. Then, with the weight set at ten thousand pounds, three teams failed, knees buckling, shoulders gleaming with sweat, and were eliminated. At eleven thousand pounds, another team was unable to make the pull. Only Denis, Ben Campbell, and a man named Tom Cushing remained. Campbell was first to go. His powerful horses jerked the sled forward and seemed to have no trouble for the first ten feet, but then the left-most horse hit a muddy patch and faltered. Campbell urged the team forward, but it had lost its momentum. The sled stopped, all three horses breathing heavily.

"Look at that!" Uncle Chrétien shouted to Jordi. "Didn't I tell you about Dupuy luck? Denis didn't have a chance against Ben Campbell, then one of the man's horses hits the mud."

Tom Cushing's team avoided the mud and made the distance, though it appeared to struggle over the last several feet. Then it came time for Denis' pull. With the aid of two helpers who carried the massive, triangle-shaped hitch as he guided the horses, Denis steered them toward the front edge of the sled and neatly turned them so that they were facing away from it. "Whoa!" he called, urging them backward to position the eye of the hitch over the upthrust hook on the front of the sled. The horses hoofed the ground, eager to pull. Finally, he called, "Drop it!" and the two men lowered the hitch to engage the hook. As soon as the horses heard the ring of metal on metal, they lurched forward, muscles straining, heads bobbing. Denis shouted, "Eyip!" as he held the reins and ran with tottering steps just in front of and to the side of the sled. Their hoofs throwing up sprays of dirt, the team suddenly started to swerve to the left, an indication that the right-most horse wasn't pulling as strongly as the others. Denis leaned in to his right, snapped the reins of the outside horse, and screamed "Eyip!" again. Suddenly his foot hit a patch of mud. He staggered for an instant, then fell headfirst in front of the boat. The horses, uncontrolled, joyful in the exertion of the pull, leaned heavily into the weight. The sled leaped forward. Denis screamed in agony. From the grandstand Jordi heard a sickening sound—a crunching of bones like a hundred snapping twigs.

"*Mon Dieu!*" cried Nana, making the sign of the cross.

The grandstand buzzed with a strange mix of murmurs—horror, shock, excitement, fascination.

Pip, Gil, and Chrétien bolted from their seats, hurtled down the steps and onto the track. Several officials ran ahead of them, rushing to the now stationary sled. The three horses were breathing heavily. Sweat gleamed on their flanks. They scraped the ground with their fore-hoofs, still eager for the pull.

"Unhook the team!"

The horses, startled by the many men rushing at them, lurched forward. Denis' limp body, half under the boat, was pulled forward like the coulter of a plow through the dirt and mud. More sounds of bones snapping.

"Get the Christless reins!"

Chrétien leaped between the boat and the team and picked up the reins. "Whoa!" he cried, "Whoa!" He pulled back hard. The horses stopped and started to back up. "Unhook it now!" he cried.

Two men reached down, lifted the hitch from the sled, and dropped it to the ground. Chrétien let go of the reins.

The horses strode a few paces forward then turned, stopped and gazed at the confusion around the boat. They ambled toward Chrétien.

About a dozen men frantically hauled the boulders from the sled, passing them from man to man and dropping them at the edge of the track. It seemed to take forever. Finally, the last of the boulders was removed and four men stationed themselves at each corner of the sled. "Careful, now. Lift it gently on my count. One…two… THREE!" They lifted the sled in unison, backed it away from Denis' body, and dropped it to the track.

Pip and Gil crouched by Denis. Blood frothed at his mouth and nostrils. Another man joined them. It was Evan Davids, a doctor from Blue Hill Hospital.

"Evan, thank God you're here," said Pip.

Doctor Davids folded his tall frame and knelt to place his ear beside Denis' face. "Not breathing," he murmured. He lifted an eyelid, examining the pupil, and placed a finger on Denis' neck. He felt for a pulse in the carotid artery. He frowned. Laboriously, he unwound his body and stood up, shaking his head. "He's gone. Probably half his ribs broken, pushed into his organs like so many knives. Lungs, heart, who knows what? Massive internal bleeding, no doubt."

By now Jordi had escaped his mother and made his way to where Denis was sprawled. He gazed at the lifeless body. The face was contorted, not at all peaceful and resigned like Emily's in the picture over the stove. It was a different face of death. Jordi wrinkled his brow, trying to assimilate this new knowledge. He felt like an intruder and wondered if the dead man could sense all the people staring at him, could sense that he was on public display, a curiosity.

"Jordi, you shouldn't be here," said Gil.

Jordi, pressing his lips together, looked at Chrétien, stared into his eyes. Chrétien stared back for a few moments then nodded in recognition, shrugged his shoulders, and said, "Aw Jeez, Jordi, I guess he didn't have the luck of a Dupuy after all...or else it plain ran out."

Chrétien waited until well after Denis Dupuy's wake and funeral to introduce the family to Delores. One day he rang the telephone in the Dupuy farmhouse to announce that he was bringing Delores home with him.

Nana lifted her eyes heavenward, made the sign of the cross, and said, "Mother of God, it's about time my brother gets hitched."

"Guess that's the end of Sue Harper," said Gil.

"But Zabet," said Pip, "That Delores Ludlow's pretty damn ugly."

"So what? As long as she keeps him in line and I don't gotta do it no more."

"But she's English, probably not even a Catholic."

This gave Nana a slight pause, but she shrugged her shoulders and said, "I spend my whole life worrying 'bout my brother. Thank God someone else can do it now." She assigned everyone a room to straighten out in order to make a good impression on their unexpected guest. "There's not enough time to bake a pie," she said despairingly.

"But there's blueberry pie left over from yesterday," said Lydie.

Nana nodded. "It ain't fresh, but it will have to do."

A short while later, they heard Chrétien's car coughing up the

road, and the entire family poured onto the porch to greet Delores
Ludlow. The car was towing a trailer. It ground to a stop in the gravel near the barn and Chrétien leaped out. He was alone. He ran to the
back of the trailer, lowered the tailgate, and tugged on a halter which
was attached to a cow. The family, stunned into silence, slowly walked
toward Chrétien's car.

Chrétien led the cow around to face them. "Meet Delores," he
said.

"*That's* Delores?" asked Lydie.

Nana frowned and muttered, "*Jésus, Marie, et Josef.*"

Chrétien handed the halter to Jordi. "You said you wanted a cow,
so here she is. But remember, you promised to take care of her every
morning and every evening."

Jordi's eyes beamed. "I will, Uncle Chrétien, don't worry."

Gil laughed. "When you told us you were bringing Delores home,
we thought you meant Delores Ludlow."

"Delores Ludlow! Now why the hell would I do that? She ain't
Catholic and besides, she's ugly. Why do you think I named the cow
Delores?"

The previous owners of the farm kept cows, so the barn had stalls,
their walls pitted and scarred. But they were crammed with all kinds
of odds and ends, broken tools, discarded tires. It took most of an
hour for the family, working together, to get just one of the stalls
cleaned out. In the process, they unearthed a milking stool, a water-
ing pail, and several milk cans. They stacked items into two piles: useful and junk.

Nana said, "We'll get a… what do you call them things to make
butter? In French we say *une baratte.*"

"A churn," said Gil.

"Yes. Then we can have butter instead of oleomargarine."

"And I won't have to mix in the yellow coloring anymore," said
Lydie with delight.

Later, when he was in bed listening to the wind rattle the window
in its frame, Jordi overheard Chrétien say to the others, "He's been
moping around thinking of what happened to Cousin Denis and of

the war that's coming. He needs somet'ing to keep his mind off such t'ings. I figured a cow would help, it being alive and giving milk every morning and night and all."

What they didn't know was how often Jordi also thought of Emily, almost as though she had been his sister and had died only recently, or that she was somehow connected to his father going to war. And they didn't know he thought of Lou Gehrig's death that past June, how it was almost impossible to think of the man in his grave, unable to move, never again to swing a bat or throw a baseball. He imagined the same thing happening to the great Ted Williams. Was it possible? And in ten years or a hundred years would they all be gone, his father, his mother, Nana, Pip, Uncle Chrétien... himself? Where would they be? Would they know each other? Do the dead feel anything—like rain, or snow, or the wind passing over their graves?

He tried to think of the *Mistral* sailing out from the fog, but the image kept slipping away.

chapter 4

Jordi saw that his father was in an expansive mood as he made a last check of the *Zabet & Lydie's* mooring line before lowering himself into the rowboat where Pip and Jordi waited. After a week of almost nonstop rain, the sun had burned through the fog revealing a crystalline November day. The morning had been luxuriant, overrun with sky, and sunlight pelted the hills, fields, and sea. Then it was an afternoon of refractions; their eye muscles twitched from squinting all day long. Now, the sun was sinking. In the east, Cadillac Mountain on Mount Desert Island was wreathed by a rim of bruised rose, a fading flush turning toward black. And in the west, streaks of gilded, feathery clouds floated over the hills of Camden.

The rowboat nosed onto the pebbly shore with a scrape, and the three lobstermen climbed out and hauled it above the high-tide line. As they walked toward their truck, a flock of seagulls scuttered before them, taking off with a flutter of wings. Climbing into the truck, Gil said, "Let's go see Ogden Gower. He's probably still working in his shop. Nana and Lydie will be out with their sewing club, so they won't be expecting us." They always enjoyed visiting Ogden, especially watching the man work.

They parked in front of Gott's Market to get a copy of the *Bangor Daily News*. As they climbed out of the truck, a gust of wind came up, followed by the scritch of dead leaves crabbing along the pavement. More leaves spiraled down from a large oak.

"Not long before winter," Pip said.

Already, there was the musty smell of fermenting leaves, like bad whiskey, which had brewed in puddles during the week of rain.

Jordi and Pip waited outside while Gil went in for the paper. Jordi frowned when he saw Virgil Blount come out of the store, climb into his truck, and head down Naskeag Road, the loose rear bumper of his truck rattling. The right taillight, hanging by its wires, swayed like a dim red lantern.

Gil emerged holding the newspaper before him, turning to the second page. "Churchill gave a speech yesterday. Said if we become involved in war with Japan, England would declare war on her within the hour."

"They'd better, after all we done for them."

"And I'll bet you that as soon as that happens, we'll declare war on Germany and Italy."

Jordi frowned but said nothing.

Pip said, "Sounds to me like they expect it any day. Just last week they put the Coast Guard under the Navy. They only do that in time of war."

Ogden Gower's boat shop was only a short way from Gott's, so they left the truck and walked. Darkness was descending rapidly. Cassiopeia and the Big Dipper began to emerge clearly in the northeast. Pip put out an arm, signaling them to stop. He scanned the sky. "There," he said, pointing to the east. "There's the Pleiades a little above Orion. Can you find it, Jordi?"

Jordi peered at the sky for a long time. He shook his head.

"Well, it ain't so big," said Pip. "How 'bout the Northern Cross?"

Jordi smiled. That one, he knew. He turned toward the west. "There," he said, pointing.

"Good! We'll make a star watcher out of you yet."

A hunter's moon rode high and round, seeming to shoulder Orion from the sky. Ever since Pip had heard Edward R. Morrow's broadcasts from London during the blitz the previous year, he liked to call such a moon a "bomber's moon." Now, its light rained down on the street, the buildings, and the trees, suffusing them with a ghostly, astral radiance. A wind stirred and the air swirled with dead and dying leaves.

They moved on, their steps slow in the half-light, until a lamp from the shop brought them to Ogden's door. Gil knocked.

Ogden's part-time assistant, Buddy Phelps, a skinny high school dropout who at twenty-four was still without a steady job, opened the door, undamming a flood of harsh electric light. He smiled and let them in. They were met by the smell of freshly sawn lumber—mahogany, oak, pine, hackmatack, and, dominating all, red cedar. Buddy motioned for them not to interrupt Ogden, who was bent over a long board clamped edge-up.

In the center of the shop, inverted on a cradle, was a half-finished rowboat. A wood stove sat in a corner with chairs grouped around it. Along the length of one wall, supported on wooden horses, was a long rectangular steam box for bending planks. It was connected at one end by a feed pipe to a steam generator.

This was the stuff of boat building and Jordi felt a flush of excitement. His eyes were drawn to the wall covered with half-models of boats Ogden had built. These were small-scale carvings of the boats reduced to their most essential lines—no details of deck, fittings, sail plan, cabin structures—just the elegant curves of the hull carved in bas relief, as though Ogden had slit a hull down its center line and mounted it on the wall. Workbenches took up the other walls, a variety of tools arranged on them. Saws of all kinds hung from hooks, including an old bow saw that had belonged to Ogden's grandfather, carpenter's squares, rasps, spokeshaves, calipers, hammers and, jutting from slots cut into the back of one of the benches, a huge collection of chisels and gouges. Jordi admired all the planes arranged on shelves. He recognized an old Stanley #62, the plane Pip often used. But it was when he turned to watch Ogden leaning over his work that he saw—and heard—the most magnificent plane of all. Ogden was using a wooden jointer plane nearly three feet in length to square the edge of the board. Jordi could hear the plane sing as Ogden made long, powerful sweeps. Shavings curled from it, some flying over Ogden's shoulder, most clinging to his coveralls. They were gossamer-thin like the wings of moths.

Ogden set the plane on the workbench and ran his fingers along the edge of the board. "Eyuh," he said. He turned to his visitors.

"Ready for steam bending and fitting tomorrow."

While Buddy swept up the shavings and Ogden arranged his tools neatly on the workbench, Jordi directed his father's attention to the wall of half-models. Gil examined them closely, running a finger along the lines of the bilges and the tucks, the sweeping sheerlines. Jordi followed behind him and passed his hand across the smooth surfaces.

"If you like those, Gil," said Ogden, "I have something to show you out back. Think you'll recognize her. Come with me." He lit a kerosene lantern and led the way out the back door of the shop. In the darkness, they could see the vague hulks of three boats sitting on cradles, stern to bow.

"I thought you only had two repair jobs going," said Gil. He knew of the forty-foot cutter and the old Jonesport lobster boat.

"Got the third one in last week. Man from Boston wants me to fix a leak. Turns out she needs a new garboard strake."

He walked toward the stern of the boat. They followed the bobbing pool of light. When they were all gathered in a semicircle under the transom, Ogden lifted the lantern to the full reach of his arm. The bloom of weak light was just enough to illuminate the name.

Mistral.

"Dad, look!" cried Jordi.

"She's in your yard?" Gil nearly shouted.

"Be here through the winter."

Buddy brought an extra lantern and they spent a half hour circling *Mistral,* admiring her sleek lines. "Look at that tuck. Gives it a shape like a wineglass at an expensive hotel," said Pip with enthusiasm. Ogden set up a ladder so they could climb up and explore her interior layout.

When they returned to the shop, Gil said, "Sure wish we could build something like that."

"We can," said Jordi.

"Hard to do it on a lobsterman's income, even if you also have the farm," said Ogden.

Gil smiled. "Oh, there may be ways. Meanwhile we can dream."

Jordi smiled.

"No harm in dreaming. That's what a lot of us'll be doing soon's Roosevelt takes on that Hitler fella because the gov'ment will lay restrictions on a lot of things folks have a fondness for."

Buddy slammed his right fist into his left palm. "If we get in the war, I'm gonna join up. I have an awful urge to go gunnin' for old Adolph myself, him sittin' over there smug as Billy-be-damned!"

"There'll be a line in front of you," said Gil. "Maybe I'll be one of them." Then, seeing the frown on Jordi's face, he quickly changed the subject. Nodding toward the wall of half-models, he asked Ogden, "You going to carve a half-model of *Mistral* like you do lots of boats you work on?"

"Hadn't thought about it yet." Ogden paused, then said, "Why don't you?"

"Me?"

"Good way of dreaming; gives you something solid to touch. I could show you how. Then if you ever get the means to build the boat, you got a head start on the design. Trick is, you start with *Mistral* but soon enough you want a little more tuck, maybe some tumblehome, whatever is eye-pleasing to you. Becomes your own design, then some-day…who knows?"

"But what about—I don't even know what you call it—things that make a boat sail well or not so well?"

"You mean principles of naval architecture? Mostly it's a matter of feel—eye-pleasing is the key. In the old days, even large ships were designed by hazard and by eye using these half-models. What you're trying to do is carve out of wood not so much a hull, but the *relationship* of a boat to the water and the wind. You have to imagine it with its lines duplicated on the missing side of the hull and in communion with the water and wind. If you go far wrong, I'll steer you straight."

"Like only you could," said Pip with a smile.

None of them had ever heard Ogden Gower utter so many words all at once, especially words like "communion" or "duplicated." Even Buddy stared at his mentor, mouth agape. Jordi found himself seduced by the power of Ogden's quiet passion and saw that his father was also impressed. Ogden was right; it would be a way to dream in a tangible way about the boat they might someday build.

Gil spent the following hour absorbing instructions from Ogden on how to carve a half-model (Jordi listening intently) and when he was sure he knew how to proceed, they went into Ogden's woodshed.

"Take this here piece of clear pine. It's a dite dozy, not seasoned well, but it'll do for a half-model." Ogden also gave Gil some mahogany and a thin strip of cedar. Gil's first task would be to assemble the three woods in a sandwich with the cedar in the middle where the waterline would be, the mahogany above for the topsides, and the pine below for the underbody.

Jordi couldn't wait to get home and help his father set up a place in the barn where he could do his work.

In the following days, Jordi could think of nothing but their boat. He listened as his father described the lines that began to take shape in his mind. Gil described how he saw the shear of the deck in the sag of a telephone line (not that one, where the line sags too much because of the lean of the poles, but that one, between upright poles, where the curve is shallower); the turn of the bilge in the swell of Nana's biscuits; the tuck of the stern in the smooth undercurve of a wave on the verge of breaking; the sweep of the bow in the easy droop of anchor lines from boats in the harbor. As the boat took shape, Gil insisted on stopping by Ogden's shop on their way home from lobstering so he could gaze at *Mistral* and compare her lines to the form he was gradually freeing from the glued-up block of wood.

Jordi was with him every moment, watching closely.

Soon, what began to emerge was not a copy of *Mistral,* but a variation on a theme, a shape that was both derivative and freshly inspired. In short, Gil was designing his own vision of what the marriage of a hull and the elements should be.

One day in early December, Ogden held the roughed-out half-model in his hands and viewed it from several different angles. "You gave her more hollowness in the bow…a slightly deeper keel. I think

your boat will sail better to windward. Gave her a nice long spoon
bow, too, like the raking overhang of a batteau—" he said, referring to
a Penobscot River logging boat. Then turning the half-model and
sighting from behind, he added, "—and less fullness in the run aft.
She'll be a little less sea-kindly in quartering waves, but still good."

"You think she'd sail, then?"

"Eyuh. Nicely, too."

Jordi felt a flush of pride.

"So would you say I've got the right shape? Just some smoothing
to do?"

"Can't say. That's up to you." Ogden smiled, then said, "This may
sound downright mystical to you, but sometimes I think a design's finished when it makes you think that maybe, *just maybe*, the finished
boat will have blood running through its veins like a living thing."

Everyone stared at him.

"Told you it'd sound a dite mystical," Ogden said with a laugh.

Inspired again, Gil and Jordi returned to the barn to refine the
half-model. It excited Jordi to see his father so passionately involved
with imagining their boat because he spoke less often about the war in
Europe. Jordi hoped the half-model had magical power that would
keep his father from going to war. He watched his father fair the lines
until the model was pleasing from every angle. Then Gil sanded the
half-model smooth and, each day for the following week, applied a
coat of tung oil until it gleamed, the light breathing life into its lines.

They were in the barn the next Sunday afternoon, Gil polishing
the half-model with cheesecloth, when Lydie came running out of the
house. "Gil…Jordi. Come listen!"

Gil dropped the cheesecloth on the workbench. "What's the matter?"

"The Japanese have bombed us…some place called Pearl Harbor!"

chapter 5

Jordi chased his father toward the back door of the farmhouse with a lump of fear swelling in his chest. He remembered Pip saying that if America went to war with Japan, we would also go to war with Germany; and he knew, as surely as he knew anything, that his father would want to fight Hitler. He burst into the kitchen close on his father's heels. Passing through the kitchen into the living room, he stole a glance at the photograph of Emily. He wondered if she was in heaven somewhere, able to see what was going on. Would she understand how some voice they didn't know could come through their tiny radio and announce that other people they didn't know were somehow trying to destroy their family, to steal their dreams? He hated that radio, the scratchy sound of it. How could it have such power over people's lives? The radio was like a crack in the wall that let the war stealthily slip into their lives. It was no different from the gaps in the house and the barn that let the wind whistle through.

...began at eight o'clock this morning Hawaiian time, that's...uh... one o'clock in the afternoon here in New York, just four hours ago. As far as we know, the bombing was concentrated on the American Naval Base at Pearl Harbor which is near Honolulu. Reports are sketchy, but there has certainly been loss of American lives...

Jordi tried to interpret what all this meant. What right did this voice have coming into their lives like this?

The next day, they listened to President Roosevelt:

...The attack yesterday on the Hawaiian Islands has caused severe damage to American naval and military forces. I regret to tell you that very many American lives have been lost. In addition, American ships have been reported torpedoed on the high seas between San Francisco and Honolulu...

I believe that I interpret the will of the Congress and of the people when I assert that we will not only defend ourselves to the uttermost but will make it very certain that this form of treachery shall never again endanger us.

"Damn right!" said Gil.

After that fateful broadcast they settled in to wait—to see how their lives would be changed. Jordi felt they no longer had any control over what happened to the family. They were no longer free to dream. It was Hitler and Roosevelt and Churchill and Tojo who would determine what happened.

Along with the rest of the country, the Dupuy family waited.

One day, Jordi helped his father and Pip dig a hole. When it was finished, they poured concrete and erected a flagpole. Like most of their neighbors, they would fly the American flag every day. Flags were everywhere, attached to slender poles lashed to car bumpers or hanging like bunting over doorways. People even started to greet each other with broader smiles born of a new sense of solidarity and patriotism.

Jordi wondered which of his father's two impulses—building the boat or serving his country—would win out.

Over the long weeks of waiting the sun slid into cold Capricorn. The North Pole tilted away from the sun like a boxer slipping a punch, and the shores of Eggemoggin Reach and the islands beyond wore lacy hems of salt-rime. Mooring lines were stiff and crickled when Jordi, Pip, and Gil strained to bend them around cleats with gloves that stuck to the ice-encrusted rope.

Inland, the freezing pond was never silent. It cracked and groaned, boomed and whined, as the ice flexed against confinement. On clear days, the shadows of birds glided over the ice. The woods rang with the blows of axes, the bark of foxes, the cry of blue jays. Here and there, they saw the tracks of snowshoe rabbits and bobcats. Occasionally, the tracks converged in a patch of distressed snow turned pink where two animals had met in a frenzied, bloody tangle.

All the while, Jordi watched for signs that his father had made a decision. So far, there had been none. He gazed often at the half-model, hoping it would somehow keep his father home.

Shortly before Christmas, snow settled over the farm like a down comforter, sealing it off from the rest of the world. Roads remained unplowed, fields untracked. Outside the house a corridor of packed snow stretched across the yard from the foot of the porch to the barn where small cascades of drift-snow, stirred by breezes, floated to the ground. To provide footing Gil had forked hay from the loft and Pip had strewn it along the path. From distant chimneys, curls of smoke against the steely blue sky assured them their neighbors were still there.

One evening, Jordi followed his father and Pip into the house, pulled off his mittens and knit cap, shrugged off his blue reefer, and joined them, hands extended, over Nana's red-hot cast-iron stove. The dank smell of heated wet wool filled the kitchen.

After dinner, they moved into the balsam-scented living room where there was talk of the war around the Christmas tree, which glistened with dust of mica. Later, Jordi and Pip tracked the latest progress of the war on maps of Europe and the Pacific. Then they went to bed.

An hour passed before Jordi got to sleep. He couldn't help but hear the intense conversation his parents were having in their room next door. As much as Jordi tried, he couldn't make out the whispered words. On some nights the tones had been angry, on others, pleading. But tonight the voices were hushed and tender and punctuated with cries of delight. He felt warmer, and eventually the tick-tock of the grandfather clock in the hall lulled him to sleep.

When he woke, it was to the drip-drip of the water faucet left running to prevent the pipes from freezing. He dressed and walked downstairs. He struck a match to light a lantern, but the flame guttered momentarily before going out. No matter how hard they tried, they could never totally seal the house off. Sometimes the wind moaned, sometimes sighed, but it always let them know it was there. And when a nor'easter blew, it caterwauled through the cracks, whistling into every room of the house.

Jordi struck another match, shielding it with his cupped hand, and this time he lit the lantern. He went out into the barnyard lit by the faint glow of starlight in the hour before dawn. Cold silence greeted him. The only sound he heard was the distant, muffled snore of waves hitting the shore of Eggemoggin Reach. He gazed up at the sky and identified the constellations Pip had taught him—the Little Dipper, pointing to the faint freckle of Polaris; the Big Dipper, low on the horizon this morning, only its ladle showing; the "W" of Cassiopeia—all of them in the northern sky. And to the east, the belt, legs, and arms of Orion stood out clearly, Rigel and Betelgeuse especially bright. He extended an imaginary line from Orion's belt, just as Pip had taught him, but he was still unable to identify the Pleiades with any certainty.

Bucket in hand, Jordi walked to the barn. Starlight sizzled on the packed snow that crunched under his boots. He slid the barn door open. It squealed on its metal track, the frozen rollers turning sluggishly on their shafts. Delores gave a soft low of recognition. The slobber from her nose had frozen around her mouth, but when Jordi pulled out the milking stool and reached under her, he saw that her udder steamed with body heat. Her teats were warm to his touch.

By the time he left the barn, the snow-covered fields were glowing with an inner radiance. The ragged outlines of the spruce, swaying in the wind, emerged against the brightening sky. The snow was mounded on the trackless road. It was as though the farm were the only inhabited place in the world. There was no Hitler, no Tojo, no Roosevelt, no Churchill. He looked to the east and frowned to see a rim of flame expand and swell even as he watched.

And he thought: If only the sun would not rise and melt away the snow.

On Christmas Eve, Winston Churchill spoke on the radio from Washington to the American people. Jordi and his family, wrapped in the warmth of the living room, listened intently. What would next Christmas be like? It seemed impossibly far away, but Jordi couldn't help wondering. From the living room, he stared through the kitchen door at the half-model on the wall near the stove.

Mr. Churchill said he felt a sense of unity with the United States, particularly now that they shared a common purpose. He also said how strange this Christmas Eve was:

Here in the midst of war, raging and roaring about us over all the land and seas, creeping nearer to our hearts and homes; here amidst all these tumults, we have the peace of the spirit in each cottage home and in every heart. Therefore we may cast aside, for this night at least, the cares and dangers which beset us, and make the children happy in a world of storm. Here then, for one night only, each home throughout the English-speaking world should be a brightly lighted island of happiness and peace. Let the children have their night of fun and laughter…

But Jordi didn't feel full of fun and laughter. He felt like the outside world was intruding into the privacy of his family. Lydie put her arms around him and held him close to her.

On Christmas Day Jordi's unhappiness deepened when President Roosevelt called the nation to *"unsheathe its sword in the cause of Honor, Truth, and Justice."* He said that this was a war *"of the dignity and brotherhood of man which Christmas Day signifies."* Then the Reverend Joseph M. Corrigan gave an invocation:

We pray for all who hold power over human life…for the one we have chosen. Keep him in Thy grace, through this stress of war, strong and tender, wise and fearless, nor let his hand be stayed until he can sheathe his nation's sword.

Nana made the sign of the cross and the others followed. But Jordi shuddered when he thought of those who could hold such power over human life.

The family spent evenings together in the living room, listening to the radio. Often, they listened to Amos 'n' Andy or to Kate Smith, especially when she sang "God Bless America." But mostly, they listened for news of the war.

In early March, Jordi went with Pip and his father into Brooklin. Outside Gott's, the air was redolent with radiator alcohol. Inside, cigarette smoke and the rank scent of unwashed hair and clothes filled Jordi's nostrils. But no one that day could say the smell came from Buddy Phelps and Wilbur Cribb; they appeared unnaturally clean-cut in their only suits as they sat at the center of a large group of men. That afternoon Ogden Gower was scheduled to drive Buddy and Wilbur into Blue Hill where they would catch a bus to Bangor and then a southbound train to Boston, then New York, then westward to California where eventually they would end up on some warship in the Pacific. One night, a few weeks before, they had drowned themselves with whiskey and patriotic fervor and woken the next day to find themselves in the Navy. Now they were being celebrated as the first Brooklin men to leave for war in twenty-five years.

"Why the Navy?" Gil asked.

"They was the first recruiting station we came to," answered Buddy.

"After we *came to*," added Wilbur, drawing a storm of laughter.

Gil laughed with the others, then said, "But Buddy, not long ago you said you wanted to go gunning for Hitler. You won't get your shot at him in the Pacific."

Buddy shrugged. "Japs, Krauts…same thing."

"Not to me they ain't. If I go, it'll be to Europe."

Virgil Blount said, "Count me out. I don't plan to risk my neck for no gov'ment."

They all ignored him. Niall Macgrudder turned to Gil. "You planning to join up?"

Gil glanced at Jordi, then Pip. He shrugged.

Several days later, Jordi settled into his bed with a Hardy Boys book, *The Tower Treasure*, for an afternoon of reading. The snow was drifting down in large lazy flakes. Before he got to Chapter Three, the wind had risen, and the window rattled in its frame as needles of snow sissed against the glass. He propped the book like a tent on the bed and shuffled to the window in his heavy woolen socks.

Everything—the sky, the fields, the snow-draped spruce, the barnyard—was a shade of murky pewter. The rectangle of ice on the frog pond, which they had cleared for skating, was now a dim outline. It lay under three inches of new snow and was framed by more than a foot of old snow that extended to the edge of the spruce. Jordi slipped into his lumberjack shirt and put on his pants and boots. He would persuade his father that they needed to clear the ice again before supper.

As he headed down the stairs he was hit by the smell of freshly baked blueberry pie. Instead of pleasing him, as it usually did, it stopped him in his tracks. He realized his mother had begun baking every day in order to keep her men at home—to keep Jordi's father here on the farm. Maybe this wasn't even conscious on her part, maybe it was just some instinct women have, but as soon as the thought came to him, he was certain of its truth. What bothered him even more was that his mother thought this was necessary. If she was going to these lengths, she must also be afraid that his father would decide to go to war.

Everyone was in the kitchen. Pip and Gil sat at the table, large pieces of pie in front of them, while Lydie carved out another slice and slid it onto a plate for Jordi. "I was just about to call you, Jordi. Here's a nice, hot piece of pie for you."

"What's got into you, Lydie?" Pip asked with a chuckle. "You trying to fatten us up for the slaughter with all this pie lately?"

Jordi flinched at the word "slaughter." He looked at his father's face to see if there were signs that he had made a decision. But his father's expression was only one of contentment. And he saw, with pleasure, that his father was studying the half-model that hung gathering dust on the kitchen wall.

"I like baking pie for my men. You know that, Pip." Lydie smiled.

Jordi glanced at the picture of Emily, then at the half-model. He looked back at his father. *Doesn't he realize we may never get to build the boat if he goes to war?*

When everybody had a piece of pie, Lydie went into the next room and came back with several samples of yarn. She showed them to Gil. "Which colors would you like for your sweater? Brown and green? Blue and red?"

"What sweater?"

"The one I'm going to knit for you."

"When did you decide to do that?"

"Just the other day. Which colors?"

Gil examined the samples. "The blue and red."

Lydie beamed and nodded. "Yes, these are the ones I like, too. I'll need to take your measurements so I can get started. And, naturally, you'll have to keep trying it on as I go along."

Jordi knew exactly what his mother was up to; it would take her months to finish the sweater.

Of course the blueberry pies and the promise of a sweater didn't work. Explaining that he could never live with himself if he didn't do his duty when a man like Hitler was on the loose, Gil announced that he was joining the Army.

Jordi feigned indifference, spending most of his time in the woods. But he fooled no one. On the one hand, he acted as though his father was already gone. On the other, he would stare at his father over supper, as if he were trying to fix his father's image in his mind.

And he would stare at the half-model mounted on the kitchen wall.

The Saturday night before Gil's departure, the men at Gott's held a going-away party for him. The store was stocked with beer and booze and closed to the public. Just about everyone involved with lobstering came and the party got predictably rowdy, especially after Chrétien arrived with two bottles of single malt whiskey. Late, after many of the men had gone, Jordi found himself trapped at a table with just barely enough room for his chair where two walls formed a corner. He was dismayed when Virgil Blount, obviously drunk, plopped himself into the chair next to Jordi.

"What the hell're you drinking?" asked Blount, his words slurred.

"Moxie."

"Soda pop?" cried Blount. His voice was so loud the room went silent as men turned their attention to him and Jordi. "Christ! That's no drink for a man. Here, have some of this." Blount snatched the Moxie from Jordi's grasp and slid a glass of beer in front of him. The glass was sitting in a ring of suds, and it made a skating sound as it slid across the varnished surface of the table.

"I don't want any beer."

Blount lifted the glass and held it in front of Jordi. "Aw, c'mon kid. It ain't polite to refuse when a man offers you a drink."

Jordi snapped his head back and waved at Blount's wrist. "I told you I don't want a beer." He felt his body trembling with a mixture of rage and fear. He glared at Blount, holding his gaze, though he desperately wanted to look for his father or Pip.

"What are you afraid of? Don't you want to celebrate your dad goin' off to war?"

"I don't want any beer."

Blount slid the glass closer. "C'mon, kid, drink up."

To Jordi's relief, his father reached between them and slid the glass back toward Blount. "Leave my boy alone, Virgil. He doesn't want the beer."

"I was just trying to be friendly."

"Fine. But now, leave it be."

Blount smiled. "Okay, Mr. Big Shot Hero."

"Just leave, Virgil," Gil replied. "You're nothing but drunk."

"You gonna go win the war for us?"

Niall Macgrudder stepped between them. "Virgil, you can be some kinda jerk when you put your mind to it. Hell, you wear on people like a long, hard winter." He looked over his shoulder at the other men. "Guys, help me drag him out of here and throw him in his truck."

Blount was too drunk to put up a struggle and within minutes he was gone.

"Hope he drives himself into the bay," said Travis Lathrop. Then he turned to Gil. "Sorry 'bout that, Gil."

"Aw Jeez, you can't account for *him*." Gil turned to Jordi. "You all right, Son?"

"I'm all right." Jordi felt a surge of pride not only for his father but also for having stood up to Blount.

Soon, much too soon for the family, the eve of Gil's departure arrived. Jordi could not sleep. He lay in the darkness and listened to the murmur of conversation coming from his parents' room. After a while, the talking stopped and the house fell silent. He said his prayers. He said the "Hail Mary," first in English, then in French just in case Nana was right when she said, as she often did, that God understood French better.

He couldn't sleep. With his head buried in his pillow, Jordi could hear the blood rushing through his veins like the hiss of a distant surf or the soughing of wind in the trees. He heard and felt the beat of his heart. He didn't know when he finally drifted off to sleep. All he knew was that his mother was standing by his bed, gently shaking his shoulders. "Jordi, honey, it's time to get up. We have to leave in an hour."

Sluggishly, Jordi rose to go to the bathroom. After a night of little sleep, he felt as though sand had mixed with the blood in his veins and little drops of syrup had somehow dried on the edges of his eyelids. The steady tick-tock of the hall clock seemed preternaturally loud that morning, as if all of Jordi's senses, though tired, were especially sharp, almost raw.

The bathroom door was open. Gil was at the sink, dressed only in his best trousers, suspenders hanging down the back of his pants. "Good morning, Jordi," he said. His voice sounded strained.

Jordi mumbled, "Morning," then leaned against the door frame to watch his father shave. He had done this often, but today he studied his father's every movement. Gil scritched the back of his fingers against the grain of his whiskers, testing their prickly length. He leaned over the sink and held a steaming hot cloth to his face for several long seconds. The mirror clouded with mist. Then he twirled the shaving brush in the soap dish, worked up a rich lather, and pressed the bristles against the grain of his whiskers. With long, even strokes, he drew the razor down first one cheek, then the other, which made a scratching sound like dead leaves on the pavement. Jordi saw his father's reflection smile at him. It was partially obscured by the mist in the mirror.

The kitchen smelled of oatmeal. Nana always made oatmeal when one of the men had to travel. The family gathered silently at the table. Few words were spoken as they ate breakfast. Jordi spent much of the time stealing despairing glances at the picture of Emily and the half-model.

When Jordi and his parents stepped out into the cold March morning, Pip was already in the truck with the engine running. Silently, they filed along the path, crunching dirty snow, and climbed into the truck. Jordi looked over his shoulder to see Nana staring out the window. She could not go to Bangor with them because there was not enough room inside the cab, and it was too cold for anyone to ride in the truck bed. She had said her goodbyes to her only son earlier that morning.

They drove to Bangor mostly in silence, passing boulder-strewn heaths mottled red with clusters of winter-burnt heather. During the night, rain had fallen on top of the old snow and it had frozen solid. A low sun flared off the glazed surface giving it the appearance of crusted meringue.

The train station was abuzz with a strange and new commotion; a mixture of sadness and excitement hung in the air as the men going to war glanced at each other proudly while their families looked on with fear and worry. Pip took Jordi aside and reminded him that this same scene was being played out in train stations across the nation. There were signs of the war everywhere. Several men wore buttons that said "To Hell With Hitler." Taped to the walls of the station were the torn-off covers of several recent issues of the *Saturday Evening Post*. Each featured a painting by Norman Rockwell of the fictional soldier,

Willie Gillis. One in particular caught Jordi's eye because it reminded him of himself just a few hours before. In it, Willie was asleep in his bed under a sign that reads "Home Sweet Home," his soldier's uniform draped carelessly on one of the bedposts.

"Jeez, look at that," said Pip when they passed the newsstand. He pointed to a row of small statuettes of Hitler showing him bent at the waist, his butt thrust out behind him. A tag attached to each figure read: "HOTZI NOTZI. It is good luck to find a pin. Here's an 'axis' to stick it in." Several pins and an American flag protruded from Hitler's butt. "I'm gonna buy you one of them, Jordi. You want one?"

Jordi shrugged his shoulders and nodded. He was amused, but he didn't want to smile for fear that it would somehow mislead Pip and his parents about his true feelings.

The rest of the time before the train departed passed in a blur. Jordi spent most of it with Pip because his mother and father were clinging to each other. Across the station, he saw another boy reading a *Superman* comic. Here he was seeing his father off to war when even Superman, in a recent strip, had been declared 4-F because his X-ray vision caused him to read the wrong chart, the one in the next room. Jordi looked up at the station clock. Despite the clamor of the crowd, he heard the tunk of the big hand every time it ticked off another minute. He was overwhelmed with a sense of helplessness, of being at the mercy of events far larger than himself, larger even than his parents and Pip. All time stopped for him when a conductor stepped to the platform and called, "All aboard!"

Then his father was gone.

Jordi hadn't had the chance to pull his thoughts and feelings together, let alone share them with his father. There was one last embrace and his father's voice, seemingly from a distance, saying, "Take care of your mother, Son, until I get back"; his mother standing next to his father, crying; Pip coughing, stubbing out a cigarette; the last-minute hugs and murmurs of other families; other wives quietly crying; the hiss of the locomotive as it built up steam pressure; the heartless clunk of the station clock's minute hand; the cry of a newspaper boy; the blare of a car horn from outside the station; the nearby cry of a child much younger than him; and the cry of the conductor again, "All aboard!"

All these sounds replayed in Jordi's mind as Pip drove them, in the truck that now seemed too roomy, back to the farm, to what would be a far different life. He wondered if he had actually said to his father, "When you come back, we'll build the boat."

Or if he had only thought it.

chapter 6

Jordi remembered the photograph clearly. He saw it once while thumbing through Pip's old *Life* magazines and now something made him want to see it again. Late one afternoon he went into the shed where Pip kept a small rolltop desk and a bookcase filled with old magazines. The issues of *National Geographic* filled the top two shelves of the bookcase; the middle two shelves were taken up with the *Saturday Evening Post* and other magazines; and the bottom two with *Life*. He sat cross-legged in a slant of sunlight that illumined a cloud of dust released from the magazines. He sifted through the magazines looking for the right issue.

At last he found it: July 12, 1937. The cover reminded him of his mother; it was a portrait of a mannequin with high cheek bones, a long graceful nose, elegant mouth and chin, and soft eyes. He looked at the cover for a while then started turning the pages, looking for the image that had been burned into his mind. When he found it, his heart skipped.

The photograph was of a fighter in the Spanish Civil War at the instant a bullet had hit him. Where his right ear should have been, there was an eruption of white. An imperfection of the photograph? Exploding bone? The man's knees were buckled as though he was falling back into a chair that was not there. His upper body was arched backward and his face was turned slightly to the left. His left arm was hidden by his body, but his right arm was fully extended. The rifle he had been carrying was suspended, forever, in midair, touched only by the tip of the man's thumb as if he were flinging the gun away. It was early morning or late afternoon, for the man's long shadow stretched out behind him.

Jordi gazed at this man frozen in time. He knew that an instant before the picture was taken, the man had been alive, blood pumping hard through his veins. And an instant after the picture, he would have been lying on the ground, probably on his back, blood pouring out onto the grass. But in the precise instant of the photograph, he straddled the divide between the living and the dead.

The photo was by Robert Capa. It was called "Moment of Death." Jordi stared at the picture, trying to understand what it was that separated the living from the dead. It was the same thought that preoccupied him every time he looked at the picture of Emily.

The first letter arrived a week later as the farm crouched against a driving nor'easter. Rain splattered against the windowpanes as Jordi peeled potatoes with Pip and Nana at the kitchen table while Lydie sat in the living room listening to Dinah Shore singing "You'd Be So Nice to Come Home To," one of the songs of separation that were becoming so popular as the war wedged families apart.

The wind whistled through the house and rattled the windows. Jordi could see his mother was oblivious to the storm as she sang along with the Victrola. Who could blame her? Weren't they all thinking of his father all the time? Jordi often found himself staring at the half-model, trying to imbue it with the power to bring his father back to them. When his father had said at the train station, "Take care of your mother while I'm gone," it was as though he had also said, "Take care of our dream till I get back."

Over the roar of the storm they heard someone pounding on the door. Pip said, "That'll be Virgil Blount coming 'round to remind us again about the blackout curtains. Ain't he got not'ing better to do?"

Lydie frowned as she walked into the kitchen. "Oh, I was hoping it was the mailman."

"In this weather? Besides, he'd leave it in the box." Pip opened the door. A blast of cold air entered the kitchen, flipping the pages of the *Bangor Daily News* that was sitting on the table.

Virgil Blount said, "Afternoon, Pip." He bowed toward Nana and

Lydie. "Ladies."

Jordi thought the man looked at his mother a little too long. "Came by to remind you 'bout the blackout curtains. Saw you had mail, so I brought it to the door for you. Wind's blowing awful strong out theah." He held out a handful of mail. Rivulets of rainwater dripped from his hat and slicker; one drop snaked down his forehead, skidded along his nose, paused for a second at the tip and dropped onto the topmost envelope.

Lydie hurried to him, took the mail, flipped through it and gave a cry of joy. "It's a letter from Gil!"

Pip said to Blount, "Thanks for the reminder...an' the mail." His tone made it clear that Blount was not invited to stay.

"Welcome," said Blount. "See ya at the lookout station." Manning the coast lookout station in East Blue Hill was another of Blount's volunteer jobs. Pip, Lydie, and Jordi also stood watches, and it seemed their shift was always just before or after Blount's.

"Yuh, at the lookout station," said Pip, holding the door open even before Blount had turned to leave.

Lydie tore open the envelope, unfolded several sheets of paper, and started to read.

"Ma, read it out loud," cried Jordi.

Lydie looked up, blushed slightly. "Well, some of it." She dragged her forefinger down to the middle of the first sheet. "The first part's addressed to me...let's see...Uh, here we go. She read what Gil had to say about life at Camp Blanding in Florida; about the buddies he had made; about how they were all eager to be shipped overseas; about seeing Negroes for the first time when they were in Jacksonville; and about the cigarettes that cost only twenty-five cents for two packs. And when she finished and folded the letter and put it in her apron pocket, she said, "I can't wait till tomorrow's mail."

But there was no mail from Gil the following day.

On the day after that, bathed in the warmth of Nana's baking bread, they were all at the kitchen window when the mailman arrived. "I'll get it," Jordi shouted as he threw on his pea coat and bolted out the door. He returned clutching several envelopes in his hand. "There are *four* letters from Dad. One for each of us!"

They spent the next hour reading the letters to each other, thus beginning a new family ritual. As winter gradually eased its grip on the land, the arrival of the mail became the main event of each day. On warmer days, Jordi would wait on the porch listening to the twangs and snaps of the pond ice beginning to break up until he saw the mailman coming up the road. If there were letters from his father, he would rush into the kitchen where Nana would pour tea, Lydie would set out pieces of blueberry pie, and they would all sit down to relish Gil's news.

One day, while they were still glowing from an afternoon of letters, Pip, Lydie, and Jordi took up their posts at the lookout station in East Blue Hill. As usual, Pip began their shift by sweeping the sky and the horizon with his binoculars. "Not'ing." Then he added, "Can't see much 'cause it's already getting dark." He steadied the binoculars by propping his elbows on the cinder-block wall.

Jordi stared at the drama unfolding in the sky. It was as though the sun and the moon were on opposite ends of a giant, invisible seesaw, and the sun, swelling as it approached the rim of sea, seemed to get heavier as the moon rose into the eastern sky. Jordi wondered what his father was doing at that very moment. Was he also watching the sun and moon? Jordi thought like this often; whenever he heard Pip stropping his razor, he wondered if his father was shaving at that very moment, too; whenever he heard his mother listening to the Victrola, he wondered if his father was listening to music, perhaps even the same song. He wondered if things worked that way.

He was wrenched from his thoughts by the scritch of Pip's wooden match along a seam of mortar.

"Pip, do I see two planes coming over Mount Desert Island?" asked Lydie. As she turned, a gust of wind came up and flicked at her long, chiffon scarf. It floated out, caught a simmer of moonlight, then settled on the cinder-block wall, where it snagged. She carefully lifted it from the wall.

A Chesterfield pressed between his lips, Pip swung the binoculars, twisting the focusing knob at the same time. "Yup. Bet they ain't the Luftwaffe, though. Just our own coastal patrol planes." There was a hint of disappointment in his voice. He dragged deeply on the cigarette, let the blue smoke stream from his nostrils, and continued to peer through the binoculars.

Lydie reached into the pocket of her culottes and pulled out a peanut. They were her chief vice these days and since they were so hard to get, she hoarded them, saving a dozen or so for each of the long watches. She pried the meat from its shell which she then flipped into the breeze.

Rapidly, the sky darkened. Moonlight twitched and shivered on the water.

"The moon looks like a whale's eye," Jordi said.

Lydie and Pip looked up. "A surprised whale," Pip said.

"Yes, a surprised whale," said Jordi.

"So, what do you think surprised the whale?"

"A harpoon," replied Jordi instantly.

Lydie said, "That's cruel. It looks more like a pie covered with powdered sugar to me." She cracked another peanut on the cinder-block wall.

Pip laughed. "You're always seeing pies, Lydie."

"Well, what do *you* think the moon looks like?"

"It's a bomber's moon."

"No it's not! It's the eye of a whale," Jordi shouted, causing Lydie and Pip to stare at him bewildered. Then, more softly, he said, "Who's been harpooned."

Later, when Virgil Blount came to relieve them and Pip and Lydie chatted with him for a while, Jordi remained silent. He watched Blount's eyes and tried to calculate how many seconds they looked at Pip versus how many seconds they looked at his mother. He determined that the man spent at least three times as long looking at his mother.

Why didn't she just look away?

March brought a rebirth of scent. The almost odorless, sterile smell of winter, like the odor of chrome, was gradually replaced by the malty smell of mud then by the more yeasty aroma of the earth in estrus. The sun one morning, at first fuzzy-edged and faint behind a gauze of cloud, broke through to radiate, not with the cold dry brilliance of winter, but with a new heat. Stems swelled with sap. In the woods out back old spruce with brindled barks were limned with the light green of new growth.

Jordi sat on the porch enjoying the warmth. Ice melted from the gutters and the roof valleys, dripping in continuous streams into the winter cistern under the southern corner of the kitchen. The sun had finally come around the corner to flood the kitchen with light each morning. The day before, Nana had placed several Chase & Sanborn coffee cans containing earth and tomato seeds in the kitchen window. Pip had stacked heavy planks against the barn wall, preparing to lay them between the house and the barn for that time between winter and spring that in Maine is called mud season. Jordi knew that throughout the next month—on days of warm blue skies and cold mud—he would hear a thousand times, "Eyuh, nice weather...overhead" or "Bottom's fallen out of the road."

Something back near the line of spruce caught his eye. He looked up to see a small flock of crows. It was still a little early for the sparrows. He knew that beyond the farm streams were beginning to trickle, veins of life opening in the comatose earth. And as the snow melted up on Caterpillar Mountain and on Stover Hill and on Seven Star Hill, rivulets of melt-off would begin to etch their way down the slopes. The lacework trails of rabbit and mice tracks would dissolve and vanish. Jordi would see geese going north. Because the lakes and ponds would still be frozen, the geese would follow the coast, settle down in tidal estuaries or on the shores of the reach where a tracery of ice would be cradle-rocked by sluggish waves. Soon, Jordi knew, he would forget how silent the winter woods could be.

The mailman's car appeared just as a patch of snow slid from the barn roof and fell with a whumph. The newly-exposed patch of tin roof started to steam. The mailman leaned out the window, looked up at the roof, nodded, and said, "Guess we're coming up March Hill at last. Weather's awful nice overhead."

Jordi smiled.

"Got a letter from your dad. You're lucky, he sure writes an awful lot. Wish I could say the same for my son." The mailman tipped his cap, put his car in gear, and drove off.

Jordi burst through the front door and into the kitchen. "Letter!"

Nana emerged from the pantry, tying her apron. Lydie ran in from the sitting room, her knitting in hand. Behind her, the strains of a song, like a trail of perfume, followed. It was Frank Sinatra with the Tommy Dorsey orchestra singing "I Think of You."

The three of them pulled their chairs up to the table as Pip pounded down the stairs, shaving soap on one side of his face, a towel draped around his neck. His suspenders bounced uselessly against his hips. He pulled up a chair and touched a finger to his chin where he had nicked himself. While he examined the drop of blood he asked, "Who's the letter addressed to?"

"All of us," said Jordi. "It says 'The Dupuy Family'."

"Then you read it, Jordi," said Lydie.

Nana pulled a handkerchief from her apron pocket and patted Pip's chin. Jordi tore open the envelope. A photograph fell out onto the table. Lydie reached for the photograph. She studied it for a moment before showing it to the others. Gil stood in his uniform in front of a long barracks between two puddles of shade. Tall trunks capped with bursts of palm fronds formed the background. Though his lower body and head were squarely facing the camera, Gil's upper torso was twisted as if to call attention to the insignia on his shoulder, a large red "1" on an olive-green patch, the emblem of the 1st Infantry Division. He was smiling brightly. His forehead shone and there were dark patches of sweat under his arms.

"He looks wonderful," said Lydie.

In the living room, the voice of Frank Sinatra was replaced by Vaughn Monroe singing "My Devotion."

"Read the letter, Jordi."

Jordi cleared his throat and read. The letter was mostly about Gil's unit. "It's called 'The Big Red One' just like the patch on my shoulder says," he wrote. "Here is how I am known:"

UNIVERSE
WORLD
AMERICA
U.S. ARMY
1st INFANTRY DIVISION
26th INFANTRY REGIMENT
3rd BATALLION
L COMPANY
SERGEANT DELANEY'S PLATOON
CORPORAL MILLER'S SQUAD
PRIVATE DUPUY

Jordi held up the letter to show the others. "See how he wrote it."
Lydie looked at Pip. "What does that mean?"

"What? The units?"

"No, the way he wrote it, all in a column and in capital letters. Is he making fun of it? You were in the Army."

Pip shrugged. "He feels like anyone at the bottom. That's how me and Chrétien felt until we made buddies in our units. 'Bout as significant as farts in a hurricane."

"He must be depressed." Lydie's brow wrinkled. She looked at Nana who also looked sad and concerned.

"Of course he's depressed," Pip replied with a laugh. "Who wouldn't be? You're *supposed* to be depressed in the Army. Proves you're not crazy."

"But I worry for him."

"Of course you do."

"But…"

"We all should be *happy* he's depressed. It means he misses us. Jeez, we all feel bad. That's the way it is in war. You're supposed to feel good that you feel bad."

Lydie frowned. She looked at Jordi. "What else does he say?"

More details about daily life at Camp Blanding followed, then, to

Jordi's delight, his father devoted the rest of the letter to a discussion of the boat they would build when he got home. He talked of the layout below decks, the way they would rig the sails for ease of handling, even the dark blue they would paint the topsides. That night Jordi resolved to make a half-model of his own so he would be ready when it came time to build the boat for real.

The next morning, Jordi woke early and went downstairs before the others were up. He couldn't wait to go into the barn, milk Delores, and begin his half-model. Early sunlight covered the cast-iron stove with a buttery light. Jordi hooked one of the stove plates with an iron lifter and raised it to see if any fire was left. There was enough of a hunkering red glow deep in the heap of coals for him to revive the fire with a little prodding. After stirring and poking new life into the embers, he closed the small door, poured fresh coal in through the top, and slipped the plate back in place.

It was only then that something new about the kitchen caught his eye. There, up on the shelf above the stove, next to the jar of stove polish, the statue of Saint Francis of Assisi, and the fading picture of Emily, was the picture of his father in uniform. It was in a new frame.

He stared at it, his stomach churning like the slush-filled water that still rimmed Eggemoggin Reach. *How could Ma have done that? Didn't she know that was the wrong place?* He snatched his father's picture from the shelf and took it into the living room, where he placed it on a doily on the lamp table, wondering if it was already too late.

Jordi was back in the kitchen drinking a glass of milk when Nana came downstairs. "You're up early, Jordi," she said. "Aw Jeez, an' you fixed the stove." She lifted a stove plate, examined the coal, and shook the grate vigorously, the flesh on the back of her arm jiggling. She pressed her fingertips to her lips and touched the picture of Emily. "Good morning, Em," she whispered. Then she started to make coffee.

Lydie appeared, yawning. She kissed Jordi on the forehead then looked up to the shelf above the stove. "What happened to Gil's picture?" she cried.

Nana looked up from the pot of oatmeal she was stirring. "I don't know. I forgot you put it there."

"*I* moved it, Ma," said Jordi.

"You moved it? Where?"

"Into the living room."

"But why? I want his picture in the kitchen where I can see it first thing in the morning."

"You can see it in the living room." His voice was pleading.

"But I spend more time here. This is where I want it." Lydie frowned. "What is the matter with you?"

Pip appeared in the kitchen doorway. "What's going on?"

"Jordi moved Gil's picture into the living room. Last night I put it up there over the stove." She turned back to Jordi. "Why?"

"I just don't want his picture...I just don't want..."

"You don't want his picture...*what?*"

"I don't want his picture in the same place as Emily's."

Lydie gave a surprised expression. "But why?"

"*Because.*"

"Because *why?*"

"Because...because she's dead, Ma. She's dead!"

Everyone froze. Pip glanced at Nana. She was staring at Jordi with a stunned expression, like someone who has just come to understand a deep truth. She had no idea that what brought her some comfort would have such a profound effect on Jordi.

Nana looked at Lydie, her eyes sad and knowing.

Lydie brought a hand to her mouth. "I'm...I'm sorry, Jordi. I wasn't thinking," she said. "Of course Dad's picture can stay in the living room."

But Nana shook her head. She looked at Pip, who placed his arm around her and squeezed her shoulder. Then she took Emily's picture in her hand, gazed at it a moment, and started toward her and Pip's bedroom.

"No, Nana," cried Lydie. "Gil's picture can stay in the living room. Emily's should stay here."

"No," replied Nana. "Gil belongs with us here in the kitchen. This is where we spend most of the time, this is…the real *living* room." She disappeared into the bedroom.

When Pip came down to breakfast the next day, he said to Jordi, "How 'bout we take the day off an' go fetch some mussels?"

"You mean not go to school?"

"What's one day gonna hurt?"

"The boy needs to go to school," said Nana. "An' you got a job to do, too."

Pip gave a dismissive wave of his hand. "Nah. It ain't gonna hurt us to mess around for one little day…spend some time together." He looked at Nana and nodded, as if to say Jordi needed some special attention, especially from a man. Nana caught on immediately; with a wide smile she said to Jordi, "I suppose it ain't gonna hurt." Then she put the dishcloth on its rack and headed upstairs. "Where is that Lydie? *Jésus, Marie, et Josef,* she is sleeping late these days."

After breakfast, Pip and Jordi set out for a small, nameless cove they had dubbed Mussel Cove. They walked a little more than a mile along a narrow scrawl of a dirt road that ran along the ridge above the coast. Orcutt Harbor was on their left, but they could not see it for the dense growth of tall spruce that descended a hundred yards or so from the road to the water's edge. Yet they could sense its presence in the fetid smell of the broad, exposed intertidal zone.

After a while, they left the road and descended through the woods toward the harbor. They followed a grassy path between the tall spruce. Shade fell over them. Above, the tips of the spruce prickled the blue sky, and as the wind blew through the trees, it made a sort of sizzling sound close to silence.

Jordi looked up. Pip was gone. He had disappeared around a bend and Jordi had to hurry to catch up. This path, he imagined, had been cut by the Indians who inhabited this coast hundreds of years before—the Abenaki, and perhaps the Passamaquoddy and the Mi'kmaq too. Pip said that some Indians believed their souls inhabited the living trees after death, that they returned to the earth not in the way white men thought of it, but in a more vital way. He told

Jordi that he, himself, wanted to believe in the possibility and hoped it was true. Jordi also found the notion comforting. Now, he looked to the left and right hoping, as always, to detect some sign of the ancient people. He saw none. But they were here, weren't they? Didn't they have as much presence for him as his father? And as little?

He remembered the day his father left, the crowded train station, the locomotive belching steam, the heat of his skin where it tingled with his father's last touch. He remembered how the train had pulled away and he had closed his eyes to summon his father's face but couldn't. Or he could only see the features vaguely, and the harder he tried, the less clear the image became. He could close his eyes and summon an image of the big oak tree near the barn, or the house, or the shape of the frog pond, or the half-model on the wall in the kitchen, but he could not cling to a clear image of his father's face.

"Why are you so slow? *Dépêche-toi.*"

Pip's voice jerked him out of his reverie. He hurried to catch up to his grandfather. Their footfalls were soft on the beds of pine needles. Sea air, cool and salty, mixed with the scent of balsam fir. Jordi heard the slosh of waves before him and soon they descended to the rock-strewn beach of Mussel Cove. A band of reddish-brown seaweed marked the reach of high tide and mustard-colored lichen covered the larger rocks. A gentle breeze pushed soft waves onto the shore. They came one after another, one after another, and Jordi knew they would keep coming in like that until the very Earth itself shuddered to a stop. After some practice, he found he could breathe in unison with the waves. Out ten or twenty yards beyond the shore, seawater wheezed between two jutting rocks.

Pip snapped open his lighter, lit a Chesterfield, put the lighter back in his shirt pocket. It was the Zippo with the insignia of the First Infantry Division that Gil had sent him. "Lots of mussels over there to the left." He coughed and sputtered a wad of sputum up his throat and spit it out onto the rocks. He only spit when Nana wasn't around.

Jordi looked to the left. He saw several large outcroppings of rock and, at their bases, skirts of olive-green knotted wrack spreading and waving in the quiet water. He knew that just beyond, where the rocks were exposed to waves from the southeast, the skirts would be of bladder rockweed. He marveled, not for the first time, at how precisely each species kept to its own habitat. So it was with the organisms that clung to the rocks facing him, each colony providing its own field of color: white where the rocks were encrusted with barnacles, black where they hosted periwinkles, and shining blue-black where the mussels were motionless until the next tide when, in a sudden moon-drawn agitation of life, they would feast on millions of microscopic water-borne plants and animals. Jordi imagined the mussels clung to the rock as though they felt the pull of the earth's spin through space.

Jordi leaned against a rock. He watched a water droplet, heavy with salt, hover at the top of the rock near his head—a single, thin membrane of hydrogen and oxygen containing how many living organisms? Tens? Hundreds? Thousands? And then slowly it gathered weight and started to slide down the face of the rock, borrowing, as it traveled, the colors of the rock and lichen it slid over. The droplet fell toward the sea with increasing speed, subject to a force like the one that feeds the outgoing tide, that drains the Bay of Fundy to the north, and reveals the millions of microscopic deaths that have occurred since the last tidal change. Pip taught him to look at the world this way, to open himself completely to it.

He watched his grandfather flip the stub of his cigarette into a tiny tidal pool and open a pocket knife. Pip knelt, selected a mussel, and started to cut through the strong hair-like threads that it used to attach itself to the rock. When it was free, he dropped it into the tin bucket Jordi held.

"Pip?"

"Uhmm?"

"How much would a train ticket to Florida cost?"

Pip dropped another mussel into the bucket and regarded Jordi for a long moment. He grabbed a handhold on the rock and levered himself to an upright position with a groan. His knees cracked. He put his hands on the small of his back and eased his hips forward to stretch. He looked at Jordi, gave a knowing nod, and said, "Miss him that much, eh?"

Jordi frowned, nodded. "I want to talk to him about the boat." He paused, then said, "How come he has to go, and guys like Virgil Blount get to stay here?"

Pip didn't answer. Instead, he took the Chesterfields from his shirt pocket, tapped one free, flipped open his Zippo, and lit the cigarette. He took a long drag, exhaled the smoke through his lips and nostrils, and finally said, "Well, there's the way you would like t'ings to be, and there's the way t'ings are, and those are two different t'ings."

"But why? What does that mean?"

"Look at those mussels on the rock. They might want to feed all the time, but that's not the way t'ings are. They got no elbow room. It's the tides that says when they eat. And it's the moon that tells the tides when to ebb and when to flow."

"What are you saying, Pip?"

"Listen, Jordi, what kind of mussel would you be if you could be a mussel?"

"What do you mean, what kind?"

"Yuh, what kind?"

When Jordi didn't answer, Pip said, "If you was a mussel, you could only be one kind because a mussel can only be what it is. It has no choice."

"But, Pip, that's okay for mussels, but what about people?"

"Same tides, same moon. There are always t'ings bigger than you. Sometimes they're t'ings that men make up themselves. Like war."

"Are you saying there's nothing we can do?"

"Oh, no! Never think that. There's plenty a man can do. We always have some sea room." His eyes twinkled. "Instead of letting the wind have its own way all the time, a man can build a sailboat that shapes the wind. People have choices. You can choose what kind of person you are. You can be anyt'ing you want. For example, a man ain't able to help it that the war has caught up to him, but he can choose how he behaves—what kind of man he is in the war. Sure, war is like a hurricane; it's too big for us and we're too small. We're no more than farts in that hurricane. But it don't mean we can't have a plan."

"But Dad didn't have to go to the war. The war didn't catch him."

"Yuh, he wasn't drafted," Pip took a long drag on his cigarette, "but the war is there and he, well, he kinda had a choice not to go, and he kinda had no choice *except* to go."

"I don't understand."

"Because of the way he's made up. Sometimes the t'ing that controls a man is his own conscience." Pip blew out a stream of smoke. "But, you know, it's better to be controlled by that, than by t'ings outside yourself."

"Like what?" The skepticism in Jordi's voice was unmistakable.

"Like all the t'ings that are bigger than we are: storms, wars, disease…time."

"But you said that's just the way things are and we can do nothing about it."

Pip nodded. "Yuh, it's how t'ings are. Like time…" He looked at Jordi as if trying to decide whether or not to continue. Finally, he said, "You been thinking a lot about people dying lately, so I guess you're old enough to talk about it. You remember old Peter Nutt, the one they called 'Peanut'?"

Jordi nodded.

"Small man, but tough as anyt'ing. Best lobsterman I ever knew. He was out there many times when the wind and the waves were bigger than him and everybody else just turned over in their beds and went back to sleep. He told me once he didn't try to beat the wind, just to work wit' it. And he always got his catch. Know what I mean?"

Again, Jordi nodded.

"Well, do you remember how he died?"

"He was washed overboard in a big sea."

Pip nodded. "Yuh, that's what most people think."

"Well, isn't that the way it happened?"

"Maybe yes, maybe no. But as for me, I don't think he was just a helpless victim. I think he had a part in it."

Jordi furrowed his brow. "I don't know what you mean."

"Well, you know that Nana and me was good friends wit' old Peanut and his wife, Gladys. So we know t'ings about him that most people don't. For example, he knew he was gonna die."

"Before he went out?"

"Even before that. He had somet'ing called cancer of the pancreas. The doctors said there was no cure and he had only a few mont's to live." Pip observed Jordi intently.

"I don't know what you're saying," Jordi said.

"Well, he had been too weak to go out for almost a mont' and he was getting weaker. And I know for a fact that he and Gladys, that they..." Pip's voice caught. He paused, then said, "...that they...that the night before he went out, they spent the entire time just kinda holding hands."

"You mean he killed himself and she knew?" Jordi's mind was swirling the way it did when he surveyed a star-strewn sky.

Pip shook his head. "Maybe, maybe not. But I'd say he knew he was gonna die and he couldn't do not'ing about that. But he could decide the *how* of it and, up to a point, the *when* of it. Gladys said he didn't want to die in bed wit' people crying all around him." Pip took a drag on the cigarette. "See that mussel?" he asked. "It can't decide when and how to die. No animal can. You ever seen an animal take its own life? That's what makes us different; we got a little extra power."

They remained silent for a long while. Jordi watched the thinning fog slide away from the black navigation buoy out in the bay. The sun appeared as a great, blurred light shrouded in cotton gauze. Out beyond the point, the red and white bell marked "EG" rang clearly to the rhythm of the swell. The day was brightening over Eggemoggin Reach but confusion still clouded Jordi's mind. Everything Pip said amounted to a great mystery which he would now have to sort out for himself. Finally, he asked, "Pip, what did Nana think?"

"About what?"

"About what Peanut did."

Pip gave a knowing chuckle. "You know your grandmother good, don't you? Being so damned religious like she is, of course she didn't believe it. Or, I should say, she didn't accept it. It goes too much against the teachings of the Church for her taste."

"But Peanut wasn't Catholic, was he?"

"That don't matter to Nana. The whole idea of it is just beyond her, way beyond." He chuckled. "Like, say, the Pope takin' up with some floozy."

Jordi didn't say anything for a long while. Finally, he asked, "Pip, is Dad going to be killed?"

Pip threw an arm around Jordi's shoulders and pulled him in tight. "Jordi, most soldiers don't get killed in wars, only somet'ing like one in ten at most. And don't forget, there's the luck of the Dupuys and the Bastaraches."

An image of Denis Dupuy lying under the weighted sled came to Jordi. He burrowed himself deeper into Pip's embrace. The smoky smell of Pip, permanently imbedded in the woolen shirt, gave him comfort.

That night, instead of preparing the mussels himself as was his habit, Pip asked the women to do it while he and Jordi poured over maps of Europe.

chapter 7

In August they received what Gil said would be the last uncensored letter he could send them. On the porch, Pip absently waved at a swarm of mosquitoes as he read, "…because we are soon to leave for our P.O.E. (Point of Embarkation), which remains unknown to us. But I know you all want to follow my adventures and that you won't be talking to anyone, never mind the Krauts or the Japs, so I'm going to tell you where I am through a code. In my letters, I will spell out where I am through the first letters of each sentence of the first paragraph. That way you can follow me on the map. Also, this might make it possible for you to get more information about what I'm doing from the newspapers if they give a location that matches where I said I would be on that date. By the way, Lydie, I will use this code only in the letters I send to the entire family, not the ones I send to you alone."

Several days later, Gil sent a letter that started, "Anchors aweigh! That means, as I'm sure you can guess, that I am on my way. Last night was awful what with the wind and the pitching and rocking of the ship. And that wasn't the worst of it! Nobody could keep their dinner down. Three times I had to go on deck to heave. Imagine, me, a lobsterman! Coupled with the smell of puke below decks, was the constant smell of greasy food, which they cook all hours of the day and night—worse than old bait in the bilge!"

When Pip finished the letter he said, "So, Jordi, where is your dad?"

"Can I see the letter?"

Pip handed it to him. Jordi studied it for a minute then cried, triumphantly, "Atlantic…he's on the Atlantic Ocean."

Now that an ocean infested with warships and submarines separated them from Gil, they all felt his absence more keenly. They continued to gather to read his letters. And, as a family, they listened regularly to the news on the radio. They heard Walter Winchell whose
staccato voice Jordi learned to imitate: *"Good evening Mr. and Mrs.
America, from border to border and coast to coast and all the ships at sea."*
Or they tuned in the wonderful broadcasts of Edward R. Murrow,
who made you feel that you were really there. Of course, there was also
Teddy Thibodeau. But Jordi took most comfort from the broadcasts
of Gabriel Heatter who always began by saying, *"There is good news
tonight."*

They had an unspoken agreement that they would share these
times together, yet they were also beginning to inch away from each
other, ever so slightly, into private worlds of longing. Jordi soothed
himself by spending more time with Pip, and in doing so he failed to
notice how both Nana and his mother were withdrawing, too.

Jordi kept himself busy with building a half-model of his own.
One day, when Pip was feeling too sick to go out on the *Zabet &
Lydie,* Jordi rode his bike all the way into Brooklin. He heard that
Ogden Gower had finished the repairs to *Mistral* and he wanted to see
if the boat was still in the harbor. Also, he wanted to visit Ogden's
shop and ask for some scraps of wood and some advice.

Caterpillar Hill was too steep to ride up on his bike, so he walked,
stopping at the top to catch his breath. He scanned the horizon. Far
below him, the shattered crystal of Eggemoggin Reach flashed a million tiny explosions of light, stirred by the wind. The shadow of a
cloud drifted across the reach and dipped and rose over the bordering
land. Below and to his left, looking like a toy in a Lionel model rail-
road layout, was the Deer Isle Bridge rising out of the tree canopy to
span the reach. In the foreground was a field mottled with purple
ragged robin, and beyond, a burned-out blueberry field where magen-
ta fireweed thrived among the blackened boulders.

The fog stayed to the east, so his view stretched well out to sea. Far in the haze-blue distance to the west, the hills of Camden rose out of the ocean like bulwarks of the continent. Out beyond the reach and Deer Isle, smaller islands gave the appearance of a pod of whales making its way westward across East Penobscot Bay. The illusion was heightened by the shadows of clouds gliding across the ocean in the opposite direction.

When at last he arrived in Brooklin, *Mistral* was just leaving her mooring. He watched as the sails filled and the boat leaned to the wind heading for the southeast opening of Eggemoggin Reach. He remembered Pip saying that such a boat shapes the wind, gives it meaning, order, and now he could see how. He was overwhelmed by its beauty.

"Pretty, ain't she?" said Ogden.

"Sure is."

"What're you doin' all the way down heah, Jordi?"

Jordi explained about wanting to build a half-model.

"Like your dad, eh? Well, then, you can have the roam of my woodshed. Pick up any scraps you find. Then when you're done, I'll give you some tips on how to get started."

After Jordi had gathered some scrap mahogany and cedar, Ogden came to talk with him.

Jordi said, "Pip says that a boat like *Mistral* is beautiful because it controls the wind."

"No, not *control*, Jordi. Ain't nothin' can control the wind."

"Well, he actually said *shape* the wind."

"Eyuh, that's better," said Ogden. "Wind is kinda formless. Used to think it was sort of mindless, too. But was talking with one of my customers once, Mr. E. B. White over to Allen Cove, the writer. We were talking about how sails *absorb* the wind to make a boat come to life."

That evening, before supper, Jordi began his half-model, all the while dreaming of the boat he and his father would build together. After thinking about what Pip and Ogden Gower had said, Jordi came to sense that the boat had a mysterious life force, one he hoped might protect his father.

Nana kept herself busy by launching her own campaign against Hitler. She told everyone that the war was on their very shores and for proof she pointed to the fact that there was often static on the radio. "You see? You see? It's Germans, they're fooling around wit' the radio. *Jésus, Marie, et Josef,* give me the strength!" Prodded into action—and convinced that her frequent visits to church, where she lit countless votive candles, had enlisted the help of God—she organized the family and demanded everyone comb the house and barn for metal, tinfoil, or rubber that was not absolutely essential. They found a number of old inner tubes, along with worn truck and tractor tires that could not be retrod. From the barn, Pip heaved a bumper that had long ago fallen off the front of the truck, then went back and took the rear bumper as well. More than a dozen license plates sailed out of the barn, too. They were followed by rusted padlocks, rusted nails, bolts, nuts and the Chase & Sanborn coffee cans that contained them. Jordi brought out two old milking pails that were worn through on the bottom. Because of the clatter and clanging, the birds disappeared from the barnyard. Even the crows fell silent.

Jordi hoped all the surplus metal going to make ammunition would help keep his father safe. He also realized that, with all the ancient junk cleared from the barn, there would be room for him, his father, and Pip to build their boat. He spent hours scraping dried puddles of paint and shellac from the work bench, to create a clean work area for his father.

They gathered all of the junk into two piles by the porch for the Boy Scouts to pick up. Nana and Lydie contributed all the tin cans they could spare, holding aside only half a dozen or so to collect bacon grease, meat droppings, and frying fats. These they would take to the nearest collection station set up by the War Production Board, from where the waste fat would be shipped out to a rendering plant to make glycerin, which in turn would be used to make explosives. Nana said, with a satisfied giggle, "I am going to bomb that Hitler fella wit' bacon. He will learn to leave *my* son alone!" When they gathered up all the scrap metal, rubber, and waste fats they could find, Nana turned her attention to paper. She demanded Pip construct a bin beside the porch steps into which they would throw all newspapers, old magazines, and other waste paper. But only after cutting out any columns or articles that might interest Gil and sending them off to him. Pip and Chrétien began to strip empty cigarette packages of their outer paper and drop the foil liners into the same bin Lydie used for her chewing gum liners.

One day, after a frustrating half hour searching all the usual places, Pip asked if anyone had seen his second pair of binoculars only to learn that Nana had sent them off to England to help in the war effort.

"You sent my binoculars?"

"You still have a good pair for the lookout station."

Nana was not finished. She pulled the Frothingham Fertilizer Company calendar from the wall and laid it on the table. She counted the weeks left until they could expect the first frost and announced, "I will plant a Victory Garden of fall vegetables just like I did during the Great War." She was determined to be one of the first in Brooklin to "grow food for victory," as the posters encouraged.

"But, Zabet, it's already August. There ain't time," said Pip.

"There's time. I counted the weeks."

"But there ain't more than eight weeks to the first hard frost."

"It's enough, especially since I will pray to God to hold back the frost. I will light many candles."

Pip shook his head, but when Nana insisted he paint a sign to herald their patriotism, he could only comply. Two days later, Pip planted the sign that said:

WE HAVE A VICTORY GARDEN

in big black letters across a red, white, and blue background, exactly according to Nana's specifications. Nana planted spinach, turnips, carrots, radishes, and beets. With Lydie's help, she planted the seeds twice as deep as usual to protect them from an early frost. Just in case.

Privately, Pip whispered to Jordi, "She can be a pain in the butt, but at least she's got us all doing somet'ing. Shows she ain't gonna take things lying down."

Lydie followed Nana's lead and dutifully did her part. But as soon as her chores were done, she would retreat to the sitting room with her knitting and listen to records on the Victrola. Her companions became Dinah Shore and Vaughn Monroe, Bing Crosby and Frank Sinatra, Perry Como and Jo Stafford. On some days, when she took a break from her knitting, piles of peanut shells could be found in one of Pip's ashtrays.

One day Jordi walked into the sitting room while Lydie was listening to Helen Forrest singing "I Don't Want to Walk Without You." The recording sounded scratchy, so Lydie lifted the Victrola's arm gently, and removed a knot of dust from the tip of the needle. She leaned over and blew on the needle to remove any last trace of dust then lowered it carefully to the record. Still there was a scratching sound. Then the needle skipped and skated across the grooves with a shrill skirl.

Lydie gave a frustrated cry. "What's wrong?"

"Maybe it's the record, Ma," said Jordi. "Here, let's try another one." He took the top record from the stack and handed it to her. It was Vaughn Monroe, "My Devotion," which was high on the "Lucky Strike Hit Parade" and which Lydie had bought little more than a week before.

"No, not that one, Jordi. It's one of my favorites, and I don't want to ruin it if it's the needle that's bad. Here, we'll try this one. It's hardly been played because I don't like it. I don't know why I got it." She fitted the record over the spindle and lowered the arm. The Andrews Sisters started the song, "Don't Sit Under the Apple Tree with Anyone Else But Me" but they were drowned out by the same scratching noise.

Lydie shook her head. "It's the needle." She turned to Jordi. "I need to help Nana prepare supper, we're having pork pie and that takes a while to make. Will you do me a favor and go over to the general store and buy a new needle?"

"Sure, Ma."

"Come into the kitchen. I'll give you the money."

Later, Jordi was still a quarter mile from the Brooksville General

Store when some kids, four boys and a girl, approached him. At first he didn't notice them because his attention was focused on the lonely sound of one or two halyards slapping masts in Buck Harbor. At this time of year, the harbor would normally have been full of sailboats, but since the war started, there were few boats on the water. Even though the other lobstermen rejoiced that the waters were now left to them and the shore patrol, Jordi missed the sight of the graceful sailing yachts.

Then he saw the kids. He recognized all of them and knew they were trouble. The girl was Felicity Griswold and two of the boys were her older brothers George and Jack. The other two boys were Jared Hollis and Leon Molesworth, both in Jordi's class at school.

"Hey, it's Frenchy Dupuy!" cried Felicity. A spray of spittle shot from her mouth when she spoke. This happened so often nobody wanted to sit in front of her at school.

"Hey, Frog," said her brother Jack with a sneer.

"He ain't no Frog, that's a Frenchy from France," said George. "He's a Frenchy from Canada and they're called Gorfs, *backwards* Frogs."

The others shrieked with laughter. "Hey, Gorf!"

Jordi felt heat rise in his cheeks but he ignored it. He pushed past the gang and continued on to the general store.

"Hey, where do you think you're going, Gorf?"

Jordi felt a hand on his shoulder and turned to see Leon Molesworth looking down at him. "Leave me alone," he said. He felt a trickle of sweat snake down his back. To his horror, his knees started to shake and this only made him angrier. He twisted his shoulder and with his right hand slapped Leon's hand away.

Leon shoved him with both hands. "Don't you swing at me, you little French shit!" He shoved Jordi again, causing him to stumble backward.

"Leave me alone," Jordi said a second time. "I didn't do anything to you."

Leon turned to the others. "Hey, Frenchy says to leave him alone. He doesn't want to fight, just like his chickenshit dad." The previous spring, one of Jordi's teachers had asked the students who among them had fathers in the military and Jordi raised his hand. Afterwards, the Griswold brothers, whose father was in the Pacific and had already seen action in the Battle of the Coral Sea, said that Jordi's father joined the Army because it was only the Navy and the Marines who were doing any real fighting. "Leave it to a chickenshit Frenchy," they said.

Jordi hurled himself, fists flailing, at Leon. He caught the taller boy by surprise and smashed his fist squarely into Leon's nose. He heard the crunch of cartilage and the sound sent a wave of pleasure through him. Blood started to spurt from the boy's nose. Jordi reared back and took another swing, aiming again at the nose. Before he could connect, he was tackled from behind by all three of the other boys. He found himself on the ground with George, Jack, and Jared on top of him. He threw his arms in front of his face and felt the pain as his forearms and biceps were pummeled. He felt someone reach into his pocket where he had put the money his mother had given him. He tried to twist away, but the weight of the boys on him was too much. He heard Felicity yell, "Kill him!" He could barely breathe under the crushing weight.

From somewhere beyond the spasm of fear and rage that was his entire universe, he heard a man's voice. "Hey you kids, stop that. Get off him."

One of his attackers was suddenly pulled off him, but the other two kept swinging away.

"Stop it, I said!"

A second boy was jerked off him. Only Jack Griswold continued to fight. At least Jordi could breathe now. Then a man's hand grabbed the back of Jack's shirt and yanked him to an upright position. Through tears of pain and rage Jordi saw the man's distorted image, the wire-rimmed glasses, the cigarette behind his ear. It was Virgil Blount.

Blount helped Jordi to his feet. "Say, ain't you Lydie Dupuy's boy? Jordi, ain't it?"

Jordi said nothing. He knew Blount knew very well who he was. He rubbed his left forearm.

"Well, looks like you got yourself a real baster of a fight there, but it don't seem fair what with four of them and just one of you."

"He started it," said Felicity Griswold.

"I don't give a damn who started it, four against one just ain't fair." Blount paused then said, "Now I'll let you all fight and get it out of your systems, but you can only come at him one at a time." He turned to Jordi. "That okay with you?"

Jordi nodded without looking at Blount. He was glaring at the Griswold brothers.

"Okay then," said Blount, "who's first?"

The four boys looked at each other. The biggest and toughest among them was Leon Molesworth, but he was holding a handkerchief to his nose and tears were streaming down his cheeks.

"Shit," said Jack Griswold, "he ain't worth it, the little Gorf." All four boys turned and walked away, Felicity trailing behind them.

Only after they disappeared, did Jordi remember the money. "They have my money!" he cried.

"What money?"

"The money my mother gave me."

"Lydie?"

"My *mother*...to buy a new phonograph needle for her."

"A phonograph needle? That the whole of it?" Virgil Blount paused. "Come on, we'll go over to the general store and buy the needle. I'll get the money from those kids' parents later."

Jordi was horrified. How could he let this man, whom he detested, help him like this. How could he let him help his mother? His horror turned to anger at himself for getting into this situation. How could he? "I don't know..." he said.

"What do you mean you don't know? Lydie...your mother... wants the needle, don't she?"

"Yes, but..."

"But nothing. We're going to get it and bring it to her."

Bring it to her? Jordi was sick with the sudden realization that Virgil Blount intended to go all the way home with him, but he didn't know how to prevent it. The last thing he wanted was his mother feeling grateful to Blount. Especially since, he was certain, that was exactly what Blount wanted. None of this would have happened if it hadn't been for those kids—or if he had been more careful about protecting the money. Now he desperately tried to think of something to say that would stop Blount from helping him. Maybe he would be lucky and they wouldn't have the needle in stock at the General Store.

But they did. Soon he and Blount were heading back to the farm. All the way from the general store, Jordi was silent, furious with himself. He knew he would have to tell his mother the whole story because, besides the fact that Blount would tell if he didn't, he felt a thickness around his left eye. It was probably already swollen and discolored. His mother would notice it immediately and he would have to confess that he had been in a fight and that…that Virgil Blount had saved him.

And that was exactly how it happened. But, it was even worse than he had imagined. After his mother soaked a face cloth in cold water, folded it in two, and made Jordi hold it against his eye, she thanked Virgil Blount effusively and invited him to stay for a piece of pie. *Stay for a piece of pie!* Jordi's cheeks flushed with a mixture of anger and shame as he was forced to sit holding the dripping cloth against his face, while his mother chatted happily with *that* man. He burned with hatred for Virgil Blount for taking advantage of him.

"That's kind of you…ah…Mrs. Dupuy, don't mind if I do. I ate a big bowl of stew at noon, but I s'pose there's room for more."

"Oh, please call me Lydie."

Jordi glared at his mother. He wondered where Pip and Nana were.

Blount bowed his head slightly. "Lydie."

Lydie placed a piece of pie in front of Blount and one in front of Jordi. "I guess you can take the cloth away from your eye long enough to eat some pie," she said.

Blount had already taken a bite. "Uhm, uhm, this is some good pie. Better'n at Kate's Diner over to Blue Hill."

"I'm glad you like it, Virgil."

Virgil?

"Eyuh, I have a liking for blueberry pie something awful." Blount's eyes danced.

Jordi ignored his pie. *Where were Pip and Nana?* He glanced at his father's half-model and a wave of guilt came over him. Then anger. How could his mother do this?

When Blount finished his pie, Lydie said, "Feel free to smoke. It's okay, Pip smokes at the table all the time."

"Thank you." Blount reached behind his ear, took the cigarette, and lit it. He sighed, let smoke drift lazily from his mouth and sucked it into his nostrils, then expelled it from them in parallel streams. The smoke licked at his wispy blond mustache. He reached into his vest pocket, pulled out a pack of Lucky Strikes, removed one, and wedged it behind his ear. "Listen to music much, Lydie, do you?"

"I enjoy playing the Victrola when I'm sitting alone and doing my knitting. Pip and Nana, they don't much like my type of music. "

"What're your favorite songs lately?"

Where were Pip and Nana?

"I like Vaughn Monroe a lot."

"Do you? Me too! His new song especially, you know...ah..."

"My Devotion."

"Eyuh, that's it."

Jordi saw his mother's eyes brighten with pleasure.

"Mostly I listen to songs that...well, you know, what with the war and all there are lots of songs that..."

"Tell about how lonely people are?"

Jordi saw his mother blush.

"I suppose," she said softly. Then she looked up and said, more brightly, "You're very lucky to have a deferment."

Blount adjusted the glasses on the bridge of his nose. This time it was he who blushed. "Eyuh, I s'pose. But to tell you the truth, I'd rather serve. I feel guilty and all, what with other men like your husband...like Gil...going off and I can't go."

"Oh, don't be silly. Every man can't go. We need men on the homefront, too."

Jordi was so angry that his hands started to tremble. He tried to steady them but it was too late. His mother had already noticed. She frowned. "Jordi, what is it? Are you in pain?"

"Yes, Ma," Jordi replied through clenched teeth.

"Well, Pip and Nana are in the barn. We'll go see what Pip says. Maybe we'll drive you in to see Dr. Davids."

Blount stood. "'Pears you have things to do. I'll take my leave, now."

Lydie nodded. "We should have his eye looked at."

"Eyuh, I'll be leaving."

"Thank you again," said Lydie.

Jordi watched Blount leave, trailing a coil of smoke. He ground his teeth together so hard that the grinding sound was audible. His cheek muscles were clenched. He wore the anguished expression of someone who has just discovered one of the sad truths of the world and wished he hadn't.

"My poor Jordi, that's really hurting you, isn't it?" asked Lydie.

The next day, Jordi was still blue about the affair of the phonograph needle, but he cheered up when the mailman delivered a letter from his father.

When they finished reading Gil's letter, which told of his trip across the Atlantic, Pip got out a map of Europe. He spread it out on a folding card table and he and Jordi tacked it to the table at the four corners. Pip then took a small pin with a red head and stuck it upright in the center of England. "That's Gil. It'll have to do until we get an exact location from his next letter."

In the morning, a soft southwesterly breeze was blowing up over Deer Isle, eddying down to the landward side of Eggemoggin Reach. The water was wrinkled here and there with cat's paws, yet there were no waves. But within an hour the wind backed ninety degrees and a strong southeasterly funneled straight into the seaward mouth of the reach, roiling the waters and snatching spindrift off the tops of newly born whitecaps. Shadows of clouds chased each other across the water. Several seagulls flew into the wind but were unable to make forward progress. They rose up, stalled for an instant, and shot downwind at a tremendous speed, their shadows darting over the waves. The piebald surface of the reach, all whitecaps and black troughs, heaved and fretted against the shore. The *Zabet & Lydie* and a half dozen other boats lurched and pitched like unbroken horses in the short, hard chop— spray splattering their windshields. Aboard their boat, the wind insinuated itself into a slot where the roof and side of the wheelhouse had begun to separate. The slot resonated like a flute's sound chamber, and the *Zabet & Lydie* moaned. The red and white bell buoy by Hay Island Ledge clanged fitfully in the sharp chop.

Jordi staggered aft to right a bait bucket which had overturned. When he turned to make his way back to the wheelhouse, the *Zabet & Lydie* plunged into a wave. Spray, filled with tiny, sharp, salt crystals, bloomed around him, stinging his face. He staggered toward the wheelhouse.

"I'd say, t'irty knots," said Pip. "Strange how she come up like that, all at once."

Jordi didn't answer.

"Yuh, wind is a strange thing. I remember back in '34, wind from the Rockies blew clear 'cross the country. Scraped soil from the plains. That's what caused the dust bowl. Wind just ripped up the soil and blew it east. There were dust clouds here in Maine. Dirt from the Midwest here in Maine. Imagine that." Pip stole a look at Jordi, then looked out the windshield again. Spray sissed against the glass. He was being careful to keep the bow pointed into the waves in order to minimize the tendency of the *Zabet & Lydie* to yaw. "Yuh, that's the wind for you." He paused for a moment, then continued, "War's like the wind, you know. Like a hurricane, if you know what I mean." He snuck another peek at Jordi, who stared straight ahead. "I mean, a man can hang on to his mooring and hope to hell that it holds, which it likely won't. Or he can do somet'ing. Me? I'd leave the mooring and fetch myself some sea room, that's what I'd do. I'd take some action." He paused again, apparently waiting for Jordi to respond. When Jordi said nothing, Pip said, "Don't be too hard on her, Jordi. It ain't not'ing but the war."

"What do you mean?"

"Your ma. You're mad at her for not'ing more than smiling and laughing wit' that Blount fella."

"But why does she? He's a zero who's too afraid to join up!"

"Would you be happier if he was some nice guy who just came back wounded from the Pacific?"

Jordi glanced at his grandfather, shook his head. "No."

"See, your problem is you don't want her to have no contact at all except us, but that ain't natural."

"I don't know what you mean."

"She needs to talk with people of her own generation. They're the ones who are most involved in this war. Me and Nana, we already had our war. You? If this war drags on like the last one, it may be your war, too. Another six or seven years and you could join up. But in the meantime, it's their war and one thing about it, it brings the generation that's involved in it together. Like they're all in the same boat in a hurricane."

"But we're involved in it too, you and me and Nana."

"Yuh, but it ain't the same."

"How?"

Pip stuck a cigarette between his lips, hunched against the wind eddying under the wheelhouse roof, and lit it. He dragged in smoke until the ash at the tip glowed bright orange, then released the smoke in a stream that fanned out against the windshield. "Ah, that's a tough one." He paused, then said, "I guess for the *before* generation and for the *after* generation—that's you and me and Nana—the war makes things kind of…dull. It's like we're drugged or somet'ing. It's going on but we're not directly involved so we can't do anyt'ing but wait for it to be over. Like we're paralyzed. But for the generation that's fighting the war, everyt'ing is much sharper. It's like they have a raw spot. I know, I've been there. And when people feel like that, it's as though they have a secret code between them that says 'Aw Jeez, we're the ones that are doing this. Only *we* really know the pain and excitement of it.' It's as though a whole generation of people have, all at the same time, come to believe that life is short and you better do somet'ing now. Know what I mean?"

"I guess."

"Life seems kinda more precious to them, the life of *that* moment, and they want to share it wit' someone, anyone, of the same generation—their favorite songs, for instance, which the other generations don't much like. You like the music your ma plays?"

Jordi gave a short laugh. "No."

"There, see what I mean?"

"But can't she talk with other *women* her age, women in her sewing club? Does she have to talk with someone like Virgil Blount?"

"Most of the time she does talk wit' her women friends. He just happened by, and she was probably feeling lonely." Pip paused, then hurriedly corrected himself. "Lonely for someone of her generation, I mean."

"He didn't just happen by," said Jordi morosely.

"Ah, yuh, that's eating you too, huh? Well, it wasn't your fault. The jerk just took advantage of a situation."

Jordi was silent for a while, bracing himself against the lurching of the *Zabet & Lydie*. Finally, he said, "When you said that the people involved have their whole minds on the war, does that mean that Dad isn't thinking of building our boat when he gets back?"

"Aw Jeez, I'm sure he's thinking of it. Except there ain't much he can do about it now. But don't worry, he'll be all hot to trot when the time comes."

Jordi was silent. After a time, Pip said, "You still don't like him, that Blount fellah, do you?"

Jordi shook his head.

"Well, me too. The man is a complete zero."

Then Jordi laughed.

chapter 8

Lydie organized a St. Valentine's Day dance to sell war bonds. She formed a committee, which included two members of her women's club and Virgil Blount. She hadn't asked Blount to work with her, but when he heard about the committee, he said it was the least he could do seeing as how he couldn't actually "go over there and serve." The committee met several times at the Consolidated School's gymnasium, where the dance was to be held, and on each occasion Blount came by to pick Lydie up. He said that it was better for him to drive her to Blue Hill than for her to drive Pip's truck as he wasn't subject to gasoline rationing because he had to drive around every evening to ensure that blackout curtains were in place.

Each time there was a meeting, Jordi would stay awake until he heard the crunch of Blount's truck picking its way up the snow-packed road. As soon as he heard the truck, he would turn off the light and open the blackout curtain. He could see the bloom of the headlights sweep across his ceiling when the truck's front end bounced up the crest of the hill. That was his signal to crouch at the window and peer over the sill just enough to spy on his mother and Blount. He always heard a murmured thank you and good night. Then soft laughter.

And what about the rest of the evening? The long drive to Blue Hill, the long drive back? Was it possible his mother let Virgil Blount kiss her? So what, as Pip said, if his mother needed the company of people her own age? He still could not shake the fear that she would abandon his father and, in doing so, him too. By the time she made her way upstairs, Jordi was so worried that he would pretend to be asleep so he wouldn't have to talk with her.

The war continued day after day, week after week, month after month, until it seemed a permanent part of their existence. Another winter surrendered to another spring and still the war continued.

The geese flew in from the south, lingered a week, and continued their migration north. The robins came, then what the locals called a robin-storm of spring snow fell, then it melted away.

The winter constellations of Orion and Gemini ceded the sky to Cygnus and Libra. Cassiopeia migrated from west to east. A million chrysalides yielded butterflies, and butterfly shadows flitted over the flowering meadows and fields. The swallows, sparrows, and grackles appeared. The fields were furrowed by the men not at war. The rhubarb ripened and alewives flashed up the Damariscotta River as they did every year, drawing with them the gulls, ospreys, and eagles. Bluebottles and dragonflies and deerflies came; a blue heat haze settled over the farm; and fireflies flared at night. The bobolinks appeared with their bubbling songs and the hermit thrushes with their clear flute-like phrases.

The mud in the barnyard slowly turned to early summer dust. Nana placed a nosegay of wildflowers in an old Chase & Sanborn coffee can and placed it on the sill of the kitchen window—Quaker ladies, English cowslips, and buttercups at first, later oxeye daisies, black-eyed susans, and harebells.

As the war went on, the Dupuy family clung to its routines. In addition to her Victory garden, now famous throughout the county, Nana stepped up her food fight against the Germans with a vengeance. No longer was perfectly good food to be thrown out. So Pip and Jordi had to make do with day-old sandwiches wrapped in Victory Pack extra-heavy waxed paper. Evenings they were treated to wartime dessert recipes that Nana took from the back panel of packages of Minute Gelatin—plain, unflavored—which they ate huddled behind the blackout curtains in a pool of light from the lone bulb above the table. This, after a meal prepared with the aid of a newly published pamphlet called "Victory Meat Extenders," which contained a disheartening number of bland and grainy recipes. As for feeding others, people said Nana was canning so many fruits and vegetables that she was posing a threat to Herrick & Allen's Canning Plant in Sedgwick.

She was not the only Dupuy digging in. On the top shelf in the pantry, Pip stored three different helmets near the binoculars (which he forbade Nana to touch)—each helmet with a Civil Defense insignia identifying him as an Air Raid Warden, an Auxiliary Fireman, or an Auxiliary Policeman. He read the *Handbook for Air Raid Wardens* published by the Office of Civilian Defense and could answer any question posed by his fellow volunteers. This was in addition to his regular shift at the lookout station. At home, he removed all light bulbs from the porch, and from the wall of the shed near the chopping block, so there was no chance of showing up in the sights of a German bombardier.

The family played nightly games of poker crouched behind the blackout curtains, under a canopy of smoke from Pip's cigarettes. Sweatered against the evening wind, they played with a deck of Uncle Sam cards that had pictures of allied and enemy planes on the backs. The cards were designed so people could become expert plane spotters. Nana never stopped complaining that two Heinkels, a Stuka, a Focke-Wulf, and a Messerschmitt beat a P-38 Lightning, a Wildcat, a B-26 Marauder, a British Hurricane, and a British Halifax. "Kraut planes ain't s'posed to beat Allied planes," she insisted.

Jordi was the true expert because, in addition to the nightly card games, he built models for the U.S. Navy Bureau of Aeronautics. Indeed, he had developed a reputation since nearly all of his wooden aircraft identification models had been accepted by them. This was a remarkable achievement because the specification and accuracy requirements stipulated by the bureau were very tough.

Jordi also continued to work on his own half-model.

Lydie busied herself trying to keep up with Nana's frenzied pace. The Valentine's Day Dance was such a success, she set about organizing more bond rallies. Unfortunately for Jordi, she continued working with the same committee, which meant Virgil Blount still showed up to drive her to planning meetings.

Though they all managed to stay busy, the highlight of this time was still reading Gil's letters. They sustained the family as the war stretched on. The family hoped their letters to him provided comfort, too.

But the tone of Gil's letters had changed. They seemed to lack the high spirits that had always characterized them. Now they read like the letters of a man who was reaching the end of his endurance.

On July 18 they received a letter in which Gil, through his coding system, told them that he was now in Sicily. Pip rose from the table without a word, walked over to the map, and moved the red pin from Africa to Sicily. He exhaled a stream of smoke that settled over the map. Then they received a second letter, one which started without a code, since they already knew where he was.

July 20, 1943
Dear Lydie & Jordi & Ma & Dad,
Couldn't sleep much so I thought I'd write. The mail hasn't caught up with us yet so I'm really looking forward to a bunch of letters when we finally settle in somewhere.

I never spent a more restless night than I did the night before this invasion. It was almost impossible to sleep below decks so I went topside. Except for the wind (and the waves which were just beginning to build) it was hard to believe that a lot of shooting was about to take place. H-hour was just before dawn (0400), but my outfit wasn't scheduled to go ashore until about one and a half to two hours later. So I was able to watch things from the deck as long as I stayed away from the guys assembling at the rail to climb down into the waiting boats. What I saw was one of the most strangely beautiful sights I've ever seen. As I looked toward the beach, I saw what looked like a fireworks display. But after a while, I noticed the sky brighten over the mountains behind the beach. The sunrise came flaming red and yellow, more brilliant than I think I've ever seen it, even after countless sunrises on the reach! It was like God was saying, "Who the heck do you little men think you are? You're small and weak, and your silly little business on that beach is meaningless. It's just another day like the millions before and the millions still to come." I tell *you, it was an oddball thought, but it was a <u>comforting</u> thought. Dad, to use your expression, I felt about as big as a fart in a hurricane! Which I guess means I couldn't change anything out there so I was free to worry only about myself and how I would do what I had to do. Does that make any sense to you? I hope so, because I don't know how to explain it any better.*

Anyway, I made it okay on the beach and that was that.
July 21, 1943
Still here. Still on the move! Can't write much.
July 23, 1943
Bivouacked. Field train finally joined up with us. Everyone is tired, but we're winning. We're kicking their goddamned butts! (Sorry, Ma.)
July 24, 1943
Moving out again! More trucks over bad roads. More marching!
July 26, 1943

Although he had entered the date, Gil made no entry here. He had written several words then crossed them out so thoroughly it was impossible to make out what they were.

July 27, 1943
We beat them. The Germans retreated in total disarray sometime in the wee hours this morning. Have slept for several hours. Now I'm feeling refreshed and I guess a little better. I don't know how much I can tell you, but we were in one heck of a battle! Our casualties have been extremely light. I mean, we really hurt the Germans bad. It's probably all over the newspapers stateside.

Now I'm going to close because I want to be sure to make mail pick-up. I don't want you to wait another day! Hopefully, I'll be able to write again on a regular basis. Love, Gil

Nana spread the letter out on the table and tried to smooth its wrinkled surface with the edge of her hand. She took a handkerchief from her apron pocket and wiped at the mud stains that covered the pages. Her eyes welled with tears.

One evening in early December Jordi reached across the coat-check counter and accepted Ogden Gower's heavy, government kersey coat. In the steam heat of the Consolidated School's gymnasium, vapors rose up from it, giving off the smell of wet wool. He hung the coat on the crowded rack and gave Ogden a numbered plastic tag.

"Thanks, Jordi. How's the fishing?"

"Pip and me had a big catch today. He saved one for you."

"Gory, I'll say it was a big catch," said Niall Macgrudder who appeared brushing snow from his navy pea coat. The snow sifted to the floor and melted instantly. "Best in a month!" He nodded at Ogden. "Keeping warm?"

"Eyuh, warm's I can."

Ogden turned to Jordi. "How's the latest half-model coming, Jordi?"

"Not great. I did something wrong…messed up the measurements, I guess. I'm gonna have to start all over again."

"Eyuh, easy to do. But keep at it, you'll get it right."

At that moment Lydie approached. "Niall, Ogden, I'm so happy you could come. Thanks for your help." She wore a stylish blue dress with a Peter Pan collar and a bow tie. Her long, soft neck seemed even more elegant. Her legs were bare, but a carefully drawn seam along each calf simulated the nylon stockings which were now impossible to get.

"Least we can do for Gil and the boys over theah fighting," said Niall.

"And you can buy some bonds." It was Virgil Blount appearing at Lydie's side. He wore a brown Victory suit—narrow lapels, short jacket, no cuffs, no vest.

Jordi glared at him.

Lydie herself seemed to think the man was standing too close, and, to Jordi's satisfaction, she took a step sideways, leaving a gap between them. "Yes, please do buy some bonds. You, too, Ogden. We need all the help we can get."

Niall laughed. "Gorry, with you and your bond drives and Zabet and her...her...her everything, the Dupuys will finance the whole goldang war!"

Lydie squeezed his elbow. "Everybody who contributes makes a difference. And speaking of Nana, she and Pip are right over there speaking with Gladys Nutt and Rufus Metcalfe if you want to say hello."

"How's Gil doing?" asked Ogden.

"As well as can be expected," said Lydie. "He's left Sicily and he's in England now and seems homesick."

"Eyuh, that's understandable. It's something, what men like him are doing. Heard about the Fournier boy over to Winterport?"

"No. I don't think we know him."

"Thought you might, him being French with a name like Fournier. Guess it'll be in the papers tomorrow. They gave him the Medal of Honor...posthumously."

Lydie put her hand to her mouth. "Oh, dear, what happened?"

"It was at Guadalcanal. Him and another guy held off damn near all the Japs in the place with one machine gun...till they was killed."

Lydie shook her head. "Was he married?"

"Don't know."

Lydie bit her lower lip. Jordi, who was now as tall as his mother, put a hand on her shoulder.

Jordi couldn't sleep. Each night, in bed, the war started up again, planes falling from the sky, buildings blowing up. Like that picture in *Life* magazine, he saw soldiers crumbling to the ground.

He tried to read a Hardy Boys book but couldn't concentrate. So he turned the light off and raised the blackout curtain. Only a few thin, stray clouds crossed the full moon's face. Its glow limned the horizon and Jordi could see the illumined rim of the earth. He imagined he could hear the faint pop, pop, of gunfire beyond the horizon. He closed his eyes to drive away the thought, then opened them again. Below the window moonlight puddled in the barnyard like thinned milk and glanced off the hood ornament of Pip's truck. The barn and house seemed to fret like insomniacs. He heard the distant bark of a neighbor's dog. It was fitful, perhaps made uneasy by the fat moon. Wind sizzled through the treetops, rattled the window, and wheezed through cracks in the east wall of the farmhouse.

Jordi resolved to begin a new half-model first thing in the morning, after milking Delores. He was determined to get it right this time.

December 15, 1943
Dear Lydie & Jordi & Ma & Dad,
I suppose I need to tell you that I was awarded the Distinguished Service Cross. If I don't tell you, it will appear in the Bangor Daily News and the Ellsworth American and you'll find out anyway. Then you'll all be mad at me. So I'll tell you what happened myself. The first thing you need to know is that I was wounded, but not seriously. I didn't mention this to you before because I didn't want you to worry. But now everyone will know because of the citation. Here it is:

"Pfc. Guillem H. Dupuy, 11702032, United States Army, for extraordinary heroism in connection with military operations against an armed enemy. On July 26, 1943, near St. Venera, Sicily, Pfc. Dupuy saw that his platoon was pinned down by intense enemy machine gun fire. Pfc. Dupuy, along with Pfc. Angelo Cirillo, carrying carbines, advanced on belly through a field without protection in order to flank the enemy machine gun nest. They started to take heavy rifle fire and Pfc. Dupuy was hit in the shoulder. Despite his wound, Pfc. Dupuy asked Pfc. Cirillo to cover him while he continued toward the machine gun position. Pfc. Dupuy managed to surprise the three men in the machine gun nest by approaching from the side. He killed all three men before the enemy could turn the machine gun around. Pfc. Dupuy's initiative and his bravery under fire, despite the risk to his own life, eliminated a serious threat to his platoon and allowed it to continue its advance which, in turn, helped lead to the total defeat of the enemy in this engagement."

I've quoted the whole thing like that not to brag, but because it will be printed in the paper anyway. But I have to tell you, the medal gives me no personal pleasure. I just reacted. We were pinned down and Angelo and me, we happened to be closest to the machine gun. That was all. It was either them or us.

Well I guess you can see I'm feeling pretty rotten about the whole thing, so I'm going to close this letter before I depress you all any more than I already have. Don't worry about the shoulder wound. The bullet didn't even penetrate, and I'm fine. Love, Gil

"That's Medal of Honor stuff!" said Pip. "I wonder why they didn't put him up for the Medal of Honor like the Fournier boy from Winterport?"

"Pip, that poor boy was killed," said Nana. "Don't wish that on our son."

"Damn it, Zabet! You know I ain't wishing that. That's a goddamned stupid t'ing to say. But they give the Medal of Honor to guys who survive, too. That's all I'm saying."

Nana whipped her dish towel at Pip. "Don't you swear at me, Mr. Pète-sed!"

Lydie was riffling through the shoe box that contained all of Gil's letters. Finally, she said, "Here, I found it."

"What?"

"Do you remember the strange letter where he wrote down a date but crossed out whatever he had written? Do you want to guess what the date was?"

"July twenty-sixth?" asked Pip.

Lydie nodded.

February 2, 1944
Dear Lydie & Jordi & Ma & Dad,
Dad, you always used to say that whatever life gives you, no matter how it seems to tie you up, it always leaves you a little sea room, enough room to make personal choices so that you aren't stuck like a boat in a wind storm without a motor or a sail. Do you remember saying that? Well, I've made such a choice. You all better sit down, because this is going to come as a surprise.

I'm now a combat medic!

And yes, before you ask, this has a lot to do with what happened in Sicily. I guess I can't explain it fully, so I won't even try. Let's just say I think I can help the war effort just as much by patching up guys on our side as I can shooting at the enemy. I won't pretend that it was easy getting the transfer. Some of my commanding officers were pretty hot and bothered since, as they said, having just won the DSC I should be an example to the other guys, instead of exchanging my "bullets for bandages." (That's exactly what the captain said.) But it turns out that Lydie's cousin, Teddy, plays bridge with our commanding general and I guess he put in a word for me. (I think he's friends with everybody over here! I wouldn't be surprised to see him playing cards with Ike and Churchill and de Gaulle!)

He spent the rest of the letter describing his medic training in detail. Also, he included a new photograph. In it, his torso was twisted to the right to display the white band with red cross that wrapped his upper arm. He stood in front of a long row of Quonset huts and he was grinning, but it was a grin that looked as though it had been pasted on his face. In his right hand he held out a helmet to show that it, too, had a red cross on it.

"Chrétien, I seen that kind of face before." Pip handed the photo to his brother-in-law. Chrétien was on one of his infrequent visits, since he was working full-time on warships at the Bath Iron Works now.

Chrétien examined the picture for a moment. He nodded. "Adam Bandrowski."

Pip nodded sadly.

"Who is Adam Bandrowski?" asked Lydie.

"A guy me and Chrétien knew in the Great War. He was in our outfit. In the Meuse-Argonne. Them Germans was coming at us out of the trees. One came straight at Adam Bandrowski. Well Adam, he takes his bayonet and he jams it into the man's belly and he pulls the trigger at the same time. And when the man went down, sure as hell dead, Adam yanks the bayonet out and shoots the guy four, maybe five more times. After the fight, poor Adam, he couldn't stop shaking."

Pip flicked the photograph of Gil with his finger. "And he had this kind of look on his face…"

"Like a man who just killed another man," said Chrétien.

Lydie snatched the photograph from Pip. "You know goddamned well that Gil wouldn't do that kind of thing! What the hell are you talking about?"

Jordi backed away from his mother, startled at her sudden burst of anger.

"Lydie," snapped Nana. "You don't talk to Pip that way." Then she turned to Pip and, with even greater anger said, "*Jésus, Marie, et Josef,* you know your son ain't like that."

"Zabet, it's war," said Chrétien. "No man, I don't care who—"

Pip grabbed his arm. "Of course, you're right Lydie, Zabet. We ain't meaning to say Gil would do what Adam Bandrowski did. Not like that. It's just that in war you got to kill the other guy and it kind of gets to you."

"Yuh," said Chrétien. "It kind of gets to you. Me and Pip felt the same way even though what we did was…clean…you know, not like this Adam." He looked at Pip and they exchanged nods.

Lydie gazed at the two of them for a long while. Then she asked, "Will he be all right?"

"Oh, sure," said Pip. "It just takes getting used to. I don't know anybody in our whole outfit that didn't need time to get used to it."

"Yuh," added Chrétien. "Look at Pip and me. We came out of it completely normal and all." Then he laughed.

They all laughed. But Jordi could see his mother didn't believe them for a minute.

Neither did Nana.

Neither did he.

chapter 9

Jordi and Pip parked the truck and walked toward their inverted
rowboat on the beach at Naskeag Point. The sky started to go from all
black to blue-black. Stars, fading in the east, still pricked the darkness
in the west. Though it was bone cold from a long night of cooling, the
first hint of light was rising over Cadillac Mountain on Mount Desert
Island. There was little breeze and the great rollers from a storm far
out to sea that had punished the coast for three days had subsided.

By the time they turned the rowboat over and Pip smoked a cigarette and stretched his back, the rim of the sun appeared blood red
above the horizon. A seagull lifted into the air. Others joined. They
swooped up invisible slopes, spun round unseen threads, traced out
lines, loops, spirals, arabesques—geometries of flight that disappeared
the moment after Jordi saw them.

The rowboat scraped softly on the sand as Pip and Jordi dragged
it into the water. They rowed out to the *Zabet & Lydie*, started the
engine, and cruised into open water from the northeastern end of
Eggemoggin Reach. As always, they scanned the horizon, looking for
the great whale they, along with Gil, had seen before the war.

That day, years ago, the whale rose silently up out of the vast
waters of Jericho Bay, heralded only by a scurry of seagulls. The whale
breached the surface no more than twenty yards to starboard in a long
parabola of flesh. And in that instant, the whale set against the vast
sprawl of blue saturated sky, Jordi's mind reeled with all the details
of its form. An impression of large white flippers spread heavenward,
of a mighty head, a massive sloping rostrum, long parallel throat run-

nels, huge bifurcated flukes—a great bulk of flesh swaddled in light. For an instant it was surrounded by a nimbus of spray, millions of sun-suffused droplets forming a glistening counter-sun with the whale at its center.

"Mary, Mother of God," Pip whispered.

Jordi and his father were unable to utter a word. All three—grandfather, father, son—stood at the starboard gunwale of the *Zabet & Lydie* eyes wide, barely moving, even when the whale reentered the water, raised its flukes, and lobtailed, slapping the surface of the sea with such force they were doused with spray. The *Zabet & Lydie* rocked in the wash of waves.

Gil finally spoke. "Holy mackerel." Then he laughed nervously. "It's enough to give a man religion."

"Or take it away from him," Pip said.

They watched as the whale disappeared and the roiling of the sea's surface diminished.

Jordi said, "It was a humpback."

"*Keporkak*," Pip replied. There was reverence in his voice. His eyes glistened.

"What?"

"There's an old Mi'kmaq legend says it was a great humpback—they called him *Keporkak*—that lobtailed with such might it set the water to sloshing back and fort' across the Bay of Fundy. They say that's what made the tides. After seeing that fella, I believe it."

Later, they saw what they assumed was the same whale, bubble-cloud feeding. From below, it circled, exhaling a mist of bubbles that rose to the top forming a columnar net that trapped sand lances which were unaware they could swim through the wall of bubbles. The whale rose up through the column, mouth agape, sucking in hundreds of the long, thin, undulating fish as seagulls squalled about its mouth.

Pip said, "Poor, dumb fish. If they only knew they had a chance to escape."

"Not much of a chance," Jordi's father said.

And Pip replied, "A chance is a chance."

Jordi remembered the day clearly. But today he saw no whales. Only an expanse of water and a faint line where the sky met the ocean.

Throughout the day they hauled traps, removed the lobsters, sent the crabs and other creatures pinwheeling through the sunlight and back into the ocean, rebaited the traps, and lowered them again. For most of the day, the world had a big-sky look, rows of clouds stretched toward a vanishing point. But as the day wore on, the breeze picked up and storm clouds began to appear over the hills of Camden.

"Mackerel sky all day, now looks like a blow coming," said Pip in the late afternoon. "Maybe we won't go out tomorrow."

"Good," said Jordi. "I can work on my half-model."

Pip let Jordi pilot the *Zabet & Lydie* homeward. Jordi held the wheel low on the rim, palms facing up. It was the same peculiar style of steering his father always used.

Jordi threaded the *Zabet & Lydie* around Lazygut Ledge and between Stinson Neck and Crow Island, taking a course they would have avoided if visibility were poor because of the rock, exposed at low tide, midway between Stinson and Crow.

"Is this the kind of thing you meant when you told Dad about sea room?" asked Jordi.

"Taking this course? Yuh, I guess that's part of it. The weather allows it today. But it don't always, eh? In a storm or in a fog a man would be a fool to go this way. Sometimes you have more or less sea room depending."

Jordi waited for Pip to continue. When he didn't, Jordi asked, "Depending on what?"

"Oh, I don't know... Storms and fogs and t'ings are dumb. They ain't got will, they're just strong as hell, that's all. They put you in a kinda box. War and disease are the same way. A person has all the sea room he wants inside the box, but he can't get outside the box. Know what I mean?"

"Yuh, I guess."

"Now your dad, he's inside the box of war, which, by the way, includes his own ideas of what that means, but he sure did somet'ing with the little sea room he had. There's always sea room, but most guys ain't got the guts to use it. They just wait for t'ings to happen to them, good or bad, like never leaving your mooring and hoping it will hold."

Pip was so preoccupied looking at Jordi as he spoke that he didn't notice they were approaching Niall Macgrudder's dock until Jordi throttled back the engine. This was the first time Jordi had taken the *Zabet & Lydie* all the way into the dock, and Pip was just about to take over when he changed his mind. Jordi reduced his speed and turned downwind of the dock in order to coast up to it going into the wind. Pip stood behind Jordi until the *Zabet & Lydie* was about to stop, then, without a word, he went forward and threw a line to Niall Macgrudder. When he came back to the wheelhouse he said, "Good job."

Jordi beamed. He knew this was an important test of his ability and someday he'd be able to bring a big sailboat into a dock, too. After selling their catch to Niall, Jordi piloted the *Zabet & Lydie* around to Naskeag Harbor and their mooring. As was their habit since the war started, they gave the horn four blasts: three short, one long—*de... de... de... daaaah*—the Morse code for "V," *Victory*, like the Beethoven symphony they sometimes heard on the radio. They cleaned up the *Zabet & Lydie*, lowered themselves into the rowboat, and rowed ashore.

One day that spring, Lydie planted impatiens all along the base of the porch and along the southern side of the barn. She opened the living room window and turned the radio up. While she planted her flowers, Pip repaired lobster traps, Nana tended her victory garden, and Jordi worked on his latest half-model. They listened to "Lucky Strike Hit Parade" songs. No one spoke. It was as though they had somehow agreed to take a break from the war's constant worry and speculation, especially now that Gil was in England preparing for the invasion of France everyone said was inevitable.

Mid-morning, Pip nudged Jordi and nodded toward Nana and they both snorted, trying to stifle a laugh. Nana was swaying to "Besame Mucho," her broad backside setting her dress to shivering. When the song ended and Bing Crosby and the Andrews Sisters came

on singing "Is You Is, Or Is You Ain't, My Baby?" Nana really began
to gyrate, her dress flapping like a flag. Jordi could no longer hold
back his laughter. He dropped what he was doing and watched, wide-
eyed as Nana thrust her hips right and left to the slow striptease-blues
intro played by a wrawling trumpet with a mute. When the orchestra
picked up the tempo, Nana quickened her step and added a bounce.

Jordi rose and, holding his hands high above his head, mimicked
Nana's moves. Pip joined Jordi. Lydie burst out laughing, which startled everybody. They hadn't heard her laugh much the last few years.
Nana turned, saw what Jordi and Pip were doing, and stuck her
tongue out at them. "*Les malades!*" she snapped. Then she, too,
laughed and they all danced together.

Nana thrust her hips more zestfully and they followed, each trying
to outdo the others. Pip threw his hip to the right, then yelped, then
pressed the heel of his hand against it, then groaned, then laughed
again. Lydie took Jordi's hands and they danced a dance that was equal
parts jitterbug and hootchy-kootchy. The song slowed and Bing
Crosby and the Andrews Sisters came together to sing in unison. So,
too, did the Dupuy family, coming together in a circle with their arms
around each other. They laughed with the kind of abandon that
cleanses—if only for a short time.

A moment after the last notes of the song died away, Walter
Winchell came on to report the taking of Santa Maria Infante by the
Americans and Sant' Angelo by the British. He closed his broadcast by
saying the Poles were facing stiff resistance at Cassino:

*But be assured that Rome will soon fall and then it remains for the
allies to open another front in France. Nobody knows when the invasion
of Fortress Europe will begin, but it can't be long coming...*

Their laughter died away. Lydie went back to her planting. When
the music resumed, she sang along quietly to Jo Stafford's "I'll Be
Seeing You," her voice quivering.

Nana, Pip, and Jordi fell silent. Nana looked at Pip and shook her
head sadly.

May 23, 1944

Dear Lydie & Jordi & Ma & Dad,

Yes, I have heard "Is You Is, Or Is You Ain't, My Baby?" and it must have been quite a sight to see Ma dancing to it! I only wish I could have been there. My medic training has been going well. I've learned how to apply a tourniquet, how to give plasma, how to debride a wound (that means clean it), apply sulfa, and inject morphine. At first, I was nervous. Morphine can be very dangerous. But it turns out that the army has supplied us with what they call morphine syrettes. They're like toothpaste tubes with morphine and a needle and it's pretty easy because the dosage is all measured out. If we give a guy a shot of morphine, we pin the empty syrette to his collar so there's no danger of somebody coming along and giving him a second shot (which could be fatal). I'm feeling pretty comfortable now with this medic business. I figure I'll be of some help when we get the word to go. Anyway, I've got some studying to do before lights-out so I'll close. Love, Gil

The next week passed with no word from Gil. Pip said he thought that meant something was up—everybody knew that the allied invasion of Europe was imminent—and the family went about their daily chores as best they could. Tension and fear saturated the farmhouse. They began to snap at each other, giving voice to those little annoyances usually held to oneself, those emotional abrasions that come from living with great stress. Lydie complained about Pip smoking in the bathroom; Pip nagged Jordi for spilling milk on the table from his cereal bowl and Lydie for leaving peanut shells all over the place; Nana complained about the volume at which Lydie played her music and about having to empty Pip's pockets before washing his shirts; Jordi complained that Nana nagged him about washing his hands before supper. Each day they apologized to each other, then the next day they complained about something else. Day after day passed as they waited for news that the invasion was on and that Gil was once again in combat.

And when they turned on the radio, they learned that the whole nation was waiting along with them.

Jordi spent much of his time working in the barn by himself on his new half-model. He was becoming good at woodworking, and he ached for the day when he could use his new skills alongside his father and Pip when they built their boat.

One Tuesday in early June, Pip and Jordi left for an early breakfast at Gott's before going out for a day of lobstering. When they got there, an unusual number of trucks and cars were parked in front of the store. The lobstermen, who usually left early for Naskeag Point, must be getting a late start, Jordi thought. Pip was forced to park across the street in front of the library. They stepped down from the truck and looked up the road at the First Baptist Church whose bells were ringing. In the weak first-light, they saw people gathering in front of the church.

Pip shook his head. "Jeez, I don't understand Protestants. What the hell are they doing out so early?"

Inside Gott's, they were enveloped by a cloud of cigarette smoke and through it they saw twice as many men as usual for five in the morning. Ogden Gower saw them come in. "Pip, it's on!" he shouted.

"What's on?"

"The invasion. It started this morning!"

Pip sucked in his breath then waved his hand dismissively. "Aw Jeez, we hear that every other day."

"No, Pip, it's true," added Niall Macgrudder. "I heard it myself more than an hour ago. It's the Krauts who made the first announcement. But then the Allies confirmed it."

Pip stared at Niall, then Jordi. He made the sign of the cross. "*En nom du Père, et du Fils, et du Saint-Esprit.* Dear God above, protect my boy."

A violent shudder passed through Jordi. His eyes welled up. "Pip?"

Pip put his hand on Jordi's shoulder. The room went silent for a long heartbeat. Pip exchanged glances with Eddie Grindle, the only other man in the room to have a son stationed in England for the invasion. The sons of other men in Gott's that morning were in the Pacific. Eddie nodded to Pip. Pip nodded back, then turned to Niall.

"Where?"

"Northern coast of France. That right, Walter?"

Walter Smollet put down his coffee and took a scrap of paper from his shirt pocket. "I wrote it down. Heard about it at four this morning." He slid his glasses down his nose and read, " *'Under the command of General Eisenhower, Allied naval forces, supported by strong air forces, began landing Allied armies this morning on the northern coast of France.'*"

"Gorry!" said another man, "Sends chills up my spine every time I hear it!"

"But that's a big area. Ain't they said where, exactly?"

"'Fraid not. Just the northern coast."

"Did they say anything about resistance, about how the fighting's going?"

"NBC came on 'bout an hour ago. Their reporter had flown with an airborne division. Said he saw lots of smoke, ships, and planes. But there hasn't been any word from the beaches."

"Been listening for more news," said Ogden Gower, "but all they keep saying is the invasion's on. No details. Maybe they went in with no opposition, Pip. I wouldn't worry 'bout Gil. He's a good man and knows how to handle himself."

"Oughta give us more news," groused Rufus Metcalfe. "Here we are nervous as long-tailed cats in a room full of old folks."

The others looked at him quizzically.

"You got it wrong," said Ogden Gower. "Goes: nervous as long-tailed cats in a room full of *rocking chairs.*"

"Eyuh, that's what I said: Old folks in rockers."

Pip turned to Jordi. "I think we better go home to your ma and Nana."

They drove as fast as they could on the worn, irreplaceable tires, ignoring the signs that said "Victory Speed, 35 mph." Pip slowed only when they passed through patches of early-morning valley fog that wrapped around the truck.

When they got home, Nana and Lydie were already in the living room listening to the radio.

"We heard at Gott's," said Pip.

"Pip! Our boy…"

"Yes, yes, I know, Zabet." He held her for a long moment. Then he took Lydie in his arms. "He'll be okay. You'll see."

"Yes, I know, Pip," Lydie said. But her voice betrayed fear. Her eyes were rimmed with red. "Do you two want some coffee?"

Pip and Jordi both nodded.

"Have they said anyt'ing about the fighting?" asked Pip.

"No, nothing. Do you think Gil's there?" Lydie asked.

"No way of knowing. Most of the Army don't go in wit' the first waves. There's a good chance his unit will go in later, even tomorrow or the next day. Remember Sicily? He didn't go in until hours after it started."

"But we don't know. That's the awful part."

Pip put his arms around her again. "Aw Jeez, I know. All we can do is wait. That's all we can do."

They listened to the radio constantly, eating in the living room. Early in the morning they had heard a rebroadcast of General Eisenhower's order of the day:

Soldiers, Sailors, and Airmen of the Allied Expeditionary Force: You are about to embark on the Great Crusade toward which we have striven these many months. The eyes of the world are upon you. The hopes and prayers of liberty-loving people everywhere march with you…

After Eisenhower's speech Nana made the sign of the cross and slid from her chair to her knees. She led the family in the Hail Mary. "*Je vous salue, Marie, pleine de grâces, le Seigneur est avec vous…*" saying it so rote-fast that it came out as one long breathless plea for mercy.

At seven in the morning they heard the bell at the Methodist Church toll solemnly. Nana said, "We gotta go to church. We can listen to the radio later."

"Of course, *ma chère*. We'll go right now."

An hour later, they pulled up in front of St. Mary's Star of the Sea

Church in Stonington. Built for the Italians who worked the Deer Isle and Crotch Island granite quarries, it was the closest Catholic church.

Saint Mary's was a small, white building on a rise overlooking the water. It had a tiny belfry topped with a cross and, in both of the long walls, three lancet-arch, stained-glass windows.

They were greeted at the door by old Father Battisti, a thin, balding man who reminded Nana of the Pope. Father Battisti put his hands together and bowed to the family. "Ah, Zabet and Pip, Lydie and Jordi. I told people that you would come today and here you are. We pray hard, very hard, for Gil and all the others."

Nana thanked him, reached into the font of holy water, and crossed herself. "I will light candles," she said.

"Yes, of course, Zabet. We put out many, many extra candles today. And in an hour, I will say a special Mass."

The tiered racks of votive candles on both sides of the altar pulled Nana forward into a field of radiance. At the head of the aisle she genuflected, rose, and moved to kneel in front of the rack to the right of the altar. Lifting a long wick from the tray, she began lighting candles. A shaft of morning sunlight flooded through the stained glass window and fell on her, deepening the dark depressions under her eyes. She lit a dozen candles, dropping a dime for each one into the tin tray in front of the votive lamps. All the while, she whispered prayers. The others also lit candles. Jordi lit several for his father and then lit an extra one for his father's boat, hoping God would understand.

Nana returned to the pew and took out her rosary beads, the special ones made of walnut. The rest of the family took out their own rosaries. Nana prayed in a soft whisper, her beads clicking against the back of the pew in front of her. The others prayed in silence. As they prayed, person after person came to the front of the church to light candles. Several acquaintances smiled and whispered, "For Gil." The smell of melting wax permeated the church. After saying the Rosary, Nana rose shakily from the kneeler and led her family in the Stations of the Cross.

They were at St. Mary's for more than two hours. Upon leaving, they spoke briefly again with Father Battisti, who said he would have more candles tomorrow. "And Zabet, you must rest. God does not want you to exhaust yourself."

They spent the rest of the day moving in and out of the living room listening for fresh news about the invasion. But there was little. They reconciled themselves to the prospect that it might be days before they heard anything definite about Gil.

At ten o'clock that night President Roosevelt broadcast a prayer on the radio and the entire Dupuy family knelt and prayed with him. When they finished, Nana said, "*Ainsi-soit-il,*" and the others said, "Amen." Nana said, "This is a good prayer and we should say it every day until we hear that Gil is safe."

They spent much of the next day in the living room listening to the radio. Pip went to Buck Harbor to get the evening newspaper, but it had no more news.

Late in the afternoon, Lydie said she needed to be alone for a while and went for a long walk. When she returned, shortly before supper, she was carrying a brown paper bag. She pulled a bottle of Jack Daniels from it and placed it on the kitchen table.

"Lydie, what are you doing?" cried Nana. "You ain't a whiskey drinker."

"I just thought it would be a good idea to have some around," Lydie said. She turned to Pip. "Here, I bought you some cigarettes."

Pip smiled. "Where did you find the whiskey? It's hard to get these days. Even Chrétien has had problems."

"I was at the market trying to decide what to buy. Virgil Blount happened to be there. He said he had some whiskey in his car and would I like to buy a bottle so I said sure, why not?"

Jordi gave his mother a disgusted look, which she apparently didn't see.

"Where the hell did *he* get it?" asked Pip.

Lydie shrugged. "I didn't ask."

Pip laughed. "Well, wherever he got it, at least Blount is good for somet'ing. You want me to pour you a drink?"

"Yes, I'll have it with supper."

All through the evening, there was no news.

In the following days, every ordinary thing took on new meaning for Jordi. If he could stay in bed an extra five minutes, even though he desperately needed to pee, then his father would be safe. Or if he looked out the window and saw a gentle breeze in the tops of the spruce, his father would be safe. Suddenly, the number of eggs he found in the chicken coop each morning, the flight of seagulls, the call of songbirds, the appearance of dogs, or cats, or foxes offered proof that his father would be safe. Jordi would say to himself, "If no car appears in the road in the next minute, then Dad will be okay." And if a car did appear, he would start again. "Okay, *now* if no car appears in the road in the next minute..." He would count the seconds faster than Nana could say the Hail Mary.

Thursday morning, two days after the invasion, the *Bangor Daily News* carried the first picture from the landings. It was a Coast Guard photograph, transmitted by Signal Corps Radio. It showed several columns of ships, blurred and seemingly tethered to barrage balloons hanging above them, moving in a line toward a vanishing point, presumably the Normandy beaches. The accompanying article said there was fierce fighting near Caen, and that reinforcements were streaming across the Channel. But it didn't say what they most wanted to know: which units were involved in the fighting and which were in reserve? Had Gil's outfit been among the first to hit the beach? Was he part of the reinforcements now crossing the channel or was he still in reserve in England?

Was he safe?

Nana insisted on going to St. Mary's again and since they were already out, they returned by way of Blue Hill to say goodbye to Evan Davids who had joined the Medical Corps and would soon leave for Europe.

"I'll be setting up field hospitals," he told them. He explained, with enthusiasm, that medical care in the military began with the aid station near the front lines and included field hospitals, evacuation hospitals, and hospitals stateside. "It's a pretty sophisticated system, but do you know where it all begins? It begins with the Combat Medic, men like your Gil. They are the real heroes of the system."

"Do you know where you'll be stationed, Dr. Davids?" asked Lydie.

He shook his head. "It'll be close to the front, wherever that is."

"We think Gil was in the invasion," said Nana.

"Yes, I know. If I go to France, who knows? I might meet up with him."

In the evening paper, they saw the first picture of what was called "6-6-6," the sixth hour of the sixth day of the sixth month—D-day, H-hour. It showed a blurred view of a beach, savage obstacles partially submerged at the water's edge, and dozens of landing craft in the background. And it showed soldiers sprawled, lifeless, on the sand.

Jordi couldn't sleep that night.

On Friday, Pip returned from the market with the paper. They sat around the kitchen table as he turned the pages, searching for fresh news. The headline said that twelve towns had been stormed and that the Allied armies were moving inland. Pip read that two of the units that spearheaded the initial assault on D-Day were the British Fiftieth Northumbrian Division, and...the American First Infantry Division.

And now they knew.

Pip was seized with a coughing fit. Nana pulled a handkerchief from her apron pocket and handed it to him. His face was red. The others watched and waited while he coughed into the handkerchief then took several deep, rasping breaths before settling back into his chair. Nana and Lydie looked at each other, but nobody said anything.

Knowing Gil was back in combat, the fear they had been holding at bay filled the room. No one said a word and, one by one, they drifted away from the table. From the growing pile of newspapers, Pip removed the issue with the picture of dead American soldiers on the invasion beach.

The following morning, Pip and Jordi drove toward Brooklin. Pip said, "Goddamn this weather. Why is God playing games wit' us?"

Jordi looked at Pip who leaned over the steering wheel and peered out the windshield. All they could see was the bloom of their own headlights bobbing back at them, blurred in the thick fog that had rolled in from the reach. The truck lurched along in second gear. Pip's knuckles were white from gripping the shift knob hard to prevent the truck from slipping out of gear. Jordi snuck a quick peek at Pip before returning his attention to the road. He didn't know what to say.

"I mean, God knew damn well why we couldn't get out to the traps the last two days," Pip continued, "and now we hafta go out today. So why does he give us two good days while we're waiting for news, but this shit weather when he knows we *hafta* go out? *Merde!* Don't he know there's a goddamned war on?"

A few moments later, they saw a faint yellow glow.

"I think it's Gott's, Pip."

"We been driving so long, it could be England!"

The yellow light grew larger until the two-story structure of Gott's loomed out of the mist. They stopped for a quick breakfast before heading out to Naskeag Point.

Pip's foul mood was caused by more than the weather. Jordi heard him and Nana arguing that morning. Pip said he was in no mood to have Nana's religion shoved in his face and when she asked him if he had said his prayers for Gil, it set him off.

"You think God is going to listen to you just because you say the Rosary over and over and over again? What does he care? Look outside. Look at the goddamned fog!"

"What does the fog have to do wit' it?"

"If he listened at all, he would have given us a good day today since he knows we spent the last days waiting for news of our boy."

"God listens to me," Nana replied with quiet assurance.

"Why you? You think nobody is holier than you?"

"No, I don't think that. I think God listens to anybody who prays. If you prayed more—"

"I go to church, don't I?"

"Church on Sundays ain't enough."

"Zabet!" Pip snapped. "Are you trying to make the rest of us feel like sinners so that if Gil gets hurt it will be our fault for not praying enough?"

"*Fermez la bouche!*" Nana shouted. "*Fermez la bouche!* God will protect Gil if we pray to Him." She stormed out of the kitchen and Pip flew out of the house so fast Jordi had to run to catch up.

After a sullen breakfast, they left Gott's and headed for the harbor. At Naskeag Point, visibility was poor and there were no signs of other lobstermen. The trees appeared half-formed, like images pulled early from the developing bath. Pip cut the engine and they heard, without seeing, the suck and swell of the waves. It was an asthmatic, gasping sound that, every time Jordi heard it, seemed to compel his own lungs to mimic the same rhythm. It was almost as if he would dissolve into vapor. Who was to say the fog wouldn't swallow him up? Or Pip? Or Nana? Or his mother?... Or his father? What would stop the fog from swallowing them all up?

And the thought occurred to him: What was the point in building a boat after all?

As they walked through the fog, objects emerged slowly before them, first the ghostly outline of their rowboat, then, nearby, the weed-skirted, barnacled rocks with the sea wheezing and rising against them.

They dragged the rowboat into the water, slipped the oars into the oarlocks, and climbed aboard. Jordi rowed while Pip sat on the thwart facing forward and calling out directions. The oars groaned and creaked in the oarlocks. Water dripped from the blades. With a radius of visibility only about three times the length of the rowboat, they had carefully noted their angle to shore when they shoved off, so they had no difficulty finding the *Zabet & Lydie.*

"That was not'ing. Now we gotta try to find the traps," said Pip. He started the engine. "Jordi you go up on the bow and keep a sharp eye. I'll keep her going just fast enough for steerage way."

They followed the sound of the Hay Island Ledge bell. It swayed slowly, giving an indifferent clang as the seawater moved sluggishly beneath it. They turned to the southeasterly course Pip had plotted on the chart that morning from the bell to the string of pots. They coasted for a long time, holding steady on their course.

"Anyt'ing?" called Pip.

"Nothing."

"*Merde!*" said Pip. "We're going so slow the lobsters will probably outrun us."

"I think I hear the lighthouse horn, Pip."

"A horn?" Pip ran forward. "Where?"

"Listen. Almost dead ahead."

Jordi peered into the fog, expecting to see a familiar blurred light swing across their path. But, of course, the light had been turned off at the beginning of the war.

Then Pip heard the horn. "Mary, Mother of God, that's the Halibut Rocks light! We've gone too far." As if to answer him, the lighthouse sounded its booming horn again and the boat shuddered. Pip worked his way back to the wheelhouse and turned the *Zabet & Lydie* on the reverse of their previous course. "Keep a sharp eye to port. I'll watch to starboard," he called.

Ten minutes later, Jordi shouted, "There they are, Pip. Two points off the port bow. We're almost on top of them."

Pip cut the engine and they pulled up alongside the first buoy. They began to haul traps. The traps came up spilling cascades of water and bumping against the rail of the *Zabet & Lydie*. Most of them contained more than one lobster. Pip and Jordi slipped pegs into the claws of the keepers and threw the others back, along with assorted other sea creatures. When they finished, they groped their way into Center Harbor, sold their catch to Niall Macgrudder, and cruised slowly back to the mooring, which they found only after several passes. It was late in the afternoon when they were finally back in the truck. The fog was still as thick as Nana's lobster bisque.

"We'll stop by Gott's," said Pip. "Give a couple of lobsters to Ogden and Rufus." Pulling up to Gott's, Pip said, "Don't tell them we missed the pots the first time."

Jordi smiled. "Okay, Pip."

On the night of the eleventh, after weeks without a letter from

Gil, they heard Lydie's cousin Teddy Thibodeau give a special report from the front lines:

I'm reporting to you from a field hospital not far from the Normandy beaches and I have just had one of those intensely personal experiences that leaves a person shaking his head and saying what a small world it is.

I was touring the hospital, interviewing some of our wounded boys and some of the wonderful docs and nurses who are caring for them. Most of the boys were slated to be sent back to an evacuation hospital, some even back to the States. I saw one boy who was so bandaged he looked like an Egyptian mummy. Above his chest only his mouth and right hand were exposed. So what do you think the boy says? 'Gosh I'm lucky!' and I say, 'Lucky?' And he says, 'Yeah, my hand's free, my mouth's free, so I can smoke.' Of course, I laughed. I asked him how many cigarettes he had on him and he said, with a smile, 'Well, now, that's the problem.' So I gave him all my cigarettes. And while we smoked together, he told me how he was wounded by shrapnel in the hedgerows and how a medic spent almost an hour patching him up enough just to get him back to the field hospital. And all the time, they were under fire. 'Man,' the boy said to me between drags of his cigarette, 'those medics are something else!'

Later, I saw one of these medics leaning against a jeep, taking a break, smoking a cigarette. Since I had just given all mine to that severely wounded boy, I thought I'd bum one. I tapped the man on the shoulder and said, 'Say, buddy, do you have a smoke?' And the man turned around and, lo and behold, it was my cousin's husband.

Lydie gasped. They all leaned toward the radio as though they could see into it.

Nana made the sign of the cross, a tear in the corner of each eye. "*Merci, Mon Dieu.*"

I know that you in the States, because of the need for secrecy, have been starved for news since the invasion began. So I believe those of you listening to my voice now will understand and forgive me, if I end with a personal message. And it is this: Lydie, Gil's okay.

This is Teddy Thibodeau somewhere in France with the American Army, and, oh yes, this medic was the one who helped the boy who was so terribly wounded by shrapnel.

Jordi shuddered. He looked at his father's half-model on the kitchen wall. It appeared wavy through the tears in his eyes. He smiled.

chapter 10

On a sultry August evening with mosquitoes swarming the darkened porch, the Dupuy Family listened to a disturbing broadcast:

This is Teddy Thibodeau somewhere in France with the American Army. And a fast moving army it is now that we have broken through the hedgerow country. So fast, in fact, that we have trapped the entire German seventh army in a pocket known as the Falaise Gap. I could tell you of the glorious advance of our soldiers, of their skill and heroism, of the greatness of their leader General Patton; I could tell you of all these things because they are true. But I have a different story to tell you. It is the story of the horror of war.

Yesterday I saw a boy walking alongside a road with a cow. He couldn't walk on the road because our artillery and planes had trapped and slaughtered a battalion of German soldiers and the road was impassable because of the carnage. The bodies were so numerous, in many places you could walk the length of a football field without setting foot on solid ground. The boy was leading his cow, probably the last one his family owned, away from the killing fields. The cow's bell sounded strangely peaceful against the background of explosions that were still rending the air. And oh, those explosions! All around us, as far as the eye could see, were naked, blasted trees like exposed nerves and ganglia. Along the road, German vehicles were smoldering piles of metal. Hundreds of dead cows littered what was left of the fields. On and beside the road, countless corpses sprawled, legs and arms fixed in the odd poses of the burnt dead, and along with them a couple thousand putrefying horses.

Anyone who passed through here had to keep a handkerchief to his nose. I'm told that even pilots of low-flying Piper Cubs were so overwhelmed by the stench that they vomited in their cockpits.

In one place I saw German prisoners. They all had glassy, unseeing eyes, expressions that seemed to look at you from souls that were already dead. Some were eating bread green with mold. I talked with several of them, the ones who could still hear my questions and who could still speak, and they mentioned the sound and the confusion, the horrible nightmare of the anger unleashed upon them by the Americans.

It is hot and sunny here which makes things all the worse. For our boys, this is the stuff of daily life now and we must pray for them. We pray that our boys won't be wounded or killed as, of course, we should. But we must also pray that our boys are able to come through this living hell, this horror of horrors, with spirits that are not diminished, with a hope that is not dashed, with a faith in humanity, and God, that is not betrayed.

This is Teddy Thibodeau, somewhere in France.

Good night.

Sleep did not come for anyone in the Dupuy family that night. And in the morning they sat around the breakfast table staring at the walls with sleep-deprived eyes.

Pip remembered the Meuse-Argonne and shuddered.

August 19, 1944.

Dear Lydie & Jordi & Ma & Dad,

Better late than never! As I'm sure you know from reading the papers, we've been pretty busy. God only knows when I get time to write these days! Now that we're really pushing the Krauts, we're on the move all the time it seems. Of course, now and then we stop to let supplies catch up and that's when I get to write. Last night some of the men were permitted to go into a nearby town to see a movie. Everybody says that means we'll stay here a while. So maybe I'll be able to write more, but don't count on it.

Ma, Lydie tells me that you are setting the whole state of Maine on fire with votive lamps and prayers for me. Thanks. I feel well-protected. Believe me, it must be working because things are pretty easy around here. It's been really hot and sunny here, which makes things easier. And for the

first time in weeks we were even able to get showers. And today I was able
to attend Catholic services in the battalion area. We also had a movie and
a USO show, so you see it's been almost like a vacation! Just an hour or so
ago the Red Cross donut wagon came to our area and passed out donuts
and coffee. So, all in all, life has been good. If we don't move out again,
I'll try to write tomorrow. Love, Gil

Pip searched the map until he found the town of Bagnoles de l'Orne, where he placed the pin representing Gil. He studied the map further and said, "That's part of the Falaise Gap where we're kicking the Germans in the pants."

"The place Teddy talked about?" asked Lydie.

Pip nodded.

Nana said, "Our boy is seeing all that horrible stuff Teddy talked about?"

"I'm afraid so," answered Pip. He shook his head. "No man should have to see that."

"That's strange," said Lydie. "He doesn't mention any of the horrible things. He only says how pleasant it is…"

Pip rose from the table and put a hand on Lydie's shoulder. "I remember how it was in the Meuse-Argonne. It gets so a man doesn't want to think about it. It's a way of dealing wit' it and keeping from going crazy."

"Are you saying that he won't write about it in his letters?"

Pip nodded. "*I* never did. And I saw some bad t'ings. But I don't think I saw t'ings like what Teddy described. No, not that bad…not *that* bad."

September 2, 1944.
Dear Lydie & Jordi & Ma & Dad,
Lately it seems this war will never end! I guess I'm just being impa-
tient, though. Every day brings us closer to the Rhine. Germany is next
and we can't wait to take the war to them in their own homeland.
Everybody is itching to get across the river and move on to Berlin.
I can't wait to get home. I've had enough of this damned war. All I

want is to be with all of you and to get out on Eggemoggin Reach behind the wheel of the Zabet & Lydie. Remember that G. I. Bill they passed back in June? Maybe it will provide us with enough funds to build our boat, who knows?

The letter closed with several paragraphs about Gil's work on the front lines, but Jordi could hardly listen because of his excitement that his father had mentioned their boat.

Pip said, "He's in Liege. That's close to the Meuse-Argonne, where I was." He shook his head sadly.

"Isn't Liege close to Germany?" asked Lydie.

"Not far."

"Then maybe he's being too pessimistic about the war not being over soon. Maybe he still can be home for Christmas."

"I don't think we should get our hopes up," said Pip. "Once we're across the Rhine, the Krauts will fight like cornered animals."

"But still…"

"Lydie's right," said Nana. "There's not'ing wrong wit' hope. I will say extra Rosaries so the war will be over by Christmas."

"My teacher says that we're just catching our breath and we're about to roll all the way to Berlin," Jordi said.

"Your teacher ain't over there, Jordi," said Pip. "He don't know what the hell he's talking about."

"*She.* Mrs. Gray."

"Then *she*, goddamnit! *She* don't know what the hell *she's* talking 'bout."

"Pip, there's no need," snapped Nana.

"Yes there is. Everybody sits here and thinks how easy it will be to finish the job. But I been there. I know it ain't easy."

Pip's neck flushed red and the others stared. He didn't lose his temper often. He was seized by a fit of coughing. When it subsided, he pulled a cigarette from the pack, tapped it against the back of his hand, and lit it with an angry snap of his lighter. He drew in a lungful of smoke, held it deep in his body, then exhaled forcefully. The stream of smoke curled around the hanging flypaper, setting it to swaying. Finally, in a more subdued voice, he said, "Me and Chrétien were there and we don't like to remember." Then he went out on the porch.

Nana watched him go. She fingered the rosary beads that she kept constantly in her apron pocket. "It ain't easy for him," she said, looking from Lydie to Jordi. "All his life he's been a father who could protect his boy. When Gil was little and other kids called him Frenchy or t'ings like that, well Pip, he always took care of it by talking to their parents. But now Gil's over there and Pip's here and he can't do not'ing about it. He can't talk to that Hitler fella, you know."

December 1, 1944.
Dear Lydie & Jordi & Ma & Dad,
Well, we're in the same place. How's that for progress? Here's the situation as I see it. [Here, several paragraphs were blacked out by the censor.] *So you can understand why I'm pretty depressed.*

I can't remember if I told you the expression that guys use about the morphine syrettes we carry around. They say, "One for the pain, two for eternity." Well, I've been forced to go all across France and Belgium with that expression in my head and now it looks like I'll have to go halfway across Germany, too!

The letter ended with sketchy details of Gil's daily life and a litany of complaints. When they finished the letter, Lydie asked, "What does he mean when he says 'One for the pain, two for eternity'?"

"Just an expression, I guess," said Pip. He lit a cigarette and said, "Well, I gotta go out to the barn and repair some traps." Sleet from an early winter storm pelted the kitchen window.

"Wait a minute, Pip. There's something you're not telling us."
Nana said, "Lydie, maybe it's just like he said. It ain't not'ing."
Lydie squared her eyes at Pip. "Pip?"
"Lydie, let the man fix his traps," snapped Nana.
"No, I won't. He's not telling us something and you know damn well he isn't. You just don't want to hear it."
Nana said nothing. She fingered her rosary and glanced at Jordi.

She looked back at Lydie as if to ask her not to press this in front of Jordi…or her.

Lydie ignored her. "Pip, we're all big enough to take it. We have a right to know what's happening to Gil."

Nana turned her back and started to move dishes from one side of the sink to the other.

Pip stared at Lydie. A tear formed in the corner of his eye and Lydie's face fell. "Pip, please?" Her voice quavered.

Pip dragged from his cigarette, sighed deeply, and said, "Maybe it means sometimes he has to give guys two shots of that morphine stuff."

"What does that mean?"

"He would only do it if the guys were wounded real bad."

"Go on."

"Real bad like they ain't gonna make it."

"You mean Gil is forced to…to…put them down?"

Pip didn't answer. He let Lydie's odd euphemism lie like a dead bat nobody wanted to touch.

Still facing the sink, Nana gripped the handle of the pump. "Only God has the right."

Nobody else spoke.

Nana said, "What if they're Catholic and ain't had the Last Rites? Does my boy think he's a priest, too, and gives them the Last Rights?"

Pip put a hand on her shoulder. "Aw Jeez, you know better, Zabet. And about the morphine, it's war. God forgives such t'ings in war."

"God can't forgive that."

"Don't worry, Zabet. It's just a saying. Our Gil would do the right t'ing." Pip kissed her on the cheek.

Nana smiled. "You're right. Our boy wouldn't do that. It's just a saying, is all."

"We need to help him," said Lydie. "He's over there and suffering and he has no one to talk to. He's got so much all bottled up inside him."

"We can pray for his eternal soul," said Nana. "That he never is tempted to do that t'ing that he said."

"Fine, Nana," said Lydie. "You pray for his eternal soul. Right now I care more that he's alive today. I'm going to write him a letter. I'm going to beg him to tell us what's going on. Maybe if he writes about it…"

They fell silent and in their silence they heard a crack from inside the icebox. Lydie rose and put her arms around Nana. "I'm sorry. I didn't mean to snap at you. Of course we'll pray. We'll pray our hearts out. But I'm still going to write that letter."

Suddenly, and for no apparent reason—there had been no news of any major battles that would keep him too busy to write—Gil's letters stopped. More than a week passed without the mailman driving up with a smile and an envelope. And this was the week before Christmas when they would have expected Gil to write more than ever.

Again, time slowed to a painful crawl.

One day, Jordi carried a small stack of firewood that Pip had chopped up to the porch. At the southwest corner of the barn, the air buckled every time Pip brought the ax down on a dried, quartered log of birch with such force that pieces leapt from the chopping block and splinters flew in the air. Jordi came back and stood behind Pip, waiting for another load of split logs.

Snow fell softly—small, light flakes like flour spilled from some celestial sifter. The cries of blue jays from the copse of spruce behind the barn made Jordi look up. Often their cries warned of a hawk or an osprey, but Jordi saw nothing. He heard a fox bark in the woods.

Over Pip's shoulder, he saw the kitchen window, frost forming an irregular border around its edges. Through the small clear spot at the center of the window, he saw Nana moving between the table and the coal stove and back again. He knew she was baking bread—that was why the inside of the house was so hot.

"Jordi, you sleeping or somet'ing. There's another load ready." Pip took a checkered handkerchief from his coat pocket and mopped his brow. He took several deep, wheezing breaths.

"Sorry, Pip." Jordi squatted and gathered the pieces of birch until he had a full load, then rose. He turned toward the porch when he saw, a quarter mile away, a car coming up the road. He stood frozen to the spot, watching the car's progress, hoping it would continue on past the entrance to the farm. He thought, "If the car goes past our road, then…" But his fear was confirmed when the car slowed and made the left onto their road.

"Pip, a car." Jordi dropped the load of wood. He moved closer to Pip and reached for his hand. Pip fumbled in his pocket for a cigarette before realizing he already had one lit between his lips.

It was a dark green Plymouth, its hood ornament missing, black-out blinders mounted over its headlights. It approached slowly, eddies of light snow swirling in its wake. When it came to within twenty yards or so of them, they could see that the driver wore a military uniform.

Was this how they were to be told, then: a visit from an officer? They had heard somewhere it was done that way. The car stopped several yards in front of them. The door opened. A cane emerged first, followed by the tentative step of a black shoe. A somber-looking man stepped out of the car. He walked stiffly toward them, dragging one foot in the snow. Jordi saw the large red insignia on the shoulder of his overcoat. It was the numeral "1," the "Big Red One" of the First Infantry Division.

"Is this the Dupuy residence?" the man asked, clearly nervous.

"Yes," answered Pip. He extended his hand. It was shaking. "I'm Hippolyte Dupuy."

The man stared at Pip's hand for a moment as if confused, then grasped it, visibly embarrassed. "Oh, yes, yes of course. I'm Sergeant Ken Elder. I'm with the 26th Infantry Regiment. Your son, Gil, was with my outfit."

Jordi's heart hammered in his chest. *Was?*

Apparently Pip heard the word, too, for his voice faltered when he said, "You've come to tell us somet'ing about Gil."

"Yes, of course, sort of. You see, I have a—"

Pip stopped him. "Please, come inside. The whole family must hear what you've got to say."

"Sure. Okay, sir."

Lydie and Nana were already standing on the porch. They had no overcoats. Nana's hands were covered with flour. She wiped them absently against the sides of her apron. She was breathing hard, almost panting, as though she had run over from the barn. Lydie stood with her arms folded under her breasts, her hands gripping each forearm just below the elbow. Her chest was heaving as though she was trying to catch her breath.

"This here's Sergeant Elder," said Pip.

Sergeant Elder removed his cap, bowed twice. "Ma'm... Ma'm."

They both nodded.

"I was with the Twenty-Sixth Infantry Regiment," said Sergeant Elder. "Your Gil was with my outfit."

There was that word again.

Lydie and Nana simultaneously fell back against the wall with soft thuds.

Seeing the way the two woman reacted, Sergeant Ken Elder said, "Oh, no, no! It's not what you think! Oh, please! I just have some papers he wanted me to give you."

They stared at him dumbly.

"I'm here because I was wounded over in France. Lost a foot. Makes it tough to drive."

They continued to stare at him uncomprehendingly.

"I mean that's not, of course, why I'm here. Actually, yes it is...it is why I'm here...because Gil knew I was coming stateside. You see..."

Pip stopped him. "Sergeant Elder, please. You are torturing these poor women. Just say it. Is Gil okay?"

"Yes! Yes, of course. He..."

They ignored him. They looked at each other. Tears flowed down Lydie's and Nana's cheeks. Nana clutched her rosary beads and said, "*Merci, Dieu!*" They came together in a circle and put their arms around each other, laughing softly.

Sergeant Elder stood outside the circle fidgeting with the cap he held in his sweaty hands. A blush suffused his face. Pip turned to him and placed a moist hand on each shoulder. His eyes were wet. "Please.

Please forgive us. It…it…it's a wonderful relief!"

"Yes, sir."

"I mean we thought you were gonna…we thought he…"

Sergeant Elder's blush deepened. He was now as red as a cooked lobster. "Yes, sir. I understand. I guess I…messed it up. I'm…"

"Aw Jeez, no, no, no. You didn't screw up," laughed Pip. "We just jumped to conclusions, I guess." He reached a trembling hand into his coat pocket. "Here…here, would you like a cigarette?" He put one between his own lips and held one out for Sergeant Elder.

Elder took the cigarette. "Thank you, sir."

"Oh, enough of that 'sir' stuff. I was in the last war and I was the one saying 'sir' all the time. Please, call me 'Pip.' Everybody does 'cause they can't say my real name." His words came out in a rush. "Hippolyte. Some kinda name, huh? It was Jordi, here, when he was young who first gave me the name 'Pip' 'cause he couldn't say Hippolyte so they all call me 'Pip' now. Most people don't even know my real name! Ain't that somet'ing?" He gave a strangled laugh. His entire body shuddered.

Sergeant Elder stared at Pip, his hands working so hard it appeared he was trying to tear his cap apart.

Lydie reached over and put a hand on his wrist. She smiled. "You'll destroy your cap. Here, let me take it."

"Zabet!" Pip boomed. "We must invite Sergeant Elder for supper."

"*Jésus, Marie, et Josef,* Pip," said Nana. "You think a man comes to tell me my boy's okay and I ain't gonna invite him to supper? You crazy or somet'ing?" She was crying now. She turned to Sergeant Elder and said, "Please come into our house and have supper wit' us and tell us all about Gil."

chapter 11

"I have a package for you from Gil," Sergeant Elder said as he took off his coat. He reached behind him and pulled a thick, folded envelope from his hip pocket. He handed it to Lydie. "It's letters he wanted to get to you without them going through the censors."

Lydie took the envelope and stared at it. She looked up at Sergeant Elder. "Why?"

"Well, sometimes there's just things a guy wants to say to his family that the censors would never let through. Guys like me who get wounded and sent stateside suddenly become very popular." He gave a little chuckle. "Five other guys gave me letters to take home for them, too."

Lydie placed the envelope on the shelf by the telephone. "We can all read them together after supper."

"Excuse me Ma'm, but I'll be going after supper. You'll want to read them alone. I pretty much know the kinds of things he wants to tell you. You see, me and Gil, we talked a lot together. I was with him that time in Sicily, and also just after D-Day at Coleville-sur-Mer."

"Coleville-sur-Mer? He never mentioned that place."

"It was D-Day plus one."

"Is that where you were wounded?"

"No. That was later. Some god-awful place in the Falaise Gap."

"The Falaise Gap?" asked Pip with a glance to the others. "We heard a broadcast about that place. Sounded pretty bad."

Sergeant Elder nodded but said nothing.

"But we got a letter from Gil about the same place," said Lydie.

"He said you were seeing movies in towns..."

"And USO shows," added Nana. "He said he saw Bob Hope."

"I'm afraid I didn't see Bob Hope," Sergeant Elder said, stealing a look at Pip.

Pip caught his glance and said, "Well, what's the difference? Let's all sit down and eat. I'm starving. C'mon Zabet, what're we waiting for?"

Pip, Jordi, and Sergeant Elder sat at the kitchen table while Nana and Lydie got supper ready. Sergeant Elder looked around. "Is that the boat Gil kept telling me about?" he asked, pointing to the half-model.

"Yuh," said Jordi. "That's a half-model; it's a plan for a boat. When Dad gets back from the war, we're going to build the real boat together, Dad, Pip, and me. Ain't that right, Pip?"

Pip smiled, nodded.

"Oh, Jordi," said Lydie. "That's a silly dream and you know it'll be too expensive."

"It *not* a silly dream, Ma. Dad will be able to afford it. Everything will be different after the war, won't it, Pip?"

"Sure, t'ings will be different, Jordi."

"See, Ma?!"

Lydie looked at Sergeant Elder with an amused expression as though to say, "What can a person do?"

Meanwhile, Nana busied herself at the coal stove, using a long-handled spoon to stir the contents of a large pot. Soon the kitchen was filled with a savory smell.

"What are you making, Zabet?" asked Pip.

Nana gave a satisfied chuckle. "Well, I was gonna make a fish stew, but something told me to make a lobster bisque. I guess God knew Sergeant Elder was coming."

"But Nana...rationing," cried Lydie. "That requires a lot of butter and whole milk. And a couple of eggs."

"So, don't tell Mr. Roosevelt. Sergeant Elder came to tell us that Gil is okay. We owe him somet'ing special."

While they ate, the family listened to Sergeant Elder talk about Gil. When they were done and Sergeant Elder had his coat on, Lydie said, "Are you sure you won't stay, Sergeant Elder? It's difficult driving at night around here, with the blackout and all, and we've got plenty of room."

"No, no," he replied. "I need to get back and besides, you'll want to read Gil's letters in private."

"You're sure?"

"I'm sure." He moved toward the door, which Pip held open. He turned back to Lydie. "I guess I can figure what those letters say." He paused as though unsure what to say. "I just want to say…well, I guess…Gil was one of a kind. Don't let those letters upset you too much. Sometimes a guy's gotta get things off his chest, if you know what I mean."

Lydie glanced at Nana and Pip, then put her hand on Jordi's shoulder. "Thank you, Sergeant Elder," she said.

They went onto the porch to see him off. When his car disappeared, they went back inside. A gust of wind sent a sprinkle of powdered snow after them. Nana put on some coffee while Lydie fetched the envelope from the telephone shelf. She opened it. Several sheets of paper, obviously torn from a notebook, were enclosed within a V-mail form addressed to Lydie. Silently, she read. When she finished, she looked at Jordi.

"What's he say?" asked Pip.

"It's just a cover letter to me…sort of explaining what's in the envelope. He says he's replying to my letter asking him to tell us more about what he's thinking. He says this is the 'straight dope.'"

Lydie focused her gaze on Pip then turned to Jordi.

"What, Ma?" asked Jordi.

"Nothing. Noth—" She paused, then continued in a more resolute voice. "Dad just wanted to be certain that we all thought you were old enough to listen to what he has to say."

"But I'm fourteen."

"Yes. Yes, I know. Of course you're old enough." She looked at Pip for confirmation. He nodded his head. She looked at Nana who, despite a worried expression, also gave a slight nod.

Lydie unfolded the sheets of paper. She placed them on the table before her. Jordi saw that each page was filled with doodles along the margins as though his father had spent a long time thinking about what he was going to write.

Lydie read aloud:

September 1, 1944.
Dear Lydie & Jordi & Ma & Dad,
This is a tough letter to write. Partly because I'm not totally sure what I mean. I don't want you to worry too much about me. On the other hand, I think you have a right to know a little about what it's really like, maybe because talking about it a little will help, maybe because you should know (especially you, Ma) what exactly it is you should be praying for. (You'll probably receive this letter long after I write it because what I'm going to say will never pass the censors so I'll have to wait until I can send it with one of my buddies when he returns to the States.)

This war is not just the good guys against the bad guys as I'm sure it's being represented at home. The generals only talk about this objective, or this town, or that position. To them, it seems, it's just a matter of advancing so many yards or so many miles a day. And, as I'm sure Dad can tell you, they have an amazing ability to screw up. I think more men die on both sides because of screw ups than because of intelligent, planned action. Please forgive my language, but we even have a word for it: FUBAR— F—-ed Up Beyond All Recognition.

Here, Lydie, with a slight blush, pronounced it "Effed."

Sometimes it seems like the side that screws up the least will be the one that wins. But you know what? I don't blame them. This thing is just too big for everybody. So one of the things you should be praying for is that our generals just plain get lucky most of the time.

But to the men in the front lines, the ones I have to patch up, the war's a totally different thing. There's no flag-waving here, no patriotic songs, no Fourth of July parades. It just one long slog of evil versus evil. You only have to look at the thousands of German corpses in this place to realize that, sure, we're fighting the Wehrmacht and the Nazis and we're winning and we're determined more than ever to beat them, but we're also fighting the evil that lurks in all of our souls.

Two guys died in my arms today. One was a friend of mine, the other was a young German boy. And it wasn't like you see in the movies, a clean shot to the forehead and the man drops dead painlessly. You don't need to know the details, but I can tell you it's almost never like that. They both suffered a long time while I held them in my arms. And you know the funny thing? They both asked for their mamas. The word's almost the same in German. There was no hope for either one of them. I hate everything about this.

Sometimes it seems to me that while the generals play their games of strategy and tactics the real men <u>on both sides</u> are fighting the same enemy. Does that sound too philosophical?

So anyway, that's what I wanted to say. I wanted to ask you to pray for an Allied victory, of course. But in addition I wanted to ask you to pray especially for all the soldiers on the front lines. Pray for the Americans and the Brits and the French, but also pray for the Germans and the Italians. Heck, we're all in this together. It's bigger than all of us. And, Dad, there isn't a whole lot of sea room here but, like me, every last one of these guys is using what little he's got.

Gil went on over several pages describing things like his personal living conditions; his lack of good reading material; screw-ups with supplies; and so forth. Finally, he ended the letter.

Now don't take any of this to mean you should worry about me. I'll be fine. I just wanted to give you some flavor for what it's like without the lousy censors looking over my shoulder all the time. Just like you asked me to do. Love, Gil

"Mary, Mother of God, he never used language like that before!"

"Nana, for Chrissake," cried Lydie. "Didn't you hear what he said? And you talk about his language?"

Nana made the sign of the cross. Her eyes were filled with tears.

Jordi looked at Pip. "Is he really asking us to pray for the

Germans?"

All Pip could offer was a weary, sorrowful expression. Suddenly, he burst out angrily. "Why the hell couldn't he keep this to himself? You don't need to know that! None of you need to know that!"

"Pip, for more than a year he kept it to himself. And all it did was eat him up. How can he pretend one thing when, when…"

"A man keeps it to himself!"

"Pip, Goddamnit, you—" Lydie stopped abruptly. There was a tear sliding down Pip's cheek. They had seldom seen Pip cry before. The room was silent.

Finally, Lydie said, "The Meuse-Argonne?"

Pip said nothing. He stood, walked over to the coat rack and fumbled through the pocket of his jacket for a cigarette. He lit it and took two quick puffs. He exhaled a stream of smoke that curled slowly upwards and fanned out along the ceiling. No one spoke for a while. Nana gathered each of their cups and poured more of the coffee that they had been hoarding. Then she reached for the canister of flour and removed the lid. She placed a rolling pin beside it. She went into the pantry for something but returned empty-handed. She stared at the flour and the rolling pin as though wondering what she had planned to do with them.

Lydie rose and walked into the pantry. She returned with the bottle of Jack Daniels. "Pip?" she asked, proffering the bottle.

He nodded.

Nana frowned.

Lydie took two glasses from the cupboard and poured a large shot each for herself and Pip. "Did you notice," she said to no one in particular, "that he wrote that letter shortly after the one in which he made it all sound like some kind of vacation?"

Jordi stared at the others. He had experienced the shock and, yes, the pleasure of being considered an adult. Now the awful weight of it came down on him. He no longer felt, as he often had before, like an observer. Now he wanted to do something to fix the situation, to make it come out right, to restore…to restore what? What was it that had existed just a few minutes before? Whatever it was, it didn't matter now, and he was suddenly yoked with the others in a new way.

Nana was praying. The silver cross at the end of her rosary clicked as it swung against the chair with the movements of her hands.

Pip sat rigid in his chair, expressionless, smoking.

"He needs to see a priest," murmured Nana, shaking her head.

No one spoke for a long time. Finally, Lydie said, "How can we get him help?" She carefully folded the pages and put them back into the envelope. "He's crying for help."

"I don't think there's anyt'ing we can do," replied Pip, lighting a fresh cigarette with the butt of his old one.

"I feel so goddamned helpless," cried Lydie.

Nana said, "I'm scared that Gil is going crazy wit' hate. I hope he sees a priest. He needs somebody to talk to. What if he does that t'ing he talked about wit' the morphine?"

Pip reached for the bottle of Jack Daniels. "Listen to you. What he's saying is the most sane thing any man can say about war. It's the sanest thing I've ever heard! What I could tell you about the Great War!" He lowered his voice and said, "Zabet, I ain't sayin' our boy did that t'ing wit' the morphine, but if he ever had to help those boys that way, then that's love. That's love, Zabet, it ain't a sin."

Before anyone could respond, Pip threw his jacket on and pushed through the door, muttering something about repairing lobster traps.

Several days later, they got another letter from Gil.

December 25, 1944.

Dear Lydie & Jordi & Ma & Dad,

Merry Christmas! We have plenty of snow on the ground here so it seems like Christmas even though Jerry is trying his best to ruin it. I'm sure you've read about their latest, desperate offensive. Everybody here is confident that we'll throw him back over the border then we'll sweep all the way to Berlin. But in the meantime he's making it difficult to do things like have a decent Christmas meal.

But none of that can take away my real Christmas present: they've

finally decided that we medics deserve combat pay! Every little bit helps!
I'm hoping to have enough put aside to start that boat. Are you keeping
that half-model dusted?

We've been in constant action and the V-mail forms (and all writing
paper) are running low, so I'll end this letter. I want to save enough to
write again on New Year's Day. Love, Gil

After reading the letter, Pip went out onto the porch to gather up
more firewood. While he was gone, Lydie said to Nana, "That letter,
it doesn't sound like the same person. Maybe he's got his good spirits
back. After all, he did write that letter Sergeant Elder delivered way
back in September."

Nana nodded eagerly. "Mary, Mother of God, I hope so."

"Yes," said Jordi, feeling for the first time that his opinion was
welcomed. "He's going to be okay."

Pip shouldered the door open, and backed into the room, his arms
full of wood. He went into the sitting room. As he passed, the flames
from Nana's votive lamps twisted, writhed, then stood upright again.
They were the candles Nana had persuaded Father Battisti to let her
borrow from the church. After he deposited the wood, Pip came back
to the kitchen. He swung the kitchen door closed and the little flames
buckled, almost going out. Nana rushed to shield them with cupped
hands.

"What do you think, Pip? Didn't Gil sound a lot more cheerful?"
Lydie asked.

"He sure did to me," said Jordi.

Pip looked from one to the other. "Sure," he said, "he sounded
better."

"You don't sound convinced," said Lydie, a note of accusation in
her voice.

"I said he sounded better. What do you want me to say? I can't
read the boy's mind, for God's sake."

"Jesus, Pip, I only asked—"

"And I answered. He sounded better, okay? Now I gotta put more
wood in the living room stove." He stormed out of the kitchen.

Nana stared after him. She muttered, "*Jésus, Marie, et Josef,* I don't understand that man sometimes."

January 1, 1945.
Dear Lydie & Jordi & Ma & Dad,
I finally got a break. I'm manning the aid station for a change and things are pretty peaceful right now. We're in a house, one of the few that hasn't been completely destroyed in this town, so things are pretty comfortable. Anyway, it sure beats a foxhole!

I told you I would write on New Year's Day! The Krauts are still giving us a tough time, but it looks like we broke the back of their offensive. In no time we'll be sweeping across Germany. The war will be over this year!

Damn! I just got started and here come some jeeps with wounded! Gotta go. Love, Gil

"That house, that's Dupuy-Bastarache luck," said Chrétien, who was visiting for the weekend. He turned to Pip. "Remember the house in Bouligny?"

Pip laughed. He turned to Jordi and said, "The family who had lived there had left the silverware. So there was Chrétien and me eating our rations wit' silverware and napkins tucked under our chins. I tell you, it was—"

"Did he sound okay to you?" asked Lydie.

Pip paused for a moment then said, "Aw Jeez, Lydie, he sounded okay."

"Yes, that's what I thought," said Lydie.

Chrétien put a hand on her shoulder. "Lydie, stop worrying. Gil has the Bastarache-Dupuy luck. Look he's made it all the way from Africa to Germany, t'ree years, and one little scratch in Sicily. And the war's almost over."

Jordi was furious with Chrétien for saying this and tempting fate.

After what was being called the Battle of the Bulge was over, they got letters from Gil on a more regular basis. And they were all cheery, all filled with the expectation that the war would be over and that he would be home soon. Then in April they received the most hopeful letter yet.

April 17, 1945.

Dear Lydie & Jordi & Ma & Dad,

Well, we're deep inside Germany as you know and it's only a question of time now. In a matter of days or, at most, weeks, the war will be over and I'll be on my way home. Let me tell you why I say that. We've heard pretty reliable rumors that the army has developed a point system for deciding who goes to the Pacific when the war in Europe is over, who remains as part of the Army of Occupation, and who gets to go home. Everybody will get so many points for things like total length of service, number of months overseas, battle decorations, age, marital status, and dependents. We had a sample of the "Deployment" form that they will use and I out-scored everybody. Not only out-scored them, but did it by a lot. It seems hard to believe after all this time, but our long nightmare is about to end. I'm guessing that next month, or June at the latest, Germany will surrender and there's a good chance I may be back for July 4th. What do you think of that?

Anyway, dust off that half-model of mine. I may be using it soon to loft lines for THE boat. Wow, it's a real pleasure just to think about it. And going back out on the reach with the Zabet & Lydie. And eating your wonderful food again, Ma. And holding you all. (Lydie, I'm writing a letter just to you to describe what <u>we</u> can do when I get home.) See you all soon. Love, Gil

Lydie brought her hand to her cheek and gave a squeal of delight. "I've got to hurry and finish that sweater. I don't know what's taken me so long."

Pip said, "Maybe Chrétien is right after all about the Dupuy-Bastarache luck." He started for the pantry. "How 'bout a little whiskey to celebrate, Lydie?"

"Don't mind if I do."

"And Nana and Jordi will drink wit' us."

Nana said, "I ain't gonna drink no whiskey! And Jordi is too young."

"Well, *you* can refuse the whiskey, Zabet, but you can't stop Jordi from having a little sip to celebrate such good news. He's almost a man now. Hell, he's taller than all of us."

She gave a mock frown, then laughed. "Just don't get him drunk."

Pip poured for himself, Lydie, and Jordi. He offered his glass in a toast first to Lydie, then to Jordi.

The whiskey burned Jordi's throat.

Nana said, "Well, when you bums are finished drinking, I want to go to Saint Mary's and thank God for listening to our prayers."

Jordi stayed home from school the following day to clean out the barn. He cleared the work bench, arranged all the tools the way he thought his father would want, and swept the floor.

Pip came in during the afternoon and watched silently for a while. His cigarette smoke mingled with the dust from the floor. Finally, he said, "Cleaning out to build the boat?"

"Yuh. I want everything ready when Dad comes home."

"Ain't big enough."

"What?"

"The barn ain't big enough to build the kinda boat your dad wants to build. Ass end will stick out."

Jordi stopped and surveyed the barn's length. After a while he said, "Maybe we can build a covering with canvas coming out from the door, like the temporary sheds Ogden has over some of his boats."

Pip shrugged. "I dunno, maybe. We'll see when your dad comes home."

chapter 12

Jordi recognized the speck in the dazzling blue sky as an osprey long before he could make out its shape. It glided with its wings cupping the air in a wide, inverted "V." He admired its effortless flight and hoped to see it dive for a fish, striking feet first in a lightning attack. The sight always thrilled him. The woods where Jordi stood on the shore of the reach suddenly became quiet, a sign of the approaching raptor. For long moments, no other birds, no squirrels, made a sound.

The osprey glided on at twice the height of the surrounding trees. It dipped a wing and banked toward the reach. Then it spiraled up until it was again just a speck in the vast sprawl of sky.

Jordi knew an attack was coming.

If it catches a fish, he thought, then Dad will be home by the Fourth of July. He felt confident because he had never seen an osprey miss. He stepped from the shelter of the trees for a better view. He held a hand over his brow and squinted upward.

From a tremendous height, the osprey shot down a long, silent shaft of air, its wings folded back against its body, sending it straight downward. Jordi sucked in his breath. Instead of diving for the water, the osprey swooped away from the shore, over the spruce lining the reach, and down onto a brushy, boulder-strewn field. Jordi heard the frantic barking of a fox. He ran through the stand of spruce. When he came out on the other side, he saw the osprey rise with heavy wing-beats. It carried a tiny, struggling fox cub in its talons. The mother fox was running frantically toward a bloodied spot of grass where the osprey had apparently dropped the cub and picked it up again.

For days afterwards, Jordi thought of what he had seen. Ospreys feed almost exclusively on fish, only occasionally snatching up a rodent or a snake. He had never heard of, much less seen, one attack a fox.

After the April 17 letter from Gil, there were no others. Nana made pilgrimages to St. Mary's in Stonington to light votive candles. Lydie redoubled her efforts to finish the sweater. Pip busied himself with his traps, making small repairs that were not really needed, and checking and rechecking the fluids in the truck.

And Jordi worried, thinking about the osprey.

As Jordi worked the pump in the kitchen sink, priming it so he could fill a pewter pitcher with water, he looked out the window and saw fog rolling in, lifting its skirts over the farm. Water gushed from the pump's spout and he turned his attention back to the pitcher. Something else made him glance out the window again. He paused in mid-stroke. The rhythmic suck and wheeze of the pump stopped, causing everybody to look up.

"Jordi, what is it?" asked Lydie.

Jordi didn't answer. He was frozen, his hand gripping the raised pump handle.

What he saw was Niall Macgrudder's Chevrolet pull up beside the truck. He saw Niall emerge from the driver's side and run round to the passenger side to open the door. He helped an old man from the car. It was Father Battisti from St. Mary's. Jordi's heart caught in his throat.

Pip joined Jordi at the window. After a moment, he said, "Jordi, get the door." He turned to the others and said, "It's Niall Macgrudder...and Father Battisti." His smoke-cured voice was barely audible.

Niall and Father Battisti came into the kitchen looking nervous and uncomfortable. A gust of wind followed them in, carrying with it some dead leaves from the previous autumn. The leaves scattered to the corners of the kitchen.

Niall clutched a piece of paper in his shaking hand. "Pip, Nana,

Lydie...Jordi...You know young Johnny Crockett who works for Western Union...well, he got this heah telegram to deliver...I figured it'd be better if I delivered it...along with Father Battisti." He held out the telegram. "Goldang it, I'm so sorry."

Everyone in the kitchen froze. Niall held the telegram before him but no one would touch it. Finally, Pip sighed and took it into his trembling hand. He opened it. He held it in the hand that held his cigarette and smoke seemed to be rising from the telegram itself. He read. He rocked forward slightly and grabbed the table with his free hand to catch his balance. He opened his fingers and the telegram fluttered to the floor.

With a soft groan, Lydie doubled over as though kicked in the belly. She raised her head and stared at Pip with blank eyes. Then her knees buckled. Nana caught her, steadied her, but then her knees, too, collapsed and they sank together to the floor. They put their arms around each other and rocked.

Pip stood frozen, looking down at them. He held his cigarette between two stained fingers and the blue smoke coiled up toward the ceiling. He looked at the cigarette dumbly. He stubbed it out in an old sardine tin, grasped the edge of the table with his gnarled, trembling hand, and lowered himself to the floor. He rocked forward to embrace Nana and Lydie. He looked over their shoulders to Jordi, beckoning him. Jordi, fear frozen on his face, walked toward them like a zombie. He walked past Niall Macgrudder who shifted nervously and kept mumbling, "I'm sorry...I..."

Father Battisti held his hands apart. He murmured, "*In nomine patris et filii et spiritus sancti...*"

Jordi joined his family. He smelled Pip's cigarette-smoked clothes, starchy potato from Nana, his mother's bath soap. He looked in amazement at how the linoleum curled up in the corner by the kerosene stove and he stared at the puckers of linoleum where the stove's legs dug into it. And he saw a tiny spider web between one leg of the stove and the wall.

The telegram lay under the table. Jordi saw only a block of text. He couldn't read the words. And then a breeze swept under the door and the telegram skidded away from him across the floor. He felt something he could not put a name to. It was something in the way Pip held his shoulders; the way the flesh on the back of Nana's arms jiggled with her heavy sobs; the way his mother's entire body sagged.

Jordi said, "Dad?" and when he said it all the agony that was frozen inside each of them was released. It emerged as a wail from somewhere deep within the embrace. Was it Lydie? Was it Nana? Both? Later, reliving that moment, Jordi would still not know. He would remember only that it was a woman's voice, and that it said, "Oh, Gil."

And then Pip said, "Why us, God? Why us?"

That night, Jordi couldn't sleep. He saw German soldiers before him. They had rifles and were firing at him. He saw his father, exactly like the soldier in the *Life* magazine. He thought about the mystery of time and that instant between life and death.

And he thought of his horrible wager with the osprey.

He rose from bed and groped his way downstairs, afraid to turn the lights on in case anybody was awake. He went out onto the porch. Above him, the sky pulsed with stars. He used the Little Dipper to find Cygnus low on the northeast horizon and there it was... the Northern Cross. At this angle, it appeared upended, like an overturned grave marker. And over there, a star was perversely out of place until he realized it was the pinpoint of a lone masthead light pricking the sky.

When he turned to look in the other direction he saw, at the end of the porch, a tiny red glow in the darkness. It was the end of a cigarette. It floated up and down. And he could hear the soft creak of Pip's rocking chair.

Jordi became conscious of a divide between his family and their neighbors. One Sunday, the family, along with Chrétien, attended a tearful memorial service for Gil, then left the church and saw Elwood Morton walking happily arm in arm with his wife in the bright sunshine. Like most American soldiers, Elwood had survived the war and felt the joy of reunion and a new future. Jordi caught Elwood's gaze and read in the man's sympathetic eyes a kind of guilt. It startled him.

Pip nodded a greeting to Elwood, patted Jordi on the shoulder and said, "I know it's hard. It feels like the whole nation is having a party and we ain't been invited. But that's just the way it is. We gotta live wit' it."

When they received Gil's personal effects, including the Distinguished Service Cross, they found an unfinished letter, his last to Lydie. In it he spoke of coming home soon and of a new song he liked a lot. And he offered Lydie new lyrics for the song "I'll Be Seeing You." He wrote:

In Gray's Ice Cream Parlor, the beach at Naskeag Point,
at the Blue Hill fair, that big oak tree, the skating pond...

It was too cruel. Lydie dropped the letter onto the kitchen table and ran into the sitting room. One by one, she flung her records onto the floor. She lifted Nana's bronze statue of the Virgin Mary and began to smash the records with it.

Nana cried, "No, Lydie, please, no, no!"

Jordi felt his mother's pain. Along with the pain he felt a hatred for all of the things, all of the forces, that had brought his mother to this, that had brought his family to this. He hated Hitler, and Churchill, and Roosevelt. He hated all Germans. And yes, most frightening of all, he hated his father for dying on them. Then, as though to run as fast from this as he could, he thought instead of Virgil Blount, and hated the man for staying home and not getting killed.

Because none of it made any sense unless there was someone to blame.

The May 26 *Saturday Evening Post* arrived, a cruel interloper mocking the family's grief. Its cover, by Norman Rockwell, was called "The Homecoming." In some nameless neighborhood a young soldier, satchel in hand, appears before a brick tenement house. Laundry stretches across the yard. People gather on the small porch and at the windows to greet him.

"A goddamned slap in the face," Pip muttered, slamming the magazine to the table.

Jordi jumped.

Chrétien shook his head sadly.

Nana, who had put Emily's picture back on the stove shelf next to Gil's was muttering the Hail Mary and lighting votive candles, which she had placed alongside the photographs. She looked over her shoulder at Pip to see what had so angered him. The smell of melting wax permeated the kitchen, evoking the inside of a church.

"Do you hafta light those goddamned candles here?" snapped Pip. "I can't stand the smell."

"You always said you liked the smell of candles."

"In church, not in the kitchen. The kitchen ain't supposed to smell like that."

"They're for Gil. They're for our son, Pip."

"Candles ain't gonna bring him back."

Nana fumbled with the knot on her apron. Her hands shook. "They're for his soul," she said softly. "God will take care of him."

"How the hell do you know what your God will do?"

"*My* god?"

"Well, he sure as hell ain't *my* god!"

Nana made a frantic sign of the cross. "*En nom du Père et du Fils et du Saint-Esprit!*" Nana whipped her apron off, threw it into Pip's face, and stomped out of the kitchen, slamming the screen door behind her. Pip swiped at the magazine with the back of his hand, sending it flying across the room. It hit the water pump and fell into the sink.

Chrétien nodded to Pip, then went after his sister.

Father Battisti visited the next day to recite the Rosary with Nana. "Everybody at Saint Mary's sends their condolences," he said.

"Do you see my gold star?" asked Nana.

Father Battisti glanced at the gold star that Nana had pasted in the kitchen window signifying that she was the mother of a boy who had been killed in the war. "Yes. You must be very proud."

"He got the Distinguished Service Cross."

"Yes, yes, I know."

When Nana and Father Battisti started to pray, Pip went out onto the porch, hesitated, then headed for the barn. Jordi followed him.

Pip leaned his back against the old, idle tractor, which still smelled of diesel fuel, and lit a cigarette. A barn swallow, who had made a nest up in a corner, flitted about the roof beams, disturbed by the sudden presence of humans. It flew through an oblong patch of sunlight, then settled back on its nest, twittering: *vit, vit.*

"Pip, why do you say those things to Nana?" asked Jordi.

"What t'ings?"

"Like you said yesterday…about her god not being your god."

"Because he ain't." Pip paused, drew on his cigarette, studied Jordi for a moment, then said, "Because sometimes when your heart is broken, you do and say the wrong t'ings."

Jordi said nothing.

After a few moments, Pip said, "What am I doing telling *you* about a broken heart?"

Jordi moved closer to Pip and lowered his forehead to Pip's shoulder. He smelled the tobacco in Pip's shirt, felt his grandfather's big hand ruffle the back of his hair. "Oh, Pip," he moaned.

They stayed like that until they heard Father Battisti's car start up with a cough and the tires crunch the gravel of the road; they went out to the barnyard.

"Will you tell Nana you're sorry?" asked Jordi.

Pip stopped and gazed at the kitchen window. "Nana, she prays until she's blue in the face, but bad things keep happening to her. I can't tell you how long she prayed, down on her knees, for little Emily."

"Will you tell her you're sorry?"

"Now she's got to pray for her boy, too. It ain't fair!"

"Pip, will you say you're sorry?"

Pip turned to face Jordi and said, "Yes, I'll tell her I'm sorry. But between you and me, I ain't taking back what I said about God."

He may have been smiling, but Jordi wasn't fooled. He saw the awful truth in Pip's tortured face.

The next day, Jordi burned all the half-models he had made.

part 2

1946-1950

By the breath of God they perish, and by the
breath of his nostrils are they consumed.

— Job 4:9

chapter 13

In the summer of 1946, Pip and Jordi took the train from Bangor to Boston, where they would catch the subway to Revere Beach.

After Gil's death, the family had tried several times to escape the heavy burden of grief that settled over the farmhouse like a fog. There was a trip to Prince Edward Island to see relatives, another to Chelsea, near Boston, to see yet more relatives, but nothing eased the pain of the loss. Indeed, their sense of isolation was heightened in August 1945 by news of the surrender of Japan and of victory celebrations in Times Square and by the renewed sense of vigor and joy they saw all around them. Grief became a wedge between them, with Jordi and Pip retreating to the sea, and Nana and Lydie to the kitchen. But Pip refused to accept such a state of affairs. "We can't just whine about t'ings and do not'ing," he said, trying to reunite them and bring them out of the agony. He looked around and saw how quickly others recovered from the war; he read in the newspapers of a new prosperity sweeping the nation, of a new spirit of good times. When he walked into Gott's, he saw faces transformed from the grim resolve of the previous years to a kind of careless joviality. But he did not see that happy renewal in his family. That's why he proposed a trip to Revere Beach, where they had spent great times before as a family. Maybe they could recover those times again.

But Nana and Lydie refused to go, perhaps because Gil had been with them that last time and the memories would be too painful. Still bent under the unspeakable sorrow of losing Gil, they both made excuses.

Lydie. What everyone noticed about her was not that she spent hours sitting alone by the silent Victrola, or that she often disappeared for whole afternoons, returning to say only that she'd been walking, or that she talked no longer in a musical voice but in a dull monotone. Rather, it was her eyes. They had lost their sparkle and become like tiny mud puddles. She had grown thinner.

"You must eat somet'ing," Nana would say.

"I'm not hungry."

"Pip, you talk sense into her."

Pip tried, but deep down he knew Lydie would have to pull out of this herself. Nothing he could say would make a difference because her hurt was too private; it had contours to it, depths to it, which no one else would ever understand. No, he could not presume to know what Lydie was going through. Just as only another mother could imagine Nana's grief and a fatherless son Jordi's pain.

And who else could feel the agony of the father who, in the end, was unable to keep his boy from harm, to shield him from the insatiable and omnivorous appetite of war?

Did they have no choice but to let sorrow separate them? Pip didn't want to accept this. He wanted to somehow banish the sorrow, but he could find no place to begin.

So he and Jordi went to Revere Beach alone.

Jordi settled into the plush, red seat of the train and watched in the window as his own ghostly image whizzed through trees and poles and over stretches of water. Once, as he was drifting into a trance, lulled by the rhythmic click-clack of the train wheels, he was startled by a flight of ducks from a pond. The half-model his father had carved years before came into his mind. For months it had been too painful to think about. But now he pictured its lines which fell into place as naturally as snow on a wire, how the sweep and curves of the hull were as smooth as sand dunes gently mounded by the wind. The lines of his father's boat, all rhythm and proportion, refinement and symmetry, were the antithesis of chaos, a concept he'd recently become familiar with in long discussions with Pip and Ogden Gower. The boat's sails would conform to the wind, working with it and giving it meaning.

As Ogden said, sailboats *absorb* the wind and become animated by it. For all its destructive power, the wind can give life. And with a flash of insight, he guessed that his father's dream of the boat had been a reply to the confusion and ugliness of the world.

The idea of the boat now took on a deeper meaning for him. It was no longer the dream of a young boy; now it was the symbol of a young man's newfound hope, an antidote to all the impersonal, form-less forces, the wind, the war, and death, that had so deeply affected him. Building it, as Pip might say, would be *doing* something. It would mean taking a stand. Eking out some sea room.

Soon, he fell into a true sleep filled with strange dreams that, when he woke in Portsmouth, New Hampshire, he could not remember. But he did remember the half-model, and he said to Pip, with new confidence in his voice, "Do you think Dad would have built that boat...you know, if he had come home from the war?"

"Your dad was a hard man to say 'no' to. He usually did what he pleased when he wanted it bad enough."

"And he wanted to build that boat real bad, didn't he?"

"Real bad. It wasn't just a boat to him."

Jordi nodded, a smile spreading across his face. They were silent for a long time. Finally, Jordi said, "Why don't we build the boat, you and me, Pip?"

Pip laughed. "You know, I thought about that myself a lot after... after we got the telegram."

"You did? You never said anything."

"That was somet'ing good your dad wanted to do. That was somet'ing real good."

"Let's do it, Pip."

"Can't. It's an awful lot of money, you know. And time. It would take us years and we can't just stop fishing our traps."

"We could work at it a little bit at a time."

"It sounds real nice, but it just ain't practical."

They arrived at Revere Beach tired and hungry and immediately checked into the Parkview Hotel where the family had stayed in 1937.

They rose early the next morning and, after a heavy breakfast of bacon and eggs and pancakes, stepped out onto Revere Beach Boulevard. They had talked at breakfast about taking a flight in Holt's seaplane, something everyone had enjoyed back in '37, but when they looked out at where Holt's Pier and the plane should have been, they saw only a double row of twisted pilings leading to nothing. The pilings had at one time supported the quarter-mile long boardwalk that led out to the elegant dance hall on Holt's Pier where the seaplane was always docked. The doorman at the hotel told them the seaplane was wrecked in the Hurricane of '38 and the pier itself was destroyed by fire the next year.

"Well, I guess there won't be no airplane ride," said Pip. "But there're plenty of t'ings to do. Let's go see if the Cyclone is still here."

Jordi experienced a sinking sensation in his stomach just like the one he felt when the roller coaster plunged down the big hill during his first ride when he was six years old. But now that he was a man, he decided he would no longer be afraid of the Cyclone. "Let's go," he said.

They strolled north under the arched promenade of the Spanish Gables, which housed an opulent ballroom. Across the boulevard, deeply tanned bathers were assembling on the sand. Parents, balancing blankets and towels in one hand, dragged children behind them with the other. The children carried little tin pails and shovels. The sea air, a heady mix of salt water, perspiration, and suntan lotion, was warmer and more moisture-laden than they were used to in Maine. Across the water, the peninsula of Nahant was barely visible in the haze.

"How much would it cost?" Jordi asked.

"What? The boat?"

"Yah."

"Aw Jeez, I don't know. All that wood an' stuff…t'ousands."

"That's a lot of money."

"I told you."

They passed the Beachview Ballroom with its round, domed towers and flags snapping in the breeze, and came to the Derby Racer which had a pair of parallel tracks so that the two roller coasters could race each other.

"Want to?" asked Pip.

"Let's ride the Cyclone first. Then if we want, we can ride this one on the way back," Jordi answered.

Jordi and Pip abandoned themselves to the Cyclone. After the first ride they bought a fistful of tickets and rode for an hour. When they were at last finished, Pip said, "I think it's time for somet'ing to eat before we find another ride."

They stopped at Kelly's Roast Beef stand, ate a sandwich each, then turned to retrace their steps. After a few minutes, Pip suddenly stopped.

"What's the matter, Pip?" asked Jordi.

Pip took a deep breath and said, "Not'ing…not'ing. I'm just a little winded. Let's go sit down for a little while."

At Mary A'Hearn's they bought frozen custards then crossed the boulevard to sit under a pavilion to eat them. The pavilion's concrete floor was muddied with sand from hundreds of bare feet. The peaked roof seemed to trap all the sun-leached fumes of body heat and suntan lotion from the streams of people who passed through. They squinted out at the still water.

"Hardly a breat' of wind out there," said Pip.

Jordi nodded. "Yuh, the beach is pretty well protected. I'll bet it doesn't ever get much of a blow."

"Aw Jeez, I don't know. Seems to me if the wind has a mind to raise some hell, it'll do it no matter what stands in the way. Just look at what happened to the seaplane."

"Pip, what if we put a little money aside every month. Maybe put in some extra traps?"

Pip laughed. "*Jésus, Marie, et Josef!* You can change a subject faster than anybody I know. An' stubborn."

"No, I mean it. I don't mind working extra hard."

Pip's eyes turned soft. "Yuh, just like your dad when he wanted somet'ing real bad."

"So what's wrong with that?"

"Not'ing. Not'ing at all."

"See?"

"Except Nana an' your ma."

"What do you mean?"

"Soon's we said we wanted to fish more to build a boat, they'd say don't it make more sense to build another lobster boat first, then fish more. They'd say we can fish twice the number of traps."

"There you go. They'd be right. It's time I should have my own lobster boat. We could make twice the money."

"An' then Nana and your ma would say we'd be crazy fools to build a sailboat wit' the extra money since the farm needs so much work."

"I'll do the work on the farm in my own time."

Pip shook his head, amused. "Gonna do it all, are you?"

A small orchestra played in the bandstand nearby. They listened for a while in silence, Jordi turning the conversation about the boat over and over in his head. But when the orchestra started to play "I'll Be Seeing You," they rose without a word, immediately crossed the boulevard, and lost themselves in the strip's sea of noise.

They went back to the hotel.

In the lobby, they found an empty sofa where they sat and enjoyed the cooling breeze from an overhead fan. They had been sitting for little more than ten minutes when they heard, "Pip! Jordi!"

They turned to see Chrétien, a straw hat jauntily perched on his head, coming toward them. "What are you two doing here?" he asked with a bemused grin.

"We been riding the Cyclone an' t'ings like that. What the hell are *you* doing here?"

Chrétien pulled a booklet out of his jacket pocket and sheepishly held it out to them.

"What's that?" asked Pip.

"A racing form."

"A racing form? You been over to Suffolk Downs?" The racetrack was less than a mile from Revere Beach.

"Yuh, I come here a lot."

Pip's face lit up. "So this is where you come whenever you disappear."

Chrétien smiled. "Couldn't tell Zabet. You know what she t'inks of gambling."

Pip nodded and laughed. "It'd be worse than that Sue Harper woman you used to talk about. Remember how Zabet always tut-tutted about that woman?"

"Sue Harper was a horse."

Pip and Jordi stared at Chrétien. "A horse?" Pip's eyes grew round with delight. "You mean all that time we thought Sue Harper was a woman who was giving you money and she was not'ing but an ordinary horse?"

"Aw Jeez, no ordinary horse." Chrétien took a bag of Rotherham's saltwater kisses from his coat pocket and offered some to Jordi and Pip. The paper crinkled when they unwrapped them. "One day back before the war—in '40, it was—I was at the track and she was listed at two-twenty-one to one."

"Two-twenty-one to one! And you bet on her?"

"Just got the bet in at the last minute. Biggest return ever at Suffolk Downs."

"Mary, Mother of God. How much did you bet?"

Chrétien smiled broadly. "Two hundred dollars."

Pip whistled. "That's almost fifty t'ousand!"

Chrétien nodded. "In the beginning. But then I used the money to bet on other horses. I guess I had a run of good luck."

"You mean there were other Sue Harpers?"

"Aw Jeez, not *that* good, but yuh, lot's of them."

"How did you pick 'em?"

"I know this guy at the track. I give him a little money an' he lets me in the stable area."

"You don't mess wit' the horses, do you?"

Chrétien laughed. "What? You think I'm crazy? That's a good way to get killed. No, I just look 'em in the eye."

"The horses? You just look in their eyes?"

Chrétien nodded. "I seem to be able to tell a good horse from a

bad horse by the way they look at me. I can tell if a horse has the fighting spirit. I ain't always right. Sometimes horses are like women, they
can fool you wit' their eyes. But I'm right enough times to win a lot
of money."

Pip shook his head and laughed. "First, Delores turns out to be a
cow, then Sue Harper turns out to be a horse. You're somet'ing else,
Chrétien." Then he narrowed his eyes and asked, "How…how much
money do you got, anyways?"

"Enough so we can do anyt'ing we want." Chrétien turned to
Jordi. "Like I said to you before, Jordi, there's enough to send you to
college an' I intend to do that. Even Harvard, if you want."

"But why keep it such a secret all these years?" asked Pip.

Chrétien gazed at his brother-in-law with a sardonic expression.
"You think if I said how much money I had that Zabet would let it go
at that? Are you crazy? She'd pester me an' pester me about how I came
by the money until I'd have to break down an' tell her. Then she'd be
on me, her little brother, for gambling and she'd never stop praying for
my soul. I think I could take the screaming, but I couldn't take all that
damned praying!"

Two days later, they drove back to Maine in Chrétien's Packard.
Jordi slept much of the way, but when they crossed the Kennebec
River at Bath, seeing the shipyard made him think of his father's half-
model. He brought it up again.

Chrétien asked, "Why not do it?"

"Pip's right, it'd be far too expensive."

"I'll pay for it," Chrétien said with the same calm firmness he'd use
to say he'd pay the next toll on the highway.

"What?" Jordi sat bolt upright.

"I'll pay for it."

"Just like that?" Pip asked.

Chrétien lifted his hands from the wheel just long enough to
shrug his shoulders. "Why not? I got the money. You know that. And
except for what I've put aside for Jordi's college…and a few other
expenses…I got not'ing better to do wit' it. Think of it as an invest-

ment."

"An investment?" asked Jordi, leaning forward from the back seat, his head between Pip and Chrétien.

"Well, ain't you said before how much you admire the men who build the boats? I figure if you build a boat wit' a man who's as good a carpenter as Pip here, then go to school to get a degree in naval architecture…well, by then, you'd be ready to open up your own boat-yard. It's a much easier life than fishing for lobster." He glanced over at Pip. "No offense to you, Pip."

Pip shook his head. "No, you're right, Chrétien, it would be better for him." He paused a moment, then said, "You mean it? You really want to pay for building Gil's boat?"

Chrétien stopped at a traffic light. He leaned back in his seat and looked squarely at Pip. "He was not my son, Pip, but he was my nephew. I loved Gil. His boat should be built by all that's right in this goddamned, lousy world."

It was late afternoon when the Packard turned off Route 176 and climbed the rutted, dusty road to the barnyard. When Jordi, Pip, and Chrétien piled from the car, they saw Nana rush out onto the porch still drying her hands with a checkered dishcloth. "Oh, it's you," she said.

"Aw Jeez, how 'bout that for a greeting?" laughed Chrétien. "She sounds like she's disappointed to see us."

But Pip cut him off. "Zabet, you look worried. What's the matter?"

Nana glanced at Jordi then said, "It's Lydie. She's been out all afternoon. I expected her back two hours ago."

"Where'd she go?" asked Jordi.

Nana frowned, looked from Jordi to Pip then back to Jordi again. "On a picnic."

Jordi's face flushed, his cheek muscles fluttered. "Who with?"

"*Jésus, Marie, et Josef!* You know who wit'," Nana snapped. Then, in a voice filled with more resignation than anger, she said, "That Virgil Blount."

"Damn him," said Jordi. "Where'd they go?"

"I don't know." Nana was wringing the cloth in her hands.

Jordi looked up to see a coil of dust kick up on Route 176. A truck came over the rise and slowed, then made the turn onto their road. It was Virgil Blount's beat-up '38 Ford pickup. The sagging dropgate clanked as the truck bounced up the bumpy road.

"That good-for-nothing zero," Jordi muttered.

Pip put a hand on Jordi's shoulder. "Settle down, Jordi. There ain't not'ing you can do. She's a grown woman. It's her choice."

"But why would she choose a lout like him?"

Pip leaned toward Jordi and spoke harshly. "Don't you go putting your nose in your poor mother's business. Remember what we talked about in the car? You and me, we got plans and you need to focus on that. Now settle down."

The truck lurched to a stop behind Chrétien's Packard. Lydie sprang from the passenger side and ran toward Jordi. She threw her arms around him and looked into his eyes. "You're home early. How was Revere Beach?"

The top of Lydie's head came only to Jordi's chin. He saw a few strands of grass in her hair and he smelled alcohol on her breath. It mixed with her perfume, the one his father had liked so much. Jordi said nothing. He stared past her shoulder at Virgil Blount who remained in the truck with the window closed.

Lydie stepped back and said, "I asked you a question. How was your trip?"

"Fine," he replied curtly. He continued to stare at Blount's truck.

Blount rolled down the window and leaned his head out. He nodded politely. "Hello, folks." He looked at Lydie and said, "I'd best be going now." He stuck his elbow out the window, turned to look over his shoulder, and backed the truck away from Chrétien's car. He ground into first gear, spun the wheel, and headed down the road toward Route 176, his elbow hanging out the window.

Once the truck was out of sight, Jordi turned to his mother. "Goddamn it, Ma! Did you give him the sweater you were knitting for Dad?"

"No! Are you crazy? I would never do such a thing."

Jordi narrowed his eyes. "It sure looked the same."

Lydie shook here head. "Dad's sweater is...was...blue and red. That one is green and red. And it's much cheaper yarn."

"Why did you have to knit him a sweater? What difference do the colors or the yarn make?"

Lydie opened her mouth to say something, then stopped, sucked in her breath. "It's wrong, I know. I knew it even when I gave it to him."

"Then why did you?"

She shrugged her shoulders, gave a helpless look. "I don't know. I...He's given me a few gifts and I just thought..."

"Jesus Christ, Ma!"

"Jordi!" snapped Nana. Her eyes were moist and her hands were trembling.

But Jordi persisted. "Of all people, you just *had* to give a sweater to that...that...jerk."

"Jordi, I..."

"Goddamn, I hate him."

"Jordi, it's been more than a year, you know. I've got a right—"

"I know exactly how long it's been."

"Other people should be able to..." Her voice trailed off. Tears had formed in the corners of her eyes. She pressed her lips together angrily. "Has it ever occurred to you that I have to get on with my life, too? I like to knit sweaters; it gives me something to do. What's so wrong with that? I've knitted them for you and Pip and Uncle Chrétien, too." She whirled around and stomped up onto the porch stairs, brushing past Nana. She disappeared into the house, letting the screen door slam behind her.

Everyone stared at the door. A moth clung to the middle of the screen, apparently undisturbed.

Finally, Nana sighed and asked, "Will you stay for supper, Chrétien?"

"I plan to stay for the weekend, if that's all right."

Nana gave a smile of pleasure. Then she said, "She has so much pain."

"We all do," replied Chrétien.

A week later Pip and Jordi felt ready to announce their plans to build Gil's boat. During a supper of pork pie, which Nana always made with extra thick crust, Pip pointed his fork at the half-model on the kitchen wall and said, "Remember when Gil made that? Back in '41, wasn't it, just before he went off to the war?"

Lydie nodded sadly.

"He dreamed of using it to lay out the lines of a real boat," Pip said. "It was his dream, that boat…his dream."

Nana reached for Jordi's empty plate. "More pie?" she asked. When Jordi smiled and nodded, she slipped a large slice onto his plate and slid it across the table toward him.

"Yuh," Pip continued, "you know, we been thinking, wouldn't it be somet'ing if me an' Jordi built that boat? It would honor our Gil, know what I mean?"

"It would be lovely," said Lydie, "but there's no way this family can afford that sort of thing."

"What if we *could* afford it?" asked Pip.

Nana snorted. "Who do you think you are, some rich guy who can afford to build a yacht?"

"It's not a yacht. It's a simple ketch."

"*Jésus, Marie, et Josef,* it's a sailboat. It's a silly t'ing to spend money on."

Pip's face flushed. "Who are you to speak of spending money with a closet full of dresses you hardly wear?"

"Dresses ain't boats."

"You got that right. Dresses just sit in the closet, a boat can take you places."

"If you got to build a boat, build a lobster boat like everybody else."

"We have a lobster boat already."

"Build another one. Jordi can use it and we'll make more money."

"Goddamn it, Zabet, it ain't that easy. The water is already overcrowded wit' traps now that the men are home from the war. If we try to set out more traps, try to carve out a separate area for Jordi, you know what will happen? The traps will be cut. Don't you remember how it was when we first came here an' everybody said there was no way they was gonna let us 'Frenchys' fish their territory?"

Lydie spoke up. "Pip, Nana, this is a foolish thing to argue about. We don't have the money to build the boat anyway, so what's the point in arguing about it?"

Pip slipped a mouthful of pie into his mouth, wiped crumbs from his lips, and smiled first at Lydie then at Nana. His eyes danced. "We got the money," he mumbled through the pie.

"What?"

"I said we got the money. Ain't we, Jordi?"

Jordi smiled. He nodded to both Nana and Lydie, then lifted a forkful of pie to his mouth.

"Where did you get this money?" asked Nana.

"Chrétien wants to give it to us."

"Chrétien?" Her eyes narrowed with anger. "Is it that Sue Harper tramp again?"

Pip laughed. "Naw. I think he's finished wit' her. Said she was just a horse's ass, didn't he, Jordi?"

Jordi laughed.

Pip continued. "Let's just say he's got the money an' he wants to spend some of it helping Jordi." Pip shared the details of their plan, which he and Jordi had refined in the last week. Building the boat would give Jordi basic boat-building skills and then they'd send him to school for a degree in naval architecture, which would set him up to open his own business.

When he finished, both Lydie and Nana stared at him, mouths open. Finally, Lydie turned to Jordi and asked, "Is this what you want to do?"

"Yes, Ma, all of it. I want to build *that* boat," he said, pointing to the half-model, "and I want to become a boatbuilder."

Lydie looked at Nana, then back at Jordi. "I don't know what to say."

"Do you know what Uncle Chrétien said when we talked about this? He said that he loved Dad and that his boat should be built by all that's right in this goddamned, lousy world. That's exactly what he said."

"And is that what you want me to say, too?"

"Ma, I just want you to say that you understand why it's so important for me and Pip to build the boat. You see, to me and to Pip, that boat is part of Dad."

"Jordi's right," said Pip. He was looking at Nana, imploring her to understand.

For a long while neither Nana nor Lydie said anything. Finally, Nana asked, "What about the lobsters?"

"Oh, we'll still fish," replied Pip. "We'll do bot' t'ings. It'll be long hours, but we'll do it." He hit the table with his fist. "We're gonna do this t'ing!"

chapter 14

In the fall, they rented Rufus Metcalfe's old two-story barn near the Benjamin River to build Gil's boat. Rufus' brother was killed in the Spanish-American War, both of his sons were killed in the First World War, his one grandson was killed shortly after the invasion of Normandy, and his wife Ada died while the Battle of the Bulge was raging. She died cursing the Germans to the end. So the broken man had nobody to run the farm now that he was too old and worn, and he was happy to let Pip, a compatriot in grief, use his old, battered barn. At first, he refused to take money for it, but when Pip insisted, he finally gave in. But when a new woodstove showed up along with boards to repair the flooring on the second story, Pip had a good idea how old Rufus was using the money.

"Stove's for me," said Rufus. "I intend to watch some, an' I been spleeny something awful lately." He was a man in his middle eighties who, ever since his wife died, always appeared unshaven, the coarse white whiskers making his craterous face look as if it could be used for a rasp. He carried a malodorous pipe in his craggy, macula-spotted hand, and a stench of old urine fumed up from his clothes. People said that he was a proper Down-Easter, since all the sentences he ever uttered in his entire life wouldn't make up a single chapter in a book.

When Rufus said he would order wood to rebuild the cracked walls, Pip said it would be better to let the wind in. "This boat will live or die wit' the wind so it better get used to it. Besides, if we keep the wind out now, it will only take it out on the boat later." So the wind, on most days, penetrated the barn, carrying with it the salt-sea smell of high tide or the decay of low tide. But the interior was often striated with blades of sunlight as well, lending warmth to the barn.

Once they had cleared out the second story and repaired the floor and leveled it with replacement boards to make a loft, Pip persuaded Ogden Gower to spend two days helping them get started lofting the lines from Gil's half-model. First, they used calipers to carefully plot key reference points of sections and waterlines—vertical slices across the breadth of the hull, and horizontal slices of the hull from the deck to the bottom of the keel. They scaled these measurements to full size and developed a table of offsets which would allow them to lay down the lines on the lofting floor which they had painted dull white so the lines would show up well. They drew a grid representing the sections and waterlines, scaled up, then overlaid it with a profile drawing show-ing the deck line, the sheerline, and the rabbet where the hull joined the keel. To save space, they superimposed on the grid the half-breadth plan, or the seagull's view of the boat. Next, they fashioned a separate large panel on which they laid out the body plan with but-tocks, waterlines, and sections. They completed this view by fairing in diagonals and projecting the curved and raked transom.

When they finished, late on a Wednesday, Pip rose creakily to his feet. "All this time kneeling on the floor has done my knees in," he said. "In the last few days I been on my knees more than Nana and all her praying." He put his hands on his hips and stretched his back.

"Yuh," said Jordi, "but look at the result."

The three men stared at the complicated network of straight and curved lines which had an abstract beauty of its own. They all thought of Gil.

Finally, Ogden said, "Ain't the same as building something square. Curved lines require a whole lot more figuring." He paused, then added, "But Gil sure thunk up some pretty lines!"

"He had the eye for it," said Pip.

"Most lobstermen, this kinda boat would never occur to them," Ogden said. "To their way of thinkin' a good lobster boat's the only *real* kind of boat."

That evening, they returned late to the farm. When they climbed the porch steps in the gathering darkness, they were startled by a voice from the other end of the porch. It was Lydie. "Where have you two been?" she demanded. She was sitting in a rocking chair and it creaked as she rocked back and forth.

"Ma, we didn't see you there. It's dark," said Jordi. "We were working on the boat."

"I know it's dark. That's my point. You usually come home early on Wednesdays because that's the day I make blueberry pie for you."

"Oh, gosh Ma, we forgot…"

"You think of nothing else but that boat these days."

"We're sorry, Ma, it just slipped our minds." An edge of anger tinged Jordi's voice. "I'd love to have a piece of your pie now."

"Well, it's a little late for that. Nana has supper just about ready. You're not going to eat pie right before supper. You can have it for dessert."

"Okay."

"By which time, of course, it will be cold."

Over supper, Pip and Jordi tried twice to turn the conversation to the boat, but neither Lydie nor Nana wanted to talk about it. Instead, they asked after Rufus Metcalfe and how he was getting along without Ada, then they talked about their plans for the vegetables, fruits, and jams they would put up that year. After a few half-hearted attempts to join their conversation, Pip and Jordi fell silent.

One morning, Pip and Jordi were leaving for an entire day at the Metcalfe barn when a chevron of geese flew honking overhead. As they passed, several of the chickens in the barnyard ran in the same direction, wings flapping furiously. They seemed to be in the grasp of some withered impulse irritating long-dormant flight nerves.

"Look at those dumb chickens," Jordi cried.

Pip shook his head, laughing. "I guess they're trying for some kinda chicken dream, but that's crazy."

After Ogden Gower helped them develop a list of scantlings specifying the dimensions of the hull timbers, they brought in the wood they would need and stored it in racks they had built against the two long walls of the barn. There was quarter-sawn white oak, which they would use for the keel and the rest of the backbone. Ogden had advised them to be sure to get winter-felled lumber since, being cut down and sawed when the sap was not flowing, it would be stronger. They also made sure it was green, which would make it easier for steam bending. For the planking, they got white cedar, which came plain-sawn as flitches with a strip of bark along one edge. Next came the quarter-sawn white ash which they would use primarily for deck beams, and then roots of the hackmatack tree because the natural crook was ideal for curved stems and knees. Finally, they brought in some ordinary clear white pine for battens and, later, for some of the interior joiner work.

All the while, Chrétien kept writing checks.

Late on a Wednesday afternoon, they were storing the last of the lumber when Jordi said, "Oh, hell, Pip, it's Wednesday. We better knock off and go get some of Ma's pie or she'll be angry again."

They finished up quickly, bid Rufus a hasty goodbye, and hurried back to the farm. When they lurched into the kitchen, they were relieved to see that Lydie had, not long before, taken the pie from the oven. It was still steaming under its cloth. She looked over her shoulder at them, "Well, how's that for timing? I thought you were going to stand me up again."

Nana smiled at them then turned back to her dishes. Lydie seemed content to watch as they wolfed down two pieces each. When they sat back and murmured their thanks, and said, "It's one of my favorite things to do, make pie for my men. I'm glad you came home when you did. I would have hated to miss you."

"Miss us?" asked Jordi. "Why would you miss us?"

"I told you last Saturday, I'm going out to dinner tonight."

"You didn't say anything about that."

"I most certainly did. You just don't listen."

"With him?"

"If you mean with Virgil Blount, yes. What of it?"

Jordi didn't say anything. Instead, he stared at the half-filled pie plate. Nana and Pip exchanged glances.

"Now listen here, *all* of you," said Lydie. "I am fed up with your obvious disapproval of Virgil and I won't stand for it! He may not be much, he's certainly no Gil, but he likes me and he can be fun, and that's all. Everybody knows he had a terrible childhood, so you can understand why he may be a little weak here and there. Sure, he's not the man Gil was—he may look big and strong but he's afraid and needs the care of a woman...And at least he's alive!" She sucked in her breath. Her eyes grew round with horror. "I'm sorry," she said, "I didn't mean...Oh, God."

Everyone remained silent.

Lydie gave Nana an imploring look. "When I'm with Virgil, especially if I've had a few drinks, that's the only time I ever get to think about something besides Gil. You understand that, don't you, Nana?"

Nana nodded. "It's hard not to think about Gil all the time. I know."

Lydie started to walk toward the stairs, then turned and said, "I can't spend the rest of my life alone in my room thinking of the way things could have been...*should* have been. I didn't cause the war. I didn't ask Gil to go into the Army. In fact, I did everything I could to stop him... I baked pies...I knitted...But I was no match for the war and all the killing. So now *this* is all I have and I'm going to make the best of it. She looked from Jordi to Pip to Nana. "It's not your life, or yours, or yours. It's mine."

She paused and asked Pip for a cigarette. Everyone stared at her. Pip slid a Chesterfield half out of his pack and held it out to her. He took one for himself and lit first hers, then his. "When did you start smoking?" he asked quietly.

"I don't know, a little while ago. I only have one now and then," she replied, "and *that*, too, is *my* decision." A cloud of smoke settled in front of her face and she waved a hand to dissipate it. She coughed.

Nana frowned, turned her back to them, and busied herself at the stove. Pip and Jordi sat back in their chairs staring blankly at the wall.

Lydie said, "Now I'm going to get ready, but I want to say one more thing. If I decide to marry him...which I haven't...but *if* I do, then I expect each and every one of you to be civil to him." She whirled and stomped out of the kitchen.

Jordi ground his teeth together. Under his breath he said, "I'm not gonna have that man as my stepfather."

Neither Pip nor Nana seemed to hear him. Nana said, "Women shouldn't smoke."

"I wouldn't say anyt'ing to her right now if I was you," said Pip.

One morning that winter, they built a long steam box and caulked it with cotton. At one end, they attached pipes from a wood-fired steam generator and stuffed rags around the cracks to prevent steam from coming out. At the other end, they fitted a small door. They were now ready to construct the section molds and lay out the backbone of the boat. With Jordi on Christmas break, they were able to work every day.

Using the lofted lines as guides, they bent steamed oak staves to the curve of a section, holding the bend with awls firmly jabbed into the floor at intervals along the fair curve. Once the mirrored staves were properly shaped, they stayed them with plank bracing, creating a section mold. In the following weeks they repeated this process for all twelve stations, stacking them against the far wall for later use.

When they returned each afternoon and began their work, Rufus Metcalfe would emerge from his house and take up his place in the chair beside the blazing woodstove.

After all the section molds had been built, they started to assemble the backbone which would eventually include the stem, the gripe, the keel, the deadwood, the sternpost, the horn timber, and the knees. They worked slowly, bending and shaping each part carefully so that the whole would fit together perfectly in the end.

One day, Pip told Jordi and Rufus how the Cree Indians would sing special songs as they built a canoe because a canoe was, to them, a living creature. It must be able to cross lakes quickly like a caribou, move through the water the way a hawk moves through the air, obey the wishes of its riders the way a horse answers to the reins, and, above all, be a proud and beautiful woman who dances on the waves. So the songs would appeal to the spirits of all these beings, asking that they lend their virtues to the canoe.

"Ain't never heard that," said Rufus.

"It's true," replied Pip. "I read it in a book."

"Book?" Blue smoke curled lazily from Rufus' pipe.

"Yuh, ain't you never read a book?"

Rufus shook his head, champed on the crazed, yellowed stem of his pipe. "Ain't," he said with unmistakable pride.

"Do you know these songs, Pip?" asked Jordi.

"No, just read about them."

"Then you can't sing the appropriate songs to make this backbone strong as an ox?" Jordi asked with a teasing smile.

"No, 'fraid not."

"Good!" said Rufus.

Pip laughed. "What? You don't want to hear me sing?"

"Work careful. Don't use no dozy wood. Be enough."

Pip smiled. "Guess you're right. But even wit'out the songs, this here boat's gonna be a living t'ing."

One evening, after Lydie and Nana went off to a bean supper, Jordi sat in the living room when he realized he didn't know where Pip was. He went out on the porch and saw there was a light on in the shed. He crossed the yard, entered the shed, and found Pip sitting at the rolltop desk intently reading a small book.

"What're you doing, Pip?" he asked.

Pip started. "Oh, Jordi...I...I was just reading this old combat medic's manual. It belonged to your dad. I was just about to call you in here to see it."

"It belonged to Dad? Where did you get it?" Jordi reached for it and, after a moment's hesitation, Pip released it. Jordi examined it. "So, where did you get it?" he asked again.

Pip said, "Jordi, there's something we gotta talk about."

"What?"

Pip reached into the back of the desk, shifted through some papers, and pulled out a large, black school exercise book that had been hidden beneath all the papers. He handed it to Jordi.

"What is it?"

"It's a diary your dad kept during the war."

Jordi gazed at it, wide-eyed. "Where did you get it?"

"One day, not long after the war, one of your dad's buddies from his medical unit came by. You were at school and—thank God—your ma and Nana were off somewhere. The man gave me this diary and your dad's medic's kit."

"But why didn't you tell us? Why did you keep it secret all this time?"

"You'll see when you read it," Pip replied. "What it says…well, it ain't pretty. It would destroy Nana, her being so damned Catholic. Your ma, too…it would, I don't know, ruin her memories, somet'ing like that. Only me an' Chrétien know about the diary, and now you do, too."

Jordi fanned the pages of the notebook. They were covered with closely spaced handwriting and crammed with doodles in the margins. A few pages had old postcards inserted between them. "Why are you showing it to me now?"

"Because it seems right. I debated it for a long time, but I finally decided you had the right and, now that you're a man, I don't see no reason to wait any longer."

"Do you want me to read it now?"

Pip nodded. "The entries I marked wit' postcards. Then I guess we better have a nice long talk about it." He rolled the desk chair out and motioned for Jordi to sit. As Jordi started to read, Pip stood, hands clasped behind his back, looking out the shed window. A ghostly moonlight paled his face.

Jordi removed the postcard and read the first entry.

28 July, '43. Somewhere near St. Venera, Sicily.

Just told I'm being recommended for DSC. What bull! I told the captain I wouldn't accept it—not for what I did—but he told me, in so many words, to screw off. Said they wanted heroes and, tag, I was it. He read me the citation. Extraordinary heroism. Ha! It all happened so fast there was no time to make any decisions. It was just instinct. But what a lousy instinct! It was only after it was over that we realized they had hardly fired back. How could we have known they were only kids, barely older than my own son? Helmutt Pflederer. Dieter Bottiger. Ulrich Heinkel. That's what their IDs said. Given the right circumstances, they could have been friends with my boy. Why the hell are the Krauts using kids so young? All of them a lot closer to Jordi's age than to mine. Dear God forgive me. Angelo says we can't blame ourselves; they might have killed us if we had-n't fired. But that doesn't help much. I can't escape the thought that we could have persuaded them to surrender. Receiving the DSC doesn't feel like an honor—it feels like being branded a child killer. Dear God, please help me.

When he finished reading the entry, Jordi said, "Pip?"

Pip turned to gaze at Jordi. "Uhmm?"

Jordi opened his mouth as though to ask something, but he could-n't find the words.

"I know, it's tough to take," said Pip. "But there's a deeper, more important truth behind it and I think you're enough of a man to find it. Read the other ones, then we'll talk about it."

7 June, '44. Coleville-sur-Mer.

The very worst thing about war is that it brings out things that, in civilian life, we make every effort to hide—hatred, violence, inhumanity, cowardice. And how easy it is to experience all these things at once here! That's what I felt when I tried to treat Pfc. Burton. (I need to stop think-ing of them as people, and shouldn't learn their names. Either that, or I'll never make it through this war sane.) Sure, he had both goddamned legs blown off and his intestines were spilling out of his belly. And, sure, there was no way in hell that he was going to make it. And he sure as hell knew it! So why didn't I give him a second syrette of morphine like he asked? Why did I give him only one, just enough to knock him out, but then intentionally not pin the empty syrette to his collar so somebody else would come along and "accidentally" give him the "second for eternity"? Isn't it just pure cowardice to trick some unsuspecting slob into doing the deed so that I wouldn't have to trouble my own sensitive little soul with such a decision?

Jordi flipped the pages and removed the next postcard.

19 August, '44. Bagnoles sur L'Orne
If I thought war was a nightmare before, I realize now that I hadn't seen the half of it. This so-called Falaise Gap is the worst hellhole I have ever seen. The stink of rotting corpses—men, horses, cows, everything—is more than just nauseating, it is pure evil. Can any of us survive this? This stench really is the smell of a rotting Hope. What we have done here is kill Hope and now nothing matters. Maybe that's why I didn't feel a damned thing when two of the guys executed those ten Krauts by shooting them one by one in the back of the head. Nothing in this pit deserves to live anyway! How many boys did I send off today? Two? Three? I can't even remember it's becoming such a habit. I even dispatched one of the Germans who was crying for his mother. Hell, some of the guys even call me the angel of mercy.

"Pip, is he saying that he killed those men?" Jordi asked, his voice shaking.

"No, Jordi, he's saying he made their deaths less painful…and quicker. And you listen to me, Jordi, that's *love*…that's *love!*"

Jordi gazed at Pip for a long while, then flipped to the last postcard-marked page.

1 December, '44. Vicht.
So now I'm a mother! I didn't ask for this! God knows I tried to stop the kid's bleeding but there were just too many holes. That blood was damned and determined to pour out. The shrapnel had ripped him up as bad as I've ever seen. Tore through God only knows how many organs— liver, kidneys, stomach. It would have been better for him if it had blown his heart to pieces, or his head. At least that way he would have died quickly. I gave him the two syrettes. Maybe I should put notches on my

medic's bag! No, I'll put notches on my DSC and when people ask me about them I'll say they represent the enemy. And hell, it'd be the truth because anyone who dies here is the enemy! There are just two sides—the living and the dead.

What was his name? Johnny? I didn't ask him to tell me but he told me anyway, damn it! Barely old enough to enlist, for Christ's sake! He knew he was going to die. I knew, too. There was just no damned doubt about it. So he calls "Mama, Mama" over and over again. People back in the States, they'd never believe me if I told them that guys don't say "Go on without me" or "Give 'em hell for me" or some other John Wayne bullshit when they die. They all call for their mothers. So the kid, Johnny, calls "Mama, Mama." All the time he's calling "Mama, Mama." And what was I supposed to do, let the poor kid die alone? So I lay down with him and I put my arms around him just like we were in his mother's bed somewhere back home. Just like we were going to go to sleep together. I held him and I said, "It's okay Johnny, It's okay" just like I figured his mother would say. All the while he's spilling his blood on me. "It's okay, Johnny," I kept saying. It took a long time, God, it took a long time! But eventually I felt him start to go limp, start to leave. His eyes were opened wide but the pupils had contracted to pinpoints—classic signs. I could see he was in shock. And he looked straight at me and he said, "Mama." But he wasn't crying it out anymore like he was searching for her; he just said it quietly like he had found her. His cries of "Mama" stayed with me all night and the next night and the next night. I'll probably hear them again tonight. God damn this war; it's chickenshit! I guess it's time to see the Division priest. I didn't ask for this. I'm only a simple lobsterman!

When Jordi looked up at Pip, his eyes were wet with tears. Pip put a hand on his shoulder and said, "Just tell me what's on your mind and we'll talk about it." He removed a cigarette, snapped open his Zippo, and lit it.

"Goddamn it, why did he have to shoot those German kids?" Jordi wailed. "My dad would never do that sort of thing."

With a sudden movement, Pip passed the still lit Zippo under one of Jordi's fingers.

"Ow!" cried Jordi, pulling his finger back. "What the hell?"

"Because that's about as much time as your dad had, goddamnit! Don't you go making judgments about him unless you been there too. Don't you *dare* do that!"

Jordi was breathing heavily, licking his finger. He gave Pip a hard look. "So is that the deeper truth. That we all kill?"

Pip shook his head. "That's too simple. You're smarter than that Jordi." Pip reached for Jordi's hand, examined the burn on his forefinger. "Come on inside, we'll put some salve on that."

Once Jordi's finger was smeared with salve and they'd wrapped a Band-Aid around it, Pip said, "The deeper truth is this, Jordi: even in hell—and there ain't no doubt that your dad was in hell—there's always some sea room. There's always a way to make t'ings just a little bit better, a way to make choices. Sure, his instincts made him kill them Germans, just like you pulled your finger away from my Zippo. And that's the one place, instinct, where nature kinda has us by the balls. But look what he did out of it. He became a medic and he started helping people. And when he couldn't help them live… he helped them die. He used all the sea room he had. And that's why you should be proud of him. Just like I am, goddamnit. That's why I wanted to show you the diary, because I figured you were man enough to understand. It's one thing to be brave when you ain't got no decision to make, when you ain't got no choice. But to be brave enough to make a decision even when it hurts so bad you want to scream… now *that's* courage."

Jordi reached out, he grasped Pip's hand, squeezed it, and said, "Thanks, Pip."

Pip gave a short laugh. "Sorry 'bout the finger."

"I don't even feel it."

Pip took on a serious expression. "Now that you know what's in your dad's diary, you gotta promise me that Nana and your ma will never, ever see it. Maybe your ma would understand; she's kind of a modern woman. But Nana? Never. Never in a thousand years. She would go to her grave believing her son was a murderer because that's what her damned religion would say."

"I promise, Pip. On Dad's soul, I promise."

"I made Chrétien swear."

"I swear, too, Pip."

When they returned to the shed to lock the diary away, Pip gave Jordi a copy of the key to the desk. "Read the rest of it only when your ma and Nana ain't around."

Jordi nodded. "Didn't you say that Dad's friend also gave you his medic's kit?"

Pip slid the desk out away from the wall and lifted a pair of khaki-colored pouches which he dropped on the desk. He opened the left pouch and spread the contents across the desk. There was a small pencil, something that looked like an emergency medical tag of some kind, eight first aid packets, each about half the size of a pack of cigarettes, and a strap Pip thought must be for carrying a litter. He spread out the contents of the right pouch and showed Jordi an ammonia flask and cup, iodine swabs, various gauze bandages, rolls of adhesive plaster, bandage scissors, and a tourniquet. Pip reached behind the desk and took out three more small cases. In the first was a collection of scissors and tweezers of different shapes and sizes plus a white arm band with the medic's red cross. Jordi remembered the photograph in which his father showed off an arm band just like it. The second case was a tiny pouch containing a red tin marked "Sulfanilamide." The third contained several toothpaste-sized boxes which were labeled "Solution of Morphine Tartrate."

Jordi's heart skipped when he saw those boxes.

They heard Mrs. Winter's car turn onto their road. She had given Nana and Lydie a ride to the bean supper. Hurriedly, Pip and Jordi slid the pouches and other equipment behind the desk, shoved it against the wall, buried the diary under a sheaf of papers, and locked the desk. They were just emerging from the shed when Mrs. Winter's car pulled to a stop in front of the house.

chapter 15

It was Pip's hands, ridged and pitted like a glacier-scoured landscape, that caught Jordi's attention one early winter night out on the
reach in 1948. Pip's hands had always been strong. Jordi had once seen
Pip win the bat toss before a baseball game by holding onto the mer-
est sliver of the bat handle between his thumb and forefinger. Jordi
had studied those hands as they confidently guided tools giving form
and purpose to the boat taking shape in Rufus Metcalfe's barn. But
now, two years after starting the boat, Pip's hands seemed weak as they
gripped a castnet in the stern of the *Zabet & Lydie*.

Pip was showing Jordi how to throw the castnet, since they had
decided to give the lobsters a break and do some shrimping, something many lobstermen did in the winter months if they thought they
could make more money.

"Hold the t'row-line like this," Pip said, showing Jordi how he had
coiled the line in his right hand. "Then place the net between the forefinger and the middle finger of the right hand like this. Now take the
bottom part of the net with the weights in the left hand…" Pip leaned
over to lift the net, but dropped it twice before finally grasping it in
his left hand which, Jordi noticed, trembled slightly. "There, like that.
Now check and make sure not'ing is tangled up." Pip stepped closer
to the stern rail. "The way you t'row it is a lot like the pictures you see
of a discus t'rower in the Olympics. You turn to the right… like this…
Then you spin to the left and let the net go. Watch." He rotated his
body slowly to the right, then unwound with a quick spin to the left.
He heaved the net out. It went only a short distance before wafting
down to the water too close to the stern, like a veil descending.

"*Merde!*" He hauled the net back.

Earlier that evening, the reach had been swaddled in a cold fog. But as night came on, the fog dissipated and the moon rose yellow and fat. The sky went from dark blue to cold black. Stars were strewn here and there in the vast dome of night, but where the moon rode, it rode alone.

On the reach the running lights of a half-dozen boats bobbed on the black waters. Jordi and Pip noticed that the boat nearest them on the starboard beam belonged to Virgil Blount. They ignored him and focused on their own shrimping.

Pip was breathing hard. "Let me take a short rest," he said. He snapped open the Zippo, spun the wheel against the flint several times before it sparked, and lit a cigarette. As he smoked, he held the cigarette between the forefinger and middle finger of his left hand and watched the tendrils of smoke rise into the still air. With the thumb and forefinger of his right hand he absent-mindedly spun his wedding ring around his finger.

Jordi watched for a moment, then said, "Nana's right, you're losing weight. Look how easily you can move your ring."

Pip held his left hand before him. Blue smoke curled from the cigarette and licked at his nostrils. He coughed. "It's not'ing. Weight goes up an' down. Nana ain't happy unless people are fat."

"You're sure you're okay? Maybe you ought to see Doc Davids."

"Aw Jeez, what do I want to see Evan for? He'll only say he's glad I lost some weight. All the time he's telling me to lose weight, Nana's trying to fatten me up. Well, this time he wins."

"All the same, Pip…"

But Pip gave a dismissive wave of his hand, smoke trailing it like incense from a swinging censer. He took a deep drag from the cigarette, leaned back and looked up at the vastness of the sky. "Funny how when you look up at the sky and see all the stars, they seem so cold. But what we're really looking at is the heat of a million suns." He paused, then murmured as though to himself, "Arcturus, Orion, and Pleiades, and the chambers of the sout'."

"What?"

"All the stars in the chambers of the sout'. It's from Job." After a while, Pip said, "The Egyptians figured if a man was good during his life, then he would become immortal, spend eternity as a star. I'd like to believe that. I'd like to believe that the heat of the stars comes from all the good people who've died."

Jordi hugged his arms around his chest. "Well, I don't feel any of that heat now. It's sure as hell cold out here. Why do the goddamned shrimp have to run at night?"

"But there's heat up *there*. It's just that they're very far away." Pip lowered his gaze to the ocean. He scanned the water, moving his gaze slowly from right to left.

"What are you looking for?" asked Jordi.

Pip smiled. "*Keporkak*."

"That humpback whale? Christ, Pip, it's dark out there. You wouldn't be able to see him." Jordi remembered the whale bursting from the water, its great white flippers spread heavenward, the mighty head, and the massive sloping rostrum.

"You can see him if you look hard enough. All you gotta do is find the wake, you know, the way it kinda lights up. What do you call that?"

"Phosphorescence? The light that plankton gives off?"

"Yuh, that's it. You know what that light is?"

Jordi smiled, shook his head. He thought he was about to hear another one of Pip's fanciful explanations. "No, Pip, what is it?"

"That's starlight. It's the light from all the stars in the chambers of the sout'. That's what *I* believe."

Jordi scanned the water but could see no phosphorescence. "Pip," he said, "do you remember years ago when we saw the whale— *Keporkak*—breach just a few yards away from us? You said something then that I guess I've never understood."

"What's that?"

"Well, first, Dad said that seeing the whale like that was enough to give a man religion, then you said 'or take it away from him.' What did you mean by that?"

"I said that, eh?"

"Don't you remember?"

"Yuh, I guess I do." Pip paused a moment, then said, "See, it's like this: I guess I don't think any religion is big enough to hold somet'ing like that inside of it. No priests, no Latin prayers, no stained-glass windows, no rosary beads, no churches—none of that stuff helps to explain t'ings like whales or hurricanes." He turned his gaze upward. "Or the stars."

They were silent for a while. Pip lit another cigarette from the stub of the old one. He continued to gaze upward. Finally, he said, "Imagine that light coming from so far away."

As he said it, they could hear the sound of a voice close by.

"A lot farther away than *him*," Jordi said. "Christ, I can hear him singing to himself."

"You mean Blount? Stop being so bedeviled wit' him. Keep your mind on the fishing…and building the boat."

"But he's drifting toward us."

"If he gets too close we'll tell him to screw off."

"I wish to hell he'd fish someplace else," muttered Jordi.

Pip ignored him. "All my life, I been trying to think about the stars. Trying to imagine the distances, you know, get so's I understood it all. But there are some t'ings you can't even begin to understand. It's like if you put your foot in the ocean, you can feel how cold it is on your foot, but you can't know how deep it is, or even how really cold it can be somewhere else in the same ocean. You can only let it tickle your foot the way some ideas tickle your mind. And that's the closest you ever get to it."

A breeze started to blow, an easterly slipping up the reach from Nova Scotia. Its cold fingers found the skin on the back of Jordi's neck between his wool cap and his thick coat collar. He hunched his shoulders to raise the collar up his neck.

Pip shook his head. "The crazy t'ing about it is that as soon you accept that there ain't no meaning to it all, that's when there suddenly seems to be some meaning." He flicked the cigarette away and buttoned his coat all the way up. He sighed. "Well, let's give that sucker another try," he said, reaching for the castnet.

Once again, he arranged the net in both hands then rotated his hips to the right before uncoiling himself in a rapid spin to the left. This time, he heaved the castnet with such force that he threw himself off balance and started to stagger toward the stern rail. Jordi watched, frozen. Pip lurched three steps before the stern caught him just above both knees. At precisely the same instant a wave lifted the *Zabet & Lydie's* bow, dipping the stern. With a cry of "*Merde!*" Pip hurtled over the stern and into Eggemoggin Reach.

Jordi ran to the back of the boat. At first, he saw nothing. He whipped his overcoat off so fast that two buttons popped and clattered along the floorboards. Pip bobbed to the surface several feet astern of the *Zabet & Lydie,* sputtering. He struggled in the water, but the weight of his clothes seemed to be pulling him down. Jordi bent down to lever his boots off. He stood on one leg. The boat rocked and he fell. Cursing, he sat on the wet floorboards and struggled with his boots until he was finally free of them. He stood. Out of the corner of his eye he saw Blount's boat to starboard. It was even closer than before. "Man overboard!" Jordi cried at the top of his lungs.

He turned to find Pip again. He was now ten feet astern, flailing helplessly. Jordi climbed up on the stern rail. He grabbed the life ring from its rack and the stern line, which was still attached to a cleat, and plunged into the water. The shock of the cold water sucked his breath away. Blackness closed around him. He clawed at the water, trying to pull himself up. It seemed to take an eternity during which all he saw was an image of Pip struggling, weighed down by a heavy coat and boots. Finally, Jordi bobbed to the surface. Frantically, he looked around. He saw Virgil Blount's boat riding high on its bow wave. It was speeding away from them. He wanted to scream out, then he felt a hand grasp his shoulder. It was Pip who sputtered, "Line!... Get a line!"

"Here!" replied Jordi, pushing the life ring toward him. "Grab this!"

Pip slapped the water several times in vain before he finally got hold of the ring.

"Hold on!" shouted Jordi. He pulled himself back to the *Zabet &*

Lydie by the stern line he was still clutching in his right hand. He tried to pull himself up over the stern, levering a foot against the transom, but his foot slipped and he fell back into the water. He reached up, grabbed at the rail with numbed fingers, got a handhold, tried again. Pulling himself with so much force that a searing pain tore through his arms, he raised his body so that his chest was balanced on the stern rail. He kicked his legs up and toppled over the stern, crashing onto the floorboards, his entire weight landing on his right elbow. Again, pain shot through his body. He scrambled to his feet, his wet socks slipping on the floorboards. He heard Pip's voice. "Jordi! I'm slipping!"

Jordi lurched to the stern rail and watched Pip haul himself up to the transom. But he was unable to clamber aboard. He still clutched the life ring. Jordi wedged his knees against the inside of the transom, leaned way over, and extended both arms. "Grab my hands!"

Pip grasped each hand but as Jordi tried to lift him, their wet hands slipped apart. Pip seemed too weak to hold on.

"Can you grab the stern?" Jordi cried.

Pip placed both hands on the top edge of the stern. He was now high enough so that Jordi could grab him under the armpits. Jordi pushed his knees into the transom until they were shrieking with pain and leaned back in a mighty heave. Pip flew over the transom like a huge fish and flopped onto the floorboards.

"Christ, we need to get these wet clothes off before we freeze to death," said Jordi. He fumbled at Pip's buttons with numb fingers. "Shit! I can't get the damned buttons!"

"Get the knife," gasped Pip.

Jordi stumbled under the wheelhouse and pulled the knife from its sheath on the bulkhead. He returned and began working at Pip's buttons. One by one, they popped off the coat. Finally, the coat was open and Jordi was able to get behind Pip and pull it from his shoulders. He pivoted in front of Pip and began working at the boots. He twisted and pulled at them, drawing cries of pain from Pip, until both were at last off.

"I'll take care of the rest," said Pip through chattering teeth. "You get your own clothes off."

The two men worked frantically, shivering and struggling with stubborn buttons and zippers, until they were finally both naked. Jordi scurried into the tiny cabin and returned with two wool blankets. He wrapped one around Pip's shoulders and arranged him so that he could crouch against the bulkhead of the wheelhouse, sheltered from the wind. He wrapped the other blanket around himself like a toga and staggered forward to the wheel. He fumbled with the starter until the engine caught and soon the *Zabet & Lydie* was leaping over the waves towards Center Harbor and Niall Macgrudder's dock. The boat threw sheets of spray far out on each side.

Jordi was having difficulty breathing. It felt like the time he had the wind knocked out of him while playing football. He looked over his right shoulder. Pip was curled up in the corner of the wheelhouse, trying to draw the blanket tighter around him.

At last they saw the dock. But Jordi was bringing the *Zabet & Lydie* in with too much speed. He saw Niall Macgrudder run out from his shack, waving his arms frantically. He threw the engine into reverse and the bow fell off its wave. Then their own stern wave caught up to them, lifted the boat, and sent it careening toward the dock. Niall, who had positioned himself to fend the bow from the dock, suddenly seemed to think better of it and jumped back out of the way. The *Zabet & Lydie* struck with a sickening crunch, her bow sliding up onto the floating dock for an instant, then slipping back into the water.

"Jesus Christ!" shouted Niall. "What the hell are you doin' honkin' in heah something awful like that! Gory! You coulda—" He stopped abruptly, stared goggle-eyed. "You're all nekid!"

"Fell overboard," said Jordi. It came out as "bell oberbud."

"*Bell* what?"

"F-f-fell overbud, ba chrissake!"

"Gory!" Niall reached for the painter and tied the *Zabet & Lydie* to a piling. "How in hell'd you manage that?"

Jordi cut the engine, ignoring the question. "We need to get Pip warmed up."

"And you, too, from the looks of it."

Niall helped Jordi half-carry Pip into the shack. Both Pip and

Jordi clutched at the blankets wrapped around them and walked halt-
ingly in their bare feet across the dock. When Niall opened the shack
door, the scent of burning wood and coffee came spilling out at them.
After the anesthetizing cold of the water, the heat was almost overwhelming.

Rufus sat by the stove smoking his pipe. "You fellahs are nekid,"
he said matter-of-factly.

Niall helped each of them into a chair. "Here, let me get you some
coffee." He went over to the wood-burning stove where an old, dented coffeepot sat.

"Do you have any extra clothes here?" asked Jordi.

"Eyuh. An' you can have 'em 'cause I ain't aiming to spend my
time staring at your ugly, nekid bodies. But drink some coffee first. I
ain't embarrassed having two nekid men in my shack, so you oughtn't
be. I expect Rufus can handle it, too."

"Eyuh," said Rufus, sucking on his pipe.

Niall handed each of them a steaming cup of coffee.

With a weak voice, Pip said, "Ain't you got no whiskey?" They
were the first words he had spoken since Jordi had stuffed him into
the corner of the wheelhouse.

Niall laughed. "Eyuh. Ain't Chrétien's, but it'll do I s'pose." He
went behind the counter and retrieved a half-empty bottle. "In the
coffee or from the bottle?"

By way of an answer, Pip held the cup out in front of him, shivering. Niall grasped Pip's hand to steady the cup, and poured in a generous dollop of whiskey. "Folks call it Irish coffee, but I don't hold that
against it." Then, saying he'd be back momentarily, Niall went across
the road to his house to fetch some dry clothes.

While he was gone, Pip and Jordi sipped their coffee silently.
Rufus gazed at them, shaking his head. He sucked on his pipe and
said, "Flung yourselves overboard! I ain't never done that in seventy
years on the reach. Wouldn't know how to explain it to Ada."

Gradually, warmth returned to their bodies. By the time they
stopped shivering, Niall had returned with some spare clothes and a
hot bowl of fish chowder for each of them. "The wife wanted to come

over, but I told her you was all nekid. Should'a seen her blush. When she could speak, she said to make sure you ate up all the chowdah."

As they ate, Jordi asked, "Niall, did you see Virgil Blount earlier tonight?"

"Eyuh. Came in just before you two. Said nothing. Just took off."

"That son-of-a-bitch was out there. He saw us go overboard."

Niall stared at Jordi. "You sure 'bout that?"

"He was no more than fifty yards off our starboard beam. Ain't that right, Pip?"

Pip nodded.

"You saying he saw you but didn't help?"

"That's what I'm saying. I screamed 'man overboard' and the next thing I know, he's taking off!"

"Man's a zero," said Rufus.

"That's some kinda serious charge," said Niall, a note of warning in his voice. "Any man of the sea who refuses to help his brother—"

"That's my point!" said Jordi fiercely. "When I see that son-of-a—"

"Be careful before you go honking off at full speed. Give the man a chance to explain himself. Maybe he ain't heard you."

"Didn't hear me? I screamed as loud as I could."

"Maybe he had a radio on."

"Don't make excuses for him, Niall."

"Jordi, why in hell would a lobsterman see another lobsterman in the water and not go to help? It ain't the way we do things."

"Because that water's freezing. You know damn well that Pip and me came close to dying out there. He probably figured it'd be too risky—"

"All I'm saying is you shouldn't let your personal thing with him get in the way of—"

"You mean about him and my mother?" Jordi felt a flush of anger rise in his cheeks.

"Now, Jordi, I ain't—"

"It has nothing to do with my mother. The man just left us there to die."

Niall held up his hands. "Okay, okay. That's the way you see it. All

I'm saying is give the man a chance to explain before you go off smug as Billy-be-damned that you know the truth of it." He looked to Pip as if asking for support.

Pip nodded slowly. "Seems to me Blount couldn't help but hear Jordi. Jeez, even *I* heard him an' I was drowning with half of Eggemoggin Reach in my ears." Then Pip turned to Jordi. "All the same, it's best to be careful. We don't want to start trouble. The way you feel about him, if you tangle wit' him it'll bring trouble wit' the law, sure as hell. It'll ruin everyt'ing—the fishing, what's between you an' your ma…the boat, everyt'ing."

After an hour, both Pip and Jordi started to feel better. By the time Niall returned from putting the *Zabet & Lydie* on a mooring for them, they were ready to go home.

"You sure about going home now?" asked Niall.

"I'm sure," replied Jordi. "I'll drive. After a good night's sleep, we'll be fine."

After they both thanked Niall, Jordi helped Pip into the truck and went around to the driver's side. As he passed behind the truck, Niall grabbed his elbow. "Try to persuade him to see Evan Davids," he said. "He ain't looking all that swell."

"I'll try."

"And be careful 'bout Blount."

Jordi's face darkened at the mention of the man's name. But he said, "I'll be careful. If he doesn't have a good explanation, though, I'm not going to let him get away with it."

When they arrived home, Nana and Lydie knew immediately that something was wrong. "What happened to you two?" cried Lydie.

"What are those clothes?" asked Nana.

Jordi told them the story while Pip sagged in a kitchen chair. He left out the part about Virgil Blount. As Jordi spoke, Pip smoked a cigarette. It was the first since he had carried nearly a full pack into the reach with him. He played with the smoke, letting it curl from his mouth to his nose.

When Jordi finished, Nana said, "*Jésus, Marie, et Josef!* You gotta see Evan Davids right away. I told you somet'ing was wrong wit' you.

You ain't the kind of man to try to t'ro a net overboard and instead t'ro himself overboard."

"I'm fine," muttered Pip.

"Nana's right," said Lydie. "You haven't been yourself."

"All I need's a good night's sleep."

"Not until after you have some food," said Nana. She had been heating a pot of baked beans. Now she shoved two large bowls in front of them and added, "And not until you promise we'll all go into Blue Hill in the morning to see Evan Davids."

Pip cursed under his breath, but finally said, "I'll go just to get all of you off my back!"

chapter 16

The hospital was on Water Street at the foot of Blue Hill Harbor. At low tide, the harbor was brindled with salt rime and frozen mud, its bottom ridged and runneled by the scouring action of the waves. The hospital building was a three-story, large Colonial faced with white clapboard siding on the front wall and brick on the end walls. In front was a row of oak trees, whose stiff, bare branches were like exposed nerves. Jordi parked the truck so it faced the harbor. He got out and opened the passenger door. Lydie, who had been sitting in Pip's lap in the front seat, handed him the lap robes that had covered them, then slid out of the truck. Jordi tried to help Pip down to the icy ground. "Careful," he said, reaching for Pip's arm.

Pip snatched his arm away. "I can help myself, goddamnit. Help Nana."

Jordi shrugged and turned to Nana, offering his hand. He laughed when she stuck out her tongue behind Pip's back. "*Il est une patate,*" she muttered.

They entered through the main door and headed up the stairs.

"There's an elevator," said Jordi, wary of Pip's anger.

"I'll walk," Pip snapped.

"But maybe Nana—"

"Leave the elevator for the patients," she said, charging ahead of them up the narrow staircase.

By the time they reached the third floor, where the doctors' offices were, both Nana and Pip were breathing with great difficulty. Pip's rasping breath came so hard that it provoked a fit of coughing, and they had to pause at the top landing until he caught his breath.

They stood in a long hallway with doctors' offices to the sides under the sloping roof. A radio played softly. Jordi recognized a melody he had heard often. It was "Peg O' My Heart." He realized this tune had been playing silently in his head all morning long. Was it possible he heard it the previous night out on Eggemoggin Reach? Was that what Virgil Blount was singing to himself? Had the man, indeed, been listening to the radio?

Several secretaries were sitting at desks in the open space. One of them approached Pip. "May I help you?"

"My husband has an appointment with Dr. Davids," said Nana. "We called last night. His name is Hippolyte Dupuy."

"I can tell her, dammit," said Pip. He turned to the woman. "I have an appointment with Dr. Davids. We called last night. My name is Hippolyte Dupuy."

The woman smiled. "I see. I'll go tell Dr. Davids you're here, Mr. Dupuy." She walked across the room toward a closed door.

"He knows me better as *Pip*," Pip called after her.

"Yes, Mr. Dupuy," the woman said over her shoulder, "Pip it is." She knocked on the door and entered.

The radiator at the far wall hissed and spat. Then it clanked loudly.

Nana and Pip jumped simultaneously. "Mary, Mother of God," they cried in unison.

"I'm sorry," said a woman at one of the desks, "We've been asking the janitor to fix that for nearly a month."

Jordi stared at the narrow-board oak floor, biting the inside of his cheeks to stop from smiling.

The first woman emerged from Dr. David's office and said, "The doctor will see you right away, Mr. Dupuy."

Pip started toward the office then stopped abruptly. Nana, Lydie, and Jordi were all following him. "Where the hell're you all going? I'm the one who has the appointment."

"Jordi is coming to tell Evan what happened last night," said Nana. "And I'm coming to make sure that you tell him *everyt'ing*. So you don't expect us to leave Lydie out here all by herself, do you?"

Pip rolled his eyes toward the ceiling and muttered, "Dear God."

Evan Davids' office was small with a built-in desk and cabinets along one wall. The outside wall, where the eaves came low, had two double-hung windows. Davids stood up from his chair and walked toward Pip, his head bowed, until he came to the center of the room where he could at last stand at full height. He extended a hand. "Pip, it's so good to see you." He nodded to the others, acknowledging each in turn. Then he turned back to Pip. "So what's been bothering you? Zabet sounded quite concerned on the phone last night."

"Humph! *She* might as well tell you. She will anyway."

Davids turned to Nana, eyebrows raised. "Zabet?"

Nana was sitting in the chair beside the doctor's desk, her cloche hat, a relic from the twenties, in her lap. "He t'rew himself overboard last night because of weakness. Jordi will tell you. Besides, his cough is getting worse and he wheezes a lot—"

"My cough is just the same," Pip protested.

"No it ain't," said Nana. Gesturing to Lydie and Jordi, she said to Davids, "Ask them."

They each nodded to say that, yes, it was getting worse.

"Do you produce sputum when you cough?"

Pip nodded.

"What color?"

"Ugly," said Nana. "Kinda green or yellow."

Pip glared at her.

"Any blood in the sputum?"

Pip shook his head vigorously. "No."

"Don't believe him," said Nana.

Davids placed a finger on each side of Pip's neck just under the curve of his jawbone. "Any shortness of breath?"

"No," said Pip.

"Pfouf!" cried Nana. "At the top of the stairs we had to wait for him to come back from the dead."

"How much are you smoking these days?" Davids asked Pip.

"One—"

"*Two* packs," answered Nana before Pip could finish. She glared at

Pip with a righteous expression.

"Is the cough persistent?"

"If you mean is he always coughing," said Nana, "the answer's yes." Then she turned to Pip. "Show Evan how you can move your ring."

"What?"

Nana grabbed his hand and vigorously moved his wedding band back and forth on his finger. She looked up at Davids. "It shouldn't be that loose. He's lost too much weight."

Davids smiled. "Considering your cooking, Zabet, that's indeed very serious. How much weight have you lost?" he asked Pip.

"Not much," Pip replied with a growl. "I'm getting ready for the Olympics."

Davids laughed. "Then you'd better stop smoking." He asked Pip to remove his shirt, then used a stethoscope to listen to his lungs. He examined Pip for a long time in silence. Finally, he said, "Well, it could be a number of things..."

"What kind o' things?" asked Nana.

"The coughing, the wheezing, the shortness of breath... they're all consistent with, say, bronchitis...or asthma...Is there any asthma in your family?"

"I don't think so," replied Nana.

"Well, that doesn't rule it out. It could be any number of things."

"What else? What kinda things?" demanded Nana.

"What I'd like to do is order some tests—X-rays, blood tests, that sort of thing—just so we can start ruling things out."

"Not today,' said Pip. "Look at the weather. It's perfect and a storm's forecast for tomorrow. If Jordi and me don't pull traps today, we'll lose a bundle. We should be on the reach already."

"Can you come in tomorrow?"

"Sure, if it's storming like they say it will."

"I'll be waiting for you at eight o'clock, then. Okay?"

Pip nodded as he buttoned up his shirt. "I'll bring you a couple o' lobsters."

Outside, Pip expanded his chest and took in a bellyful of the cold salt air. "Well, Jordi, let's go get us some lobsters," he said with a grand show of enthusiasm.

The day after Pip's visit to the hospital, a nor'easter swept down on them. Although the waters of the reach were relatively protected, Pip saw no point in taking chances and insisted they move the *Zabet & Lydie* to a safer spot up the Benjamin River. Over Nana's vigorous protestations, he promised he would go into Blue Hill for tests as soon as he possibly could.

In the afternoon, Pip and Jordi stopped at Gott's where a crowd of lobstermen, all kept ashore by the nor'easter, sat smoking and drinking coffee. Jordi's eyes were stinging with the smoke that coiled around their heads. Niall Macgrudder came up to them. "Well, how are you two feeling today? All recovered?"

"Better'n ever," said Pip.

"It's good to see you with clothes on."

"We'll be fine," said Jordi as he scanned the crowd. He spotted Virgil Blount.

"Now be careful," Niall said.

"Excuse me," replied Jordi. He slipped past Niall. He moved through the crowd and stood facing Blount who was sitting with his back against the wall and his legs stretched out across a chair. "I want to know if you saw what was happening the other night, if you heard our calls for help."

"What in hell are you talking 'bout?"

Jordi saw the fear etched in Blount's expression. He was both encouraged and disgusted by it. His loathing for the man grew. "I'm talking 'bout how you hauled your ass out of there the minute Pip and me needed help."

"You're full of shit!"

"Then explain how you could be no more than fifty yards off our beam and not see us or hear me scream 'man overboard' at the top of my lungs."

"It was dark. I had the radio on."

Jordi remembered hearing "Peg O' My Heart" in his head the previous day. He hesitated a moment, then said "Bullshit! You're a god-damned liar and a coward!"

Jordi felt a hand on his shoulder. It was Pip. "Leave the man be," he said with quiet authority.

Jordi turned. "But Pip, he left us for dead."

He felt a hard push from behind. He stumbled forward into the arms of Niall Macgrudder, then whirled around to see Blount glaring at him.

"I ain't that kinda man!" Blount said.

"Any man who runs away from the war and lets other men fight for him is that kind of man," Jordi shouted back.

"You son-of-a-bitch," muttered Blount as he moved toward Jordi.

Jordi met the charge with two hands to the man's chest. He shoved with such force that Blount careened backward into a table. He teetered, then slumped to the floor. His eyes, fixed on Jordi, were filled with mal-ice. He picked himself up and edged toward the door. "I ain't gonna fight you; it ain't worth it," he said, opening the door. Then, as he start-ed to step outside, he looked over his shoulder and said in a voice drip-ping with sarcasm, "I ain't that kinda man. Ask your mother."

Jordi lunged toward the door, but Pip stepped in front of him. "That's enough."

"But—"

"I said that's *enough!*"

Jordi took a deep breath, dropped his shoulders, and let the mus-cles in his arms relax. He sat in a chair and picked up the cup of cof-fee Niall had brought him.

In an obvious effort to relieve the tension, Ogden Gower asked, "Say, how's the boat comin'?"

"Just about ready to start the setup and framing," answered Pip, still looking at Jordi. "That is if we can get any goddamned time to work on her. I promised Evan Davids that I'd go and see him tomor-row, which means I'll hafta spend the next few days full time wit' the traps."

But of course, Pip didn't go to see Evan Davids the next day, nor the day after that, or the day after that. Jordi noticed that whenever

Pip seemed to feel a particularly violent fit of coughing coming on, he went into the barn where Nana and the others couldn't hear him. Nonetheless, Nana reminded him every day that he had to go in for tests and every morning, Pip found a reason not to drive into Blue Hill. After a while, Nana gave up in frustration.

A week later, as they were approaching the turn into Rufus Metcalfe's barnyard, they saw an old Ford pickup parked by the side of the road. As they neared, it lurched forward and drove off hurriedly, kicking up a cloud of dust. The tailgate rattled against its latch.

"That's Blount's truck," said Jordi. "What the hell's he doing here?"

"Maybe Rufus'll know," replied Pip.

But Rufus didn't know. "Saw nobody," he said when they asked him. Jordi didn't like it, but he said nothing.

The three men hurried to the barn and pulled the doors open. They looked around for any signs of mischief. "Not'ing," said Pip. "Whatever he was up to, he ain't done no harm."

"Maybe we caught him before he had a chance," said Jordi.

They talked about Virgil Blount a little longer without coming to a conclusion, so they dropped the matter and turned their attention to the boat.

They had built the backbone of the boat on the ground floor of the barn with the bow facing the doors. The built-up keel was supported by hefty blocks of oak and they had used scrap planks of wood to brace the transom, which rose almost six feet off the floor. They were now ready to set up the station molds, like ribs along a spine.

It was spring and by the time they arrived each day to work for an hour or two—Jordi from school, Pip from lobstering—oblongs of late sunlight sprawled through the open west-facing barn door. Outside, the returning swallows sat on a telephone wire facing the sun, the catenary of the wire reminding Pip and Jordi of the graceful sheer that they would be building into the boat. In April, they parked the truck on dry ground some distance from the barn and walked along planks to cross the mud field that was the barnyard. Each day, Rufus Metcalfe greeted them with the same words. Eyes lifted to the sky, he would say, "Fine weather overhead."

Setting up went slowly. They took their time fixing each mold to the backbone, truing it, then bracing it to overhead rafters. When, by midsummer, they had at last finished attaching the molds, the boat looked like the desiccated carcass of some prehistoric animal dried out by the wind and sun. It was now time to tie the station molds together with ribbands—strips of wood that were bent around the molds to provide a form. The frames would then be shaped to the form.

By the fall, when this was finished, the lines of the boat emerged as a gracefully curved lacework of wood.

The newly revealed form was so pleasing that one morning, before going out to Naskeag Point and the *Zabet & Lydie*, Pip and Jordi stopped by the Metcalfe barn to view the boat in the low angle of first light. Pip said every small difference in the angle of light would reveal new subtleties about the lines, and they had never seen the boat in the early morning light. In fact, the double, east-facing back doors to the barn hadn't been open in all the time they had been using it. They even wondered if they would have difficulty with the rusted runners. But when they drove up and parked the truck, they saw a shaft of sunlight shooting through the barn and out into the barnyard. The back doors were already opened. They entered.

As they gazed bow-on at her, the boat seemed luminous, as though the sunlight came from within her. Every line—the upward thrust of the stem, the sweep from stem to stern, the reverse curve of the turn in the bilge, the gentle hyperbola of the sheer line, the fair curve of the run aft from sternpost to transom—every line rhymed with those in Gil's half-model. But in full form, the lines, which before had been merely pleasing to the eye, were now iridescent and breathtakingly beautiful.

"God," Jordi said, "Dad would be proud."

"My dad, too," Pip replied.

"Your father?"

"He's the one who taught me carpentering. His skill is partly in this boat… And his father before him…"

Jordi gave a knowing nod. "I get what you're saying."

"Yup. This was some kinda idea your dad had."

They stood shoulder to shoulder marveling at the form before them.

From the back of the barn came a hoarse voice. "Pretty, ain't she?"

Jordi and Pip were startled. "Rufus, that you?" asked Pip.

"Over heah."

They peered into the darkened corner at the back of the barn where they saw Rufus sitting on a folding chair. Smoke from his pipe shimmered in the low sunlight.

"We came to see what she looked like in the morning light," said Pip.

"Been doin' that myself for a week or so."

All three of them fell silent as they admired the boat. Swallows flitted among the rafters. Outside, several mourning doves called and from some tree, a titmouse added his piccolo notes. Jordi heard Rufus sucking juicily on his pipe. Finally, the man cleared his throat and said, "I know what you're doing."

"What?"

"Said, I know what you're doing."

Neither Pip nor Jordi spoke. Rufus stayed silent, apparently feeling no explanation was necessary. Finally, he spoke again. "Was sitting heah thinking 'bout my sons lost in the Great War." And after a long pause, he added, "And Ada, I s'pose."

Pip and Jordi waited for him to continue but he just sucked on his pipe, biting into the cracked stem. Pip walked over to the stove and felt the coffeepot with the back of his hand. "Coffee's still warm from last night. Guess the fire kept goin'. Want some, Rufus?"

For a moment, Rufus didn't answer. Then he said, "Thought I might be of some help. I'll fetch wood if that's all I can do."

"Some help?"

"Buildin' the boat. Seems right."

Pip laughed. "Aw Jeez, Rufus, there's a hell of a lot more than fetching wood you can do."

"Seems kinda respectful to them that's gone." Rufus rose and shuffled toward them from the darkened corner. He stopped and placed a gnarled hand on the rise of the horn timber which connected the sternpost to the transom. He ran his hand along it, reaching high where the stern soared. "Feels like I'm joining the enemy, though."

Pip gave a bemused laugh. "Why?"

"Lobstermen and yachts. Don't generally get along, all tryin' to use the same water."

"Well, don't worry, Rufus. We'll always be lobstermen first."

Rufus nodded, sucked on his pipe. "Gil have a name for this heah boat?"

"No," replied Pip, "but I do."

"You do?" cried Jordi. He was surprised because they had never discussed a name.

Pip nodded. "*Trobador.*"

"*Trobador*? That's nice. But why *Trobador*?"

"It's the Occitan word for troubadour. They were the singers in the Middle Ages who always sang songs of love—and pain. And if you read the lyrics, they had a lot of pain. But they didn't let life beat them down. Instead, they sang of their suffering and of their love of life. They were doing what they could, if you know what I mean."

Jordi noticed that Pip was twirling the wedding band on his ring finger again. It was too loose.

One stormy day, a delegation of lobstermen arrived at Rufus Metcalfe's barn to see the progress being made on the boat. They arrived in three trucks, laughing and joking and carrying a pot of coffee from Gott's. At first, Jordi was happy to see them. His spirits were high as he described what they were currently doing on *Trobador*. But his mood changed quickly when Virgil Blount showed up.

"Making some good progress," Travis Lathrop said, walking the length of the boat and looking up at the shapely turn of the bilge.

"She's coming along," replied Pip.

"When do you expect to have her in the water?" asked Niall Macgrudder.

Pip shrugged, started to say something, when Virgil Blount said, "Stupid thing for a lobsterman to be doing."

"Aw, Virgil," said Lathrop, "You're just a crab."

Blount sneered. "Next thing you know they'll be *yachting* and lording it over us."

Jordi glared at the man.

"Ain't yachting," said Pip. "It's sailing. That's a whole different thing."

"It's still a stupid idea."

For the rest of the afternoon, Jordi did his best to pretend Blount wasn't there. He couldn't help wondering why his mother couldn't see the man for who he was. His good spirits returned only when Blount finally left.

Late that summer, Pip caught a bad cold and stayed home while Jordi went out by himself on the *Zabet & Lydie*. But it was only midmorning when Jordi stomped into the living room, red-faced and sputtering.

"What the hell's wrong wit' you?" asked Pip, putting down the book he had been reading.

"Blount's cut some of our trap lines."

"Blount? Trap lines? How many?"

"Five. Jesus, I'm going to kill that man, I swear it!"

"Now hold on, Jordi. How do you know it was Blount?"

"Who else would cut our lines? He's still pissed off from the time I accused him of leaving us to drown."

"Coulda been some goddamned motorboat...or a ship."

"What makes you think that?"

"What makes you think it wasn't?"

Jordi shook his head in frustration. "You know damn well he has it in for us, Pip."

Pip nodded. "An' I know damn well you have it in for him because of him an' your ma."

"That has nothing to do with it."

"The hell it don't." Pip rose, placed the book on the lamp stand next to his reading chair and took out a cigarette. "Now I admit the man is capable of doin' anyt'ing 'cause, as they say, he's a zero. But you ain't got no proof and you ain't gonna get none. The only time you'll have proof is if we *see* him do it or if he's stupid enough to brag about it." He lit the cigarette, inhaled, and grimaced. "These taste like shit when you got a cold."

"Then why don't you quit like Evan Davids said?"

Pip ignored the question. "The lines, were they cut cleanly like they would be if they was cut wit' a knife?"

"No, they were made to look like they were cut by a propeller."

"Wasn't there fog this morning?"

"Yes. But, Christ, Pip, the traps are way outside any channel. They *had* to be cut intentionally. They were set in a long curve. Somebody would have had to steer very carefully and exactly on course to get all five of them."

"Maybe," said Pip. "But things have a way of screwin' wit' us just to confuse us. Sometimes I think God has a lousy sense of humor."

"What are you saying?"

"I'm saying there are t'ree t'ings it could be. It could be you're right and it was Blount who cut the lines and if that's what happened, then I understand the *why* of it. But it could also be that God made some-body or somet'ing cut the lines by accident because he likes playing games wit' us and if that's what happened, then I don't understand the *why* of it. Last, it could be just blind, rotten luck and there ain't no *why* of it." He blew a stream of smoke from his tightly pursed lips. "I hope to hell it was Blount, because I don't like t'ings that have no good reason."

"But you don't think it was him."

Pip shook his head slowly. "You ain't got no proof it was Blount."

"Maybe so, but I intend to keep an eye on him anyway."

"Jordi, I gotta tell you. I have a bad feeling. You're as big and strong as he is, now, and a damn sight tougher. You can hurt him real bad; ain't no doubt. But if you do, it's plain as a day wit'out fog that you'll be in trouble wit' the law and if that happens there ain't no way we'll get to finish the boat." Pip paused, then added, "So you control yourself when you see him tonight."

"Tonight?"

"Your ma says she's goin' to the pictures wit' him."

Several days later, Pip exclaimed, "Rufus, you're a genius!" as he examined the chain of pipes which ran from the small farm pond to a cistern outside the barn. Near the pond was an old pump with just enough power to suck water into the cistern.

The previous day, while attempting to steam the first frame for bending against the ribbands, they had discovered they were boiling off water too rapidly to keep the steaming process going. Each frame of unseasoned white oak required at least two hours in the steam box before it was ready for bending, and they found they were hard put to keep the old boiler filled with water, and the fire beneath it fueled with wood. So the next day, as Pip and Jordi tried to come up with a solution while out on the reach, Rufus quietly rigged up his pipe and pump system. When they arrived in the late afternoon, he had just started the pump for the first time and was standing watching the water flow into the cistern.

"Always figured I'd have a use for that pump," said Rufus. It had also been his idea to use an old boiler—propped on two rows of bricks so that a wood fire could be built under it—as a source of steam.

Pip rubbed his hands together. "Okay, now let's give this steaming business another try."

They added wood to the fire Rufus had already lit and soon it was roaring and spitting. Once steam started to flow into the steam box, hissing at the tiny openings in the rag-wrapped pipes, they inserted the first frame. For the next two hours, they kept a steady stream of water moving into the boiler. Rufus and Pip took many breaks, wiping the sweat from their foreheads and the backs of their necks as they smoked and watched Jordi, who worked without rest until the frame was ready to be bent.

Pip and Jordi stood before the steam box and each took a deep breath. Earlier, they had both admitted to being intimidated by this new process, especially because, once removing the plank from the

steam box, they would have to work quickly in order to get the frame
bent before it cooled. Exchanging nods, they opened the small door
and, with gloved hands, slid the frame out of the box. They rushed it
over to the boat's framework and lowered it down to the keel. Quickly,
Pip fit the heel of the frame into the keel slot, and nailed it into place.
Then, working rapidly, they forced the frame against the ribbands
with their feet, bending to the flat of the grain as they pulled the top
in. As soon as it was bent properly against a ribband, they toenailed it
in place. As they progressed from keel to sheerline, they had to twist
the frame so it would fit flush against each successive ribband. Rufus
stood outside the boat's skeleton, armed with c-clamps in case a frame
needed to be clamped temporarily before being nailed into place.

When at last they finished, Pip and Jordi stood looking at each
other with deep satisfaction. "Well, Pip, looks like we did it," said
Jordi.

Pip laughed. "Holy mackerel, that was tough. And remember, we
started amidships because that's where there is less bend." He was
seized with a fit of coughing. He bent over at the waist, supporting
himself with a hand on the newly bent frame. When at last he
straightened, his face was beet red.

"You okay, Pip?" asked Jordi.

Pip nodded, still gasping for breath.

"I got some whiskey I use for that," said Rufus. He turned and
made for the house.

"Pip, you've got to get those tests Evan Davids was talking about."

"Yuh, yuh, I know."

"Will you promise me you'll do it?"

"Yuh, I'll do it."

"When?"

"Goddamn, I said I'll do it."

"Good. I'm glad. When?"

"I don't know."

"Tomorrow, Pip."

Pip looked at Jordi. His eyes were moist from coughing. He nodded. "Will you take me in?"

Jordi smiled. "You bet. And this time we'll really go, not like the last few times when you told Nana you went and everything was okay."

Pip smiled. "It's lucky she didn't ask Evan about it."

"Has it occurred to you maybe part of her is afraid to?"

"Uhmm. You got a point there."

Jordi helped Pip climb out of the boat's skeleton. By the time they stepped down onto the barn floor, Rufus was back with a bottle of whiskey and three water glasses. "Stuff's good for a cough," he said, pouring Pip a generous dollop.

"Hell," Pip said with a laugh, "this stuff's good for anyt'ing that's bothering you."

In the morning, Pip and Jordi drove out of the barnyard and turned right on Route 176 as though they were going to Naskeag Point and another day of lobstering. But at Sedgwick, they turned left onto Route 172, an alternate way to Blue Hill. Pip insisted on not telling Nana and Lydie where they were going because the last thing he wanted was to have Nana tagging along to oversee things the way she usually did. Also, if Evan Davids again told him to do or not do certain things—like give up smoking, for example—he wanted to make his own decision about whether or not to follow the doctor's orders.

"How come it's always low tide when we're here?" Pip asked as they stepped from the truck across the road from the Blue Hill Hospital. The end of the harbor was drained of water and the runnels of the exposed seabed glistened in the morning sunlight.

They started to cross the road but stopped when a Chevrolet tooted at them and pulled into the space next to Pip's truck. It was Evan Davids. "Pip, have you come for those tests?" he called.

"Yuh."

"Well, it's about goddamned time."

Davids walked them into the hospital and ushered them through reception. "Follow me," he said.

They followed him through a long corridor until they came to a door marked "X-RAY." Davids knocked, then opened the door without waiting for an answer. He introduced them to a technician and told the man that he wanted a series of chest X-rays for Pip, *stat.* He talked a little longer with the technician, using medical terminology Jordi didn't understand, then said, "When he's finished, send him up to my office. And I'll want to see the films right away."

An hour later, Jordi was chatting with Davids in his office when Pip appeared on the arm of a nurse. "Here he is," the nurse said to Davids. "He didn't want to take the elevator, but I insisted."

"Good for you," said Davids. Then he turned to Pip. "Here, have a seat. I'll go take a look at the films."

Davids left and returned ten minutes later. He closed the door behind him and looked into Pip's eyes for a moment before saying, "Pip, I want you to go to the hospital in Bangor for more tests. I'll go with you."

"Why, Evan? What's up?"

"I suspect you know damn well what's up. You may have cancer. You knew that, didn't you?"

Pip nodded. "Somet'ing like that."

"Because the coughing's been getting worse, hasn't it?"

Pip nodded but said nothing.

Jordi muttered "Shit!"

Davids put a hand on Pip's shoulder. "Why don't you and Jordi go on to Bangor now? I'll call ahead, then after I take care of a few things here, I'll follow along."

"Today?" said Pip. "Now?"

"It's as good a time as any. My guess is Zabet figures you're out on the reach, so you've got all day. Isn't that right?"

"How'd you know?"

Davids laughed. "She'd be here if she knew what was going on. She's a good woman, you know."

Pip lowered his eyes. "I've known that for fifty years."

"Does she know you haven't been seeing me?"

Pip shook his head. "I lied. Said everything was okay."

"Why?"

"I don't want her to be hurt again. Not after everyt'ing else… Emily…Gil." He raised his eyes to Davids. "How long I got?"

Davids shrugged. "I think it's in the early stages so I suspect you'll be around a while yet, especially knowing you."

Pip gave a nod of satisfaction.

In Bangor, the diagnosis of lung cancer was confirmed. Pip made Jordi swear he would say nothing to Nana or Lydie about it. They drove back home in silence and when they walked into the kitchen, they found Virgil Blount sitting at the table eating a piece of blueberry pie. Lydie was sitting opposite him. As soon as he saw Pip and Jordi, Blount started to rise from his chair but Lydie put a hand on his shoulder, urging him to stay. All four people stared at each other for a moment before Pip finally smiled and said, "Wednesday, eh?"

Lydie nodded. "I can't remember the last time you two decided to come home for pie—the pie that I have baked each and every Wednesday since Jordi was barely old enough to feed himself."

Jordi, his face red with anger, felt the flush deepen. Blount was wearing the sweater Lydie had knit for him. "Jesus, Ma."

Lydie smiled. "Well, you two may not like my pie anymore, being so busy with that damned boat, but Virgil here sure likes it."

Pip said, "Lydie, there ain't no way in hell you can think we don't like your pie. We just have our heads buried in that boat." He pulled out a chair and sat. "Okay if we have some now?"

Lydie sighed. "Sure, why not?" She rose to get some plates and the pie from the top of the stove where it was warming.

Pip gripped Jordi's arm. "Sit down," he said with an authority Jordi hadn't heard since he was a boy.

Jordi sat.

Pip asked, "Where's Nana?"

"Taking her afternoon nap."

"Well, let's not bother her." He looked at Blount. "How's the fishin'?"

"Good catches lately. You?"

Pip nodded. "Same."

Finished with his pie, Blount placed the fork neatly on the edge of his plate and wiped a few crumbs from his mustache. They fell to the table like dandruff. He cleared his throat and asked, "How's the boat coming?"

"We've begun framing. It'll be another year or so at the rate we're going, is my guess."

"I think it's swell what you two are doing," said Blount in a low voice. "I mean, not many people can build a boat like that just for... I don't know...just for the building of it."

Jordi stuffed his mouth with pie so he had an excuse not to say anything, because he had no idea what to say. He had not been prepared for anything but outright hostility from Blount and was confused by this show of civility. He guessed it was all for the benefit of his mother and the thought fueled his hatred of the man.

Blount took out his pack of cigarettes and offered Pip one.

Pip glanced at Jordi and gave a sardonic laugh. "Sure, why the hell not?"

Jordi watched Pip lean forward to accept a light from Blount. The flame from Blount's lighter made Pip's skin shine where it was drawn tightly over his cheekbone.

Another year to finish the boat, Pip had said. Now, as Jordi studied the sharp ridge of Pip's cheekbone, which was accentuated further as he sucked on the cigarette, Jordi wondered if they had that much time left. Wouldn't Pip grow weaker? Would it even be fair to Pip, given his condition, to expect him to work on something that would take so long to complete?

Jordi was sure of one thing: without Pip there would be no point in finishing the boat.

chapter 17

They were removing the last cant frame from the steam box, the one which would complete the framing of *Trobador*, when it slipped from Jordi's hands and caught Pip squarely at the hip. Pip collapsed with a yelp of pain. He lay in a mess of wood shavings, gritting his teeth and holding his hip.

Jordi crouched over him. "What's the matter?" he asked urgently.

"I don't know," Pip said with a gasp. "Mary, Mother of God, it's my hip. It hurts like crazy."

"Broke it, maybe," said Rufus. "Ada did that once."

"How the hell could it be broken? The frame hardly hit it."

"Maybe we'd better call Evan," said Jordi.

"Aw Jeez, the t'ing just brushed me. I'll be okay."

But after ten minutes, there was no easing of the pain. Rufus stayed with Pip while Jordi took the truck and went for help. He returned with Niall Macgrudder and Ogden Gower. Pip was still on the floor, wood shavings in his hair. A wedge of late afternoon sunlight lay across his ashen face, giving him an otherworldly appearance. He held his left hand over his hip. His right hand, stretched out to the side, clutched a glass of whiskey with a straw in it. Rufus leaned against a sawhorse sipping from his own glass. When the three men entered the barn, Rufus said, by way of greeting, "Think whiskey's helped with the pain. Eyuh."

After discussing what to do, they slid the wide lofting board, on which was drawn the body plan of *Trobador*, under Pip and carried him to the truck. Carefully, they slid the board onto the flatbed, and Niall and Ogden climbed up to sit beside Pip, who still clutched his glass of whiskey. Rufus struggled into the cab beside Jordi, who eased the truck out of the barnyard and onto the road.

Jordi drove slowly, trying not to jostle Pip, so it took more than half an hour to reach Blue Hill and the hospital. Rufus went into the hospital and returned with three young orderlies. They carried Pip on the lofting board, like pallbearers, in through the main door of the hospital, down a long corridor and into a vacant examining room.

Moments later, Evan Davids arrived. He looked at Pip, smiled, and took the glass of whiskey from his hand. He sniffed it. "Some of ol' Chrétien's stuff. I thought that was long gone."

"Got a couple bottles left," said Rufus. "Slowed down my drinking after Ada died."

"Good for you, Rufus. You'll live longer."

"Can't be much longer. Leastwise, I hope not. Come by. I'll crack a bottle for you."

"Well now, thanks. I'll do that." Davids cocked his head and examined the board under Pip. "That the boat you're building?" he asked Jordi.

Jordi nodded. "We're naming her *Trobador.*"

"Aw Jeez, Evan," moaned Pip. "Can you be social later? This hurts like hell!"

"I figured it hurt some if you're drinking whiskey through a straw. How many times have I told you, morphine and whiskey don't mix?" He cautiously probed Pip's pelvis. He looked up at Jordi. "How many times have you heard me tell him?"

Jordi shrugged. "Lots."

Davids prodded more. Pip winced.

The doctor nodded gravely. "Well, Pip, I'd say you fractured your pelvis."

"But the damn frame hardly hit me!"

Davids took a deep breath, looked at the others. "That's what has me concerned. We need to do some tests."

"What for, Evan?" asked Jordi, afraid he already knew the answer.

Davids sighed. "Now you know me, I don't pull punches and none of you guys believes in that sort of thing anyway. So I'll tell you straight. I think it's spread. I've almost been expecting this. Lung can-cer often metastasizes—spreads—to the bones. Makes the bones frag-ile so they fracture easily."

After giving Pip some morphine, Davids arranged for X-rays to be taken. An hour later, the X-rays confirmed Davids' diagnosis.

As Pip and Jordi left the hospital, Davids said, "You can no longer hide this from your wife, you know. Do you want me to tell her?"

"No," replied Pip. "No, I'll tell her."

Pip chose the following Sunday, after they returned from Mass, to break the news to Nana and Lydie. While they sat in the living room digesting the pot roast Nana had prepared, he said, "Saw Evan Davids the other day."

Jordi glanced over the newspaper at Pip. Chrétien put down the book he was reading.

"How is he?" asked Nana.

"Oh, fine, I guess."

"Has he found a woman yet? A good-looking man like him."

"Said I'm sick."

"Well, I hope he told you to quit smoking. Did he give you some medicine?" Almost in the same breath, she said, "Now I've always thought the Taylor woman would be good for him. She's about his age. A widower. Pretty."

"It's cancer, Zabet."

Lydie's knitting needles stopped.

Nana sucked in her breath. She turned to Lydie. "Don't you think so? The Taylor woman?"

"Nana—" said Lydie.

"Millie is her name, isn't it?"

"It's lung cancer, Zabet, and that ain't good."

"—or is it Mindy?"

Lydie rose. She went to place a hand on Nana's shoulder.

Nana looked up at her. "You know Arthur Blaire on the church committee? He had cancer then it went away entirely. It's prayer that did it." She paused for a long time then said, "I'm making tea. Who wants some?" Without waiting for an answer she struggled up from her armchair and went into the kitchen.

Lydie turned to Pip. "Should I go to her?"

Pip shook his head. "Give her a little time by herself. When Emily died—"

Lydie rushed across the room, threw her arms around Pip. "Oh, Pip."

Jordi went to stand by the kitchen door. He watched Nana fill the tea kettle and put it on the stove. Then she reached for the photograph of Emily. Her arms shook.

Jordi heard her say, "My sweet Em, do you know Saint Peregrine? Please talk to him. Tell him I will pray to him every day."

Jordi went back to the living room. "Who's Saint Peregrine?" he asked.

"Patron saint of cancer victims," replied Pip.

With Pip's health declining, work slowed to a crawl on *Trobador*. Evan Davids insisted Pip give up lobstering, arguing that with all the hauling and the bouncing around in the waves, the risk of more fractures was too great. Therefore, Jordi had to do the work of two men and that left little time at the end of the day to work on *Trobador*. Besides, Jordi was reluctant to continue working on the boat alone for fear that it would be an admission of some sort and would accelerate Pip's illness. He was afraid that once they took that step, Pip would never again work on the boat. But Pip said, "To hell wit' what Davids says. When I'm feeling better, we'll get back to work."

They were ready to begin the planking of the hull by that fall.

Pip said, "This is where we put skin on the skeleton. After this, *Trobador* will really come to life."

After drawing up a layout of planking butts to ensure strength, they laid out the width and the run of the planking seams until it was, as Ogden Gower liked to say, "eye-pleasing" from every angle. They decided to use the method called carvel planking, in which planks were cut to fit tightly on the inside of the hull but beveled on the outside to leave a gap, called the out-gauge, which would later be stuffed with cotton caulking to make the hull watertight. They started with the sheer strake, locking in that most beautiful line, the one that had so inspired Gil when he had seen *Mistral* come out of the fog so long ago, and which he had carefully carved into his half-model. Next, they fitted the garboard strake which rabetted into the keel, followed by the two adjoining broad strakes. After that, they alternated, fitting a strake in under the sheer, then one above the broads. Their plan was to work their way toward the turn of the bilge and the last strake, appropriately called the shutter.

It was then that Jordi came up with an idea. One day he said to Pip, "You know, I was reading through Dad's diary the other day and I realized the diary sort of represents his soul, if you know what I mean."

"I suppose you could say that," replied Pip.

"It's as though all his suffering and all his goodness during that time is in the diary and that's why he had to write it."

"What are you getting at?" Pip asked with a tender smile.

"I don't think it belongs hidden away in that old rollup desk. It belongs here, aboard *Trobador*."

"Aboard *Trobador*?"

"Yes. But not just aboard her, *built into* her."

Pip gazed at him a moment, smiled, and said, "You want to build your dad's soul into the boat?"

"Something like that."

Pip smiled. "Sounds like a great idea to me."

"We could wrap it in some oilskin and place it in the space between the inboard and the outboard planking."

So one morning, just as the rising sun struck *Trobador* and before Rufus showed up, they held a private ceremony. It consisted of nothing more than a nip of whiskey each, a toast to Gil, and Jordi saying, "Welcome home, Dad" before they wrapped the diary in oilskin and put it in the space beside the port quarter berth, the traditional captain's berth.

Jordi said, "Now, when we finish the interior woodwork, the diary will be completely built in and we'll be the only ones who know it's there."

But as Jordi was helping Pip climb down from the cockpit, they were startled by Rufus' scratchy voice. "Heard what you said 'bout putting Gil's diary in the boat—"

"Rufus! We didn't know you were there," said Jordi.

"—It's a good thing you're doin'."

Jordi saw Rufus' soft eyes. He placed his hand on the man's shoulder and said, "Thanks, Rufus. But listen, please don't tell anybody about this, okay?"

"Over my dead body, I would."

By Christmas, they still had several strakes left to go on both the starboard and port sides. About this time Pip did a curious thing. Though the cockpit wasn't completed and they were far from ready to do the final cabinetry work, Pip insisted on building the cubby for deck gear in the cockpit. Moreover, he was adamant that he, and only he, do that work. After several days he was finished and invited Jordi to inspect it. Jordi found that Pip had fitted the cubby with a small door and a lock.

"Well, that's pretty fancy, Pip," Jordi said. "Why a door and a lock?"

Pip shrugged. "Good place to keep things dry and safe."

Pip's condition was worsening and Jordi frequently drove him into Blue Hill for checkups where Evan Davids would marvel at Pip's determination. "Most people wouldn't have the strength or the guts to hang in as long as you have," he said.

"When a storm's coming, it's a good idea to get yourself some sea room," Pip answered. "A man needs time for that."

But Pip was not beating the cancer; he was simply declining slower than Evan Davids anticipated. Though he kept a brave face, the morphine he was taking more and more frequently suggested his pain was growing.

Nana frequently had Jordi drive her to St. Mary's where she lit candles and prayed to St. Peregrine.

Pip had days when he was relatively pain-free, days when he was able to do a little work on the boat. On one of these days, Jordi had just returned to the barn from getting Pip a pack of cigarettes when he heard a distinctive click. It was the latch on the deck cubby Pip had built in the cockpit.

"What are you doing up there, Pip?" Jordi called.

"Oh, not'ing," Pip replied.

Jordi shrugged. Pip had tested the cubby door several times the day he finished it. "By the way, don't forget to give me the key so I can have it copied," Jordi said.

"Sure," Pip replied. "Later. You got my cigarettes?"

Jordi climbed the ladder, handed Pip the pack of cigarettes, and went back to his own work.

Despite his occasional good days, Pip had longer and longer periods when he couldn't leave the house and when the pain could only be managed with heavy doses of morphine.

During one of these bad periods, Nana asked Father Battisti to come and have supper with them. There had been a small row when Lydie said she would not be home because she was going to the picture show with Virgil Blount, but eventually Nana decided to go ahead with the supper anyway. She prepared for the visit by placing votive candles around the kitchen. The combination of melting wax and pork pie created a strange, almost blasphemous, mix of scents.

After finishing his pie, Father Battisti sat back in his chair, causing it to creak, and said, "Zabet, that was delicious. It's amazing how you go on, considering everything that's happened."

Pip, his mouth still full from a last bite of pie, smiled. A crumb bounced around on his lips as he said, "Pardon me, Father, but what choice does she have? I mean what choice do any of us have?"

"Pip, you shouldn't talk like that," said Nana. She gestured for Father Battisti to take another piece of pie.

Father Battisti waved his hand at both the pie and Nana's reproach. "No, no, Zabet. He's quite right. It's a difficult world and we must accept what is handed to us by God. But we can accept it with grace or with bitterness. You, Zabet, have shown wonderful grace, that's all I meant to say." He paused, then added, "You…all of you…have suffered so much…"

"Why?" asked Pip.

Jordi saw from the crinkles around Pip's eyes that he asked not out of a sense of anger but out of a sense of…what?…mischief? A desire to force an entertaining discussion?

Father Battisti shrugged his shoulders. "We can't know God's will. We can only accept it."

"But is it a good question?" asked Pip.

"What?"

"*Why*? Is that a good question?"

Father Battisti shifted in his chair. He leaned forward and rested his forearms on the table, forming a steeple with the fingers of his hands. "Yes, yes…it's a very good question. It's the question Job asked. Why *do* good people suffer? It's an eternal question for which, I'm afraid, there are no easy answers. That's why we turn to faith… and a love of God and His mysterious ways."

"Do you think it's a mistake to look for an answer?"

"No, no. We should always try for understanding."

"I do."

"I don't follow."

"I think it's a mistake."

"But—"

"I think there ain't no meaning to be found, so why look for it? T'ings happen and there ain't no moral reason why."

"But everything in life has a meaning. We only have to try to discover God's purpose through prayer."

Pip winced. He placed a hand on his right hip and held his breath for a moment.

"Pip, do you want me to get your pills?" Jordi asked.

Pip shook his head. "No, Jordi, I'll be alright." He turned back to Father Battisti. "It seems to me the real question is not why good people suffer, but how do good people live well in a suffering world?"

"Well, that seems like a pessimistic view, Pip," said the priest. "I would rather say—"

"Just like the question is not how to avoid dying, but how to make a good death."

"Pip, *Jésus, Marie, et Josef,* what a t'ing to say," cried Nana. Then she put a hand to her mouth and said, "Oh, forgive me, Father."

"That's quite all right, Zabet. I understand." Father Battisti turned to Pip. "Of course, what you say is true. We all die. What is important is to die in a state of grace. That's why we have confession and why Extreme Unction is a sacrament of the Church."

"And it's also why we have a sense of dignity."

Jordi saw Nana close her eyes momentarily then open them again to stare at the photographs of Emily and Gil. She took a deep, shuddering breath, and said, "Well, Father Battisti, Lydie ain't here tonight, but she made one of her famous blueberry pies. Would you like a piece?"

Later that night, Jordi and Pip were alone on the porch. Pip lit a cigarette, one of the half-dozen a day he now allowed himself, and looked up at the sky. "Orion and the Pleiades are pretty clear tonight."

"I see Orion," said Jordi, "but I always have trouble finding the Pleiades."

"See the line of Orion's belt? Just extend it west about ten times its length."

Jordi studied the sky for a few moments. "Okay…yuh…I got it."

"Now look to the east. Do you see Arcturus in the constellation Boötes?"

"I see the Little Dipper…"

"More to the east and a little closer to the horizon."

After a moment, Jordi said, "Yuh, got it."

Pip took a long drag on his cigarette, studied the glowing end of the butt. "These taste too goddamned good. How's a man supposed to quit?" Holding it carefully so as not to burn his fingers, he took a final drag then stubbed it out in a Chase & Sanborn can on the little whicker table. "In Job, it says 'He shaket' the earth out of her place, and her pillars tremble. He commands the sun not to rise and it don't. He spreads out the heavens and He walks on the waves of the sea. And He makes Arcturus, Orion, and the Pleiades and the chambers of the sout'.'... Somet'ing like that."

"You said that before," said Jordi with a chuckle. "I didn't know you knew the Bible. Catholics aren't supposed to know the Bible. That's a Protestant thing."

"I read what I want. I know the Book of Job."

Jordi didn't answer.

"I been reading it off an' on ever since the Hurricane of '38. Even before. When little Emily died, I guess. I read it a bunch of times after your dad died."

Jordi leaned back and stared at the breathtaking spread of sky, the immense compass of stars. A haze ringed the gibbous moon, making it look more swollen than usual, but otherwise the heavens were clear and cold. An easy breeze stirred in the tops of the spruce. In the distant woods a fox barked.

"Looking up at the sky makes me feel small sometimes," Jordi said.

"Only sometimes?" asked Pip with a laugh. "I'll tell you what I think. Sometimes I think God made the stars just to remind us how big t'ings are and scare the crap out of us."

Jordi laughed. For a long while they sat in silence. Again, a fox barked somewhere in the distance, probably the same fox. Several seagulls flew over the barn with cries of "kree...kree." Their shadows disappeared into the darkness.

Finally, Pip said, "But there's somet'ing else that I think about the stars."

"What's that?"

"One time, I went to the library every night for a whole week to read *Romeo and Juliet* by that Shakespeare, and there's somet'ing Juliet says that was so beautiful I memorized it. She said, 'When he shall die, take him and cut him out in little stars, and he will make the face of heaven so fine that all the world will be in love wit' night.' Well, you know them chambers of the sout' from Job I talked about earlier? I sometimes think that's where all the people who have died are, where their souls are. They are stars in the chambers of the sout'—your dad, Emily, Rufus Metcalfe's boys, Ada Metcalfe, old Peanut—all of them."

Jordi looked back up at the star-strewn sky. He found Orion's belt and used it to locate the Pleiades.

"My father and mother, too," Pip said after a pause. "And my grandparents..." His eyes had a faraway look.

Both he and Jordi fell silent for a long time, looking up at the vast, mind-numbing splay of stars. Finally, Pip said, "Get me another cigarette from my pack, Jordi, okay?"

"Didn't you just have your one after-supper cigarette?"

Pip narrowed his eyes and glared at Jordi. "If I decide to have another cigarette, it's my choice. A man don't have many choices."

Jordi got the cigarette and handed it to Pip. He took the Zippo from Pip's hand, flicked it open, and lit the cigarette. Pip inhaled deeply, exhaled, and said, "You know, Jordi, it's real important that we finish *Trobador*."

"I know, Pip." Jordi said this only halfheartedly, wondering how it would be possible to finish the boat if Pip's condition worsened much more, as Evan Davids said it would.

"Aw Jeez, Jordi. Listen to me! I mean it! It's somet'ing we gotta do. I don't think I can explain why exactly, but it seems like we made a kind of promise to your dad, you and me, an' we gotta follow t'rough on it."

"But what if...?"

"What if I get sicker an' can't work on the boat?"

Jordi nodded.

"First of all, I'm gonna work on it as long as I can stand on my two feet. Second, when I ain't able to stand up no more, then stick me under the boat and I'll work lying down. Then when I can't even do that no more, you'll have to go on wit'out me."

"But Pip, I don't have your skill. Without you there, I wouldn't know what to do."

Pip blew out a stream of smoke. "You're a hell of a lot better than you think you are, that's for sure. Also, you can ask me questions at the end of every day."

Jordi nodded tentatively. "Maybe it'll work."

"Damn right, it'll work. *Trobador* will be built!"

But Jordi could not shake the feeling that this was just bravado on Pip's part.

Jordi sat alone in the Metcalfe barn. The first tentative probes of pink sunlight were coming through the east-facing doors. *Trobador* rested before him like a patient on an examining table. There were great gaps in her skin where her ribs showed through, where the strakes leading up from the keel had yet to meet the strakes coming down from the sheerline. She looked like a creature decomposing. He half expected that when he returned the next day or the next year, he would find more strakes missing the way the skin of a dead animal disintegrates leaving only the bony carcass.

He wondered if he was now seeing *Trobador* as complete as she would ever be. He ached to see her in the water, to feel her come alive to the wind, but he couldn't see how it would be possible without Pip. Evan Davids told him Pip probably didn't have much more than a few months or so, and Jordi had the impression even that was optimistic. It was not enough time for Jordi to finish *Trobador* single-handedly. Even if he could, would Pip, by that time, be too weak to go out on her, even for a short sail on the reach? Just one sail?

He heard a crunch of footsteps in the gravel of the barnyard. "Is that you, Rufus?" he called. When he arrived that morning, he noticed that Rufus' Studebaker was not in its usual place and he had assumed Rufus went into Brooklin to have coffee at Gott's before the lobstermen went out to their traps.

The footsteps stopped, but there was no answer.

Jordi rose and walked to the open doors. "Rufus?"

He heard footsteps again, and then they receded rapidly. He stepped out into the barnyard and peered toward the road. A figure was running, hunched over, onto Route 175. The man ran down the road and around a bend. Then Jordi heard a truck start up, its tires spinning in the dirt. With the rattle of a loose tailgate, it drove off.

He recognized the sound of that tailgate. It was Virgil Blount's truck. Jordi stared at the dust cloud left by the truck for a long while before going back to work.

An hour later, he heard the crunch of tires on the packed dirt of the barnyard. He went to the door. If it was Blount, he was determined to confront the man. But there was no sign of Blount's truck. Instead he saw Rufus easing his Studebaker into the spot near the rosebushes which had grown wild since Ada Metcalfe died. Behind the Studebaker was Ogden Gower's new Chevrolet truck. Niall Macgrudder stepped down from the passenger side and, along with Ogden and Rufus, came toward the barn.

"Jordi," said Niall with a nod.

"Morning, Niall," replied Jordi. "Ogden, Rufus."

"How's Pip?" asked Ogden. Instead of looking directly at Jordi, he peered past him and gazed at *Trobador,* which sat radiant in the morning light.

"Better some days than others. Today's not a good day."

"Is he able to work on her?" asked Niall, nodding toward *Trobador.*

Jordi shrugged. "Some days. Not many, though."

They ambled into the barn. Ogden completed a circuit of *Trobador* and, running his hand along the graceful curves, said, "Lot of work needs doin'."

"I don't think it'll ever happen," said Jordi.

Niall, Ogden, and Rufus exchanged quick glances. Niall, running a hand through his white beard, turned to Jordi. "You crazy? Can't leave a boat like this unbuilt. We come to help."

"Went over to Gott's an' told them they was needed," said Rufus.

Jordi stared open-mouthed at the three men. "Well...sure...*sure.* That's swell."

"Just like you an' Pip, we'll come over at the end of the day. Work for a few hours."

"And Chrétien's coming, too," added Rufus with a chuckle. "Said he'd bring some whiskey for when the work day's done."

Niall looked down at the floor, then up at Jordi. "How long we got?"

"Who knows? Dr. Davids is surprised he's lasted this long, said it's only because of Pip's stubbornness."

"Eyuh, he's stubborn all right," said Niall with a nervous laugh.

Ogden touched the stem of *Trobador*. "Call me Billy-be-damned, but this heah boat'll be finished before Pip's finished." He turned to Rufus, "Let's fire up the steam box. Get the whole thing started with a full day's work."

Niall added, "I can work till the boys come in with their catches."

After weeks of hard work—Niall and Chrétien working on the starboard side and Ogden and Jordi working on the port side—they were finally ready to fit the shutters. Since Pip was in one of his good periods, Jordi had packed him into the truck, placed a lap robe over him, and driven him to the Metcalfe barn. He sat in an easy chair they had brought out from Rufus' house and placed alongside the one Rufus used. Pip joked with them as they steamed the final strakes and bent them to the hull. When they finished, Chrétien opened a special bottle of single malt whiskey, refusing to answer their questions about where he got it.

"Ribs are completely covered by skin now," said Ogden.

"Reason to celebrate," Niall replied.

Chrétien poured some *Talisker* into Pip's glass. "You on your pain pills right now?" he asked. "You know what Evan said 'bout mixin' 'skee an medicine."

"Not today. Besides, I figured out that a little 'skee helps the effect of the morphine, so that shows you how much Evan knows."

They drank and chatted until they heard a truck stop out on the road. Ogden stuck his head out the barn door to see who it was. "It's that damned Virgil Blount," he said. "Stopped, then took off again. Guess he saw the trucks an' figured we was all heah."

"Damn!" said Jordi, his jaw muscles fluttering in anger. "That jerk. He's been here at least twice."

"What's he want, do you s'pose?" asked Niall.

"Wants to wreck this heah boat," said Rufus. "That's what he wants."

"Why would he want to do that?" asked Ogden.

"'Cause he's a zero, that's why," replied Jordi. "I swear, if he lays one hand on *Trobador*, I'll kill him."

Niall Macgrudder shook his head. "What in hell do the women see in that man, anyhow?"

Jordi felt another flash of anger, but he said nothing.

Niall, apparently realizing what he had said, murmured, "Sorry" and looked sheepishly at the floor.

"Forget it," replied Jordi. "Let's talk about what we need to do next on the boat."

Holding tall water glasses half-filled with *Talisker*, they gathered around the plan for the deck framing, which Jordi had spread out on the floor in front of Pip.

"Shouldn't take too long to fit the clamps and shelves," said Ogden, referring to the stiffening members along the deck line to which the deck beams would be bolted. "We can spring the shelves without the need for scarph joints."

"The breasthook will be no problem," said Niall. "Make it from the crook of a piece of hackmatack. But I think Ogden should do the quarter knees. They ain't so easy with a curved transom like this."

"As far as the deck beams themselves are concerned," said Jordi, "what do you guys think of using oak most of the way as we planned, but changing over to spruce in the ends? Since spruce is lighter, won't that help to dampen any tendency to hobby-horse in a seaway?"

They all looked at each other and nodded.

"Sounds good to me," said Ogden with a smile.

"Worthy of another drink," said Chrétien, brandishing the bottle. He went around and refilled every glass.

They talked about the half-beams and headers around the deck openings, the fastening methods, the use of tie rods and lodging knees, and the mast partners until they noticed they were starting to slur their words. Jordi looked over to Pip to say it was time to go, but both Pip and Rufus were slumped in their easy chairs fast asleep. The others laughed, then agreed that after spending a few days taking care of their own businesses, they would tackle the deck framing full time and try to push it through as rapidly as possible.

"My wife can take care of the shack for a while," said Niall. "She knows how to figure the right prices for lobster."

Ogden nodded. "An' my customers can wait. They ain't pressed for time like Pip."

Niall spoke for all of them when he looked at Pip, whose bony chin rested on his chest, and said, "I'll be goldanged if we don't finish this boat in time for him to go for a little sail."

chapter 18

"The last time you were at the barn," Jordi said to Pip as they sat on the porch, "we were just about to finish the deck framing. Well, yesterday we finished it and tomorrow Ogden is going to install the sheer plank. After that, it's just a matter of working our way inboard until we get to the king plank."

Pip nodded and smiled from the depths of the oversized navy pea coat that enveloped him. "Sounds like you're making good progress." Jordi was still not used to the new weakness in Pip's voice.

"Another few weeks and we'll have the decking done. Then all that's left is the interior and exterior joiner work and the rigging."

Pip chuckled. "Is that all?"

"Okay, we've still got a ways to go, but we're moving pretty fast."

"How 'bout the sails?"

"Uncle Chrétien's taking care of that. He's got a sail maker down in Northeast Harbor. My guess is we'll be ready to sail first good day in the spring."

"And an auxiliary engine?"

"Ogden's letting us have an old Atomic Four he took from a boat he salvaged last year. It's not much, but it'll get us back when the wind craps out and it'll keep the batteries charged up enough for running lights." Jordi paused, then he asked, "Are you warm enough, Pip?"

Pip nodded. "Had to get out o' the house. Too stuffy. Nana made me promise to stay out no more than a half hour, but you and me know she don't wear no watch an' the kitchen clock is stopped." He winked. Then he scanned the sky. "Besides, I'd better take the chance now. Looks like snow. I think we're in for a good nor'easter. Wind's been backing."

Jordi looked at the moon. It was full with a bruised halo around it. The entire southern sky was barren of stars indicating a thick cloud layer was moving in. Though the earth in the barnyard had been frozen solid for almost a month, little snow covered the ground and everybody said they were due for a whopper. Perhaps, Jordi thought, this was it. "I think you're right, Pip. I hope it's enough to keep me from going out on the water but not so much that I can't get to Rufus' barn."

Pip laughed—a dry, rasping laugh that ended in a cough. When he recovered his breath, he asked, "Any more signs of Blount at the barn?"

"No, but I promise if I ever catch him messing with *Trobador*, I'll beat him to a pulp."

"Yuh, I think you would. Just be careful."

Nana appeared on the porch. She ran her fingers through Pip's hair, making it neater. "Time to come in, Pip," she said.

"A little longer," he pleaded.

"It's cold out here. I ain't got no coat on. If you want me and Jordi to help you, it's now you gotta come in. Besides, supper's 'bout ready. It'll be on the table as soon as Lydie gets home."

Wearily, Pip rose from his chair. Jordi supported him on one side while Nana supported him on the other. The kitchen glowed with the heat of a coal fire. No one spoke of Lydie's absence because she had gone out with Virgil Blount, and they all knew that if anyone said something, tempers would flare. It had happened a dozen times before.

They had just helped Pip into his chair at the kitchen table when they heard a truck pull into the barnyard. Nana pulled the curtain back and peered out the window. "Thank God. It's Lydie."

They heard the sounds of voices in the barnyard, but they were too low to make out. Then the truck started up and pulled away. A moment later, Lydie's soft footfalls came up the porch steps. They sounded unsteady. She burst through the door. "Well, isn't this nice. Everybody's waiting for me." She started forward, then stumbled back against the door. "Whoops!" She giggled.

"*Jésus, Marie, et Josef.*" said Nana. "You been drinking again?"

Lydie feigned a coquettish smile. "You can tell?"

"Shit, Ma," said Jordi.

Lydie's expression changed instantly. She glared at Jordi. "Don't you 'shit, Ma,' me," she snapped. "I've got the right to go out just as much as anybody around here. How often are *you* here compared to the time you spend at the Metcalfe barn? Hmm? Tell me!"

"I'm not talking about you being out, Ma."

"Hell you aren't! Your problem is Virgil and the fact that I have a few drinks when I'm out with him. Well, what of it? Pip drinks. Chrétien drinks. I have a right to try to forget. Am I supposed to be some kinda saint like Nana?" She put her hand to her mouth. "Oh, Nana, I'm sorry. I didn't mean…"

"Aw Jeez, what's the problem?" asked Pip. "She *is* a saint to put up wit' all of us." He beckoned to Nana who stood beside him so he could put an arm around her waist. He fiddled with the knot of her apron, gazed up at her. "You *are* a saint, you know, Zabet."

She brushed his hair away from his brow and smiled. Her eyes were moist. She nodded. "Wit' all of you, I hafta be."

"There, see?" laughed Pip. "Now let's all sit down an' have a nice supper together, okay?" He looked from Lydie to Jordi and back to Lydie again. "Okay, Lydie?"

Lydie's expression softened. She nodded, shucked off her coat, hung it on its peg, and pulled up a chair.

Later that night, under an immense sky overspread with clouds that blotted out even the moon, Pip spoke from deep within the cave of his hooded coat. "You have to give her some room, Jordi. If she drinks too much and goes out wit' Blount just to forget things, well that's partly our fault."

The first flakes of snow fell. They flared fat and white in the warm light spilling from the kitchen window before blending softly into the darkness.

"Our fault?"

Pip nodded. In the darkness, Jordi saw only the movement of Pip's hood, which was so large his head disappeared inside it. The only sign of his presence was the red glow of his cigarette. "Yuh. All this time we spent together building *Trobador*—it was unfair to your ma. Maybe it was our way of dealing wit' what happened to your dad, but it was selfish. She's the kind of woman who needs to take care of someone, especially a man—see that he's got clothes to keep him warm, make sure he's well fed…She's like Nana in a lot of ways." He paused and drew on his cigarette. "We was hurtin' real bad, you an' me, when Gil…when your dad…was killed. We kinda took to each other. I guess we kinda let them—Nana and your ma—deal wit' their own pain by themselves. See what I mean?"

"I guess."

"No wonder they resent *Trobador*. She's taken us away from them."

Jordi didn't answer.

"I ain't saying it's wrong, our building your dad's boat. I'm just saying we ain't left enough room for Nana and your ma." He gave a chuckle. "I guess we didn't realize that you and me, *we* were kinda *their* boat, their *Trobador*."

They sat in silence watching the thickening snowflakes pass through the wedge of kitchen light, then disappear again.

From deep within his muffling hood, Pip muttered, "You'd think a man would learn. Same t'ing happened between me and your dad after Emily died. We kinda let Nana suffer on her own. You'd think a man would learn."

The following day, they got a frantic call from Rufus Metcalfe. "The goldang barn's on fire!" he shouted into the phone. "Come quick."

"Jesus, Rufus," cried Jordi. "Call the Fire Department!"

"Already have. They're comin'."

Jordi hung up the phone and told Pip what was happening as he threw on his coat. "I'm going right over there. Jesus! *Trobador!*"

"I'm going wit' you."

"Pip, you're not well enough."

"I'm going wit' you, goddamnit."

"All right, all right." Jordi helped Pip into his coat and guided him to the truck. Then Jordi hopped in behind the wheel and tore off toward Sedgwick.

By the time they arrived, several fire trucks were pulled up to the east side of the barn. Thin tendrils of smoke rose from the northeastern corner, but otherwise there was no sign of fire.

Rufus Metcalfe hobbled over to meet them. His face was covered with soot. "Fire's out," he said breathlessly. "Ain't touched *Trobador*."

One of the firemen came up to them. "You shoud'a seen it. When we pull up to the place this old coot is inside the goldang barn throwin' buckets of water on the boat. We had to pull him outa theah."

When it was clear there was no longer any threat of fire, Jordi went into the barn to check on *Trobador*. Just as Rufus said, she appeared completely untouched. But when he climbed the ladder into the cockpit he saw something that shocked him. Many of the newly installed inboard planks had been pried out. Most of the boards were split and splintered.

Then he noticed something that made him want to cry. His father's diary had been behind one of the torn-out planks and was now missing.

He climbed down from *Trobador*, his face red with fury. He told Pip and Rufus what he found, adding, "There's only one person who would do this."

"Eyuh," said Rufus.

"This time, he gone too far," said Jordi. "I'm going over to his place and we're going to have it out once and for all."

"No, you ain't" said Pip.

"What?"

"If you go over there now, the way you're feelin' you'll kill the man. Hell, if I had the strength *I'd* kill him. We're gonna calmly go to the police and let them come wit' us. I don't need you getting into more trouble than you can handle."

Half an hour later, they pulled up to Virgil Blount's place behind a police cruiser.

Of course, Blount denied having anything to do with the fire or the vandalizing of *Trobador*. But when Officer Pattison went out to his cruiser to get a notepad, Blount nervously edged out onto his porch to stay in full view of the policeman.

"If I catch you anywhere near that barn," said Jordi in a low voice, "I'll kill you. You understand me? And I want my father's diary back."

"I ain't got your father's diary."

"The hell you don't."

Officer Pattison returned to the porch. "I want you guys to stop your arguin'." He turned to Pip and Jordi. "If Virgil heah says he did-n't do nothin' and you ain't got proof of it, then that's all there is to it." He turned to Blount. "But if I was you, Virgil, I'd stay away from these folks. You've caused them enough trouble to last a lifetime." He didn't need to mention Blount's relationship with Lydie for everyone to catch his meaning. "Now you two fellahs go on home," he said to Pip and Jordi. "I'll just stay behind a while to make sure there ain't no trouble."

As they drove home, Jordi said to Pip, "You know goddamned well Blount has the diary."

"Ain't no question about it."

"So what are we gonna do about it?"

"Well if he reads it…and there ain't no question he will," said Pip, "then he's gonna think he has somet'ing to bring your dad down a peg or two in the eyes of your ma."

"The bastard."

"You'll get no argument from me there," said Pip. "But I wouldn't worry about that too much."

"Why?"

"Because he's smart enough to know it'd backfire. Lydie'd drop him like the pile of crap he is."

"Why keep the diary, then?"

"I don't know. Maybe just in case…"

"So what do we do?" asked Jordi.

"Nothing," replied Pip. "I don't think he'll be causing us any more trouble unless we stir him up. And that diary is kinda like his insurance that we won't, I guess."

"But we can't simply let him get away with it. That's Dad's diary."

"Without proof, we can't go busting in on him to get it," Pip replied. "Maybe when t'ings settle down we can reason wit' him or somet'ing."

Jordi cursed. "It makes me sick."

"Me, too," replied Pip. "In fact there's only one t'ing that would make me sicker. That's for Nana to start believing her son was a murderer."

Jordi woke two days later to find almost two feet of snow in the barnyard. The truck was buried, molded by the wind into a soft mound of curves. Nothing marred the virgin, velvet expanse of snow glittering in the morning light, not even animal tracks. Across the field, the spruce sagged under snow-laden branches. Occasionally, the wind would shake lose a powdery fall from the higher limbs. Drifts of snow had crawled high up the kitchen windows, even reaching the bottom edge of Nana's fading gold star.

When Jordi came into the kitchen, he found Nana fussing with the stove. The cast-iron door was open and she was vigorously prodding the coals. The flesh on her upper arms shook like jelly. "*Jésus, Marie, et Josef!* Why won't this fire come up?"

Jordi was surprised to hear her say this since, to him, the fire seemed to be roaring. "Is something the matter, Nana?"

"I'm just trying to wake this fire up."

"Seems to be going pretty good to me."

"The water's taking too long to boil." She grabbed the handle of the kettle with a potholder and shook it.

"But what's the hurry? It'll boil in a few minutes."

"I need to make celery tea wit' chamomile and rosemary for Pip." She turned and looked into Jordi's eyes. "The pain's real bad, Jordi. Mary, Mother of God, it's real bad." Her eyes filled with tears.

"Even with the morphine?"

"There ain't no morphine. He ran out, then the blizzard came. He was gonna call Dr. Davids yesterday, but wit' the snow…"

"Jesus, Nana! Why didn't he say something?"

"You know him. That man is so stubborn. Besides, there wasn't that much pain yesterday. He thought it would be okay."

Jordi remembered something. "Wait here," he said as he threw an overcoat on and started out the door.

"Where you goin'?"

"I'll be right back."

He slogged through the deep snow to the shed. He had to sweep his leg vigorously back and forth to clear enough snow from in front of the shed door so that he could open it. At last, he was able to force it open. He rushed to the rolltop desk and slid it away from the wall. Reaching behind the desk, he pulled out the old medic kits, laid them on the desk, and opened them. He searched through them until he found the two toothpaste-sized boxes marked "Solution of Morphine Tartrate." He tore them open.

Empty.

"Damn," he muttered. Since they'd never opened the boxes, he guessed there hadn't ever been syrettes in them. Probably the Army had confiscated them.

After stuffing everything behind the desk and shoving it back against the wall, Jordi fought his way back to the house through the hip-deep snow.

"What did you go to the shed for?" asked Nana.

Jordi ignored her. He thought for a moment. "Jesus, there's no way Evan Davids can get here for another day or two, and if he can't get here, there's no way *we* can get Pip *there*."

At that moment, Lydie entered the kitchen. She stretched and asked through a yawn, "What's the matter?"

Jordi explained.

"What can we do?" Lydie thought a moment. "You know that man who always wins the horse pulls at the Blue Hill Fair every year, the one who always used to beat Cousin Denis? What's his name? You know, he lives in Sargentville."

"You mean, Ben Campbell?"

"Yes, him. Didn't I read recently in *The Ellsworth American* that he has an old sleigh he still uses to give kids rides?"

Jordi's eyes grew round. "Ma, you're a genius!"

"But we don't know the man," said Nana.

"No," replied Jordi as he lifted the phone off the hook, "but Niall Macgrudder knows him well. They went to school together." Jordi paused, waiting for the operator to come on the line. Finally, he said, "Yes, hello Verna...yes, at least two feet. Listen, can you get me... well, he's as good as can be expected, considering... Yes, I'll tell him. Verna, please ring up Niall Macgrudder for me. It's important... Yes, yes, thanks." Jordi waited. At last, Niall came on the line. "Niall, it's Jordi... Yuh, two feet here, also. That's why I'm calling." Jordi explained the situation to Niall. When he put the receiver down, he turned to Lydie and Nana. "He said he'd take a boat to Sargentville. He promised he'd be here with Ben Campbell as soon as they could hook up Ben's horses."

"Thank God for Niall," Lydie said.

Lydie was acting with more resolve and purpose than Jordi could remember. "Let's get ready for them," she said. "Nana, you gather up a couple of down quilts to wrap Pip in. Meanwhile, Jordi and I will fight our way into the barn to get three or four bales of hay. We can pack them around Pip so he won't freeze to death in the back of the sleigh."

By the time the sleigh arrived, Pip was sitting at the kitchen table in his overcoat, knit cap, and woolen scarf. His face was ghostly white and contorted with pain. All the same, he managed a smile. Two large quilts were piled on the table beside him.

Ben Campbell and Niall Macgrudder appeared at the back door slapping their heavy coats to shake off the snow. They were followed by Rufus Metcalfe. "Thought I might be of help," he said.

"As we passed by his place, he waved us down," said Niall. "Had to carry the old geezer to the sleigh like a little kid."

With Ben and Niall's help, they carried Pip through the thigh-deep snow and arranged him as comfortably as possible in the back of

the sleigh. Lydie and Jordi climbed up onto the sleigh bed and directed the men to pass them the hay bales which they then secured around
Pip. The two Belgians, matched bays with black manes and tails,
snorted and blew ropes of steam from their nostrils. When everything
was ready, Lydie leaped down from the sleigh and said, "There's only
room for one of us plus Ben and Niall. You go, Jordi."

Jordi looked at Nana. She nodded. "Call us," she said.

He climbed aboard the sleigh and sat down in front of Pip. "All
set," he called.

"Wait!" called Rufus. "I aim to go."

"There's not enough room."

"Don't need much."

With some difficulty, Jordi helped Rufus climb onto the sleigh.

"I'll huddle close to him. Keep him warm," said Rufus. Then,
with a chuckle, he added, "Be like with Ada."

Jordi smelled Rufus' clothes and smiled, wondering if Pip would
welcome the warmth more than he would object to the odor.

Ben yelled, "Git! Git!" and the horses lurched forward. The sleigh
moved sluggishly across the field and onto Route 176, or at least
where they judged Route 176 to be.

chapter 19

The few people who were outdoors, shoveling or chopping wood, stopped and stared when they heard the muffled hoofs and turned to see the sleigh coasting by, horses snorting, bells jingling. Pip even waved to several of them despite the pain which had clearly become worse. Jordi prayed they would make it to the hospital soon.

From up front, Niall periodically called out the distance and time remaining, but Jordi quickly realized the man was—deliberately or not, who could tell?—being absurdly optimistic. The horses continued to struggle through the deep snow. All along the way, they were showered by falls of drift snow shaken from the treetops by the wind. The snow glittered in the sunlight.

Finally, they arrived at the hospital. Jordi stood to peer over the hay bales. A gang of schoolboys was busy shoveling paths and clearing snow around the hospital's main building. They all stopped and leaned on their shovels when Ben Campbell steered the huge horses off the road and straight up to the main entrance. Several people were at the door, gazing out at the sight. A moment later, Evan Davids also appeared at the door.

"Evan," said Jordi, "we were afraid you wouldn't be able to get in."

"I spent the night here. It's best not to take chances in weather like this." He stepped down the stairs in his galoshes and peeked around the back of the sleigh. "Well, well, look what Santa Claus has brought me. Pip." He studied Pip's expression for a moment. "Pain's real bad, eh?"

Pip nodded.

"Run out of morphine?"

Again Pip nodded, this time with a grimace.

"Well, let's get you inside. We'll fix you right up." He looked at Jordi and shook his head. "Damn."

Ben, Niall, and Rufus waited in the lobby while Jordi followed Davids into an examining room. Several orderlies carried Pip in on a gurney.

An hour later, Pip was sound asleep in a room on the second floor. "I gave him enough to knock him out for a while. He's going to have to stay the night."

"Is there a place where I can stay?" asked Jordi. "I don't want to leave him here alone."

Davids nodded. "Of course. We've got several empty rooms. What a lousy piece of luck for him to run out of morphine when a god-damned blizzard comes along."

"I think there must be some law saying that's *exactly* when it would happen," Jordi said grimly.

"Yuh, maybe you're right. Come to my office; you can use my phone to call your family."

Jordi thanked Niall, Ben, and Rufus for getting Pip to the hospital and assured them he was resting comfortably. All three shook his hand before piling into Ben's sleigh for the long ride home.

Jordi passed a fitful night suffocated by the antiseptic smells of the hospital ward and wakened by the muffled cries and groans of patients. He was drifting in and out of sleep when he sensed a presence in the room and opened his eyes to see Evan Davids standing at the door.

"Oh, you *are* awake," said Davids.

Jordi sat up and hung his legs off the edge of the bed. He rubbed his eyes, noticing the sunlight filtering in through the blinds. "Morning, Evan." He sighed deeply, then asked, "Have you seen Pip yet today?"

Davids nodded. "I left him five minutes ago. He's doing fine. Pain's markedly abated. You'll be able to take him home this morning, assuming the roads are clear. I'll even give you a ride. But I've asked him to take a few tests while he's here. Save you folks a trip. So come on up to my office for some breakfast. I've got coffee and donuts. If you've never tasted old Mrs. Munsby's donuts, you're in for a revelation."

It was late winter and the men worked at a feverish pace to finish *Trobador* before the first good sailing day. Though nobody gave voice to it, everybody understood that Pip would not make it to the summer, so they showed up for work in Rufus' barn at every spare moment.

This urgency even led to a brief argument—with Ogden and Rufus on one side and Jordi, Chrétien, and Niall on the other. It started when Jordi said, "Listen, we don't have to finish the deckhouse and cabin. They're for looks and comfort and have nothing to do with sailing. Why don't we step the masts and rig her? We can always finish the joinerwork later."

"Ain't right," said Rufus flatly.

"What do you mean it's not right?"

"Rufus is right," said Ogden. "Ain't the way Pip would do it. Ain't the way your dad woulda, either."

"But what's important is getting Pip out on her before…" He left the rest unspoken.

"Don't dispute that," said Ogden. "But it still don't seem right."

"Eyuh," said Rufus.

Niall said, "What's more important? Getting Pip out, no matter what, or finishing the boat and risk missing the chance?"

Rufus sucked on his pipe, slurping tobacco juice. "If I was Pip, I'd say, 'boat ain't finished; boys think I'm dyin' tomorrow.' Eyuh, that's what *I'd* say."

They stared at him in silence. He raised his eyebrows as if to ask, "You men agree?"

Jordi smiled, nodded. "We'll finish her inside and out if I have to work for the next two months without sleep."

Rufus let a stream of pipe smoke flow out his nostrils. "Eyuh, figured as much."

Chrétien looked at Jordi. "I told you long ago your dad's boat should be built by all that's right in this world. I meant it. You won't be working any harder than me."

They parceled out assignments so that the work would go even more quickly. Ogden, with Rufus as his partner, took charge of the cabin trunk, the companionway, and the cockpit coaming since it was the more skilled work. Jordi and Chrétien worked on the cockpit seats and lazarettes while Niall was in charge of precutting the wood, to Ogden's specifications, for the interior joinerwork and the cabin sole. That way, Ogden would be able to work more quickly.

In the meantime, Rufus recruited his bridge partners with a promise of the finest single malt scotch in the county. When Chrétien learned of this he agreed to have a case of *Talisker* tucked away in the corner of the barn by the time the extra men arrived.

Tommy Pretty and Wade Taggart were retired lobstermen, and Angus Sorley was a retired ship's rigger who had spent almost forty years at the Bath Iron Works. They went to work preparing the masts and other spars, with Angus in charge.

With all seven men working daily, *Trobador* quickly neared completion. But Pip was deteriorating just as quickly. He could barely walk, and Jordi had to help him shave. At first, Jordi's hand shook so much when he touched Pip's cheeks with the straight razor that Pip said, "I feel like I'm about to be sacrificed."

"Maybe Nana should do it."

"Nana already does too much for me. Besides, shaving's a man's job. You been shaving for years now, so you know how it's done."

"But I use a Gillette razor, not one of these things."

"Same thing as long as you strop it up real sharp."

"Sharp is what I'm worried about."

But eventually, Jordi got the hang of it by practicing with the straight razor on his own face. Soon, the shaving became a pleasurable daily routine for both men.

Each day when Jordi appeared at Rufus' barn, he was greeted with questions about Pip's condition, and each day his report was bleaker than the day before. The mood in the barn turned somber as the men despaired of finishing in time.

The one bright spot for Jordi in those days was his mother finally ended her relationship with Virgil Blount. Over breakfast one morning, Lydie said, "You'll all be happy to know, I've stopped seeing Virgil Blount."

There was silence except for the rustling of Pip's newspaper as he lowered it to look at her.

"Well, he kept trying to put Gil down," Lydie continued. "Finally I told him if that was the only way he could feel like a man, then I've had enough of him."

"What did he say?" asked Jordi, trying to mask the pleasure in his voice.

"He started to swear like a bandit and it only made things worse. I'll never see him again. Not after that verbal abuse."

Jordi, Nana, and Pip simply looked at one another. Finally Nana said, "I made blueberry donuts, Lydie. Do you want one?"

"How's the boat coming?' It was one of his good days, and Pip was sitting at the kitchen table, sipping the celery tea Nana made for him.

"Almost done, Pip," replied Jordi. "We'll have you out on her in another couple of weeks or so."

"Are you crazy?" cried Nana as she dried her hands on a dishcloth. "This man ain't goin' nowhere." The slant of sunlight created a play of shadows where the creases in her brow and cheeks had deepened.

"Zabet," said Pip wearily as though they had had this conversation many times before, "what the hell difference does it make?"

"How do you expect to get better if you go tramping all over the place?"

"Zabet, damn it, you know—"

"Maybe in the summer when you're recovered. It's too early in the season anyway." She hung the dish towel on its rack and moved toward the door. "Now I got to get the laundry in," she said. "Don't you tire Pip out, Jordi. He's got to save his strength or he won't get better."

When the door swung shut behind her, Pip held his hands apart in a helpless gesture. "She's a good woman. It ain't right that she's always hurt. Dear God, that woman can pray—O how she can pray! But what does she get for it? It ain't goddamn right."

"Pip, try not to get upset," said Jordi.

Pip laughed ruefully. "I been pissed off at her god ever since little Emily died. Nana is perfect in her devotion. She is pious. She loves God more than any person on this Earth does. It ain't fair what he does to her. It just ain't goddamned fair. What the hell's he doing, trying to prove somet'ing to the devil like it says in the Book of Job? Ain't he bigger than that?"

"But Nana seems to handle it. If anything, her faith is stronger than ever."

Pip sighed deeply. "Yuh, ain't that somet'ing?!" He shook his head. "That's one hell of a woman! And nobody appreciates it enough—not her god...not even her husband. And you know somet'ing else about her? She's proud as can be of your dad. In all these years she ain't never removed that gold star from the window; that's how proud she is."

"I know, Pip."

"You an' me, we bot' know I ain't gonna be around much longer—"

"Pip, I—"

"Shssh! Hear me out. It's gonna be up to you, Jordi, that she never has cause to look at that gold star an' wonder if her boy's soul is in hell. When I'm gone, don't do not'ing that will make Blount bring out that diary. You hear me?"

"Don't worry, Pip. You have my word."

Pip looked into Jordi's eyes and nodded.

Jordi pushed his chair back and went to the stove for the pot of celery tea. He filled Pip's cup and put the pot back on the stove. He looked out the window. Nana was standing motionless, a clothespin in her hand. On the clothesline, one of Pip's shirts fluttered in the breeze. Its limp, empty sleeve brushed against her face. She reached up, grasped it, and held it to her cheek. She was looking off into the distance.

Jordi turned back to Pip. "Is she serious about not wanting you to go out on *Trobador*?" he asked.

Pip gave a rueful laugh. "She'd beat me over the head wit' her broom if I made even the smallest move toward that door."

Jordi glanced out the window. Nana remained motionless except for a slight shudder of her shoulders.

"You're gonna hafta sneak me out."

Jordi pivoted to look at Pip. "And how about you? How do you feel about the whole thing?"

Pip was silent for a moment. Finally, he said, "It's kinda like there's a big storm coming—a hell of a big storm—an' that boat is my sea room."

Jordi swallowed hard.

"I gotta be on it. Know what I mean?"

Jordi put a hand on Pip's shoulder. "I know what you mean." He wondered if Pip could feel his hand shaking.

His question was answered when Pip reached up and placed his hand over his. "I just want to go wit' dignity is all."

They heard Nana's slow footsteps coming up the porch. She swung the door open, a clothes basket on her hip, and backed into the kitchen. She carried the basket toward the bedroom.

"You two having a nice talk? That's good. Jordi, pour Pip some more celery tea." She disappeared into the bedroom and reemerged a moment later with the empty basket. "Seems the laundry is never done," she said as she rushed past them. "*Jésus, Marie, et Josef*, Pip, you go t'rough so many shirts." Then she was out the door.

Pip sighed deeply. "There's another t'ing," he said. "It ain't fair to Nana for me to drag this out. Know what I mean?"

Jordi nodded.

Half the population of Sedgwick turned out in the early morning cool of a late-April day to watch *Trobador's* triumphal progress out of Rufus Metcalfe's barn. Ben Campbell's Belgians snorted and whinnied with the load. Still on her cradle, *Trobador* rolled, inch by inch, over logs placed like a royal carpet out in front of her by a gang of men.

Everybody cheered when she emerged from the barn and her topsides, for the first time ever, glinted in the low slant of full morning sunlight. Ben Campbell called "Whoa!" and reluctantly unhitched his horses. He had wanted the honor of bringing *Trobador* all the way to the shore, but demurred when Ogden Gower pointed out that his horses were okay for pulling but not much good for pushing. The water dropped off sharply beyond the low water line meaning the horses would have had to go into the Benjamin River up to seven or eight feet in order to get *Trobador* enough below the high water mark for the incoming tide to float her. Rather than risk drowning his horses, Ben yielded his role of honor to Elwood Morton and his bulldozer.

With his beefy hands, one of which clutched a cigar, at the controls, Elwood called out instructions about log placement and angles. He eased the bulldozer, which snorted almost as much as Ben Campbell's horses, up to *Trobador's* cradle and started pushing. When he negotiated the difficult turn from Rufus' property onto the road, the crowd let out another cheer. They all walked alongside *Trobador* as she moved a little way up the road before turning in and groping toward the shore.

Sweat pouring from his brow, Jordi helped several men as they pulled the logs *Trobador* had already rolled over and placed them in front of the cradle again. He looked up to see that one of the onlookers was Virgil Blount. What did that man want, he wondered? But he had no time to think about that now.

Slowly, majestically, her spars lashed lengthwise to her deck, *Trobador* slid toward the Benjamin River not far from where it spilled into Eggemoggin Reach. At last *Trobador* was poised on the top of a slight downslope, her stern almost overhanging the river bank. Greased logs were laid out in the grass and sand to fashion an improvised marine railway. Everything was ready for Elwood Morton to give the final shove that would send *Trobador* sliding down to the edge of the water's low-tide retreat.

Jordi looked toward the road. He hoped Pip would be feeling well enough to come to the launching, but so far there was no sign of him. He asked Elwood to wait. "Let's give him a little more time."

Ogden Gower came over to him, "Gotta go soon," he said. "Low tide was ten minutes ago." The plan was to push *Trobador* and her cradle as far as possible into the river at low tide then wait for the rising tide to float her free of her cradle.

"Yuh, I know, Ogden. Just a little while."

The crowd milled around *Trobador* as she hovered over them, her stern pointing out over the Benjamin River and toward the reach beyond. Her prow, angled upward, reached toward the broad sprawl of sky. People touched *Trobador's* gleaming hull as though feeling for a heartbeat. The bulldozer sputtered, waiting. Elwood Morton sat back and smoked his cigar. He seemed unable to look away from the sweeping thrust of *Trobador's* bow. Rufus Metcalfe, biting on the stem of his pipe, entertained a group of women with a detailed account of the building of the boat.

Jordi looked at his watch. It was already past seven-thirty. Low tide was almost twenty minutes before. He exchanged a glance with Ogden Gower who shook his head sadly. Niall Macgrudder put a hand on Ogden's elbow and said, "Not until the last minute. Okay, Ogden?"

Ogden nodded.

A half hour later, when Pip still had not appeared, Ogden said, "Last minute's heah. Maybe he'll make it for the floating off."

Jordi's shoulders sagged, but he knew Ogden was right. He went back to the bulldozer. He motioned to the crowd to clear the path and he looked at Ogden and Niall. He turned to Elwood Morton. "Okay, Elwood. Ease her down. And be prepared to stop the instant we give you the signal."

A puff of black smoke spewed from the bulldozer's exhaust pipe as the engine roared. Elwood moved a lever and the transmission ground into gear. Slowly, almost imperceptibly, *Trobador* began to slide down the row of logs. Everybody watched, breathless. If anything were going to go wrong, this is when it would happen. Would the logs sink too deeply into the grass or, several yards later, the sand? Was the angle of the slope right?

Jordi glanced back toward the road. Still no sign of Pip. A quickening, crunching noise made him spin around. *Trobador* was gathering alarming speed. She was in a stern-first rush toward the river. Jordi waved his hand for Elwood to back off, but he saw that Elwood had already stopped the bulldozer. *Trobador* was sliding on her own. For a long, excruciating moment, Jordi could only watch helplessly as the boat hurtled down the improvised railway. She was at the shore's edge. Then her cradle plowed into the sand and mud, and *Trobador* came to a shuddering stop.

Jordi let his breath out and smiled at Ogden and Niall. "Well, guess we'd better weigh the cradle down now."

Several men began to attach pieces of heavy scrap metal to the cradle. The idea was to weigh it down so much that it would have no buoyancy and stay put when the water rose to float *Trobador* free. It was several days before a new moon and the tidal range was almost eleven feet. *Trobador* wouldn't begin to float free until a little before mid-tide, a full two to three hours from then. Even so, once *Trobador's* cradle was settled in the mud, few people left; they planned to stick it out until she was fully launched and floating on her lines. So they drank the coffee and ate the donuts several of the women had supplied and chatted while waiting for the moon to drag the water back into Eggemoggin Reach and the Benjamin River.

Jordi, Ogden, and Niall scrambled up the cradle and onto *Trobador* to make a last check of her through-hull fittings and her stuffing box—the places where water could pour in—to make sure there would be no disaster when she was fully immersed. Then they prepared the gear that would tie her to her mooring. They passed the rest of the time cleaning her decks and polishing all of her brightwork.

Soon, water was lapping over the lower members of the cradle. Jordi glanced at his watch and then at the road.

The water reached halfway up the cradle when Jordi and the others scrambled down from the deck to await the incoming tide. Around ten o'clock, *Trobador* shifted in her cradle like a sleeper slowly waking. It wouldn't be long now, Jordi thought, as he glanced once more at the road.

Most of *Trobador's* keel was now immersed. The inrushing water cast shimmering reflections in the hull. It was as though she were coming to life before their eyes. Her bow moved slightly and Jordi could see the stern lifting from the cradle.

"She's starting to move!" shouted Travis Lathrop who had maneuvered the *Susan May* in behind *Trobador* to take her in tow as soon as she came free. A line, now slack, led from each corner of *Trobador's* transom to the *Susan May*. "I feel like some kinda midwife," shouted Travis to laughter from the crowd.

Jordi looked up the road. Nothing.

Everybody moved to the water's edge. The water swirled around the cradle's uprights. A pair of shadows gliding across the water made Jordi look up. Two seagulls were spiraling and swooping over *Trobador's* stern.

Jordi heard the blare of a car horn blowing repeatedly and rhythmically. He looked up to see Chrétien's Packard come rolling to a stop not far from the makeshift launching ramp.

When people saw the car and they knew Pip had made it, they hurried up the slope and started to applaud. The applause grew louder and was accompanied by a boisterous cheer.

Jordi ran up the slope to the passenger side of the Packard. Lydie rolled down the window, and Jordi stuck his head in to see Pip sitting with Nana in the back seat. "Pip, thank God you made it. She's almost afloat."

Pip shook his head. "Don't thank God. Thank *Nana*. She finally gave in."

Nana leaned forward. "He's had a bad morning so he can stay only a little while." Then she turned to Pip. "And you keep the window up. We don't need you to catch cold and ruin your recuperation."

"I'll clear a view for you," said Jordi. He turned and asked the crowd to step aside a little to give Pip a clear sight line to *Trobador*.

"Jordi." It was Pip leaning over the back of the front seat, calling through the open front window. Jordi went back to the car. He saw Pip's hands, gripping the back of the front seat, trembling. Pip smiled. "I can see her. She looks beautiful. Your dad would be so proud."

Jordi smiled back at him. "It's mostly your doing, Pip." He

paused, then said, "Now let's watch to see how she sits on her lines. Then we'll tow her out to the reach."

Jordi moved down to the water's edge so he could oversee things. He looked back to Chrétien's car. He could barely see Pip's refracted image through the back window.

Moments later, *Trobador* floated free of the cradle. Jordi called to Travis Lathrop, "Okay, ease her back."

Travis Lathrop, grinning through his three-day stubble, maneuvered the *Susan May* so that she was precisely on an extension of *Trobador's* center line. Then he eased his boat forward until all the slack was taken from the tow lines. *Trobador* slid easily out of her cradle stern first. When she was completely clear, Jordi could see she floated perfectly on her waterline. A rush of pleasure swelled in him.

The crowd let out a great cheer and people ran down to the water to congratulate Jordi. He turned toward Chrétien's car and gave a thumbs up. He couldn't make out Pip's image, but he was certain Pip was smiling. And then, with several toots of the horn, the car made a wide turn and headed back to the farm.

Several days after the launching, Angus Sorley pronounced the masts and rigging in perfect order. They tied *Trobador* onto a mooring. Then Jordi—along with Niall Macgrudder, Ogden Gower, and Rufus Metcalfe—plotted how to get Pip out to the boat without Nana and Lydie knowing about it.

The next morning, before sunrise and after milking Delores, Jordi moved quietly around the kitchen, helping Pip get ready. He gave his grandfather a couple of pieces of bread and a glass of milk. While Pip was eating, Jordi slipped on Pip's shoes and laced them. When they were ready, Jordi helped Pip into a heavy woolen shirt. Once Pip was fully dressed, Jordi supported him as they went out onto the porch. He eased the door shut behind them and helped Pip into his rocking chair. Moments later, he heard the others approaching the farm. As planned, they left Niall's truck down the road and approached the farmhouse on foot. Jordi was certain Nana would not wake up because

Pip, accustomed to being up before dawn all his life, had made a habit of seeing Jordi off in the morning regardless of how sick he felt. It was an opportunity to have one of the few cigarettes he still permitted himself. If she or Lydie had heard them at all, they would assume everything was normal and would just turn over in bed.

A crow cawed. Delores lowed. Pip and Jordi peered into the gloom. They saw the silhouettes of two men scurrying toward them. The four men greeted each other silently.

"Rufus is waiting in the truck," whispered Niall. "Said he can't move fast enough."

Jordi nodded. Then he communicated his plan through a series of elaborate gestures. When all were certain of their roles, Pip grabbed both of Jordi's hands and allowed Jordi to pull him out of his chair. Niall and Jordi arranged themselves on each side of him. He draped his arms around their shoulders and they half carried him to his truck. Ogden, who had preceded them, held the passenger door open. They helped Pip into the truck and closed the door.

After waiting for Niall and Ogden to reach their own truck, Jordi climbed into the driver's seat and, leaving his door ajar so as not to create the sound of a second door closing, started the engine and drove off.

They rode in silence. Only as they were pulling into Brooklin did Pip say, "I just wish I didn't have to sneak around like this. Nana can be impossible. But I love her all the same."

Jordi realized this was the first time he had heard Pip openly declare his love for Nana. It had always been something that was assumed but never spoken.

When they got to Niall's dock, the others were waiting for them. The *Zabet & Lydie* was sitting at the dock, where they had stationed her the night before. Jordi and Niall helped Pip aboard. Jordi fired up the engine and they headed out to *Trobador's* mooring. It was a short ride, and soon Jordi was easing the *Zabet & Lydie* alongside *Trobador*.

Jordi vaulted the lifelines and made his way aft to loosen the mainsheet. Then he went forward to the mast and eased off slightly on the main halyard. He reeved the main halyard through a large block he had temporarily rigged to the outboard end of the boom. When he finished, he swung the boom out at a right angle to *Trobador's* center-line so that it was hanging out over the *Zabet & Lydie*. Then he led lines both forward and aft to prevent the boom from swinging out of position, and completed the rig by leading a line straight down to a cleat under the boom. The boom would act as a makeshift crane.

Aboard the *Zabet & Lydie*, meanwhile, Niall, Rufus, and Ogden had been fitting Pip into a bosun's chair. Now, they attached it to *Trobador's* main halyard and Niall climbed aboard to help Jordi haul it up. Jordi took a few turns of the main halyard around a winch and started to lift Pip clear of the *Zabet & Lydie*.

As his feet left the floorboards, Pip started to giggle. "*Jésus, Marie, et Josef,* I feel like an old time sea captain's wife. This is how they hauled the old biddies aboard."

"Look like one, too," said Rufus.

They all laughed.

"Stop your laughing an' get me aboard. This ain't the most comfortable place I been!"

Jordi and Niall took up the main halyard and Pip swung clear of the *Zabet & Lydie*. Soon he was suspended at the height of the life-lines.

"Okay," said Jordi to Niall. "You secure the halyard. I'll go swing him aboard." He made his way to the boom and undid the lines preventing the boom from swinging, then he gently swung the end of the boom inboard. He lifted Pip's legs to clear the lifelines.

"Just like hauling a big fish aboard," said Jordi.

"*Merde,*" replied Pip.

In a few moments, Pip was sitting comfortably on the cockpit seat. Niall and Ogden helped Jordi bend the mainsail to the mast and boom. They repeated the process with the mizzen sail. Finally, they laid the jib out on the deck and attached it to the forestay, ready for raising. Then they lowered themselves into the *Zabet & Lydie*.

Jordi turned to Pip. "Any pain after all that?"

"A little."

"I thought so. Your face is a little white. Did you remember to take your pills?"

"Don't worry. I have everyt'ing I need."

Pip ran his fingers along the bright mahogany cockpit coaming and shook his head in wonder. Jordi knew the wood of *Trobador*, heavily encased in fresh varnish, felt tacky. He watched as Pip brushed it first with the pads of his fingertips then along the hollow of his palm.

Pip smiled and said, "Let's go sailing."

Jordi started the engine and eased *Trobador* away from her mooring while Niall, Ogden, and Rufus watched from the *Zabet & Lydie*. They waved.

Rufus called out, "Be seeing you soon, Pip."

Several hours later, Jordi steered *Trobador* back toward Niall Macgrudder's dock. Now that it was nearing high tide, there would be enough depth to accommodate *Trobador's* almost six-foot draft. Two seagulls hovered over the bow as though guiding them in. Their shadows swept the deck. As he neared the dock, Jordi saw that Nana, Chrétien, and his mother were there. They stood alongside Niall, Rufus, Ogden, and several other men. He also saw Officer Pattison and Virgil Blount standing together. He had expected Nana and his mother to figure out where Pip was and come down to the dock to meet them. But he was surprised to see Officer Pattison. He took a deep breath.

Trobador approached the dock and Jordi adjusted the mainsheet. He stepped over Pip and made his way forward to lower the jib. That done, he scurried back to the cockpit. As he stepped over Pip again, he returned his grandfather's frozen smile with an apprehensive smile of his own. He lowered the mizzen sail and took up his position at the helm.

Jordi turned *Trobador* into the wind and coasted up to the dock. He threw the bow and stern lines to Niall and Ogden. They snubbed the lines.

Trobador came to a stop.

Nana came to the edge of the dock. "*Mon Dieu!* Hippolyte!" she cried.

Lydie looked at Jordi, her brow furrowed. "Jordi, what happened?"

Jordi swallowed. He tried to lubricate his mouth and tongue which were dry as dust. He managed, in a near whisper, to say, "He's dead, Ma. Pip is dead." He looked from his mother to Nana and saw the horror on their faces. His words echoed silently in his mind. He was scarcely aware of someone climbing aboard *Trobador*.

He heard Officer Pattison say, "He's dead, all right." Then he heard Virgil Blount say, "And Jordi, heah, killed him. I can prove it. I told you it was important we come down here." The voices seemed to come from a distance.

Officer Pattison asked, "What about it, son. Did you kill your grandfather?"

Jordi had no answer. He could only stare at the man, disoriented and stunned.

part 3

1950

O remember that my life is wind...

— Job 7:7

chapter 20

When Chrétien paid Jordi's bail, the judge made it a condition that Jordi stay with him. Jordi hadn't seen his mother and grandmother in weeks, claiming that Chrétien, who had thrown out his back, needed his help. The real reason was he didn't want to talk about that day out beyond the reach; he didn't want Nana asking too many questions. It was enough that she had seen him arrested on a charge of murder; it was enough that she had learned of his indictment. Why should she have to suffer through the trial before it even began? Both Nana and Lydie called Chrétien's house many times to speak with him, but he would only ask about their health, mumble a few things about how he was doing, and end the conversation as soon as he could.

One night, before his September trial, Jordi lay on his back out in the night air, thinking about the coming ordeal. He let his head rest on the soft, resonating crown of earth, hoping to pick up the weak hum of the planet in motion. He fixed his gaze upward, trying to detect the slow, cosmic movement of the moon as it drifted, unmoored, along an arc between the tips of two tall spruce. This was a form of self-rescue Pip had taught him long before: to feel the Earth; to gaze up at the stippled dome of stars. When things seemed overwhelming the idea was to trump them by contemplating something more overwhelming still—something like the sound of the Earth's rotation through space, or the breathtaking straddle of stars, or the idea of eternity.

"Jordi!" Chrétien called from the kitchen window. "Telephone."

"Coming." Jordi rose and hurried into the kitchen. He found

Chrétien sitting at the table. Several columns of playing cards were arranged neatly before him. On most nights Chrétien and Jordi played poker while listening to the radio, but tonight Chrétien played solitaire thinking, perhaps, Jordi was too distracted by his upcoming trial.

"It's Ambrose Locke," Chrétien said. "Wants to talk wit' you."

Jordi went to the black telephone hanging against the wall near the pantry. Chrétien raised an eyebrow, glanced at the phone, then returned his attention to the cards.

As Jordi picked up the phone, he glanced at the issue of the *Ellsworth American* sitting near the sink. The headline read:

Jury Selection in Jordi Dupuy
Murder Trial Begins Monday.

His heart lodged in his throat. He caught his breath and said, "Hello, Ambrose. What's happening?" Ambrose Locke was a longtime friend of the family, a gentle, kind man. When it came time to find a lawyer, Jordi thought of no one else.

"Jordi, I think we have a problem. What do you know about a diary?"

"A diary?" Jordi felt the muscles of his neck tighten. Chrétien looked up from his cards but Jordi averted his eyes, staring at the notches in the doorframe that marked his height for each of nineteen years of his life. The highest mark was more than six feet above the threshold. "What about a diary?" His voice wavered.

"The prosecutor called. Said he had your dad's diary and was planning to introduce it as evidence. He's sending over a copy, but I think we need to talk about it."

"Oh, God..."

"I have no idea how he got it."

"I do," said Jordi. He told Locke about Virgil Blount stealing it some time ago. As he did, Chrétien slid his chair back and sat staring at him.

"What's in it that I should know about?" Locke asked.

"Dad talked a lot about using morphine to help soldiers die."

"This is not good news…"

Jordi remained silent.

Locke continued. "I'm supposed to get it tomorrow afternoon. But I think we'd better talk about it first thing tomorrow. I'm going to need as much time as possible to deal with this."

Jordi agreed to meet Locke at eight the next morning and hung up the phone.

Chrétien was looking at him, one eyebrow raised. "So, what's this stuff about your dad's diary?" he asked, laying the deck of cards on the table. "I hope it ain't what I think it is."

"I'm afraid so, Uncle Chrétien. The prosecution has Dad's diary."

"How the hell did that happen?"

Jordi told Chrétien about Blount stealing the diary nearly a year before.

"That diary should never see the light of day."

"I know that. But what can I do?"

"You remember how Pip made me and you promise."

"I know."

"And it would hurt your ma and your grandma real bad."

"I know that, Uncle Chrétien."

"Real bad."

In the morning, Jordi borrowed Chrétien's car to drive into Blue Hill. He drove the big Packard along the same route they drove that day when *Mistral* came bounding out of the fog quick as a deer ahead of warships that loomed out of the murk. Unlike Pip's wheezing truck, however, the Packard negotiated Caterpillar Hill with ease.

Jordi drove several blocks past Locke's office and eased the Packard into a parking space in front of the Blue Hill Pharmacy. Just as he was reaching to turn off the ignition, he saw Travis Lathrop and Ben Campbell lingering on a corner across the street. Hoping they hadn't spotted him, he pulled the car onto the road again and drove around the block, finally parking on a side street near the library. He slipped out the passenger side of the car and hurried to Locke's office, cutting across the library lawn.

Locke's office was in a small house near the library. Jordi passed under a rose arbor and walked up to the front door, looking over his shoulder to see if anyone might be passing. Suddenly, he was blinded by a flash. He raised an arm to shield his eyes, "What the—?"

"I'm from the *Bangor Daily News,*" said a short, scruffy-looking man holding a camera. A cigarette dangled from his lips.

"Get out of here!" shouted Jordi.

"Aw, come on Mr. Dupuy, let me take a few shots. You're quite a celebrity, you know."

Jordi covered his face and ran up the steps to Locke's door.

Locke's secretary, Linda, greeted him. She was a chubby, cheerful blonde woman. "There you are, Jordi. Mr. Locke is waiting for you." She looked out at the photographer, frowned, and slammed the door. "Damned newspaper people," she muttered as she moved across the room and opened a door behind her desk. "Jordi's here."

Locke emerged from his office and greeted Jordi with a broad grin. In his early fifties, Locke still looked like the halfback that he was in his days at Bowdoin College—trim, broad-shouldered, crew-cut. His right hand rested on the breast of his tan blazer under a blue ribbon. "What do you think?" he asked. "First place at the Blue Hill Fair for my banana bread."

"Mr. Locke, there's a photographer out there," Linda said.

Locke frowned, walked to a window, peered out. He turned to Jordi. "Look, you better get used to it. There'll be many more of them at the courthouse."

Jordi rolled his eyes.

"Come in," Locke said, "We need to talk about that diary." He nodded to Linda.

"I'm going over to the pharmacy," said Linda. "Be back in a while." She gave Jordi an encouraging smile and left.

Locke said to Jordi, "Have a seat. Tell me about the diary."

Jordi wondered if he could remember everything, but over a painful hour, during which he nearly broke down several times, he managed to tell Locke everything that might possibly have a bearing on his case.

When he finished, Locke shook his head silently. Then he said, "Your dad went through a lot."

Jordi nodded. "But how could that be used against me?"

"I'd have to read the diary completely to be sure, but for starters they might try to argue that you got your inspiration to kill your grandfather from your dad's diary."

"That's crazy!"

"I know it is...just as absurd as the idea that you would kill Pip. But the prosecutor, Skelly, is a very clever guy, so we're going to have to be prepared."

"Isn't all the evidence circumstantial like you said before?"

"Yes, and I still believe it is. But this diary adds just one more piece. Lots of people have been convicted on a pile of circumstantial evidence." He stood, walked to the window, peered out. He opened the window and the curtain billowed inward.

Locke took a deep breath. "Let's look at what they have. You go out sailing alone with Pip and he comes back dead. A WWII medic's manual, dog-eared at the section about administering morphine, is found at your home. It has fingerprints all over it—"

"But those are Pip's, right?"

Locke gave Jordi a tolerant look. "It has *your* fingerprints on it, too; that's the point here." Locke began to tick off fingers. "On the boat they found empty morphine syrettes, tucked away in the chart table, with your fingerprints on them. They also found a whiskey glass, again with your fingerprints. Now there's a diary by your father that, Skelly could argue, gave you the idea. No matter how you slice it, mercy killing is still considered murder, at least in peacetime." Locke paused, strode back toward Jordi, sat on the edge of his desk. "Things are beginning to pile up against us, and jury selection begins on Monday."

Jordi frowned. He rose, started toward the stuck window, stopped. "I suppose so."

There was a hesitant tap on the door.

"It's okay, Linda," called Locke. "You can come in."

"Everybody's all excited down at the pharmacy," said Linda. She handed Locke a copy of the *Bangor Daily News*. "Hurricane's coming up the coast."

Locke took the newspaper from her and scanned the front page. "It's already hitting Cape Hatteras," he said. "Winds of a hundred-and-twenty miles an hour. They're calling it Hurricane Clara."

"Is it coming our way?"

Locke flipped to the second page and studied a small chart. "Yup. And she's traveling at sixty miles an hour."

Linda said, "Heck, at that rate she'll hit us—what?—Monday?"

Jordi said, "Maybe jury selection will be postponed…"

"You don't know Judge Trench," Locke replied.

"If the wind comes from the right direction, the reach will be a mess. Given where *Trobador* is, that would be real bad."

On Saturday evening they heard on the radio that Hurricane Clara had passed Cape Hatteras and was making a beeline for the New England coast. The projected landfall was anywhere between Rhode Island and Maine.

"Sounds like we might be in for a blow," said Chrétien.

Jordi nodded. "Pip always said one of the best ways to keep a boat from going on the rocks is to sail out to sea. But because of the trial, I can't do that with *Trobador*."

"If I didn't have this bum back," said Chrétien, "I'd take her out."

"I know you would, Uncle Chrétien. I guess all I can do is double up on her mooring lines. There's no time to pull her out."

Jordi walked down to Naskeag Point before sunset. Several pickup trucks were parked at the end of the road, and Jordi knew most of the men were out securing their boats.

He looked up at the sky to see if he could detect any signs of the advancing hurricane. Long sheets of clouds were beginning to stretch out over the coast from the south. They could well be harbingers of Clara, and Jordi felt hamstrung by the trial. If the storm hit Monday, as predicted, he probably wouldn't be here with the boats and the other lobstermen. He knew the men would be working together to save their livelihoods. He should be with them, not imprisoned in a courtroom in Ellsworth.

He dragged the rowboat across the pebbly beach and started for the *Zabet & Lydie*, which he would use to get out to *Trobador*. Once *Trobador* was secured, he would return the *Zabet & Lydie* to her mooring and secure her, too.

It was the best he could do.

The next day, Jordi sat across from Locke, who said, "Well, I've read your father's diary. First, I have to say I completely understand why you want to keep it from your mother and grandmother. It would only hurt them."

"Thanks, Ambrose."

"Second, I can see how Skelly might try to use it against you and I'm prepared to fight him tooth and nail. I think the diary is irrelevant to your case, and I think I have a shot at persuading the judge to rule it inadmissible."

Jordi leaned back in his chair, breathed a sigh of relief. "That would be wonderful."

"But don't count on it. This is Judge Trench we're talking about."

Jordi looked at Locke across the cluttered desk. Though the ceiling fan rotated lazily, the tiny office was stifling. Jordi stood and walked over to a window. He tried to open it but it wouldn't budge.

Locke laughed. "That's the only one that won't open. I hope your picking it isn't a sign."

Linda came into the office with a copy of the latest *Bangor Daily News* under her arm. Locke was engrossed in what he was writing, so she handed the paper to Jordi. Jordi read that Hurricane Clara was hammering the coast of Massachusetts and was expected to hit the Maine coast the next day. That morning, as he drove along the bay, he had seen the rolling wave trains beneath scudding clouds. He thought of the boats sitting vulnerable on their moorings. The *Zabet & Lydie*. *Trobador*.

And he thought of his father.

"What's wrong?" Locke's voice startled him.

Jordi shook his head as though to clear it. "Oh, nothing." But the answer sounded hollow. And untruthful. He said, "I was just thinking about the day we got the telegram."

"About your father?"

Jordi nodded. He turned the page of the newspaper. He said to Locke, "It looks pretty certain that Clara's gonna hit us."

Linda came into the office with coffee. "They're boarding up the windows at the pharmacy," she said. "I guess it's really gonna blow."

"Looks that way," replied Jordi, thinking again of the boats in the harbor.

An hour later, Linda returned from another trip to the pharmacy. "They had the radio on over there. The Boston area got hit hard. The steeple at the Old North Church got blown over. Here's a late edition of the paper."

She handed the paper to Locke who laid it open on his desk and slid his reading glasses to the end of his nose. After a moment he asked, "You ever been to Revere Beach, Jordi?"

"Yuh, a couple of times. Me and Pip went just a few years ago."

"It's a mess," said Locke. "The double Ferris wheel collapsed onto Ocean Avenue. It says here that it's nothing but a twisted heap of broken metal, a pretzel of steel…the entire roof of the Hippodrome was blown off…"

Jordi remembered his father's hand supporting him while he rode the merry-go-round.

"Whole sections of wall were torn off the Virginia Reel," continued Locke. "Damn, I remember riding that with my prom date years ago! A wall of Bluebeard's Castle is gone…boats washed up on Revere Beach Boulevard…even a tuna boat, for Chrissake!…Jesus, they really got slammed!"

A horrifying image of boats washed up on the shores of Eggemoggin Reach came to Jordi. He remembered how Teddy Thibodeau said the wind destroyed dreams. Or did he say war? Jordi couldn't remember.

Jordi shook his head. "This storm is coming on so fast, no one had time to haul the boats so everybody's doubled up on mooring lines. I hope it does the trick, but we'll just have to wait and see."

The next morning, Jordi and Locke were in Ellsworth, the seat of the district court. Torrents of rain splattered the windows of the Central Café, and the wind threatened to rattle them from their frames. The waitress was clearing the plates and Locke was stuffing papers into his battered briefcase when Jordi said, "I can't believe the judge would start the trial in weather like this."

"That's because you don't know Trench. The guy's tough and I'm telling you now, he's the worst judge we could have drawn."

"Why?"

"Because Trench is a devout Catholic, a stickler for the law, and he tends to favor the prosecution."

"Couldn't we have gotten another judge?"

Locke took his raincoat from the rack and put it on. "What? You want me to lodge an appeal that this judge is not suitable because he's devoted to God and the laws of the State of Maine?"

"Then I guess we're stuck with him?" said Jordi, donning his own raincoat.

"You got it. But it could work to our advantage."

"How?"

"He's going to favor the prosecution most of the time. He'll let Skelly get away with murder."

"How does that help us?"

"Maybe he'll overstep and leave us room to appeal." Locke put his panama hat on and said, "Well, I hope you're in good shape, because it's two blocks uphill to the courthouse and we're going to have to leave the car here."

"Why?"

"Look outside. State Street's blocked by fire engines. Wires down from the storm. No cars are allowed through."

Jordi looked out and saw the flashing red lights of two fire engines sweeping through sheets of rain. Several firemen stooped as they walked against the wind, holding their helmets to their heads.

When Jordi and Locke pushed through the café door and onto the street, the wind snatched Locke's hat and sent it flying back into the restaurant. Locke went back for it, jammed it on his head and kept a firm grip on the brim. "Well here goes. Hope you're ready," he said. Then he started running up the hill toward the courthouse. Jordi took a deep breath and set out after him.

Huddled against the driving rain, they dashed up State Street, avoiding fallen tree limbs. They sprinted as far as the old, one-story brick jailhouse, which sat next to the courthouse, and were unable to run farther. They held their arms in front of their faces as they gasped for breath and trudged directly into the wind and rain.

The Ellsworth courthouse sat at the crest of the hill, a brick building with a granite façade facing both the street and the Congregational church opposite. Six Doric columns supported a marble lintel. A stone owl surveyed the street from a corner of the roof. Jordi and Locke trudged up the steps that led to a large double door decorated with wrought-iron bars behind a panel of glass.

Inside, they struggled to regain their breath. They shucked their sodden coats and shook them out before draping them over their arms. They climbed the metal stairs leading up to the courtroom. At the halfway landing, where the stairs turned ninety degrees to the right, they saw a window crisscrossed with tape to keep it from shattering in the hurricane-force winds expected later that morning.

They entered the courtroom and found it mostly empty. The prosecutor, Simon Skelly, was gathering up papers. He glanced at Jordi and Locke and offered a half-smile.

The clerk, a balding man with wire-rimmed glasses, came toward them. "I tried to call your office, but the lines must be down somewhere," he said to Locke. "Judge Trench has canceled court for the day. We'll start jury selection tomorrow as long as we have power and everything is okay. He wants you to call ahead in the morning."

"Thank God," said Jordi. "I'm going to call Niall Macgrudder and tell him I'm on my way. Maybe he can get me out to *Trobador*."

When they left the courthouse, they ran into Rufus Metcalfe. He was carrying a cane.

"Rufus, what are you doing here?"

"Gonna brain that bozo photographer with Ada's cane if he bothers young Jordi."

Locke gave a laugh. "Come on before you get into trouble. Jordi and I will walk you to your car."

"Ain't got my car. Don't drive this far no more."

"How did you get here?"

"Hitched."

Locke rolled his eyes. "Come on, then, we'll give you a ride home. The trial's off for today."

"Eyuh. Figured that. Honker of a blow coming."

"You've been on the reach all your life," said Jordi. "What do you think?"

"Could be a lotta boats washed up. Seen it before."

Jordi's heart sank.

chapter 21

In Blue Hill they stopped at Locke's office, where Jordi and Rufus picked up the Packard and set out for Brooklin. Jordi drove slowly because the windshield wipers were barely able to keep up with the torrents of rain. In the glare of his headlights it looked like the rain was falling sideways. The wind blew so strong that even the heavy Packard rocked. When they reached the summit of Caterpillar Hill and were exposed to the full brunt of the wind, he thought they might be blown off the road. Several times Jordi had to jerk the wheel to the right to get the car back under control. He kept glancing past Rufus, looking out over Eggemoggin Reach, but it was too rainy to see anything.

The short causeway over the Benjamin River was almost completely awash. He had to slow to a crawl as water came up to the hubcaps.

At last, they made it to Brooklin. Jordi stopped at the dock in Center Harbor. Several men huddled in Niall Macgrudder's shack.

"How's it going?" he asked them.

"So far, so good," replied Niall. "Ain't seen no boats washed up yet. Leastwise not heah."

"What about *Trobador*? Did she seem to be riding it out all right?"

"Last time I saw her everything seemed fine. But visibility is so bad we can hardly see her any more."

"God, I need to get out there…"

"Eyuh, I hear you…but can't do that," said Ogden Gower. "Everything except the rowboats are doubled up out theah on their mooring lines. And you couldn't fit enough people in a rowboat to pull against those waves—"

"—even if you could get the boat in the water in the first place," added Niall.

Ogden nodded. "Just hafta wait out the night and see what the morning brings us."

After spending some time with the men, Jordi dropped Rufus at his house then drove down to Naskeag Harbor. The place was deserted. He parked the car and peered into a wall of grayness. He saw several phantom shapes that he took to be lobster boats but there was no way of telling if the *Zabet & Lydie* was one of them. No boats had yet washed up on Naskeag Point, but given where the *Zabet & Lydie* was, and given the wind direction and the set of the waves, if she slipped her mooring she'd go clear across Blue Hill Bay and wash up somewhere on Mount Desert Island. It would take him nearly two hours to drive up the Blue Hill peninsula, go through Ellsworth, and drive down to Mount Desert Island. And even if he did that, it was a big island and the *Zabet & Lydie* could wash up anywhere on the miles-long shoreline. It was pointless. As Ogden Gower said, the only thing to do was to wait until first light to survey the damage.

He slept little that night. The wind howled outside and, ferreting out the cracks in Chrétien's house, it whistled menacingly. Every window on the windward side of the house rattled. He couldn't escape the feeling that leaving *Trobador* out there to fend for herself was some kind of betrayal of his father and Pip. Around midnight, he gave up trying to sleep and went into the kitchen. He found Chrétien sitting at the table playing solitaire.

"You couldn't sleep, either," Jordi said.

"Who could with all that racket? Besides, this kinda weather always gets my joints to aching somet'ing fierce. And now this damned back..."

"Will a little whiskey help?"

Chrétien pointed to an empty glass. "Hasn't so far."

"How about a little poker?"

By the time a sliver of light came through the window, they had been playing cards for nearly four hours. They were so tired they hardly noticed the wind had died down. So it took them by surprise to see sunlight.

Jordi rose from the table and went to the window. "Storm's passed."

"Let's go check on the boats," said Chrétien.

"Yuh. Then I better shave and clean up. I have to be at the courthouse in just a few hours."

They first stopped at Naskeag Point. Because of his bad back, Chrétien waited in the car while Jordi scanned the harbor. The *Zabet & Lydie* was there and he saw only one empty mooring. He tried to remember whose it might be, but he couldn't. When he returned to the car, Chrétien said, "Maybe it's Virgil Blount's."

"No such luck. I saw his boat sitting out there fat and pretty."

It took them only fifteen minutes to drive to Center Harbor. As they descended the road to the dock, they could see that *Trobador* was still on her mooring. Jordi was relieved. He parked the car and told Chrétien, "Travis already has his boat at the dock. I'm going to ask him to give me a ride out so I can check on her."

Travis Lathrop waved from the dock. When Jordi approached, he said, "Figured you'd want to go out. That's why I rowed out and got the *Susan May* ready."

"You're a good man, Travis," Jordi said, taking Lathrop's hand.

Within minutes they were alongside *Trobador*. Jordi climbed aboard, went up to the foredeck and made a quick survey. Moments later he was back aboard the *Susan May*. "She rode it out beautifully. Just a little wear on one of the mooring lines where the chafing leather slipped."

Jordi stepped to the dock from the *Susan May*, climbed into the Packard alongside Chrétien, and told him all was well. They set off for Chrétien's house. "I've got to get to Ellsworth," Jordi said. "Could you find somebody to give you a lift out to the farm and check on Ma and Nana? Make sure the storm didn't cause any damage?"

"I'm already plannin' on it," replied Chrétien.

Inside the courtroom, five rows of oak benches faced the judge's bench, which sat on a dais. Jordi and Locke walked through the crowded room to a table at the front. Ceiling fans spun slowly, creating a light breeze that fluttered the papers Locke spread out before him. A buzz of conversation came from the benches behind Jordi. Simon Skelly and an assistant were seated at the table to Jordi's right. Jordi avoided looking in their direction.

Jury selection took a day and a half. When it was over, Locke told Jordi they faced a mixed jury. "There are a number of Catholics and that's not good, given their strong religious opposition to mercy killing which, when you break it all down, is what you're charged with. But I also managed to get a few veterans and a couple of lobstermen on the panel."

"Why veterans?"

"They might see your dad's diary in a different light." Locke paused, added, "Which brings me to a bit of bad news. Back in his chambers, Trench turned down my motion to rule the diary entirely inadmissible. The jury won't get the whole diary, but they will get copies of the entries Scully uses to buttress his points."

The rest of the afternoon was taken up with opening arguments.

The following day, outside the courthouse, Jordi looked to the sky. Earlier that morning he heard someone say another hurricane was on the way. But now, the sky appeared harmless. If there was another hurricane, it was still some ways off. He entered the courtroom and walked quickly to his seat at the defendant's table, avoiding the stares of the many people crowding the room. Despite the clear sky, however, he couldn't stop thinking about *Trobador* as he sat waiting for the judge to appear.

The room fell silent when the clerk cried out, "All rise!"

Judge Trench swept into the courtroom, and took his seat. He was a big man with masses of curly white hair framing a coarse and ruddy face. He reached into his robe and pulled out a pair of reading glasses, propping them on his nose, and studied some papers on the desk in front of him.

The clerk announced that court was in session. Jordi flinched at the words, "State of Maine versus Jordi Dupuy."

The judge looked out over his half-glasses at the crowded courtroom. He frowned. "I hope everybody survived yesterday's hurricane without significant damage. The paper says another one may be on the way, so I guess we'd better get started." He looked down at the prosecutor's and the defendant's tables and acknowledged Simon Skelly and Ambrose Locke. "Good morning, gentlemen. Are you ready to proceed?"

"Yes, your honor," they replied in unison.

Judge Trench let his gaze linger on Jordi for a long moment, then said to Skelly, "Call your first witness."

Jordi knew Nana and his mother sat several rows behind him. He had hoped they wouldn't attend the trial at all, but now he was acutely aware of their presence. He could hear the occasional click of Nana's rosary beads and the rhythmic counterpoint of his mother's ever-present knitting needles.

Skelly called Officer Pattison to the witness box. After walking Officer Pattison through the preliminaries of his rank and his number of years on the force, Skelly asked, "Where were you on the morning of May third, this year?"

"I received a call that there could be some trouble with Mr. Dupuy out on the boat *Trobador*, so I went down to the dock in Brooklin to check on it."

"Who made that call?"

"Virgil Blount."

Jordi shot Locke a troubled glance.

"Did he say why he was concerned?"

"Said it appeared the old man wasn't fit to be down theah an' that it seemed some men were kinda forcing him onto a boat."

"Did he identify the men?"

"Said he only recognized one of them," Officer Pattison replied, looking at Jordi. "The defendant, theah."

"So you went down to the docks. What did you see?"

"At first nothing. Just lots of people talking about that theah boat, *Trobador*."

"Then?"

"Then I saw the boat come in."

"And?"

"Well, when she came up to the dock, old Mr. Dupuy, he was kinda slumped over, more like laying on his back."

"And the defendant?"

"He was steering the boat and he had a kinda dazed expression on his face."

Skelly walked toward the witness stand, cracking his knuckles. "Did you hear the defendant say anything?"

"Oh yes, sir."

"What did he say?"

"He said 'He's dead, Ma! Pip's dead!' He was speaking to his mother who was one of the people on the dock."

"Then what happened?"

Officer Pattison said Blount accused Jordi of killing Pip. He then went aboard *Trobador*, felt Pip's carotid artery for a pulse, and found none. "He was dead, all right."

"What did you do then?"

"I asked the defendant if what Virgil Blount said was true, asked if he killed his grandfather."

"How did he respond?"

"He didn't say anything. He just shook his head like he was confused or something."

"Would you call it stupefaction?"

"No. Mainly 'cause I don't know that word."

Laughter filled the courtroom.

Skelly, himself still laughing, asked, "Well, how about shock? Did he look stunned?"

Locke jumped to his feet. "Objection, calling for a conclusion."

"Sustained."

"Well, then," Skelly continued, "was the defendant crying?"

"No."

"You testified that Virgil Blount accused him of killing his grand-father and that you asked him if he killed his grandfather. On either of these occasions, did he deny it?"

"No."

"Then what happened."

"Well, I had to arrest him, of course."

Skelly walked back to the prosecutor's table, examined some papers, and returned his attention to Officer Pattison. "Did you examine the boat?"

"Certainly."

"What did you find?"

"Well, several things. Most important were two things that looked like vials with long needles in them."

"Where did you find them?"

"Under the lid of the chart table."

"In other words, hidden from view."

"Not in plain sight, no sir."

"What else did you find?"

"A broken whiskey glass."

"How did you know it was a *whiskey* glass?"

Officer Pattison smiled, "I'm familiar with the smell of whiskey."

A twitter of laughter filled the courtroom.

"What did you do with the vials?"

"First, we tested them for fingerprints."

"Did you find the defendant's fingerprints on them?"

"Yes."

"Then what did you do?"

"Took the vials to Dr. Davids to see if he could identify them."

"Did he?"

"Yes, he said they were morphine syrettes from the war."

"Did you ask the defendant where they came from?"

"Yes. He was very cooperative. Said he guessed they came from his dad's old medic's kit which was in the shed at the Dupuy farm."

"Did you then obtain a search warrant and search the shed?"

"Yes."

"What did you find?"

"The medic's kit and also a medic's manual."

"Was there anything unusual about the manual?"

"It was both dog-eared and marked with a postcard at a section describing how to use morphine syrettes,"

"Did you test the manual for fingerprints?"

"Yes."

"Were the defendant's fingerprints on the manual?"

"Yes."

Skelly turned to the judge. "That's all, Your Honor."

"Any cross, Mr. Locke?" asked Judge Trench.

"Yes, Your Honor." Locke rose, walked to the witness stand. "Officer Pattison, did you find other fingerprints on the morphine syrettes?"

"Yes."

"Whose?"

"Pip's...ah, Hippolyte Dupuy's"

"And the medic's manual?"

"Yes. His fingerprints were there, too."

"Thank you. That's all."

As his next witness, Skelly called the coroner. He questioned him at length, but in the end established only two things: that Pip had died of a morphine overdose, and that the morphine had been injected into the antecubital vein which meant that whoever had used the syrettes knew exactly what he was doing. Through the remainder of that day and all during the next, Skelly called several more witnesses, mostly people who had been at the dock that day. He endlessly corroborated one testimony with another without introducing any significant new evidence.

Locke found little to contest so he rarely cross-examined them.

On the second day of the trial, Jordi placed a call to Niall Macgrudder from a telephone booth in the Ellsworth courthouse. Niall answered on the third ring.

"Niall, it's Jordi."

"Jordi! How's the trial coming?"

"It's too early to tell. Jury selection took forever and now the prosecutor is calling witness after witness—several police officers, the coroner—and he insists on questioning them on every tiny detail. Ambrose is getting pretty annoyed that he's taking so long."

"Them goldang lawyers can go on longer than a hard winter." said Niall. "Well, hang in there. What you did was right, by God."

Jordi hesitated, then said, "Thanks, Niall. And thanks for keeping an eye out for *Trobador*."

"Listen, after all we done, wan't no way we were gonna let anything happen to her if we could help it. We was all nervous, though. Can't pull the boats too early because the boys would lose too much money. Then Clara came on so fast there wan't any time left to pull 'em. We lucked out when she went inland some." There was a pause on the line, then Niall said, "But we got another hurricane coming our way."

"I heard."

"Name's Della."

"What d'you think? Is it gonna be bad?"

"Boys say we can't get lucky twice in a row. Things don't work that way. If Della keeps coming, we're gonna pull the boats. Ain't gonna wait this time. They're getting ready now."

"What about *Trobador*?"

There was another pause. "Jordi, you know we gotta pull the lobstah boats first. It's all of our livelihoods at stake. We'll pull the *Zabet & Lydie* for you if we can."

"So you're saying that if Della hits, *Trobador*'s in trouble?"

"Look, we're gonna bust our asses, you know that. But there's only so much we can do. She's coming on faster than Clara. One thing going for us is that most of the pleasure boats were hauled out for Clara. But even so, there's a hell of a lot of work to do. Don't know if we can do it all."

Jordi thanked Niall for everything he'd done. But as he hung up the receiver, all he could think of was *Trobador*, exposed and vulnerable.

Skelly called Virgil Blount to the stand. When Blount took his seat, he glanced out to where Lydie was sitting, and then looked to the prosecutor.

"Mr. Blount, where were you on the morning of May third?"

"I was at the fueling dock in Center Harbor filling up my lobstah boat."

"What did you see?"

"I saw these men carrying Pip Dupuy out to the *Zabet & Lydie* which was Pip's lobstah boat. Then they took off for that sailboat they built, which was moored out in Center Harbor."

"Did you have a good view?"

"Hell, they was less than fifty yards from me."

"Who were the men?"

"Well, I only recognized one of them. Jordi Dupuy."

"You didn't recognize the others?"

"Never saw 'em before in my life."

"How would you characterize Hippolyte Dupuy's attitude?"

"He was struggling."

"What do you mean struggling?"

"Well, like he didn't want to go on that theah boat."

Locke stood. "Objection, the witness is drawing a conclusion."

"Sustained."

"Did he step aboard on his own?"

"No. They hoisted him aboard."

When it came time for Locke to cross-examine Blount, he simply had Blount repeat that he had a clear view and that he hadn't seen any of the other men before.

"You're absolutely certain you didn't recognize the other men?"

"Absolutely."

"And you had a clear view? No more than a few yards at one point, I believe you said."

"Yes."

"Thank you."

The courtroom buzzed when Simon Skelly called Dr. Evan Davids to the stand. Jordi leaned over to Locke and whispered, "What's this all about?"

Locke shrugged. "I don't know. I have no idea what Skelly is after. I can't think of anything I heard during the doctor's deposition that Skelly would want to pursue."

Evan Davids took the oath administered by the clerk, then settled his huge frame into the witness chair. He crossed his legs first one way, then the other, searching, apparently in vain, for a comfortable position in the cramped witness box. He gazed at Simon Skelly. It was clear from his expression that he had little admiration for the prosecutor.

While waiting for Davids to sit down, Skelly cracked his knuckles. It was an old and infamous habit. After asking Davids to give his name and tell the jury about his background and education, Skelly asked, "Have you known the defendant long?"

"I delivered him," answered Davids, a touch of sarcasm in his voice.

There was a twitter of laughter from the gallery. Judge Trench scowled over his half-glasses.

"And his father, did you know him?"

"Of course. I know his mother, too."

More chuckles rose from the gallery.

Skelly glared at Evan Davids for a moment, then walked from behind the prosecutor's table and approached the witness box. "Now let me turn your attention to the...instruments of murder...the so-called morphine syrettes. Is that the right name? Syrettes?"

"Yes."

"Did the police come to you for advice about the vials they found on the boat *Trobador*, to ask you if you could identify them?"

"Yes."

"And did you?"

"I recognized them immediately as World War II morphine syrettes."

Skelly gave a satisfied nod. "Now I have a few questions about these syrettes. Are they used in civilian life?"

"No, they were used during the war by the military only."

"By combat medics?"

"Yes."

"Like the defendant's father?"

Jordi felt a shock of alarm.

"Yes."

Locke pushed his chair back and rose to his feet. "Your Honor, I'm obliged to wonder where this line of questioning is headed."

Judge Trench looked over his glasses at Skelly and raised his eyebrows.

Skelly addressed him. "Your Honor, I just want to make certain we fully understand the nature of these morphine syrettes. We have established that they were found on the boat *Trobador*. I merely want to establish with certainty, for the benefit of the jury, that the morphine syrettes were of World War II vintage. I assure you, the relevance of the question will become clear later. For the moment, however, I'm ready to move on to a different line of questioning."

"Please do," said the judge.

Skelly returned to the witness box and rested his hands on the rail. Evan Davids sat back in his chair. Skelly continued, "Now, a moment ago you said you knew the defendant's father, Gil Dupuy. Did you know him only here, in Maine, or did you know him also in Europe during the war?"

Davids was clearly startled by the question. He looked over at Jordi.

"Dr. Davids," said Skelly, "I asked you a question."

Davids tore his gaze from Jordi and looked back to Skelly. "Uh, yes…yes, I saw Gil in Europe several times."

Jordi stared at Evan Davids. He wondered why, in all the years since the war ended, Davids had never mentioned this to him or to anyone in his family. Or why his father never mentioned it in a letter. Behind him, he heard Nana's rosary beads stop clicking and his mother's knitting needles pause.

"Under what circumstances?"

"I was a doctor, he was a medic. We saw each other at one field hospital or another several times during the war."

Skelly nodded. He regarded Davids for a long moment then returned to his table, where he picked up a sheet of paper. Whispers rose from the back of the room, but otherwise there was no sound aside from the whirring fans. He lifted another sheet of paper from the table and studied it. Finally, Skelly turned back to Davids and asked, "Was it ever brought to your attention that Gil Dupuy might have used morphine to kill wounded soldiers?"

A collective gasp rose in the room. Locke bolted to his feet. The chords of his neck stood out. "Your Honor, this is too much; Gil Dupuy is not on trial here!"

"Are you raising an objection, Mr. Locke?" asked Judge Trench.

"Yes, Your Honor. I object on the basis of relevance," Locke said, tapping his pencil on the table for emphasis.

"Overruled," snapped the judge. "Answer the question, Dr. Davids."

Locke stared at the judge in disbelief. Slowly, he sank back into his chair.

Davids glanced at Jordi, then turned to Skelly and said, "I wouldn't say *kill*. The cases I was told about—"

"Please answer the question, yes or no."

"As I was about to say, these men were already—"

Skelly stepped toward the judge's bench. "Your Honor..."

Judge Trench leaned forward. "Dr. Davids, I'm instructing you to answer the question yes or no."

"In that case, no, not *kill*."

Skelly opened his eyes wide. "No?! Need I remind you, Dr. Davids, that you are under oath?"

"You needn't remind me."

"Then let me ask you the question this way: Were you ever advised that Gil Dupuy administered *two* morphine syrettes instead of one?"

"Yes."

"Good, now we're getting somewhere. That's two syrettes, you say; the same amount that, according to the coroner, was used to dispatch

Hippolyte Dupuy?" Skelly paused, then continued. "Now, Dr.
Davids, regarding the morphine syrettes that combat medics used during the war. What was the usual dosage for pain? One syrette, or two?"

"One."

"And how much morphine is in one World War II syrette?"

"A half grain."

"Is that a lot?"

"It's the equivalent of about thirty milligrams...a little more."

Skelly turned toward the jury and smiled. "Dr. Davids, I'm neither
a physician nor a pharmacist, just a humble prosecutor. So tell me, is
that a lot in terms of the effect it would have on a patient?"

"It was enough so that, combined with exhaustion from the battlefield and from his wounds, the patient was usually knocked out and
woke up only in the hospital."

"And two doses? More than *sixty* milligrams?" asked Skelly.

"Two doses, administered at or about the same time, would be
extremely dangerous."

"Enough to kill a man?" Skelly cracked a knuckle.

"One can never know with certainty...each person is different...
A lot depends on whether the medic got the vein properly or not...or
if it was injected intramuscularly...there are other variables."

"Nevertheless, more than sixty milligrams at one time, properly
administered, would be enough to kill a soldier on the battlefield. Isn't
that the case, Doctor?"

"In all probability, yes."

"And these were *young* men at very high levels of physical fitness.
Strong men, wouldn't you say?"

"Yes, I suppose..."

"Likely to be able to tolerate a higher dosage than an ordinary cit-
izen because they were, by comparison, so strong?"

"That's a reasonable assumption."

"Stronger than, say, Hippolyte Dupuy in the last year of his life?"

"Yes, but—"

Once again, Locke rose from his chair. "Your Honor, this entire
line of questioning is irrelevant. I fail to see where this is going."

Judge Trench motioned to both lawyers and said, "Please approach the bench." When they were standing before him, he leaned forward and peered over the rims of his glasses, and quietly said, "Mr. Skelly, I share Mr. Locke's bafflement. Where are you headed with this?"

Skelly cracked a knuckle, leaned toward the judge, and whispered. "I promise, Your Honor, that all of this *is* relevant to the question that must be on everybody's mind. It certainly is the question that has plagued me since the very beginning of this case. How in heaven's name is it possible that a young man would bring himself to *usurp the power of God* and kill the grandfather he purports to love so much? How in heaven's name is such a thing possible?"

"Are you saying that your line of questioning will deliver up an answer?" asked Judge Trench.

"I am, Your Honor. I propose to show a connection between what the son did and what the father did."

The judge nodded. "Then proceed. And, Mr. Skelly…"

"Your Honor?"

"Stop cracking your knuckles. It's annoying me."

"Yes…of course, Your Honor."

Locke returned to the defense table and sat heavily in his chair. He leaned over to Jordi and whispered, "The judge is letting him get away with murder, just like I said." He slid his chair toward the table with a scrape.

Skelly turned to Evan Davids again. "Now Dr. Davids, did Jordi Dupuy ever accompany his grandfather on visits to the hospital?"

"Yes, on a number of occasions."

"In his presence, did you ever warn Hippolyte Dupuy about the dangers of drinking whiskey while taking morphine?"

"Yes, I did."

"Why did you find this necessary? What are the dangers?"

"Alcohol ordinarily reinforces the effects of any pain medication."

"In what way—with morphine, for example?"

"Some of the possible effects of morphine, as with all opioid analgesics, are respiratory depression, apnea, shock, even cardiac arrest. Alcohol potentiates these possible effects."

"Potentiates?"

"Makes them more powerful, more likely."

"And you mentioned apnea. Please tell the jury what that is."

"Apnea is the cessation of breathing."

"And in the case of Hippolyte Dupuy, was there a special danger with regard to respiratory depression or apnea?"

"Yes. Respiratory depression is the chief danger of morphine and this is especially true with older patients and patients whose lungs are damaged."

"Both of which applied to Hippolyte Dupuy?"

"Yes, obviously. He already had markedly decreased pulmonary ventilation because of his lung cancer."

"So, in short, he was much more susceptible to a morphine over-dose and/or an interaction between morphine and alcohol than a younger, less impaired person. Is that true?"

"Yes. But I should add—"

"That's enough, Dr. Davids. You've answered the question. Now back to Gil Dupuy. If it had been proven to you that Gil Dupuy *did* intentionally kill patients, even if only to put them out of their misery…like a dog or a horse…what would you have done?"

"It's hard to say. I was behind the lines; I wasn't in combat. Combat's a different thing."

"Combat is a different thing?"

"Yes."

"The ordinary rules of civilized behavior are suspended? Any ol' medic can appoint himself some kind of glorified veterinarian to put down a suffering animal?"

Locke pushed his chair back and rose again. "Your Honor, I must persist. Where is this line of questioning leading?"

Judge Trench leaned over the bench and directed himself to the clerk who was sitting at a table immediately in front of the judge's bench. "Clerk, I'm going to call a brief recess. Please escort the jury to the jury room." Then he turned to Ambrose Locke and Simon Skelly. "I think it's time for a conference in my chambers." He rose and dis-appeared through the door behind his bench, his robe flowing after him. Skelly followed.

Locke turned to Jordi. "Hang tight. I'll wangle some extra time before we start again so I can catch you up on all of this. He followed Skelly into the judge's chamber.

When Locke returned, he said to Jordi, "C'mon. We've got to talk. We have an extra half hour."

They walked down the hill to Main Street and the Central Café. They ordered coffee. While the waitress fetched the coffee, Locke said, "Well, it's what I suspected. I know what Skelly's game is, and it may sound cockeyed to you, but, hell, anything can happen with a jury. From what he said in the judge's chamber, I'm certain he plans to argue that you were acting not out of a sense of compassion for Pip, but out of some kind of desire to emulate your father. That you were playing God."

Jordi stared at Locke in utter disbelief.

Twenty minutes later, Evan Davids took the witness stand again. He adjusted his tie and waited for Skelly to resume questioning.

Skelly cracked a knuckle and began. "Now Dr. Davids, I have only one or two remaining questions. The coroner testified that the injections of morphine were given through the…" Skelly peered at his notes. "Through the antecubital vein. What, if anything, does this signify to you?"

"That whoever did the injecting knew what he was doing."

"Are you familiar with the combat medic's manual Gil Dupuy used in Europe, marked exhibit D?"

"Yes, I am."

"Does it specify where morphine shots should be delivered for maximum effect?"

"Yes."

"Where?"

"The antecubital vein."

Jordi called Niall Macgruder from the courthouse again the next morning. Niall told him the lobstermen were pulling boats but that two of the tractors had broken down and they were having a rough time of it. Back in the courtroom he showed Locke a copy of the *Bangor Daily News.* "Jesus, Ambrose, look at this. They're expecting Della to hit the day after tomorrow and if it continues on its course, the damned eye will pass right over us!"

Locke put a hand on Jordi's arm. "Look, I already talked with Trench about *Trobador.* He sympathizes, but he's not going to interrupt the trial. He asked if your lobster boat was being pulled and I said yes. Then he asked if *Trobador* was insured. I told him yes. So he said that you and your family don't stand to lose a whole lot of money so there's no hardship that would warrant interrupting the trial."

Jordi shook his head in disbelief. "No amount of insurance money can replace *Trobador*; she's everything to me; she's my *father*; she's *Pip*..." His eyes began to well with tears.

"I know, Jordi, I know. But Trench is adamant. He says you will have to call on friends and neighbors to help out."

"But I already have! I talked with Niall and, of course, they'll help. But they have to get their own boats out first and, already, two tractors have broken down. Chances are they won't have time to get to *Trobador.*"

"I'm sorry, Jordi. There's not a damned thing I can do."

An hour later, Locke called Evan Davids back to the stand.

Locke began. "Good morning, Dr. Davids. During the prosecutor's questioning you were going to offer your reason for saying that, in your opinion, Gil Dupuy did not kill soldiers with an overdose of morphine, but the prosecutor wouldn't let you finish. Would you care to finish now?"

Davids leaned forward and said, "Certainly. All I meant was that an overdose of morphine while it *can* bring on death, does not necessarily do so instantly. It takes time. In my opinion, more time than men as severely wounded as those we are talking about usually had left."

"Let me see if I have this correct. Are you saying that these men would have died of their wounds *before* the morphine had a chance to become lethal?"

"Yes, it's quite possible. Septic shock, loss of blood, these things could kill a man in that situation before the morphine would."

"Then why administer a second shot of morphine if not to *induce* a merciful death?"

"It's obvious. To *ease* the *natural* death."

"You mean to make a man more comfortable while nature works its course?"

"Yes."

"Have you ever heard the expression, 'One for the pain, two for eternity'?"

"Yes. It was a popular expression among the troops during the war, especially the paratroopers."

"What do you mean, 'popular'?"

"It was common knowledge when a man was, shall we say, obviously not going to make it, there was a way to… help him get through it, the dying part."

"Was it your experience, Dr. Davids, that other medics besides Gil Dupuy engaged in this practice."

"Absolutely. That's one of the unspoken realities of war."

"When you came across such practices, did you ever call for a psychiatric consult for the medic?"

"No, of course not."

"Why not?"

"Compassion…mercy…these aren't psychiatric issues."

"So it's your best medical and military judgment that these men acted out of human compassion rather than some form of megalomania?"

"Absolutely."

Skelly rose. "Objection. Dr. Davids isn't a psychiatrist."

"I'll let it stand," said Trench.

Locke continued. "Now, Dr. Davids, in your best medical judgment, how long would Hippolyte Dupuy have lived with the metastasized cancer he had?"

"It's impossible to say. Frankly, he had already lived longer than anybody had a right to expect."

"But is it fair to say that, in your judgment, he wasn't going to make it very much longer?"

"Oh, there is no doubt."

"Do you recall Mr. Skelly asking you about the comparative susceptibilities of Hippolyte Dupuy and soldiers to a morphine overdose, especially when alcohol is added to the mix?"

"Yes."

Locke studied a piece of paper. "And based on your reply, Mr. Skelly said, and I quote 'So, in short, he was much more susceptible to a morphine overdose and/or an interaction between morphine and alcohol than a younger, less impaired person. Is that true?' Do you remember that?"

"Yes."

"Then you started to say, 'Yes, but...' You never got to finish. Would you care to finish now?"

"Sure. I was going to say there is one factor that would make this untrue, and that is tolerance."

"How so?"

"As with all potent opioids, tolerance to morphine usually develops after prolonged use. In other words, increasingly higher doses can be tolerated and, in fact, are *needed* to manage the pain."

"Could Hippolyte Dupuy have built up enough tolerance to withstand a dosage of sixty milligrams?"

"I only meant to say it would delay the effect of the morphine."

"Long enough, say, to have a drink of whiskey?"

"Barely."

"What effect would the whiskey have had, then?"

"About as significant as throwing a lit cigarette into a house that is already consumed in flames. All it would have done is put a smile on his face."

Locke turned to the judge. "That's all, Your Honor."

When Locke returned to the defendant's table, Jordi leaned toward him. "Thank you, Ambrose," he whispered.

Judge Trench peered over his glasses at Simon Skelly. "Any re-direct?"

"No, Your Honor." After showing Locke copies of the diary entries he used, Skelly handed them to the clerk. "The prosecution rests," he said to the judge.

"Very well," said Judge Trench. "Mr. Locke, call your first witness."

"The defense calls Rufus Metcalfe to the stand."

Rufus shuffled slowly down the central corridor, Ada's cane tapping out each step. He climbed into the witness box. When he was settled, he said, "Mornin', Judge."

Trench smiled. "Good morning, Mr. Metcalfe."

Rufus turned toward Jordi and Locke. "Jordi, Ambrose. Good to see ya."

"Mr. Metcalfe," said Judge Trench with a smile, "this is a court proceeding, not a social gathering."

"Don't mean a man can't be civil."

The judge raised his eyes to the ceiling and shook his head and had the clerk swear Rufus in. When that was done, he said, "Mr. Locke, please begin your questioning."

Locke advanced to the witness stand. "Mr. Metcalfe, on the morning of—"

"Call me Rufus. Always have."

Locke smiled. Even in the jury box people chuckled. "Okay, Rufus. On the morning of May third of this year, where were you?"

"You know goldang well where I was. Me an' the others was helpin' Pip Dupuy get aboard his boat."

"What others?"

"Jordi, heah. And then there was Niall Macgrudder and Ogden Gower."

"Did you see anybody else in the area?"

"Eyuh, that Virgil Blount."

"Were you here in court when Virgil Blount testified that he recognized only Jordi Dupuy but not the other men?"

"Sure was. Coulda brained him with Ada's cane heah." He raised the cane for all to see. He turned to the judge. "Belonged to my wife, Ada. Never thought I'd have a use for her cane but—"

"Mr. Metcalfe, please confine yourself to the question," said Trench.

"No need to cut me off like that. I was only—"

Locke stepped to the witness box, placing himself between the judge and Rufus. "What was it about Virgil Blount's testimony that made you angry."

"Why, the man lied."

"How so?"

"Said he didn't recognize me an' the others when, if the truth be known, he said good morning to us by name. Now I'd say that's recognizing."

"You also heard him say Hippolyte Dupuy was struggling. Was it your impression that the man was struggling?"

"Hell no! He was laughing and having a grand ol' time."

"Was there anything, in your opinion, that could give Mr. Blount the impression that Hippolyte Dupuy was being put aboard the boat against his will?"

"Not a damn thing. Man was lying to beat the band." Rufus leaned forward and rested his arms on the rail. "Now, if you want my theory as to the why of it, it all goes back to—"

The judge hammered his gavel. "Mr. Metcalfe! That's enough. Just answer the question."

"No more questions, Your Honor," said Locke with a smile.

"Good. The witness is excused." Trench glanced at his watch and said, "And we'll recess for lunch. Please be back at one-fifteen sharp."

As he left the witness box, Rufus glared at the judge.

Ten minutes later, Jordi and Locke entered a nearby hotel. Jordi had no idea why Locke arranged to have lunch in a private room at a hotel. But when Chrétien painfully shuffled into the room, Locke's plan—and generosity—became clear. Jordi pushed his chair back. "Chrétien! God, it's good to see you. It seems like we're miles apart with me up there in front of the judge and you back in the benches."

"Figured you could use some good old family support," said Chrétien. "Nana and your ma are outside. Can they come in?"

"Nana? Ma?" Jordi glanced at the door. "Sure…sure…they can come in."

Chrétien stuck his head out the door and, a moment later, Nana and Lydie walked in. Lydie rushed over to Jordi and threw her arms around him. "Oh, Jordi."

He hugged her tightly. "Ma."

She looked into his eyes. "I never knew about your dad's diary. How did *they* get it?"

"Virgil Blount gave it to them. He's also the one who tried to burn *Trobador*."

She shook her head. "I hope his boat sinks and…"

Jordi smiled and released her. He walked over to Nana. He leaned down and kissed her on the forehead. He saw that her eyes were moist. "Are you okay, Nana?"

"I'm all right. Why don't you come to see your ma and me?"

"I thought you'd hate me after what happened."

"We could never hate you, Jordi," said Lydie. "You know that."

"After Pip's funeral, I thought it best if I just stayed with Uncle Chrétien."

"We prayed for you," said Nana. "On our knees, we prayed for you every day. I lit candles."

"Thank you, Nana."

Lydie said, "You look so lost sitting up there."

"You shouldn't be in the courtroom."

"We've been there every minute."

"*Jésus, Marie, et Josef*," said Nana, "you're just like Pip. Sometimes you can be crazy. You think for one minute we ain't gonna be here for you?" She planted her large, round body in front of Jordi and threw her arms around him.

Jordi had no words. He put his arms around Nana, held her tight.

Locke put an arm on Jordi's shoulder. "Court resumes in thirty minutes. We need to eat our lunch and get going." Nana pulled away from Jordi.

Lydie came over to Jordi carrying her knitting bag.

He laughed. "Your knitting needles have been clicking through the whole trial."

"I was finishing your dad's sweater which, as you know, I never did finish. It's done now." She pulled the sweater out of the bag, handed it to him. "Would you wear it when you go up to that witness box? It's quite cold in the courtroom."

Thirty minutes later, they were all back in the courtroom. Locke stood and said, "I call Jordi Dupuy to the witness stand."

A loud murmur rolled through the gallery.

Jordi rose and walked to the witness box.

With his back to the gallery, he took the oath, then sat. For the first time, now, he was facing the gallery and felt vulnerable. He was overwhelmed by a feeling of panic. Then he saw Chrétien sitting in the third row of benches with Nana and Lydie. Chrétien smiled broadly and gave a thumbs-up gesture. Lydie and Nana had their heads down. Jordi saw Nana fumbling with her rosary beads. In the back row, he saw Rufus sitting with Ada's cane across his lap.

He was startled when Locke spoke.

"Now, Jordi, I want to bring you back to May third of this year. You took your grandfather out on *Trobador*, the boat the two of you built together, did you not?"

"Yes."

"Isn't May third a little early to be sailing on the coast of Maine?"

"Yes, it sure is."

"So tell me, why go sailing then?"

Jordi glanced at his mother and Nana. "Because it was obvious that Pip...that my grandfather...wasn't going to make it much longer and it was important that he get out on the boat. We worked like crazy, me and some of the men, to finish the boat in time. It was tough."

He heard Rufus mutter, "Eyuh." People turned to look.

Locke said, "But you did manage to finish, and you launched the boat. Tell us about that day you and your grandfather went out sailing together."

Outside, a gust of wind splattered leaves against the Palladian windows.

"We powered out a little ways on the auxiliary engine. Pip took the helm and held *Trobador* into the wind while I raised the jib and the mainsail. I could see he was having trouble holding the wheel, so I said we should forget the mizzen sail and just go under main and jib alone. But Pip, he said, the hell with that. He said…he said…this could be his only time on *Trobador* and he wanted to have all sails pulling. So I hoisted the mizzen, then Pip bore off slightly to put *Trobador* on a close reach. We were on the starboard tack. Then I sheeted in the sails and…and *Trobador* leaned with the wind as though she was born to it. My God, it was something. I heard Pip suck in his breath. He said, 'Goddamn, she's got the wind! She's alive!' and he laughed until tears were rolling down his cheeks. He said, 'It's like she has the breath of God in her sails.' You had to know Pip. That's the sort of thing he would say."

"So it was your impression that your grandfather was happy?"

"Oh, yes. But I could tell he was in pain—he had told me after we hauled him aboard that there was pain—but he held the helm like he was never going to let go. It was something special between Pip and *Trobador*."

"Go on."

"At one point, Pip said '*Keporkak*.' That's the name that the old Mi'kmaq Indians used for the humpback whale. He said he was hoping to see *Keporkak* right then and there. He said to see *Keporkak* then would make everything perfect."

"Why do you think he said that?"

"I don't know. I'd only be guessing."

Locke started to pace back and forth in front of the witness stand. "So you sailed out beyond the reach. What happened then?"

"He asked me for some water, so I went below and got it."

"What did you see when you returned topside?"

"That there were droplets of blood on Pip's arm and two morphine syrettes were on the cockpit seat next to him. Also, Pip had a big smile on his face."

"Did you say anything?"

"No. I just gave him the water. I was stunned. I guess I was crying."

"And then?"

"He was smiling like he was the happiest man in the world, but at the same time, there were tears in his eyes. Then he said something that made both of us laugh like little kids. He said, 'So when I see God, should I be real polite and see what He has to say for Himself, or should I just flat out let Him have a piece of my mind for all the things he did to Nana?' That's just how he said it."

"Did he say anything else?"

"Yes."

"What was that?"

"He said…he said he was proud of me for helping him find his sea room. That was a special term to him. It was a way he had of describing—"

Suddenly there was a cry of "Mon Dieu!" Jordi looked up to see Nana standing and staring open-mouthed at him. Then she fell back onto the bench. Jordi bolted from the witness stand and rushed to her. People were already surrounding her—among them, Evan Davids.

"Give her some room," Davids said.

Nana stared first at Evan Davids, then at Jordi. Her hands were shaking.

"Nana, are you all right?" Jordi asked.

In a barely audible voice, shaking with emotion, she said, "My Pip… he left a note."

"What kind of note, Mrs. Dupuy?" asked Locke.

"A note to me… he was telling me… telling me…" Her eyes filled with tears.

"Telling you what, Mrs. Dupuy?" asked Locke.

"That he was gonna… die… that day."

"Do you mean that he left a note saying he was going to take his own life?"

Nana stared at him as if unable to comprehend the magnitude of it. Hesitantly, she nodded. "Oh, *Mon Dieu*," she murmured.

"Where is this note now?"

"In my bureau where he left it."

Locke turned to the judge and asked, "May we call a two-hour recess while we retrieve the note, Your Honor?"

"By all means," Trench replied. "However, I want Mr. Skelly and a police officer to go with you. And a family member has to be present."

"I'll go with them," said Lydie, "if Dr. Davids stays with Nana."

"I'll stay with Nana, too," said Jordi. Then he turned to her and said, "I'm so sorry. I didn't want you to know the truth."

The court reconvened an hour later. At Locke's request, Officer Pattison was back on the witness stand.

"Officer Pattison, you accompanied Lydie Dupuy, Mr. Skelly, and me to the Dupuy house, did you not?"

"I did."

"And what did we find?"

"A note in the top drawer of Mrs. Dupuy's bureau."

Locke advanced to the witness stand and handed Officer Pattison a piece of paper. "Is this the note?"

When Officer Pattison confirmed that it was the note, Locke asked him to read it to the jury. The policeman complied. He read slowly, apparently struggling with Pip's shaky handwriting.

Dear Zabet, Please try to understand. I had to go sailing. It's the beautiful boat our son dreamed of. I would have gone by myself (that would have been proper) but I needed Jordi's help. Don't blame him. He didn't know he would be helping me find some sea room. I love you. I'll love you for eternity. Hippolyte.

"Thank you, Officer," said Locke. Turning to the judge, he asked, "May I recall Jordi Dupuy to the stand?"

When Jordi was seated, Locke asked, "Did you know your grandfather left a note for your grandmother?"

"No, I had no idea."

Locke nodded. "So continue your story. What happened after your grandfather took the morphine?"

"A real strange thing. A humpback whale surfaced not far from us. He didn't breech like that time before the war, throwing his whole body out of the water and lobtailing and everything. He just kind of eased up and spouted. But Pip saw him and he smiled. He whispered, 'Keporkak!' Then he said that deserved a drink."

"So you got him a whiskey?"

"Yes."

"Did he drink it?"

"In one gulp. I was worried because of what Doctor Davids had said about whiskey and morphine."

"Then what happened?"

"Pip pointed out to sea and said, 'He's sounding.' I looked up just in time to see Keporkak dive and that was the last we saw of the whale."

"And then?"

"He kept staring out to sea for a while. Then he sighed, turned to me and told me not to touch the syrettes. He didn't want my finger-prints on them."

"But they were found in the chart table. Did he put them there?"

"No. I did."

"Why?"

"It was after he died. I figured my grandmother would be at the dock and I didn't want her to know what he'd done. I guess I hoped she would think he died naturally. I was confused."

"Okay, after he told you not to touch the syrettes, what happened next?"

"Pip seemed to be having trouble breathing; he was making dry sounds in his throat. So I went below for another glass of water. While I was there, *Trobador* suddenly heeled over sharply then came up into the wind. She rocked on the waves…just rocked…and rocked. I hurried up the companionway ladder. The main boom was swinging back and forth, out of control. And Pip was lying on the cockpit bench face up, smiling… His eyes were open and he was looking straight into the sun."

Jordi paused for a long time. The only sound in the courtroom was the soft clicking of Nana's rosary beads against the bench in front of her. Shadows from the blades of the overhead fan swept slowly across the floor. Jordi looked up. Nana was looking straight at him.

Jordi remained silent. He stared at the floor and the sweeping shadows. There was no sound in the courtroom, not even, any longer, the clicking of Nana's rosary beads.

After a long pause, Locke said, quietly, "When you returned to Brooklin, Virgil Blount said you killed your grandfather and Officer Pattison asked you if it was true. You gave no answer. Why?"

"I don't know. I was confused. Part of me thought it was really the whiskey in the end that did it. Another part of me didn't want my grandmother to think Pip had done it himself. I just didn't know what to say."

"And when you were charged with murder?"

"I was shocked. But I still didn't want my grandmother to know. I knew how much it would hurt her. I... I..."

"Go on."

"I didn't know *what* to do. I guess I figured that I had made my choice and I was going to stick with it. It seemed like that's what Pip...my grandfather...would have done."

Locke nodded, turned to the judge. "No further questions, Your Honor."

Judge Trench took a deep breath. "The court will stand in recess for fifteen minutes. Mr. Skelly, Mr. Locke, may I see you in my chambers?"

Much of the courtroom emptied.

Jordi remained at the defendant's table. He was drained. Nana came up behind him. "Come wit' me, Jordi," she said. "I have somet'ing to tell you." She took Jordi's hand and led him to a vacant corner of the courtroom. Nana lowered herself onto a bench and motioned for Jordi to sit next to her.

A heavy gust of wind rattled the big palladium window.

"What I got to tell you is this. That day you an Pip went out on the reach on *Trobador*, well, the night before, me and Pip stayed up together for a while. And Pip, he held my hand. Now, you know Pip, that was somet'ing he never did! And he said he loved me. And I don't know *when* the last time he said *that* was. He wasn't the kind of man who gets all mushy like that. But he didn't have to say it, because I knew... I knew."

"Nana," Jordi said, taking her hand.

Nana placed her hand over Jordi's. "No, let me finish." She squeezed Jordi's hand. "And do you know what else we talked about that night? We talked about Emily and we talked about your dad. And Pip, he said somet'ing funny. He said he was sorry like it was his fault or somet'ing. Then he asked if we could pray together."

"Nana, I—"

"*Fermez la bouche!* I will tell you when I'm finished...And that note, I guess that was his way of telling me what he was gonna do. I guess he figured if he told me straight out I wouldn't understand or believe him, knowing what the church says about...about that kind of thing. I guess I just didn't *want* to believe it. It was only when I heard you describe how it was on the boat that I figured it all out." Nana leaned forward and placed both hands over Jordi's. "So you see, Jordi, Pip...he did say goodbye to me. You didn't take that from me." She paused for a long moment, then said, "Well, that's all I got to say— you didn't take anything from me." Then she sighed deeply. "I guess I got a lot of prayin' to do. Maybe God will help me understand." She rose. "Now I gotta go to the ladies' room."

Jordi went up to the bailiff and asked if he could step outside to get some fresh air. The man smiled and nodded. "I'll go with you."

They had just stepped outside when Jordi heard a low cough. He turned to see Rufus Metcalfe approaching him.

"Rufus," Jordi said, "thanks for being here."

"Eyuh. Others asked me to say they'd be here 'cepting they gotta haul the damn boats."

"How's it going?"

Rufus shook his head. "'Bout everything that could go wrong has. Three tractors gave up the ghost. Even Elwood's bulldozer crapped out. It's a conspiracy. Probably the Commies."

"So they won't be able to get all the boats up?"

Rufus shrugged. "We'll see. They're using Ben Campbell's horses."

"So there's a chance?"

"'Cepting, that ain't the whole of it. You seen the southern sky?"

"No."

Rufus waved his pipe, gesturing for Jordi to follow him around to the front of the courthouse. When they turned the corner of the building, he pointed the stem of his pipe toward the southern sky. "Coming right at us."

A wall of clouds loomed in the south. It had an eerie, jaundiced look to it, gunmetal-gray with a nicotine stain on its ragged edge. The air felt suffocating, as though it had been sucked of oxygen by the advancing, smothering mantle of cloud. The roots of Jordi's hair felt electrified. His spine tingled.

It was clear Della was already arriving. The flag on top of the courthouse was straight out and shredding at the edges. Low scud was passing over them. The trees in front of the Congregational Church across the street were swaying and twitching like drunks.

"If *Trobador* isn't moved, she's gone," said Jordi. "It's as simple as that."

"Not much of a chance she could ride it out," agreed Rufus.

Jordi shook his head. "Not where she is. Not if the eye comes as close as it looks like it will. The wind could hit from any direction. It could come from *several* directions in the space of only a few hours."

"No way of knowing what places will be protected, if any."

Jordi nodded. "But one thing's for sure, *Trobador's* not safe where she is. The only chance is to get her around into the Benjamin River. There's no way we can haul her in time. That's our only chance."

The judge and the two lawyers returned to the courtroom and everyone scrambled to their seats. From the back of the room, some-one said, "Eyuh!" It was Rufus Metcalfe. People looked back at him but quickly shifted their attention to the judge.

Judge Trench turned to the jury. "As I had anticipated, Mr. Locke made a motion for dismissal and after some discussion with both parties, I have decided to grant the motion. I wish to thank you all for doing your civic duty. You've been a most attentive jury." He turned to Jordi. "You are free to go, Mr. Dupuy." He paused, then added, "And Mr. Dupuy...good luck with that boat... *Trobador*."

chapter 22

A veteran from the jury walked up to Jordi outside the courthouse. He was holding a hat that the wind was trying to rip from his grasp. He said, "I just want to say one thing. I was wounded on Omaha Beach. The place was hell. A medic was patching me up when he took one right between the eyes. I saw several other medics get it on that beach and all they was doing was trying to help poor slobs like me. They were great heroes, them guys... Well, that's all I got to say." He turned and walked away, leaning hard into the gusting wind.

Locke came up to Jordi and handed him the diary, neatly bound in its oilskin wrapping. He raised his voice to be heard over the shrieking wind. "The judge ordered Skelly to turn it over to me. Said you should have it. I'll make certain my copy is destroyed."

"Thanks, Ambrose. Thanks for everything."

"Thank me later. I'm going to Center Harbor with you. By the way, you should know the judge has ordered Skelly to look into Blount's testimony. It looks like he'll be charged with perjury. The judge also learned from Skelly that it was Blount who gave your dad's diary to him. Because of that, they're going to reopen the investigation into that fire out at Rufus' barn. Sounds to me like he might be facing counts of theft and arson as well."

"Have they arrested him?"

"Not yet, but it won't be long. All Skelly has to do is read through the testimony, get the precise words Blount used."

Chrétien pulled the Packard alongside them. Jordi saw Nana and Lydie approaching. Locke gave him an encouraging smile. "Your

Nana's had a shock, Jordi, but she's a strong woman. She'll survive."

"I hope so…"

"Now let's get to the harbor," Locke said.

Jordi held the back door of the car open as his mother, Nana, and Rufus climbed in. Then, after Chrétien slid over to the passenger seat, Jordi moved around to the driver's side and behind the wheel. He climbed into the Packard, placed the diary on the dashboard, slipped the car in gear, and headed down State Street. "God, I hope the roads are okay," he said.

"They'll be okay," said Nana. "I'm praying."

Jordi steered the Packard down State Street toward Route 172 and the Blue Hill peninsula. Locke followed in his Ford.

Jordi turned toward the back seat. "Rufus, tell me something. When the judge came out, before he said anything, you said 'yes.' Why?"

"Knew what he was gonna say."

"How the hell did you know that?"

"Saw the man's eyes. The way he looked at you."

"Damn!" said Chrétien. "Have you ever been to the horse races, Rufus? You could make a killing."

All along the route, tree limbs littered the roadway. In several places, Jordi and Locke had to drive on the soft shoulder to maneuver around downed power lines. Above them, the trees swayed like frenzied dancers. "Oh, Dear God!" Lydie exclaimed as they passed through Blue Hill.

Jordi looked to where she was pointing and saw a chainlink fence with dead songbirds lodged between the links.

As they approached Carter Point, Jordi had a clear view of Blue Hill Bay, and he saw the tops of waves being torn off and carried away in white, boiling sheets. All along the coast, from Blue Hill Falls to North Brooklin, the scene was the same—seething waters out on the bay throwing columns of spray into the air and tortured trees swaying along the road. Live leaves, torn from their branches, splat against the windshield.

At last, they arrived in Brooklin. They turned off Route 175 at the Odd Fellows building and drove down to Center Harbor. The hurricane warning flags were now only tattered remnants. They snapped so violently from their halyards that it sounded like rifle shots. Lobster boats were scattered around the Brooklin Boat Yard. Another boat was, at that moment, being towed up the railway by Ben Campbell's team of horses. It appeared they had managed to haul out most, or all, of the lobster boats after all.

Jordi parked the Packard and jumped out.

In the unbridled wind, the reach was chaos. *Trobador* was nearly the only boat left in the water. She writhed at her mooring among the chaotic waves. The main halyard had come loose and was flailing to leeward in the deranged wind, its shackle banging convulsively against her mast. She was like a terrified animal jerking at her leash, trying to escape. Jordi thought the wind must be shifting, for even in the midst of her struggle, *Trobador* was swinging on her mooring.

Niall Macgrudder and Ogden Gower came up the dock. Jordi shouted into the wind. "With this wind direction, she has no sea room. If she slips her mooring, she'll be smashed to bits."

"And that mooring line ain't gonna hold much longer," cried Ogden. "We went out earlier and doubled up the lines, but even so…"

"No time to haul her," shouted Niall.

"The only chance is to get her up the river."

"We know. We left one boat in the water to go out to her. We were just about to go when you showed up."

"Let's go!" shouted Jordi as he headed toward the dock.

Nana and Lydie, along with Rufus, Chrétien, and Locke, were huddled together in the lee of a building.

"Can you save her?" Nana cried.

"I don't know."

"Hop in," Niall shouted to Jordi. "We'll take you out to *Trobador*."

Jordi was surprised to see it was Virgil Blount's boat they had left in the water. The boat heaved against the dock. Already, a section of its gunwale was splintered.

"Why *his* boat?" Jordi cried.

"Because he volunteered, damn it, that's why."

Blount appeared, red-faced and shouting. "I didn't volunteer! You guys kept pushing me to the back of the line."

"Won't be needin' your boat, anyhow," said Travis Lathrop.

"Why the hell not?"

"'Cause you won't be doin' no lobstering around these heah parts."

"Who's gonna stop me?"

"We are."

"You can't do that."

"We can," said Travis Lathrop with indisputable finality. He turned to Niall Macgrudder. "You gonna buy lobstahs from this man?"

"Nope," answered Niall. As if to punctuate his reply, a wave lifted Blount's boat and slammed it against the dock. There was a loud splintering sound as more of the gunwale was torn away.

Lathrop turned to Virgil Blount. "Sorry 'bout that." Then he smiled and said, "And thanks for the use of the boat."

Blount glanced at the crowd under the roof overhang of Niall Macgrudder's shack. Officer Pattison was there. Blount approached him. "They're stealing my boat! Stop them!"

"There's too much rain and noise," Pattison shouted. "I can't see or hear a thing."

Ogden Gower called out, "Let's go, Jordi."

His father's diary tucked under his arm, Jordi leapt aboard Blount's boat and joined the men crouched under the wheelhouse. Lathrop threw the boat into gear and maneuvered it away from the dock. He headed toward *Trobador*. The lobster boat flung spray out to the side as it lurched in the steep waves. As they pulled alongside *Trobador*, the two boats rose and fell together ominously. They scissored up and down in the waves and Jordi wondered if he could leap from one to the other without being crushed between them. But when he saw that the mooring line, where it passed through the chock, was frayed almost all the way through, he decided there was no time to lose and climbed onto the gunwale of the lobster boat. Niall

Macgrudder and Ogden Gower supported him as he studied the motions of the two boats, trying to time his leap. Finally, as the two decks passed one another, he jumped, gripping his father's diary firmly under an arm. He landed hard aboard *Trobador*, sprawled on the cockpit sole. He pulled himself to his feet and shouted, "I'll take her from here. It's okay."

Ogden Gower cupped his hands around his mouth and yelled, "Ain't! We're coming with you all the way up the river in case the engine konks out. We ain't spent all that time on *Trobador* to lose her now. Towing in these waves will be tough, but we'll try it if needed."

Jordi placed the diary in the cockpit cubby and closed the door. He flipped on the battery switch and pressed the starter button. A roar came from *Trobador's* bowels. He struggled to the foredeck and, crouching against the awesome force of the wind, removed the mooring line from its cleat. *Trobador* started to swing violently away from the wind and Jordi scrambled back to the cockpit to put the engine into gear. He gunned it. *Trobador* shuddered. A heavy shudder that came from deep in her keel. Slowly, she started to move forward against the waves. When Jordi thought he had enough headway, he brought the helm to starboard and set a course for the mouth of the Benjamin River. Green water and foam roiled over the deck and burst against the mast, drenching the cockpit. Water, sizzling with salt, sluiced around Jordi's feet. The wind roared through the rigging. The main halyard, left with a little slack, slapped frantically against the mast. *Trobador* bucked and crashed into the waves and, with each plunge, the forestay sagged then snapped taut again with a sickening twang. Each time she pitched into the face of a wave, a deep shudder passed through *Trobador* and she staggered as if lurching away from the blow. Jordi's forearms ached as he tried to muscle her toward the river. The progress was painfully slow. The small auxiliary engine was barely up to the effort and Jordi worried that any minute it would give out. He looked at the engine temperature gauge. It was rising quickly. He looked over his shoulder and saw Lathrop and the others following close behind. They had a towline fixed to the stern cleats, just in case.

With each wave *Trobador* bashed into, she creaked and groaned like a wounded animal. Jordi imagined he could see the fastenings he and Pip had so carefully fitted straining to pop free of the hull. He felt the hull trying to separate from the keel, the rudder from the stern post, the rigging from the deck, the engine from its bed. He peered out over the bow, eyes stinging with salt spray, and could just make out the red nun buoy off Bridges Point on the port bow. Shallow water was no more than a few boat lengths ahead of him. He jerked the helm to port and *Trobador* shook violently. In the trough between waves, her bow gradually, laboriously, came around until it was caught by the next wave and Jordi had to throw the helm back to starboard. Again, a deep tremor passed through *Trobador* as she wallowed into a trough then floundered toward the next wave. The wave jolted her with a staggering blow and she quivered to a stop. Jordi wondered if this was it. He wondered if she'd be able to recover her momentum. He tried to jam the throttle forward, but it was already at its limit. Each time a wave lifted the stern, he heard the propeller cavitate and flail uselessly against the air until the stern dropped again and the propeller grasped at the water with a terrifying vibration. He looked to starboard and found two trees that he could line up as a range to see if *Trobador* was making headway. For a long moment, the two trees stayed in the same alignment. *Trobador* was dead in the water. But then, ever so slowly, the angle began to open between the trees and Jordi saw that *Trobador* was clawing her way forward again. He snatched another look at the temperature gauge. Still rising. He looked over the bow. Ahead was the buoy marking Stump Cove Ledge. The entrance to the Benjamin River was just to starboard. He eased the helm over and *Trobador* turned. He aimed her bow to split the two buoys that defined the narrow channel.

With the wind and the chaotic waves now fully on her beam, *Trobador* was side-slipping badly. Jordi steered a course well above the entrance to allow for drift. But he found to his horror that he had not allowed enough leeway. *Trobador* was about to slide sideways onto the rocks. With all his strength, he threw the helm over and *Trobador* turned so the wind and waves were directly behind her. She accelerated and was now heading for the opposite side of the channel. Once more, Jordi jammed the helm over as hard as he could. *Trobador* heeled over precariously then righted herself and was headed back out into Eggemoggin Reach. Jordi steered around for another try. This time, he nearly overcompensated for the drift and was forced to bear off sharply at the last minute. *Trobador's* bow plunged into a wave and came up shedding sheets of green water. From the corner of his eye Jordi saw the first buoy slide past. Now he had no room left to turn around for another pass. *Trobador* was yawing wildly, heading first for the starboard limit of the channel, then the port. For long moments, Jordi was convinced that he was going to drive *Trobador* onto the rocks and rip out her belly.

Suddenly he felt a tremendous jolt. *Trobador's* bow reared. She shuddered to a stop. Jordi was thrown violently against the wheel and the breath was knocked out of him. When he heard a loud scrape he knew *Trobador's* keel was dragging along a submerged rock. He waited in agony for the next hit which would surely tear through her cedar and oak underbelly. There were several more scrapes as *Trobador* lurched along the rock.

Then she was free. With one more tug at the helm, Jordi had *Trobador* centered in the channel. In the smaller waves she settled into a more confident progress and soon they were passing the black can marking the left side of the channel. Jordi left the red buoy, which marked the tip of the sand spit, to starboard, and at last they were in deep, protected water.

He released the death grip he'd had on the helm. Cautiously, he probed his ribs where they had slammed into the wheel and drew in a sharp, painful breath. He tried to take a slow, deep breath, but that hurt, too. With great effort, he turned to see that Lathrop and the others were close astern; they made it through the passage with relative ease on a much more powerful engine. He gave a little wave then turned to guide *Trobador* the rest of the way home. Blood started to return to his hands and he gingerly placed them on the wheel. Despite the pain in his ribs, Jordi began to laugh into the wind. It was the laughter of relief.

Now Jordi saw the Metcalfe barn where *Trobador* was born. It was barely visible in the gloom, and he realized that night had fallen in the time it had taken to bring *Trobador* to this new place. When *Trobador* was nearly stopped, he rushed forward to drop the plow anchor. He turned on the masthead light.

Lathrop and the others pulled alongside. "We'll just have to sit tight here, until she blows out," shouted Niall Macgrudder.

"You did a great job," cried Travis Lathrop. "That was some tough going on a small engine."

Jordi waved.

Ogden Gower cupped his hands to form a megaphone. "We should be all right so long as she doesn't shift to the southwest. All depends on where the eye passes."

"All the same," Jordi replied, "I'm going to set the emergency anchor as well."

He went below to the forward V-berth. The emergency anchor was stored in the forepeak. He climbed atop the V-berth, slid back the partition, and hauled out the emergency anchor, a folding Danforth type. He was surprised to find a piece of paper rolled up and lodged in a link of the anchor chain. He pulled out the paper, unrolled it, and read:

> *Jordi—if you're finding this note then it might be that you've run into a storm of some kind and you need this anchor. Set it well. You and me and your dad—we built a beautiful boat. Be proud. Love, Pip*

Jordi's hand was shaking. "Pip," he murmured.

Two hours later, when the eye of Della arrived on the Maine coast, it passed right over the Benjamin River and Eggemoggin Reach and all the islands beyond. Birds which had been trapped inside the walls of the vortex now flew overhead.

Given where the epicenter passed, they knew when the wind returned it would come from the northwest rather than the southwest, leaving the Benjamin River protected. Niall Macgrudder called over to Jordi. "Jordi, she's pulled through. She's okay."

Jordi smiled. He shrugged off his oilskins, wiped the raindrops from his brow, and saw that the water around *Trobador* had already stopped boiling with rain. *Trobador* had settled onto her moonsilvered reflection. Her anchor line had relaxed into an easeful catenary that mirrored *Trobador's* own gentle sheerline.

And through the great round eye at the core of the hurricane, a shaft of light from a full moon, a bomber's moon, fell upon Rufus Metcalfe's barn and the ridge of its roof glowed metallic. In the wash of milk-water light, Jordi saw that the trees had relaxed, their limbs quiet.

Jordi walked to *Trobador's* foredeck and grabbed the forestay. He leaned back and gazed up through the eye of the storm into a vast straddle of stars. All he saw were the stars and *Trobador's* masthead light, which appeared to ride high among them. And though Orion and the Pleiades had not yet appeared, he saw in the northern sky Arcturus, Cassiopeia, and the Northern Cross. Then he turned from the arms of the Northern Cross until he saw, high above him, all the stars in the chambers of the south.

acknowledgments

Far more than most people imagine, a book is a collaborative effort. Sure, the author spends countless hours in creative solitude hammering out a first draft. But when that's done (and even before) many individuals make valuable contributions before the book finally reaches the reader. I feel privileged to acknowledge these people in the chronological order of their contributions.

First, there is my wife, Susan M. Reynolds, who has helped in so many ways, not the least of which is participating willingly in the scary adventure of leaving a well-remunerated corporate life to try launching a literary career. She was also a great sounding board for ideas concerning story and character and she did much of the detailed research underlying the book. (She also gave her name to Travis Lathrop's lobster boat, the *Susan May*.)

Many people read the first and later drafts, giving me both encouragement and useful comments. They are Marc Gautreau and Steve Gautreau (sons and doctors both, who not only read the book but answered many medical questions); Joanne Gaffney, Janice Studebaker, Carol Bent, Bill Bent, Chris Gautreau, Bill Richard, Mimi Thein, Kristen Van Cott, Gwen Reynolds, Domonique Krentz, Kay Evans, Ron Donovan, Ruth Mott, and Ann and Steve Schmitt.

The dedicated people at the Wooden Boat School in Brooklin, Maine, helped me understand what I needed to know about boat building. I especially want to thank Eric Dow, who taught me how to carve half-models so I could write about it intelligently. He also gave me a wonderful insight into Maine humor and dialect when I called him one day to say, "Eric, I'm building a '42 sailboat in 1950 and I have a few questions." His reply: "Eyuh, 'bout that far behind in my own work!"

I thank the people at the Blue Hill Public Library, especially Fern McTighe, for steering me toward answers to my many questions about the Blue Hill peninsula during the '40s. Likewise, Leona Gray of the Brooksville Free Public Library. And thanks, also, to Laura Johns and Carolyn Heller of the Breezemere Farm Inn for being such gracious hosts during my frequent trips to the area.

Vernette Bannister of the Blue Hill Memorial Hospital very generously answered many questions, provided a history of the hospital, and gave my wife and me a tour of the premises.

Norman S. Kominsky, Esq., gave me invaluable advice concerning the legal issues that appear in Part 3. I thank him and absolve him completely of any responsibility if, for dramatic purposes, I might have taken a liberty or two.

Gary D. Hall, a professor at the Throop Pharmacy Museum of the Albany College of Pharmacy, helped me with issues concerning morphine and especially its use during World War II.

Robert Parks, archivist of the Franklin D. Roosevelt Library, provided wonderful information about FDR's stopover in Eggemoggin Reach after meeting Churchill at the Atlantic Conference in Newfoundland in 1941.

My wonderful and gracious agent, Kimberley Cameron of Reece Halsey North, contributed considerable patience, encouragement, and persistence for which I am deeply grateful. She is, quite simply, one of the best.

My editor, Emily Heckman, opened my eyes to what truly great editing is. In his book *On Writing*, Stephen King says that "...to write is human, to edit is divine." Emily revealed to me the truth of that observation. Her patience, diplomacy, and skill would be difficult to match and I am forever thankful.

And, finally, thanks go to my publisher, David Poindexter, my copyeditors Laura McGrane and Anika Streitfeld, and all the people at MacAdam/Cage who took such wonderful care to bring this book to the reader: Pat Walsh, Scott Allen, Melanie Mitchell, Amy Long, Dorothy Carico Smith, Avril O'Reilly, and Sara Cook. They demonstrate what great publishing can be.